BEAUTY QUEEN

Also by Julia London

Historicals

The Devil's Love
Wicked Angel

The Rogues of Regent Street

The Dangerous Gentleman
The Ruthless Charmer
The Beautiful Stranger
The Secret Lover

Highland Lockhart Family

Highlander Unbound
Highlander in Disguise
Highlander in Love

The Desperate Debutantes

The Hazards of Hunting a Duke
The Perils of Pursuing a Prince
The Dangers of Deceiving a Viscount
The School for Heiresses, Anthology. "The Merchant's Gift," Sabrina Jeffries, Liz Carlyle, Julia London, Renee Bernard

The Scandalous Series

The Book of Scandal
Highland Scandal
A Courtesan's Scandal
Snowy Night With a Stranger, Anthology. "Snowy Night with a Highlander," Jane Feather, Sabrina Jeffries, Julia London

The Secrets of Hadley Green

The Year of Living Scandalously
The Christmas Secret, novella
The Revenge of Lord Eberlin

The Seduction of Lady X
The Last Debutante

Contemporary Romance and Women's Fiction
The Fancy Lives of the Lear Sisters

Material Girl
Beauty Queen
Miss Fortune

Over the Edge (previously available as Thrillseekers Anonymous)

All I Need Is You (previously available as *Wedding Survivor*)
One More Night (previously available as *Extreme Bachelor*)
Fall into Me (previously available as *American Diva*)

Cedar Springs

Summer of Two Wishes
One Season of Sunshine
A Light at Winter's End

Special Projects
Guiding Light: Jonathan's Story, tie-in to *Guiding Light*

Anthologies

Talk of The Ton, "The Vicar's Daughter," Eloisa James, Julia London, Rebecca Hagan Lee, Jacqueline Navin
Hot Ticket, "Lucky Charm," Julia London, Dierdre Martin, Annette Blair, Geri Buckley
The School for Heiresses, "The Merchant's Gift," Sabrina Jeffries, Liz Carlyle, Julia London, Renee Bernard
Snowy Night with a Stranger, "Snowy Night with a Highlander," Jane Feather, Sabrina Jeffries, Julia London

BEAUTY QUEEN

THE FANCY LIVES OF THE LEAR SISTERS

Julia London

Montlake
Romance

Published by Montlake Romance

PO Box 400818
Las Vegas, NV 89140

ISBN-13: 9781477805787
ISBN-10: 1477805788

Dear Reader:

I am so happy that the Fancy Lives of the Lear Sisters trilogy is available to readers once again! I had so much fun creating these sisters. They are three privileged daughters of a wealthy magnate who learns he is dying. He realizes he has pampered his girls, and he worries that when he is gone, they will not be able to stand on their own feet. Did he underestimate them?

His oldest, Robin, loves the trappings of wealth, but it takes Jake, a man who has had to bring himself up by his bootstraps, to show her that there is more to life than things. Rebecca has it all: a beauty queen title, a baby, and a wealthy husband to keep her in the style to which she is accustomed. But when her husband betrays her, Rebecca realizes she has nothing but her looks to fall back on. Enter Matt, a guy who calls them as he sees them, who makes her see that looks are only skin-deep—its what's inside that counts. Last but not least is the youngest, Rachel, who is still in school, still trying to decide what she wants to be when she grows up, and still making bad choices. When Daddy cuts her off, Rachel has to learn how to negotiate life and to get rid of the consequences of her choices. Fortunately, Flynn is there to pick up the pieces of her messy attempts…even if he does have an ulterior motive.

I so enjoyed writing these books! As the third of three sisters, with a baby brother to boot, I could relate to how the women are alike, yet different. DNA can only do so much when it comes to the affairs of the heart. But in the end, all three sisters find their unique ways to love and happiness. I hope you enjoy these books a second time around.

Happy Reading,
Julia

If I have any beliefs about immortality, it is that certain dogs I have known will go to heaven, and very very few persons...

JAMES THURBER

An author is a fool who, not content with boring those he lives with, insists on boring future generations...

CHARLES DE MONTESQUIEU

UNDERAPPRECIATED?
WE HAVE THE PERFECT JOB FOR YOU!

WANTED!! Dynamic, Exciting, and Very Important Company seeks former Beauty Queen with no discernible skills or knowledge for any position, no experience in any job-related field, and less than 30 hours toward Bachelor of Arts degree. Will train. Will assume lack of employment history is not necessarily a reflection upon applicant, but the result of a very busy social calendar. Will consider quantifying years spent shopping as years spent acquiring a skill, like maybe, time management, or something sounding equally important. Will provide ample opportunity for applicant to demonstrate she really *is* employable and really *can* do a good job, as put forth in Chapter 2, *A Woman's Guide to Finding Meaningful Employment.*

Excellent pay and benefit packages commensurate with the lifestyle to which applicant has become accustomed, including plenty of time off to take care of the kid since the nanny will not, apparently, relocate, plus FMLA benefits so when Father calls, applicant can drop everything and dash off to tend to his cancer-in-remission neuroses. This Fortune 500 Company offers lots of exposure to successful people, preferably under the age of 50, who will admire applicant for her witty repartee and not her beauty-queen looks, because we know she can't help it! *Come join our team!*

CHAPTER ONE

You may have a fresh start any moment you choose, for this thing that we call "failure" is not the falling down, but the staying down...

MARY PICKFORD

SOMEWHERE HIGH IN THE
COLORADO ROCKY MOUNTAINS

Exhausted, her body aching deep in the marrow and covered with a three-day grime from schlepping across the mountains, Rebecca Lear could only pray that she did not stink as bad as she feared. More importantly, she hoped she would not break down and actually eat tree bark, but it was becoming a monumental struggle—she had never been so ravenous in her life.

On the bright side, she *was* feeling remarkably transformed.

Enough that she managed to give it one more *oomph*, hoisting herself halfway up the rock...only to slide helplessly back down again, unable to make the final push. *Dammit!* Tears burned in her throat; she wanted nothing more than to lie down on a bed of pine needles to die.

She was the last of seven women, her Partners in Transformation on this Journey to The Vision, and the last to climb this rock, cleverly disguised as a boulder. All the rest of them were up there in a spot that Moira, their Transformation Guide, said was heaven on earth, seated around a crackling campfire, probably roasting marshmallows. Or meat! What if it was meat? *Jesus*, she was hungry!

Dammit, if *they* could do it, then *she* could do it.

Rebecca rubbed her hands on what had once been a perfectly pressed pair of khaki cargo pants and eyed that goddamn rock.

When her younger sister, Rachel, had first suggested the six-track "Transformation Strategies for Women's Changing Lives" seminars to help Rebecca cope with the aftermath of her divorce, Rebecca thought it sounded ridiculous, and had politely declined to enroll herself in Track One: *A peaceful and spiritual communing with the beautiful and wild nature of the Colorado Rocky Mountains, where the vision of a new life plan will emerge for the transformed.*

Not that she didn't appreciate the sentiment—she'd be the first to say she needed some sort of transformation after what she'd been through. But she'd never really been into sports, and God knew "packing out" was definitely not her thing, either, which she had explained to Rachel, who had (at the time, anyway) agreed. Naturally, she was quite surprised, when her older sister, Robin, showed up a couple of weeks later to pick up her son, Grayson, to learn that she had been enrolled nonetheless, was the proud owner of a plane ticket to Denver, and her gear was already assembled. Her sisters thought this was a very cool birthday gift for her. "Go get yourself transformed," Robin had said cheerfully, foisting the seminar documents on her. "Come back like Lara Croft in *Tomb Raider.*"

While she had no intention of coming back as Lara Croft, Tomb Raider, it had been clear that Grayson really wanted to go with Aunt Robin ("She's *cool,* Mom!"), and Rebecca figured she had nothing to lose at that point, except maybe a manicure appointment. So she had accepted her gift, personal reservations duly noted, and toddled off to Denver, where she met her six Partners in Transformation, all women of various ages and backgrounds sharing a common need to be transformed from a bad situation to a new beginning.

Then entered the fearless Moira Luting, who cheerfully announced that they'd be pushed to their physical limits to clear their mind, body, and spirit, so that they'd be *completely* free for The Visioning. And lest they doubt her, Moira quickly demonstrated that she meant what she said: three days of crawling, climbing, hanging, and swimming in ice-cold streams had almost killed the group of women, none of whom had ever done anything more strenuous than a treadmill.

The funny thing, at least for Rebecca anyway, was that it worked. She *did* feel free. And alive! And she had come too far to let something like a little—okay, *big* rock stand in her way!

So she gathered up all the grit she had left and jumped again. Her knee slammed into the rock wall, but she caught a ridge at the top and struggled and scraped to hoist herself up. Somehow, she made it, rolling off the other side and landing on one foot and one knee in the little clearing where the campfire was burning.

A howl—yes, an actual howl—went up from the others as she gained her feet, and frankly, it wasn't bad for a former beauty queen, even if she did think so herself. This was her highest plateau yet, and although she was completely spent and near to starving to death, Rebecca felt nothing at all like the weak and fragile socialite beauty queen she had come to expect from herself. She felt like... *Lara Croft, Tomb Raider*!

"There we are!" Moira sang in her lilting Irish accent, cheerfully noting Rebecca's presence. "That makes seven, then! So! Good evening, ladies!" she said to them all as Rebecca half loped, half fell into their midst. "How are we feeling? Alive? Rejuvenated? A wee bit *transformed*, perhaps?"

Rebecca was feeling transformed, all right, and glanced up at the pristine dusk sky. A few stars were beginning to twinkle at them through the pines, stars that looked close enough to reach up and touch. It was *gorgeous* at the top of the world!

Not everyone was appreciating the transformation or the scenery, however. "I'm dying, Moira!" Leslie, an outspoken alderman from the Northeast, moaned, her fists balled up in her stomach for dramatic effect. "When do we eat?"

Moira flashed a mischievous grin, planted her fists on top of ample hips stacked like two beanbags on thick, muscular legs. "There now, I know you're quite exhausted, love, but that is precisely the point, isn't it? In order to transform to a newer, better, *stronger* you, we must tear down all the old insecurities and misperceptions, mustn't we, for it is only *then* that we can build up new and *fresh*!"

Leslie wasn't buying it. "*Moiii-ra*!" she wailed again. "Come on, when do we eat?"

"We'll fill your belly full, I promise! But first, I have a special treat for you!" she said eagerly, stomping over to a canvas bag. "The boys will be here with our food in about an hour, at which time we'll feast on fresh river trout, asparagus in cream sauce, squash and peppers and shallots sautéed in a buttery rum sauce, fresh new potatoes..."

They were all moaning and clutching their stomachs now as Moira withdrew a long stick, polished to a sheen and adorned with bird feathers. She straightened up, a broad grin across a broader face. "But first, we'll have our first visioning," she said excitedly. "Who can remind us all what we talked about in the orientation before embarking on the Journey to The Vision?"

Most of the women were still lost in the dream of food she had created; no one answered. Rebecca couldn't vouch for the others, but she was so exhausted she could barely remember her name.

"The first step on a journey to your vision of personal growth is *what?*" Moira prompted.

"To strip away the old so we can build the new?" June, the housewife with self-described empty nest syndrome, suggested.

"That's *it!*" Moira proudly exclaimed. "And then what, June? Can you recall for us what the next step is?"

"Er...detoxification?"

"*Yes!* Everyone, look around you now—we've stripped away the old, have we not? Not one of you has any of the trappings she came with, does she? And the last three days of physical exertion has wrung you dry of impurities, both in personal chemistry and thought, eh?"

The women around the campfire looked at one another, noses wrinkled, nodding solemnly.

"It's *true.* I feel really beat, but I feel better than I have in a long time." This, from chubby Teresa, who had cried all through Day One.

"That's *marvelous!* So who among you then can tell me what happens after detoxification?" Moira asked, and glanced eagerly from woman to woman until the flight attendant, Cindy, asked timidly, "The visioning begins?"

Moira liked that answer so much that she threw her head back and howled at the moon. Literally. Because that was what they had learned was the first step toward transformation, howling at the classroom lights during orientation. *Wolves howl to show supremacy. Women in need of transformation howl their victory over shortcomings and insecurities.* And just because they felt like it, apparently. To wit: Moira howled until she had run out of breath, at which point she lowered her head and beamed at the lot of them. "That is *exactly* the right answer, Cindy. We do the *visioning,*" she said, and dropping down to one knee, she held out the stick so they could all see it.

"*This,*" she said reverently, "is our *talking* stick. Whoever holds the talking stick will speak her vision. Who will be the first to hold it?" she asked, then startled Rebecca right out of her wits by thrusting the stick toward her. "Rebecca Lear?"

Rebecca instantly reared back and looked frantically around the group. She was a convert to transformation, but still! "I, ah…I'd rather not go first, Moira, if that's all right with you."

"*Real*ly? Why wouldn't you?" she asked pleasantly.

"I, ah…I'm not really ready to, ah…Vision. Ing."

"I know. That's why I chose you," Moira said, then surprised Rebecca by tossing the stick at her so hard that she had to catch it or be bonked in the face by it. "Now you have the stick, so there's no point in arguing, is there, love?"

"Really, I'd rather—"

"Oh come *on*," Leslie snapped. "We're *starving* here! We're all going to have to do it at some point, so suck it up and go first, or we'll *never* eat!"

The expressions on the other women told Rebecca they saw it the same way as Leslie. And if she didn't do it, they looked as if they were about one step away from spearing and roasting her right there. Reluctantly, she came to her aching feet.

"Splendid! Now hold the stick like this," Moira instructed her, indicating she should hold it to her chest. "Feel the power it gives you."

Rebecca didn't feel anything but the exhaustion and hunger that were making her dizzy.

"Now—some among you have never had the opportunity to speak. Others among you may speak and feel you are not heard. But not here, ladies. Everyone will hold the talking stick. And when you hold it in your hands, you will have the power to envision the course of your future. Your Transformation Partners will assist you by helping you to look beyond your current boundaries. And we're ready to help you find *your* vision, Rebecca."

"*Oooh-kaaay*," Rebecca responded uncertainly.

"Why don't you begin by telling us a little bit about yourself?" Moira suggested. "What brought you to the Transformation Strategy Seminar Series?"

"Oh…" Rebecca could feel the heat begin to creep up her neck. "Umm, my sisters gave it to me as a gift—"

"Could you go back a little further, love? To the beginning?"

"The beginning?"

"Of your life."

"Oh God—*now?*"

"What year were you born?" Eloise, an ad agency executive, called out.

Rebecca sighed, looked up at the purple dusk sky. "Okay. I was born in 1972, in Dallas. I have two sisters, one older and one younger."

"What did your parents do then?" Melanie, the quiet one, asked.

"Ah, well…Dad was in the freight business when I was little. And then he started his own company, and we moved to Houston." She paused there, not knowing what else to say. Mom and Dad fought all the time? She mistook Bud's teenage lust for love? There was a hole in her that was so big that she didn't know how to fill it up?

"Hurry!" Leslie shouted.

"Was your family rich or poor?" Moira asked helpfully.

That was a little personal, but okay, as she was feeling a little dizzy, she was willing to skip over mortified indignation and go right to *will do anything for food.* "Well…we were poor when I was little. And then my father started his own freight transport company in Houston, and it got really big, and now…well, now, my family is, umm…wealthy."

"Wait…are you Rebecca *Lear* as in Lear Transport?" asked Melanie, who *used* to be the quiet one and had, remarkably, developed a definite Texas accent. Rebecca nodded sheepishly. Several sucked in their breath; apparently they had heard of LTI.

"I know you!" Melanie exclaimed excitedly. "I thought you looked familiar! You're one of the Lear girls! Y'all used to be in the Houston papers all the time when I was growing up. Hey, wait a minute!" she cried again, pushing up to her knees in her delight as recognition washed over her. "Weren't you the one who was Miss Texas?"

Oh, no, please no...Rebecca had really hoped at the end of this seminar she would have transformed right out of that old tiara. "Well, actually—"

"Jesus, what are you doing here?" Melanie the Chatterbox continued, her smile fading. "Your life is perfect!" She looked at the other women and announced, "We're *starving* for someone who has a perfect life."

"No, I don't!" Rebecca irritably shot back. She was sick to death of everyone thinking that beauty queen somehow equaled perfection. "Just because someone has a little money and a beauty queen title does not make her or her life perfect, trust me."

"Then why are you here?" Moira asked cheerfully.

"Because!" she cried, confused.

"Your sisters seemed to think you needed help transforming," Moira, all atwitter, reminded her. "Why? What is it that you need? Hold that stick and let it come, Rebecca. See what you are moving past, see where you are heading! Why are you *here*?"

Rebecca closed her eyes, tried to see, even tapped the stick against her forehead to try and knock the vision loose before she died of hunger. "Because I just went through a divorce," she admitted.

"And you thought, after the divorce, you needed to be transformed because...you were not a good wife?" Moira prompted.

"No, of course not!" Rebecca said instantly, feeling suddenly and terribly self-conscious. She was not the sort of person to wear her emotions or her problems openly. Actually, she wasn't the sort to wear them at all and usually pretended they just didn't exist.

"Then were you a good wife?"

"Yes!" She was, wasn't she? At least in the beginning?

"Then what is it, Rebecca?" Moira asked, coming to her feet, her broad, smiling face peering closely at her. And as Rebecca struggled to find an acceptable answer, Moira clasped her hands, began to slowly walk around her in a circle. "What. Do. You. *WANT*?"

She swallowed a lump in her throat. "I want...*I* want..." Okay, really, if she knew what she wanted, she wouldn't be standing on top of some mountain trying to explain her existence, would she? "I want...confidence!" she blurted.

"Why should you want confidence?" Teresa groused. "You've got more money and looks than any of us will ever have!"

"That's not true! I lost it all when my husband left me for another woman," Rebecca said angrily, startling even herself. "Did *your* husband leave you for someone else? Or announce it the very day you learned your father was dying? Just look at me now! I have never been anything but a beauty queen! I gave up all *my* dreams to be *his* wife, and now I have a young son, and I've never had a job, and I never finished school, and I'm still trying to figure out why I wasn't good enough for *him*!" she cried. "I want to find out who *I* am! Who I really am! And I want to believe in myself!"

She stopped, shocked by her uncharacteristic outburst… but she clearly had their attention.

"So what you are saying is that while it may *seem* like you and your life are all picture perfect, the truth is, there's nothing really very perfect for you at all, is there, Rebecca?" Moira asked, unfazed. "You don't believe in yourself, do you? You don't believe you are worthy or capable of love or hope, do you?" she pressed, moving in closer, her face looming larger.

"No!" Rebecca cried. "And I don't know what to do."

"Get a job," Teresa suggested, her voice kinder.

"Please!" Rebecca scoffed. Were they deaf? "I have no experience at anything, and I've never worked, and everyone in Dallas knows my husband. And I don't *need* a job."

"Move to a new city," Eloise said. "Leave that cheating sonovabitch behind and go somewhere and be yourself!"

"*Move?*" Rebecca echoed weakly.

"MOVE!" someone else shouted.

"What your Partners in Transformation are telling you, Rebecca, is that you should move out from the shadow of your husband, because he represents the insecurity and feelings of inadequacy that have bubbled up to toxic levels inside of you. And whether you need a job or not doesn't really matter, does it? The point is the only way you'll ever believe in yourself is to prove that you can do whatever you set your mind to. Only *you* control your future, only *you* can prove yourself. What do you need, Rebecca? Say it!" Moira shouted, pointing at her.

"A job?" Rebecca asked.

"A job!" Moira cheered. "What do you want, Rebecca?"

"*A job!*"

"*A job!*" Moira roared to the stars above.

That was it, that simple! What had seemed so ridiculous a few months ago now seemed genius. Suddenly, everything seemed clearly genius, and Rebecca felt a burst of hope throughout her body.

She suddenly tossed back her head and howled at the moon, then lowered her head, beaming at them.

At which point, Leslie clutched her stomach and turned pleading eyes to Moira. "For the love of God, can we please eat now?"

CHAPTER TWO

I like work: It fascinates me. I can sit and look at it for hours...

JEROME K. JEROME

AUSTIN, TEXAS
SIX MONTHS LATER

When Rebecca left Colorado, all pumped up and ready to kick some ass, she had immediately set out on her newly defined path. Which meant that she and Grayson had moved to her lake house near Austin and she had begun to send out résumés. Okay, admittedly thin résumés, but résumés nonetheless, because Moira said there was no such thing as an unmarketable person.

What Moira did *not* say, however, was that there was such a thing as an unqualified person. Fortunately, *The Unqualified Applicant: Obtaining Employment in a Competitive Market,* a new addition to Rebecca's ever-expanding arsenal of self-help books and tapes, had cleared all that up for her. And here was something else Moira did not say: years of tennis and shopping had not exactly qualified her for the real world.

Seated on a park bench on the grounds of the state capitol in Austin, a bench that, incidentally, was just across the street from the Fleming and Fleming Employment Agency, Rebecca decided that her lack of experience in general was, like the rest of her miserable life, all Bud's fault for three reasons: on general principle; for having convinced her to *be* a social butterfly and waste her life; and for then cheating on her and leaving her high and dry. Asshole.

Then again, she really couldn't lay it all at Bud's jacked-up feet. Yes, he was an ass, capital *A*, capital *SS*, but it wasn't as if he had chained her to a stove or anything. In the end, he was hardly ever home; she could have flown to the moon and back for all he cared. No, *she* was the one who gave it all up for Bud. She'd dropped out of college with nothing more than a Miss Texas crown to fall back on. She'd put up with his affairs. And somehow, she'd come up with the brilliant idea that if she had everything neatly and perfectly arranged, then life would be perfect. Her marriage would be perfect. *She'd* be perfect.

It had not exactly worked out that way.

Rebecca sighed, cast a faint sneer at the shiny doors of the Fleming and Fleming Employment Agency, and recalled how Marianne Rinebergen, the less than helpful employment associate, had kindly suggested she take a class or two before seeking employment. "It will help qualify you for, ah...*positions*." And then she had smiled very sympathetically.

Rebecca had wanted to reach across the desk and rub that sympathetic smile from her face, but because she was always so unfailingly *polite* she walked away, wondering if there was anything on this planet she *could* do. In something of a fog, she had continued on across the street to the lovely capitol grounds, exchanged a greeting with a smiling state trooper who stood at the gates, and plopped down on one of the wrought iron park benches that lined the walks.

And there she almost gave in to the feeling of despair until she recalled what her self-help book *Surviving Divorce: A Woman's Path to Starting Over* said about pity parties: *Poison! Concoct antidote immediately and recite three positive things about You!* So Rebecca smoothed her hair, adjusted her jacket, and folded her hands in her lap.

*Hmm...*okay, it was a reach, but here was something positive: she knew it was over with Bud for at least two years before it actually ended, which meant she wasn't a total loser. she even managed to think this with only a slight roll of her eyes. It was amazing to think two people who had once been so madly in love could somehow come to loathe each other, but that was exactly what she'd felt for so long that it was almost a relief when Bud had made his grand announcement. (Not that she wanted to think about the loathing too terribly hard, because it always made her wonder why she hadn't ended it much sooner herself, and that was a dark and slippery little slope, wasn't it?)

Moving on to Positive Thing Number Two: she stood her ground during the divorce and did not let Bud railroad her. Sort of. Okay, the truth was that in spite of being the heir to the Reynolds Chevrolet and Cadillac dealership dynasty, apparently Bud was so glad to be done with their fifteen-year history that he gave her pretty much whatever her lawyer demanded, which was: the lake house (and if she never went back to Dallas again, it would be too soon, thank you); generous child support (guilt money to make up for his lack of visitation with Grayson); the Range Rover (because he had always hated it); her jewelry and personal articles (because he had no idea what they were). And then something about an equitable splitting of mutual assets, *blah-dee blah blah bleck.*

Could she really count that as a positive thing? Because by the time the Big Divorce Moment rolled around, Rebecca had been dead inside for so long that she had lost all interest and had wanted nothing more than to get away from Bud, their Turtle Creek mansion, and their friends, who, she had inadvertently discovered, had already become well acquainted with the soon-to-be Mrs. Reynolds the Second. Women she had once thought were her friends had dropped off like so many flies, ending with Ruth, who said, "Sorry, honey, but you know Bud and Richard are tight. I have to go along to get along." And then she proceeded to throw a very posh dinner party welcoming Mrs. Reynolds the Second into their fold.

That was when Mrs. Reynolds the First ceased to care, which infuriated her attorney, selected for her by her father, naturally. "He's a rich man!" her father had shouted at her in a fit of frustration one afternoon. "*Everyone* knows him! He's on the goddamn radio or TV probably fifty times a day for those stupid cars, and you're not going to take advantage of that? Do you know what he'd give to keep this out of the public eye? What are you going to do, depend on your beauty queen titles to feed you? Go for the jugular! Demand alimony!"

At the end of his rant, Rebecca had politely but firmly declined. She did not want Bud's money. She had just wanted to cast off all the nasty trappings and the life with Bud like a larva and become a butterfly. She had wanted to start over, to become a better person, a better mother, daughter, sister—someone who was not so stiflingly perfect and neatly arranged. And because she had been so unhappy and so uncommonly bored for so long, when her Partners in Transformation suggested starting over in Austin, she saw the brilliance in their thinking—it would be startlingly invigorating.

And it *was* invigorating. For a whole week.

Rebecca looked up to the tops of the stately old pecan trees. It was so hard to become a butterfly. When marital strife and high society were lifted from her calendar, she discovered she really had little to keep her occupied. She worked relentlessly on the lake house, rearranging things, cleaning, and rearranging again, marveling at how she had managed to live for so many years filling one empty moment after another with such meaningless pursuits as shopping and spas and dinner parties. Now that she was alone, friendless, and living forty-five miles from the nearest civilization (unless one counted Ruby Falls, which, even on International Lawn Mower Race Day, could not be considered civilization), she struggled to fill those empty moments, and discovered how pathetically ill-equipped she was to live life. She realized she had been someone's daughter or wife for so many years that she couldn't even find Rebecca in the wreckage that was now her life.

Thus had begun her maddening, so-called transformation to her place in this stupid world. "Meditation," Rachel had recommended. "Clear your mind of all the negative vibes. But definitely keep up with the transformation therapy, so you can stay in touch with your alter ego. And it doesn't hurt to have a box of Oreos lying around, either."

Grand advice, only Rebecca didn't have a clue about what ego she was in touch with, if any. The job idea was more concrete; it was the best way to rediscover the confident girl in her she had buried fifteen years ago when she latched on to Bud, the girl who wanted to be an artist and dance in the ballet and raise horses and didn't care if her spice rack was alphabetized or the stripes on her couch lined up with the stripes on the couch pillows. Having spent the better half of the last decade making sure her life and heart didn't break in two, Rebecca had beaten that girl down and left her feeling worthless and numb.

In theory, a job seemed the perfect answer to rebuilding her self-esteem—the problem being, of course, that she didn't have any actual job *skills*. Her résumé was landing in round file after round file. No one called. No one returned her calls. She had hoped that Fleming and Fleming would have the answer—*Placing individuals in esteemed positions of employment since 1942*, their ad said. But Marianne said, "There are lots of people out of work right now, *blah blah blah*," and, "You're not really quite qualified, *blather blather blather.*"

Clearly she was going to have to face the fact that she could not get a job in Austin...unless she wanted to leap into the fire and call Dad.

Eeew.

Nothing against Dad—she knew that deep down, he loved her. And she loved her father somewhere deep down there, too. But he was and had always been a hard-ass, and she honestly didn't like him very much. She kept him in the Men to Avoid category. *But,* she told herself, *it's just a phone call.* It didn't mean she'd owe him anything, an extremely important point, thank you, as she had no intention of living off anyone ever again. Especially a man, because in her reading of *Protecting Our Inner Child While Searching for the External Woman*, she had come to realize that all her life, she'd been letting men take over and then answered to them, answering and answering, until there was nothing left of Rebecca.

That life was thankfully behind her now, she reminded herself as she watched a vendor roll his cart to the gate, open an umbrella, and hang a sign that said: Dogs, Quesadillas, Tacos.

She was a new woman, right? She could make her own way in this world and she didn't need a man...well, technically, she needed Dad at the moment, but it was just for a moment, and Moira would say to quit dancing around the campfire and just *do* it. Okay. This was her, just doing it.

Rebecca got a cell phone from her purse, noticed in passing that more people were wandering into the park as the clock passed the noon hour. She punched the auto dial for the number at the family ranch.

"Hello?" Dad answered immediately on the first ring, and she had an unnerving image of him sitting and staring at the phone, waiting for it to ring.

"Dad?"

"Rebecca! Did you get my message?"

"No...what message?"

"Where is your mother? I need to know where she is. I need to talk to her."

Oh geez, not again. This little on-again, off-again thing Mom and Dad had going on was really trying. First, they'd been separated for centuries. Then Mom found out Dad had cancer, and they reconciled. Things had been good until the shock of having cancer wore off and Dad became Dad again and Mom couldn't take it any better than she ever had before he got cancer. And of course they had a huge fight about Robin, just like the good old days of high school, at which point Mom had walked out for what she swore was the last time. Only Dad always had to have the last word. "I haven't talked to her," Rebecca said.

"What do you mean you haven't talked to her? Seems like none of you girls ever talk to your mother anymore," he groused. "If I didn't know better, I'd think she was trying to avoid me."

News flash—Mom is trying to avoid you. "So Dad, how are you feeling?"

"I'm fine! I wish everyone would quit asking me that. Where's Grayson?"

"He's still in school."

"I really wish you'd bring him down to see his grandpa," Dad grumbled. "You know that boy needs some familiar ground. Maybe you don't see it, but it's not like he's had an easy time of it with the divorce and changing schools and moving," he continued, always happy to dispense unsolicited advice. Her father also liked to remind her that he thought she was a less than perfect parent, too, what with moving and taking Grayson away from Dallas.

"And he was way too dependent on that nanny, if you ask me. But it's all water under the bridge now," he said with a heavy sigh, wrapping up today's free advice segment.

"Dad, listen, I need to you ask you something."

"Do you need money?"

"Dad!" Rebecca cried indignantly. "I wouldn't call for money—"

"I'm not talking a lot. Just enough so Grayson won't want for anything—"

"He doesn't!"

"You could have gotten a lot more if you would have listened to that high-dollar attorney. Anyway, I think you ought to come out here to the ranch and stay with me for a while."

That was *so* not going to happen. "I can't come to Blue Cross right now. But you could really help me out in another way," she quickly continued, before he could begin the full litany of her faults when it came to his grandson. "I need a favor," she said, wincing. "Just a small one."

"What *kind* of favor?" he asked suspiciously.

Rebecca took a deep breath, blindly fixed her gaze on the bench across from her. "You know people in Austin, right?" she asked. "Could you maybe just call a friend and see if they might have something I could do? I mean, as in a job? Just something that would help me get my foot in the door somewhere, that's all. If you could do that, I'd take it from there. I'm not after anything fancy, just a place to start."

Her request was met with a long moment of silence, then a terse, "No."

Augh! He had to be the most exasperating man on the planet.

"Now, before you get all upset, you know how I feel. If you're really determined to try and enter the workforce, I don't think you should do it until Grayson is in elementary school. And besides, I want you to make your way and stand on your own without my help."

"Stand on my—you just offered me money."

"For Grayson. Now look, I've said this until I'm blue in the face, but I'll keep saying it until it sinks in with you girls. I am dying. Who knows how long I have? I'm not gonna be here for much longer and I won't be able to make calls for you then, will I?"

"You're not dying, Dad. You're in remission, remember?"

"You want to work?" he went on, ignoring her, but what else was new? "Then you need to figure out how to do it. But I'm gonna remind you once more that you got a pretty good settlement, enough for you to sit back and relax and take care of Grayson instead of leaving him in some nasty day care where the Lord knows what goes on."

She could really despise her father at times, like now, and considered just hanging up on him. But dammit, she was too polite to do it.

"That's the one thing I regret the most, you know, not being there for you girls."

"This really isn't about you, Dad," she snapped. "I'm just asking for a leg up. It's not like I'm going to start some company and be away all the time. I'm just looking for something to do. For *me*. Is that so hard for you to understand?"

"I understand. And whether you recognize it or not, I am helping you out by making you learn to find your own way. You've had a hard row here, there's no denying it, but the answer is not to fall back on me."

Why, oh why, had she ever talked herself into calling him?

"Now come on, tell me when you're coming out to the ranch. You're just a stone's throw now."

How does a cold day in hell sound? "We're really busy now. Oh, look at the time. I really need to run."

"Listen—stop worrying about this job thing. Good things are going to happen for you, sweetheart. When the time and place are right, good things will happen."

She wanted to ask him if a little leprechaun was going to appear or something, but just said, "Okay, Dad. I'll talk to you soon." She clicked off before he could offer any other pearls of wisdom for her to choke on, and tossed her cell phone into her bag in disgust.

She folded her arms tightly across her middle, glanced around, and noticed that the park was now teeming with people. She watched the line at the taco-quesadilla vendor for a moment and decided that it was a glorious spring day, and a quesadilla could go a long way toward cheering her up.

At the taco stand, she bought a plain cheese quesadilla and picked up some napkins. But when she turned around, she saw that her bench had been taken by a couple. In fact, all the benches that lined either side of the walk were filled, save one. Rebecca snagged it, put her purse beside her, as well as the wrapped quesadilla, and pulled out the paper to review the want ads. But when she reached for the quesadilla to unwrap it, the thought occurred to her that it might be spicy hot; she hadn't thought to ask. She couldn't eat spicy hot without something to wash it down, and wished she'd thought to buy a bottle of water.

Rebecca eyed the vendor's cart; he wasn't very far away and the line had dwindled to one guy. She could leave her paper and quesadilla to mark her spot, run over and get a drink, and run back before anyone could take it. Rebecca neatly folded the paper, put it down, the quesadilla plainly on top of it, then picked up her purse and hurried to the vendor's cart, where she bought a bottle of water.

When she had shoved her change back into her purse, she turned back to her spot—but stopped midstride, absolutely stunned. A very nice-looking, well-dressed man was sitting on her bench, reading *her* paper and holding *her* quesadilla.

Rebecca gaped at him; her mind could not even absorb such appalling behavior. How could anyone be so...so cheap? What an inconsiderate, cheap-ass thief! The quesadillas were only a dollar, for Chrissakes!

That was the last straw for the day. Rebecca's blood began to boil—this was exactly the sort of thing she was learning to overcome. Here was someone who was walking all over her, taking her for granted, using *her* things to get what *he* wanted. The old Rebecca would have walked on, indignant. The new Rebecca, however, was not going to take this lying down. She was not a doormat! She did not provide quesadillas and newspapers to the citizens of Austin at large.

The man glanced up as she sauntered toward him with a sly smile on her lips. He looked surprised, and smiled a little uncertainly as he put the quesadilla down. When Rebecca stopped directly before him, his smile broadened. It was, she noticed, a very nice smile on a very handsome face, which just made him all the more reprehensible.

"Hey," she said, smiling softly, knowing full well the effect that had on most men.

"*Hey,*" he replied, snatching the bait and coming to his feet. He was tall, well over six feet, and broad-shouldered.

He put his hands on his waist, grinning, waiting for her to say something.

Rebecca turned the charm up a notch and smiled shyly, looking up at him through her lashes. "I just noticed you sitting there," she said, moving a little closer so that she was just inches from him, "and I was wondering…" She let her voice trail off, gave him another deceptively shy smile.

The man cocked a brow and with an appreciative smile, took her in, top to bottom. "Well, wonder away. In fact, would you like to take a seat and wonder?"

Rebecca smiled lustily.

He quickly moved the quesadilla and paper, making a spot for her.

She sat. She smiled. Thought it was a pity that he was really Hollywood handsome as he sat next to her, his gray eyes shining.

"I'm Matt, by the way."

"*Hi*, Matt," she said, and crossed her legs, baring her leg and leaning forward just enough that he could get a glimpse of her cleavage, if he dared.

Oh, he dared, all right. With a quick, furtive glance, he asked, "You were wondering?"

"I was wondering," she said, lower still, so that he had to lean in to hear her, "if you're always so…" She paused coyly.

He grinned. "So…what?"

"*Cheap*," she whispered.

It had the desired affect; his brows suddenly dipped in confusion. "Excuse me?"

"CHEAP," she said articulately, her smile gone. "You know, the type to screw your shoes on because you're too tight to spend a whole buck on a quesadilla?"

He suddenly sat back, pushed a hand through his thick, sandy brown hair. "I'm sorry; I think you've confused me with someone else."

"Rockefeller, perhaps?"

His frown deepened. "Look, lady, I don't know what your problem is—"

"Other than the fact that you stole my paper and my quesadilla?"

"What?" he exclaimed, his voice admirably full of indignation for such a cheap ass. "I did no such thing!"

"Yes, you did!" she insisted. "I went to get a bottle of water—"

"Yeah, I know. I saw you," he said, relaxing enough to give her a lopsided smile. "Actually, I couldn't take my eyes off you."

Oh right, like she was going to fall for that. "Or my quesadilla, apparently."

"No, just you. Because you left your quesadilla over there," he said, pointing down the walk.

That drew her up short; Rebecca blinked, looked to where he pointed—there on the very next bench down was her neatly folded paper and her untouched quesadilla, just as she had left them. She quickly looked over her shoulder to the quesadilla guy, and realized, with a very sick feeling, that he had moved his cart between the time she bought her lunch and returned to buy her water. He had moved just enough to confuse her, which meant...Oh. Dear. *God.*

Mortified, that's what she was, absolutely paralyzed with mortification. She glanced at Matt from the corner of her eye, saw the smirk on his lips. "My sincerest apologies."

He laughed, casually draped an arm across the back of the bench. "You know, I've had women do some crazy things to get my attention, but I can't say I've ever had one be quite so inventive just to meet me."

This was absolutely horrifying. "I assure you, I wasn't trying to meet you—I made a mistake." Like she'd have to do something that manipulative to meet someone like him? It was preposterous.

"Oh, yeah?" he asked, lifting that brow again. "Then why were you checking me out?"

"Checking you—that is absurd," she said indignantly. She did not check men out. She was off men; she rarely even noticed them.

"So are you denying that when you were on the phone, you weren't checking me out? Because baby, from where I was sitting, you couldn't take your eyes off *me*."

"I was on the phone. I wasn't looking at anything."

"*Riiight*," he said with a wink. "If you need to deny it, that's okay," he said, and leaned forward. "But it makes me feel kind of special that you'd go to such lengths."

"You're out of your mind," Rebecca said, and she came to her feet. "This may come as a shock to your obviously healthy ego, but I don't need to concoct a scheme to meet a man. I am sorry to have bothered you."

"No problem. It was quite entertaining. By the way, the full name is Matt Parrish. I figure you should at least get that for all your trouble."

Of all the infuriating—"Really?" she asked, feigning wide-eyed surprise. "I'll remember that. Matt Popinjay," she said, and with a pert toss of her hair, turned to walk away, bristling. She marched to the next bench, picked up the quesadilla she bought, and tossed it in the trash. And as she departed the capitol grounds, she told the smiling state trooper that the man seated on the bench beneath the big pecan tree was bothering her. The trooper assured her he would not bother her again.

From there, Rebecca walked as quickly as her Jimmy Choos would carry her to her Range Rover, and drove out of town, periodically shrieking at the windshield. How could she have made such a boneheaded mistake? All she could see was his smug look, but fortunately, by the time she reached the Little Maverick Preschool, she was calm again, because, she realized with a sigh of relief, she'd never see that man again. Thank God!

The school door opened as she parked and kids began to spill out. Grayson was the last to emerge, walking with his head down, his backpack almost bigger than he, his sandy brown hair (Bud's hair) going in fifty different directions. The poor kid had really been down this morning when he found out that Bud was skipping out on him again. "Hey, honey," she said as Grayson opened the door and crawled in, head first, onto his booster seat.

She helped him fasten his seat belt, noticed his corduroy pants had a hole in one knee. "So what happened to your pants?"

"I don't know," he said, leaning over to have a look.

"How was your day?" she asked as she started the Rover up. "Anything new?"

"I pushed Taylor down," he said.

Rebecca frowned. "Why would you do such a thing?"

Grayson shrugged, returned to examining the hole in his pants. "I don't like him."

Grayson had always been a happy child, quick to make friends, but since they had moved to Austin, he seemed different. Not unhappy, precisely, but just not...happy. And when Bud canceled weekends on him, the boy didn't take it very well. Rebecca pushed his bangs from his eyes and brushed the bit of dirt from a cheek that still had that baby roundness to it. "You can't go around pushing kids down just because you don't like them, Gray."

He frowned, picked up her cell phone, and punched some of the buttons. "I wish Lucy lived here," he muttered.

Rebecca would extract that little dagger from her heart later, but for now, she ignored it. Lucy had been Grayson's nanny until the divorce was final, and the kid had not quite yet forgiven the universe for her loss. He had not wanted to move and he had not wanted to be with his mom. He had wanted to be with Lucy. "Maybe we can go and see her sometime," Rebecca suggested with as much cheer as she could muster. Grayson said nothing, just bent over her phone, randomly punching numbers.

Okay. Maybe not.

They pulled out onto the highway, and Rebecca turned on the radio. "*Drive on down to Reynolds Chevrolet and Cadillac! We'll beat any deal in South Central Texas!*" Bud's voice blared at them. Rebecca quickly punched another button, but it was too late—Bud's voice had registered on Grayson's young brain.

"How come Dad isn't coming?" he asked her for the third time that day.

Rebecca kept her eyes on the road, hating Bud. "He's really busy, Gray. He's trying," she lied, and thankfully, her answer seemed to satisfy Grayson for the time being.

Unfortunately, he would be disappointed again, and she could hardly bear the thought.

Yep, this day had turned out to be a real winner, all the way around.

CHAPTER THREE

Being in politics is like being a football coach. You have to be smart enough to understand the game, and dumb enough to think it's important.

EUGENE MCCARTHY

By the look of things, Judge Gambofini was about to bust a nut, which was not terribly surprising. Gambofini was one of those guys who, once he donned the black robe, thought that he ascended to sitteth upon the right hand of some Supreme Court Justice and took umbrage at every little thing. Nevertheless, Matt didn't think he'd ever seen him quite *this* pissed.

Matt and his partner, Ben Townsend (who together with a handful of paralegals constituted the Parrish-Townsend law firm), stood shoulder to shoulder in front of Judge Gambofini's chamber desk, taking their licks. Which meant they were concentrating very hard on trying to look properly chastened. At least Matt was, anyway, seeing as how he was the object of the judge's complete disdain, and he couldn't get a good look at Ben. But a moment ago, when he *had* gotten a look at Ben, he had the distinct feeling that his partner intended to kick his ass up one side of the courthouse and down the other.

Okay, all right, so he hadn't actually listed Betty Dilley on the witness list. But how was he supposed to know they'd dig her up and she'd actually come out with a couple of juicy, jury-bending tidbits about the plaintiff? The means was not as important as the end—the plaintiff was a lying cheat and had retaliated against Matt's client, big-time. Mrs. Dilley just happened to be the last nail in a coffin that wasn't quite shut. Granted, Matt could have told opposing counsel about her long before today (he'd just conceded as much to Gambofini, which made him puff up like a giant red M&M), but he had succeeded in planting a seed with the jury that maybe there was something about the plaintiff they really needed to hear. It was a move, in his opinion, that had practically saved their case. But for purists like Judge Gambofini, it was what he liked to call "courtroom theatrics." And Judge Gambofini made it quite clear that he did not like "courtroom theatrics."

"Mr. Parrish, do I make myself exceedingly clear?" the judge asked him, concluding today's rant while a smug opposing counsel looked on.

"Yes, Your Honor," Matt responded instantly and contritely.

But not contritely enough, apparently. "Look, Parrish," the judge said. "I know you're the hotshot big gun everyone is talking about, but I don't care. You will *not* be allowed to stage your dramatic little antics in my fucking courtroom." (Part of that remark—not the antics part, but the hotshot big gun part—caused Matt to exchange a curious look with Ben, who appeared to be just as mystified by it). "You may think this court is your own personal little playground for showing off, but you will abide by the rules, or you will find yourself in contempt and wearing an orange jumpsuit to bed. *Do I make myself clear?*"

"Yes, Your Honor, you certainly do," Matt said again, and wished Gambofini would hurry up so he could personally wipe the lipstick smirk off the face of the plaintiff's attorney, Ann Pritchard.

"I should hope so, for your sake," the judge said, rising from his chair. "Now clear my chambers before I get really upset."

Matt and Ben nodded, waited for Ann Pritchard to precede them through the door. Once outside the judge's chambers, Ann (who, coincidentally, happened to be one of the many women Matt had dated in the past, only now he was looking at her wondering how the hell that had ever happened) turned her smirk up to a full scoff and snorted, "I told you that would get you nothing but an ass-chewing. On top of that, the jury thinks you're a jerk."

"I guess we'll know if I'm a jerk when the jury comes back, won't we?" Matt responded with a wink.

"Dick," Ann snorted and marched away, almost knocking down the only legal secretary the Parrish-Townsend firm had.

"Harold," Ben sighed, looking sternly at their legal secretary, "Take a piece of advice from me. Never, ever, do what Matt does in a courtroom. Better still," he continued, as Harold nodded solemnly, "never take on loser cases like this if you want to feed your family…or whatever."

"Oh, you mustn't worry, Mr. Townsend," Harold said brightly. "I have no intention of ever becoming a lawyer."

Ben missed that remark; he was too busy frowning at Matt. "Look, I don't want to get called on the carpet anymore by Gambofini. Hell, I remember when he couldn't argue his way out of a paper bag, let alone preside, but he *thinks* he can, so when you bring a case before him—"

"Ah, I beg your pardon, Mr. Townsend," Harold politely interrupted before Ben could go off on what was a regular rant about Matt's cases, "but I need to inform Mr. Parrish that Senator Masters has called three times today."

"Masters?" Ben said, surprised, his rant suddenly forgotten. "Hey, that reminds me—what was that about you being a hotshot big gun?"

"Hell if I know," Matt shrugged, and took the cell phone from Harold to call Senator Masters.

When happy hour rolled around, Matt drove his silver Jaguar XK to the warehouse district in downtown Austin. He screeched to a halt in front of Stetson's, a popular steakhouse, tossed his keys to the valet, strode inside like he owned the joint, and flashed his most winsome smile at the hostess. "How're you doing, Maria?"

She, in turn, lit up like a Christmas tree. "Great, Mr. Parrish! Are you by yourself tonight?" she asked, as Matt was rather notorious for bringing his many dates here.

"Just me. I'm meeting some friends—is Tom Masters here?"

"Right this way," she said and, picking up a menu, asked him to follow her.

Matt followed her and her ass, which jiggled side to side in black spandex pants as she led him to the back of the restaurant and the table usually reserved for big shots. Matt should know—he sat there often enough. With a reputation for being one half of the best litigation team in town, his clients included CEOs of multinational corporations and heads of state and local governments who liked to be wined and dined. Matt spent almost as much time here as he did in the downtown loft he called home.

Tom Masters was the first of three men to come to his feet when he saw Matt behind the pretty hostess. "Parrish!" he called, sticking out his enormous hand. Tom had been one of the best high school linemen in Texas, but in recent years, he had gotten a little thick, both figuratively and literally. "Glad you could make yourself available tonight," he said, shaking Matt's hand with enthusiasm.

Right. Like he was foolish enough to turn down a state senator, even if it was one of his old college fraternity brothers. "Wouldn't want to be anywhere else. How are you, Senator?"

"Shit, Parrish! Call me Tom!" He laughed, slapped Matt on the shoulder. "Hey, you know Doug Balinger? And Jeff Hunter?" he asked, indicating his two companions.

Matt knew them by name only, and that they were the powerhouses behind the state Democratic Party. He shook hands, took a seat next to Tom, and asked Maria to bring him a bourbon, neat. The four men watched her walk away; Tom sighed longingly. "Now *that's* a fine-looking girl," he said with a shake of his head.

"Matt, I read you did pretty well on that theater deal," Jeff Hunter said. "What was it again?"

"The Cineworld case? We sued them over access for the handicapped," he said with a shrug and left it at that. He was loath to talk shop in situations like this, because everyone and their dog was an armchair attorney.

"The paper said you did pretty well for the plaintiffs,"
Jeff continued. "Didn't the court rule that Cineworld had
to provide so much handicapped seating on par with the
rest of the crowd? And added a cool five mil for being
inconvenienced?"

Doug snorted into his vodka tonic. "Must be nice."

Actually, it wasn't very nice at all—it was textbook dis-
crimination, and Matt couldn't stand seeing the little guy
get trounced by big Cineworld-type conglomerates. Maybe
his father was right about him—Matt could be a bleeding
heart. "The deal was that Cineworld made it clear they
weren't changing business practices for a bunch of gimps
in Austin, Texas," he said coolly. "But my clients have severe
handicaps that confine them to wheelchairs. If they want to
see a movie like all the rest of us, they have to wait for video
because Cineworld puts them down on the floor where they
have to crane their necks just to see the damn screen. My
clients asked them nicely, but Cineworld got pretty arrogant
about it." And Matt hated arrogance more than anything.

"I guess Cineworld's thinking a little differently about it
now, huh?" Tom said with a laugh.

"I guess," Matt said as Maria reappeared and placed a
bourbon in front of him.

"You're a fighter, Matt. And that's exactly the kind of
attitude the party is looking for—people who know the difference between right and wrong and have the balls to apply
that common sense to the common good and get results."

He wasn't going to get the donation speech already, was
he? The election was *months* away. Matt thought he should
have ordered a double, and quickly turned to catch Maria,
but she was too far away.

"We need that kind of thinking and that kind of person to help me win the lieutenant governor's office next November."

Just looking for a few good men, yada, yada, yada...

"We need that kind of drive and determination to breathe life into the state party apparatus."

Don't you mean breathe Cineworld's money, Tom? Matt smiled and tapped his breast pocket. "Don't worry—I got your few good men right here," he said, withdrawing a checkbook.

But Tom surprised him, stopped him with a hand to his arm. "I'm not asking for money, Matt."

Hello? Since *when?* Since when had Tom Masters ever wanted anything but money? More importantly, why was Matt wasting time here if it wasn't for a contribution?

Jeff Hunter must have been reading his mind, because he surged forward so abruptly that it startled Matt. "We asked you here, Matt, because we're interested in building the party toward the future. The fact of the matter is a lot of our state senators and representatives are nearing retirement. We need to bolster the important work of the party in this state with new blood and new, relevant ideas, or we're going to watch Austin turn from the last bastion for Democrats in Texas to a Republican stronghold to rival Waco. You can just imagine what effect that would have on our representation in Washington."

Not really, but who cared? "So what's stopping you?" Matt asked cheerfully, and picked up his bourbon.

"It's not easy," said Doug, pushing aside his vodka. "There aren't that many people out there who are willing or *capable* of leading Texas Democrats into the new century. We need smart men and women with solid foundations who can be in Austin every legislative session. We're looking for people to serve…people like you."

Matt damn near sprayed bourbon all over them. "Like who?"

"You, Matt," Tom said, and clapped him solidly on the shoulder.

Matt did the only logical thing—he laughed. Set his glass down and laughed hard and loud. The last thing he would ever aspire to be was a politician. The only reason he continued to hang with Tom was because they were fraternity brothers and because Tom was fun at a Longhorn football game. Besides, it helped to grease the wheels of government every now and again. But *become* a Tom? Still laughing, Matt clapped Tom right back on his shoulder and looked at Doug and Jeff. "I think you've got your new blood right here, guys," he said. "I'm not the political type. I've got a good practice and, trust me. I've got some ghosts in my closet that you don't even want to come near."

"Come on, Matt. Hear us out," Tom pleaded. "We're not suggesting you run for an office right now. We're only asking that you work closely with me on my campaign, see how you like Texas politics, and let us see how Texas politics likes you. You've got the right look, the right reputation. If there's a good fit, we could talk about some substantial backing to put you in an office some day…like maybe district attorney."

"You're barking up the wrong tree, Tom—I don't see myself in any office but my own."

"If everyone had that attitude, then Texas would go to the dogs, wouldn't it?" Jeff asked sincerely.

"That's not gonna work on me," Matt said. "Thanks, but I'm not interested."

Jeff started to retort something, but Tom held up his hand. "Hey, he's not interested! We gave it our best shot. I'm starved; let's order!" He picked up his menu.

After an awkward moment, Jeff and Doug did the same. Matt smiled behind his bourbon and downed it before picking up his menu to peruse the specials.

"By the way, Matt...remember Cal Blivins from Conroe?"

"Remember him? I vowed to beat the crap out of him the next time I saw him," Matt said with a chuckle. "You know that."

"Did you know he's considering a run for state senator in the next four years? Word is he's got some pretty impressive financial backers already on board."

Whoa...Cal Blivins? The Cal Blivins who attended the University of Texas at the same time as Matt and Tom? The same worthless piece of shit who had screwed Matt's girlfriend in the back of his pickup? Okay, so she wasn't much of a girlfriend, and maybe Matt couldn't remember her name anymore, but that was beside the point. Guys did not do that to guys. But Cal did. Cal was forever pushing to see what would stick. There wasn't a sleazier man in the entire state, and the bastard would sell his mother to the devil if there was something in it for him

"You're kidding," Matt said flatly.

"We wouldn't kid about something like that," Doug assured him. "Blivins has so many hands in his pockets he's already talking about cutting services. Tom said you sit on the board of the Children's Aid Services, right? Well, Blivins thinks the private sector ought to pick that up. Worse, he's

41

making noises about the unthinkable—say hello to state income tax."

Matt gasped in abject horror—the absence of a state income tax was the last sacred cow in Texas.

Nevertheless, he'd never once thought of political office. Hell, he never thought of politics at all. Then again, he'd never thought of Cal Blivens at the capitol, either. Matt made the grave mistake of looking at Tom and felt his heart flutter. Nothing against Tom, but he was in politics because he couldn't *do* anything else. Was *he* the Democrats' great hope? Matt caught the waiter's eye and held up a finger before asking, very cautiously, very tentatively, and oh so very stupidly, "So what exactly are we talking about here?"

CHAPTER FOUR

You can't play the game if you are not in the game...
A Brand-New Day: Starting Up And Starting Over

In Rebecca's eagerness to move to the lake house, she had not counted on sharing it with so many refugees.

The latest refugee to reach them was big and brown and covered with ticks. His leg had been broken and then had healed funny, which made him look like he was half drunk when he walked. Even more unfortunate for the mutt was that he was too ugly and too used up for anyone to want him. He was never going to look much better than he did at this moment, covered head to toe in soapy bubbles.

Rebecca had discovered him in the early dawn when she had gone outside to become one with nature (as advised in a new book Rachel had sent her, *Changing Lives: A Return to the Basics Through the Power of Tai Chi*). His head was deep inside her garbage can, the contents of which had been strewn about the gravel path leading up to the main road. But the poor dog hadn't found much to sustain him, and when Rebecca called to him, he didn't bolt, but banged around the garbage can in his eagerness to get out, wagging his tail like a dog who enthusiastically and firmly believed that where there was a woman, dog food couldn't be too far away.

Now that his belly was full, Rebecca and Grayson were bathing him—or rather, the unnamed Big Dog was bathing Grayson, who was likewise covered in soapy bubbles. Rebecca hadn't fared much better—her T-shirt now sported two distinct paw prints where the dog had jumped up to thank her for his Purina. He was such a gentle and loving giant, it was beyond Rebecca's ability to comprehend how someone could drive down a near-deserted road, open the car door, push him out, and then drive off. Surely there was a special place in hell for those folks—and based on what she'd seen, it would have to be a very large place, because Big Dog was the fourth mutt to have found his way to her door, in addition to a pair of parakeets who had roosted for a week in the old cottonwood tree.

Of the three prior refugees, Rebecca and Grayson had agreed to keep Bean (so named from a broken tag where only *Bean*-something was legible), because the chunky yellow dog was mentally deranged. He walked into doors, couldn't find his food bowl, and always seemed to be going in the opposite direction of the rest of the world. Rebecca and Grayson found homes for the other two by sitting out front of Sam's Corner Grocery in nearby Ruby Falls one long Saturday afternoon.

Now it appeared that loony Bean would have company. Big Dog must have known Rebecca wouldn't turn him away, that she of all humans would understand why he had come here. After all, it was the same reason *she* had come here— to escape the reality of being out there. And truthfully, she didn't mind; the dogs gave her something to do to fill the endlessly empty moments that piled up around her.

The lake house was perfect for outcasts, too. It was really an old ranch house, three-quarters of an hour outside Austin on a lonely stretch of river between the Highland lakes, and six miles from tiny Ruby Falls. The house itself was big and airy; its many windows were covered with sheer, silky drapes that lifted gracefully with each breeze off the river. A porch wrapped all the way around the big square of a house, and one corner was screened off to make a sleeping porch for those sultry summer nights. Inside, the floors were made of old timbers, and in the center of the house was a huge great room with dueling limestone fireplaces. On one end of the great room, a corridor led to three bedrooms and two baths. On the other end, just behind the enormous kitchen and utility room, another corridor led to the master bedroom and two rooms that served as storage and an office.

What Rebecca loved best about the house was the long and gentle slope of green grass down to the bank of the Colorado River, lined with pecan trees and tall cottonwoods. That was where Rebecca and Grayson were hosing down Big Dog, screeching with laughter each time the dog wound up and shook off the water, spraying them in the process.

As a phone began to ring on the porch, Grayson picked up the hose and sprayed the dog a second time. The dog resolutely shook the water off again, sending Grayson into another shrieking fit of laughter. Rebecca ran up the steps, wiping water from her face, and as she grabbed the phone, she yelled, "Don't drown him, honey! Hello?"

"Hey."

An old, familiar shiver shot down her spine at the sound of his voice. His phone skills definitely hadn't improved, but he really didn't need to identify himself, as she would know that voice just about anywhere. As would the rest of Texas, who had to listen to him at least five times a day on the radio or TV. "Bud," she said simply.

"What's all that racket?" he asked, hearing Grayson's laughter on the lawn.

"Grayson is giving a dog a bath."

"Another stray?"

"Uh-huh."

"Take him to the pound and let them put the poor thing out of his misery."

That was the last thing she would ever do, and on top of that, when would he stop telling her what to do?

"You always had such a soft heart, Becky. Remember Flopper?"

That caught her off guard—she hadn't thought of her horse Flopper in a long time. Bud had given her the gelding for their first wedding anniversary, and Rebecca had loved that horse. When he got sick, Bud was the one who took him to the vet and returned home alone. Rebecca had cried for days in Bud's arms, which she really didn't want to think about now, and asked, "What do you want, Bud?"

"Jesus," he said, "what's the matter with you?"

Of course the old Rebecca—the doormat?—would have politely carried on a conversation about Flopper, regardless of how she felt or how much she despised Bud for what he had done to her in the last few years of their marriage. Fortunately, *that* Rebecca had been put out of her considerable misery. "I'm sorry, Bud, did you forget? We're divorced."

"I *know* that," he said irritably. "But we were together a long time, and I'd think the least you could do is be friendly."

Was he seriously out of his philandering mind? He wanted to be *friends* now? "Bud. What do you want?"

"You know, sometimes you act like it was all one way. You had your part in it, too, Becky—you think you're that perfect?"

Oh. Dear. *God.* How had she endured all those years with this man? "Did you really call to discuss ancient history?" she asked (pleased that even though he was making her furious at the moment, she wasn't falling into old traps, just like her book *Surviving Divorce: A Woman's Guide to Starting Over* said: *Never let your ex-spouse drag you back into conflict. Walk tall, walk proud, but most importantly, walk away!*).

"No, I called because I ran into Robin, and she said you were looking for a job. By the way, that sister of yours still has a mouth on her."

Rebecca could only hope that Robbie had laid a few choice words on ol' Budro. "Yes, Bud, I am looking for a job."

"*Why?* And what do you think you can do?"

First Dad, now her ex. Rebecca closed her eyes, tried to draw on the inner peace she was supposed to be learning through tai chi, recognizing instantly that in spite of the claims on the back of the video box, it wasn't working for shit at the moment. "Frankly, it's none of your goddamn business."

"It's my business if it affects my son," he said gruffly. "But if that's what you're going to do, at least call one of my dealerships down there. We can put you in the office somewhere—"

47

"No thanks."

"Bec, I'm just trying to help."

Like hell he was. "Thanks, but I don't need or want your help."

He sighed again, only louder. "Fine. Whatever. Listen, Candace and I've been invited to Aspen this weekend, so I'm gonna have to bail on Grayson."

Rebecca sank onto one of the Adirondack chairs, her anger giving way to frustration. "You've bailed on your son four times in the last two months. Don't you know that he misses his father?"

"You're the one who moved, Rebecca."

"You didn't see him in Dallas, either, Bud."

"Don't try and lay a guilt trip on me. Just tell him—"

"Uh-uh, no way!" Rebecca quickly interrupted. "You tell him—I'm sick of carrying your water."

"*My* water?" he started, but whatever else he said, Rebecca did not hear, because she had already jerked the phone away from her ear and yelled, "Grayson! Your dad wants to talk to you!"

The kid's face lit up; he instantly dropped the hose, left the dog standing patiently. Rebecca winced, her heart sinking for Grayson as he rushed to the porch, struggling to take the stairs two at a time. He snatched the phone Rebecca held out to him, and she leaned back, looked up at the ceiling fan turning lazily above her head as he said, "Hi, Daddy! Guess what. We got another dog!…Huh?…No, it's brown. The other one is yellow. He was eating out of the garbage can and Mom found him, and we haven't named him yet… Huh?"

Grayson stopped; the light began to fade from his face. Rebecca could not hear him breathe; he was holding his breath, concentrating on what his father was telling him. It probably took no longer than a moment or two for Bud to tell his son that he had chosen Candace over him once again, but it seemed to take forever for the disappointment to seep in before Grayson said quietly, "Oh!" And then, "But when can I come see you, Daddy?" Another long moment passed. "Well, can I come see Lucy?...Oh...Okay," he said softly, and handed the phone to Rebecca without another word.

She watched him walk down the porch steps to the dog, his head lowered, the spring gone from his step. "Way to go," she said low into the phone.

"Don't!" Bud snapped. "I can't help that this stuff comes up on my weekend to have him. Look, I gotta go. Tell Gray I'll call him later this week." He hung up.

"*Liar*," she muttered, and hung up, too. She sat there for a minute or two, watching Grayson halfheartedly try to get the soap off Big Dog and wondered, with her new, twenty-twenty hindsight glasses, if Bud had always been so dismissive of Grayson. The Lord knew *she* hadn't been around enough—Rebecca had left a lot of the heavy lifting to to Lucy. At the time it hadn't seemed that way, but now...well, now she wished hindsight wasn't so damn clear, because she rarely liked what she saw.

What was it the book *Giving Up and Giving In: The Path to Spiritual Well-being* said? *Let the water rush under the bridge, but continue on across,* or something like that, *for the past is the past and the only direction worth looking is ahead.*

What horseshit.

Grayson was still pretty down after his nap and even his favorite cartoon, *SpongeBob SquarePants,* wasn't cheering him up. He was lying on his stomach on the thick looped rug with his head propped in his hands, staring morosely at the TV as SpongeBob made a stack of crabby patties. The dogs were lying curled on either side of him; the brown dog seemed very happy to have found a home, and a very congenial Bean didn't seem to mind sharing it—assuming, of course, he even knew he was sharing it, which was debatable.

Rebecca was also in a pretty foul mood. Bud was always a downer, but add him to the fact that she'd had no luck in getting even a nibble on a job and could see nothing but long, empty days stretching before her, and she was miserable.

Seated in her office among a neat stack of résumés and the Sunday want ads, she had a variety of self-help books to study, including two new ones, courtesy of Rachel, who was really into spiritual astrology this month. Just last night, on the phone, she had excitedly reported that Uranus was in Rebecca's house and was rising. `

"What?" Rebecca had asked, confused.

"Uranus!" Rachel cried gleefully. "The last time Uranus was in your house was like 1920-something. Do you know what this *means?*"

"No, I—"

"It means that doors will open for you that you never dreamed would open! You are going to be able to draw from energy stores you didn't even know you had! Things that seemed bleak just a few weeks ago are now wonderful new opportunities! Your karma is really going to take off, Rebecca!"

"Rachel," Rebecca said skeptically. "First, take a breath. And second, do you really believe that stuff?"

Her sister gasped. "Of course I believe it. Don't you?"

It was hard to argue with such enthusiasm, and Rebecca didn't try. But she made a mental note to have a serious talk with Rach at some future date about all this new-age guru crap she kept sending her way. It damn sure didn't feel like Uranus had suddenly moved in and taken up residence in her house, and there weren't any doors opening for her that she could see. More like they were slamming shut.

With a weary sigh, Rebecca picked up her journal (a practice recommended in virtually *all* of her books and seminars, including Moira's, so what the hey), into which she faithfully entered three positive things about her life each day. Before she attacked the new round of résumé distribution, she entered:

Positive Affirmations of My Life:
1. Shoes for all occasions
2. Dogs

She was peeking back over previous entries hoping for a little help on number three when the phone rang. She propped her bare feet on the desk and picked up the phone, "Hello?"

"Ah…Rebecca?"

"Yes?" she responded, using her extremely polite, extremely ingrained, beauty pageant voice.

"Hey, Tom Masters here."

Her feet came crashing down to the wood floor, her pulse suddenly pounding. Tom Masters was an old friend of Bud's, a state politician or something—why would he be calling her? "*Hi*, Tom! How are you?"

"Doing great! And you?" Before Rebecca could answer, he added contritely, "Hey, sorry to hear about the split. You and Bud were one of mine and Glenda's favorite couples."

"Oh...thanks." Seeing as she and Bud had seen Tom and his wife about once every other year, Rebecca thought that a little gratuitous.

"So I heard you were living down here now. That's *great*!"

"It is?"

"Sure! Didn't Bud tell you I'm running for lieutenant governor this fall?"

Oh, for Chrissakes! This was about a campaign contribution? "Bud and I aren't exactly chums, Tom."

"Oh...right," he said as if that were somehow news. "Well, I've been a state senator for a couple of terms now, and I'm making a bid for lieutenant governor. When Glenda and I heard you were down here in Austin, she said, 'Hey, Rebecca would be a great addition to your team!'"

Interesting—her relationship with Glenda consisted of complimenting each other's shoes. "What team is that?"

"My team. You know, my campaign team!"

Whoa...Rebecca sat up. "An addition to your campaign team?" she repeated dumbly.

"You bet. I've got some of the brightest folks around to help me get elected. But I just thought if you had some extra time, maybe you could volunteer. Here's the deal, Rebecca. You have a lot of important friends in this state. You know their likes, their dislikes, and I need people like you to help get the word out about my candidacy and help me develop new strategies that speak to all Texans. I need bright, clever people who can help me form an agenda that is relevant to all the many different constituents of Texas."

Rebecca was standing now—forget that she hadn't a clue what Tom did as a state senator—this was too good to be true! Was it possible that an opportunity like this could just fall into her lap from nowhere? After weeks and weeks of searching for a job? It sounded perfect, something she really could do. Wow, maybe Rachel was right—maybe her karma was kicking in! This was something she could do, something where maybe she could learn stuff about computers, and maybe even meet some people who could give her...dare she think it? A paying job!

"You want me to help you?" she asked, just to make sure she wasn't misconstruing things.

"I sure do!" Tom said enthusiastically. "You'd be a perfect asset—I mean, you've always been so clever and perceptive."

Had she really? Gee, she hadn't even known it!

"Yep, I'd be thrilled if you could see your way to spending a few hours a week with me. That's all. Just a few hours where I can pick your brain."

"I don't even know what to say, Tom," she said, feeling herself blush with his praise. "I've never done anything like this before."

"Oh, sure you have! It's not any different than throwing one of those big parties you're famous for. Listen, why don't you drop by our campaign staff meeting tomorrow afternoon? My folks are getting together to talk about next steps."

"I am so flattered," she gushed, already pulling her hair out of its scrunchie. "I'd love to give you a hand."

"Then you can make it?"

"Ah...let me look at my schedule," she said, and held the phone away from her ear as she did a silent little Snoopy happy dance, then stopped, caught her breath, and said in her best, I've-got-a-life-too voice, "I think I can rearrange a couple of things. What time did you say?"

"Around four, my office at the capitol. And thanks, Rebecca. Your presence will definitely make this the A-team."

"Oh no, thank you, Tom. I'll see you tomorrow."

She clicked off the phone, threw her arms wide, and grinned up at the ceiling. "Excellent!" she exclaimed, and abruptly pivoted about, her mind already racing ahead to the perfect outfit. As she marched from her office, she joined SpongeBob SquarePants in chanting, "*I'm rea-dy, I'm rea-dy, I'm rea-dy!*"

CHAPTER FIVE

*It is important to always look professional. Clothes should be
clean and pressed, shoes polished, and hair neatly combed.
In the words of Coleman Cox, "keeping your clothes well
pressed will keep you from looking hard-pressed!"*

THE UNQUALIFIED APPLICANT

Having no idea what campaign types wore, Rebecca
chose a demure white Chanel suit trimmed in black
after watching a Lifetime TV movie in which the female lawyer lead wore very austere business suits. Rebecca thought
she looked neither conservative nor liberal, but middle of
the road. Fair. Objective. And then she remembered that
she wasn't running for office, Tom Masters was, and spruced
it up with her favorite black pearl jewelry, and decided that
she was perfectly attired for a Campaign Strategy Meeting.

How cool! How *Uranus!*

She found Tom's office at the state capitol easy enough, but
there wasn't anyone there, just a little hand-lettered sign that said:
Back at 4:00. Rebecca tried the door; it was open, so she stepped
inside. She quietly took in the ornate marble and oak decor, and
as she was admiring a painting of Ft. Worth, she heard a faint
rustle of noise from the back offices, and decided to walk back
and announce herself, lest she startle anyone with her presence.

Moving down a corridor crowded with stacks of paper and state budgets, she peeked in each office until she finally came upon the source of the noise—at which point, her heart just stopped. Cold. No beat, no pulse, nothing but instant and potentially permanent paralysis. Common sense told her that this was impossible—it had to be some sort of setup, one of those hidden camera gags, because it was impossible for *that* man to be sitting in Tom's office now— except that it *was* him, seated at a computer, staring intently at the screen as he absently bounced a Nerf basketball against the wall.

Fortunately, he hadn't yet noticed her, thank you, God. Rebecca, recovered from her paralysis, was slowly and quietly backing out of that doorway—but not without noticing the lock of sienna-brown hair that had fallen across his forehead, slipped from a wavy crop streaked gold by the sun. He had carelessly tossed aside his suit coat and was wearing a crisp white shirt, a very hip tie flipped over one broad shoulder, and shoes polished to a high sheen. And, she noticed, as he lifted his arm to bounce the Nerf ball, he was also very trim. Funny, she hadn't remembered the pompous ass being quite so...*fine*—

"I'm sorry, I didn't hear you come in," he said suddenly, twisting when her purse inadvertently hit the doorjamb.

Rebecca froze as he came to his feet, a charming smile on his face and in his expressive gray eyes. How had she missed such a square, clean-shaven chin? Or that *smile*, for God's sake, a gorgeous white smile that ended with a perfect dimple on either end...a smile that was rapidly fading as recognition and then just plain horror swept over him.

Actually, it wasn't horror but confusion, as Matt's first thought was that she had to be some sort of weird stalker—

what else would bring her here? Nevertheless, if that's what she was, then she had to be the most drop-dead gorgeous stalker ever—his memory of her was right on about that. She was, like he'd recalled (several times), tall and thin, with silky long black hair, and silky long legs, and clear blue eyes that glimmered, demonlike, as she stared at him beneath two perfectly sculpted brows dipped in a dark vee.

"Well hello, Looney Tunes," he said, folding his arms across his chest. "What's the matter, lose your quesadilla again?"

"Hardly," she said, likewise folding her arms beneath her bosom, squaring off.

"So…you're just stalking me?"

Her demon blue eyes narrowed. "You know, you are in serious need of an ego deflation, Mr. ah…I'm sorry, what was it again? Popinjay?"

Ah yes, this was the Little Miss Perfect who had crept, uninvited, into his thoughts so many times over the last couple of weeks or so, and he grinned. "It's Parrish, thanks. So if you aren't looking for a quesadilla, and you aren't stalking me, then why are you tracking me down?"

"You should really see someone, you know, because your imagination seems to border on the delusional quite often. Now really, why would I be tracking you down?"

"Why wouldn't you?" Matt asked, just to see what she'd say.

"Here we go again," she said, sighing impatiently, "the old, 'I'm-a-stud-so-you-*must*-be-following-me' routine. That really must get so tiresome for you."

Actually, her following him wouldn't be so bad, really, because she was beautiful, really beautiful, and Matt knew from beautiful. "Can you blame me?" he asked cheerfully, taking a step forward, wanting his suit coat. "You have a habit of popping up around the capitol wherever I happen to be."

That earned him a soft laugh of disbelief. "You really *are* delusional." She shifted her weight to one hip, which put her just inside the little cracker box office and directly in the way of his suit coat.

"That's just what I was thinking about you," he said. "What is it that makes all the gorgeous ones so wacko?"

With a dainty snort, she rolled her eyes. "What is it that makes men like you so full of themselves?"

"Probably wackos like you chasing us around," he said with a grin, and took a step forward, so that they were standing almost chest to chest. "But if it's all the same to you, I'd rather just fast-forward past your little game and get down to whatever it is you're after."

She gave him a withering glance she had probably used a million times on a million guys in a million venues; a superior, don't-touch-me look that, on lesser women, Matt could usually dismantle with merely a smile. Only this woman was obviously a master at deflecting, so Matt just reached around her for his coat, his arm next to her head, his body only inches from hers. He couldn't help himself; he glanced down at her endlessly blue gaze, one that was challenging him, he could see it, and felt a smile playing at the corner of his lips. "Let's just pretend you aren't following me—"

"Oh, *let's*."

"So what are you doing here?" he asked, quietly breathing in her perfume.

She cocked her head to one side, obviously enjoying the fact that he didn't know. "What are *you* doing here?"

Matt leaned in a little closer, his mouth only inches from her face as he groped for his coat behind her back. "I asked you first, Miss Priss."

"Okay, genius," she said, tapping a finger against her bottom lip. "Let's put on our thinking caps, shall we? Why would in be the offices of a state senator?"

He wasn't actually thinking too much at the moment as his gaze wandered her lips, her little nose, and her killer eyes...until a thought suddenly occurred to him. A thought that perhaps this really wasn't about him. "You're not here to see Senator Masters...are you?"

"*Brilliant* deduction."

Matt instantly reared back, coat and all. So the little cuckoo was a friend of Tom's? Unbelievable! "You're kidding."

"I am so not kidding," she said cheerfully, smiling with such pleasure that cute little laugh dimples creased her cheeks. "Now it's your turn. What are *you* doing here?" she insisted. "Friend of Tom's?"

"Fraternity brothers."

"That certainly would explain a lot." She smiled fully at him then, almost blinding him with it.

Matt shook his head as he shoved into his coat, marveling at the unbelievable odds of this little coincidence. Too bad, really—he was enjoying their verbal fencing. But, as he really shouldn't continue to bait Tom's friend by calling her a stalker, he motioned vaguely to the office across the hall. "You'd probably be more comfortable waiting in his office."

"Oh, that's all right," she said, obviously pleased with herself. "I'm sure he'll want to meet in a larger area. I had the impression that several people would be here."

Matt paused in the straightening of his tie to look at her. "Are you sure you have the right day? Tom's got a meeting this afternoon, but it's with the campaign staff—"

"Yes, that's why I'm here."

Now Matt was seriously confused. The campaign was fully staffed, and it was too early for neighborhood volunteers. He looked at her expensive suit, her purse and shoes, the black pearl ring on her hand. "But…"

The door opened at that moment; they both turned toward the sound of several people entering the office, and squeezed, simultaneously, through the door and into the crowded hallway. "Tom!" she called, and Tom waved at her over someone's head as he came hurrying forward.

"I see you two have met!" Tom exclaimed happily before grabbing her in a big bear hug that almost swallowed her whole.

"Not really," she said politely, straining for air.

"Oh? Well, this is Matt Parrish—but you can call him Matt," Tom said, and let go of her, winking over her head at Matt. "I bet you remembered Rebecca Reynolds right off, didn't you?" he said to Matt.

Why should he—

"It's Lear," she quickly corrected him, blushing lightly.

"Oh, that's right, I keep forgetting. Rebecca *Lear*. That was your name back in the glory days, right?" Tom continued jovially, and to Matt he said, "You know what I'm talking about—Miss Texas 1990?"

Matt's jaw dropped, and he wasn't certain that his tongue didn't all but roll out onto the carpet, Tasmanian

Devil style. He looked at Rebecca Lear again, his shock mixing with a growing sense of alarm. What was Tom doing?

But Tom had grabbed Rebecca's elbow and was already steering her toward the conference room before Matt could say anything. "You were Miss Houston in 1989, weren't you, Rebecca?"

"Oh, Tom! That's such old news—"

"Nonsense, don't be modest. We're not modest in this campaign! We're going to crow about our accomplishments! Matt here is one of the state's best litigators, and don't think for a moment that he hides his light under a bushel. You wanna sue, Parrish is the man for the job," he said loudly as he practically shoved Rebecca into the conference room ahead of him, and boomed, "Hey gang, meet Miss Texas 1990!"

Three heads swiveled in their direction, all of them looking as stunned as Matt felt, gaping at Rebecca Lear as if she had just dropped in from another planet in another galaxy, far, far away. After a long moment, Gilbert, the guy with the Jesus sandals, asked laughingly, "Hey, Miss Texas, where's your crown?"

"Oh! In my purse," she said. "I was going to wait until a little later to put it on."

A silent moment or two passed before anyone realized she was actually kidding.

CHAPTER SIX

A job description is merely a guideline of what may be expected. Never use it as an excuse to avoid broadening your horizons...

A BRAND-NEW DAY

A t least the older woman with the helmet hairdo chuckled at Rebecca's little joke, but the rest of them, judging by their expressions (and particularly the state's best freakin' litigator), were clearly wondering what the hell Miss Texas 1990 was doing in their conference room.

Frankly, so was Rebecca. What in God's name had she thought this would be? Maybe they'd play a little bridge and talk politely about politics? These people had credentials and a reason to be here! They weren't insecure nobodies, and honestly, if Tom wasn't blocking her exit, she'd turn and run out the door.

But she was stuck right where she stood, feeling ridiculous with her little tiara-in-the-purse routine, until a small woman with short, magenta-streaked hair, army-surplus cargo pants, and a T-shirt that read *Keep Austin Weird* stood up and asked, "Tom, did you want to order pizza?"

"Yes, please, Angie! Rebecca, I'd like you to meet Gilbert, Pat, and Angie, my paid campaign staff," he said (Rebecca couldn't help noticing the one with the helmet-hair, Pat, rolled her eyes at that). "And you met Matt," he added. "So we thought we'd have a late-afternoon powwow. Angie, see what everyone wants on their pizza, will you?" he asked, shrugging out of his coat. "Just have a seat there, Rebecca," he said as he pointed to a chair at the conference table.

Unable to gracefully extract herself now, Rebecca sat like the good little girl that she was, but caught a glimpse of Big Shot, who, having recovered from his shock that she wasn't really after him, but merely a former beauty queen playing at politics, was looking at her now like she was some sort of freak. "Tom...a word please?" he said low, and grabbed Tom by the elbow and dragged him to the corner of the room for a little tête-à-tête.

Uh-huh, she could just imagine what that was about. It was obvious to her that the state's best litigator was busy making sure Tom understood that not only was she a fraud and had no business being here, but had probably thrown in a couple of terms like "stalker" and "lunatic" for good measure. She stole a glimpse at him again. Wow. He was really giving Tom an earful. In spite of having spent one entire evening reading *Face Value: The Art of Reading Friends and Strangers*, whose author would undoubtedly insist that Matt had something more important to speak to Tom about than her, that most people went around thinking about themselves and not her, and that what looked like a heated discussion really had nothing to do with her, Rebecca was pretty sure that it did. Call it woman's intuition (which *Our Bodies, Our Minds, Our Hearts* would say was a much more accurate perception), but Rebecca was pretty sure their conversation had everything to do with her.

"Anchovies?"

"What?" she asked, startled by the question suddenly put to her.

"Do you want anchovies?"

It was Gilbert, a guy with bed-head that looked 100 percent natural instead of affected, trying to gag her with anchovies. "I, ah…whatever the group wants," she said, pasting a smile on her face.

Gilbert plopped down next to her. "They all want anchovies. Angie's already ordered it. So no shit, you were Miss Texas?"

No shit. "Yes."

"Cool," he said, nodding.

Rebecca didn't know anymore if it was cool. She chalked that title up to something else Bud had made her do, as if the title of Miss Texas made her worthy to be his wife. What a stupid girl she had been then, her stupidity eclipsed only by her stupidity now. *Stupid, stupid…*

"Hey, ready to roll up your sleeves and get to work?" Tom called to everyone.

Apparently, Tom and Matt had finished their little talk, because Tom was sauntering back to the table. He winked at Rebecca, fell onto a plush leather chair sporting a giant seal of the State of Texas, and grinned at his little group. "Ready to talk campaigns?" he asked, to which they all nodded. "Okay, the last time we met, we decided to get a manageable list of campaign issues together to include in the literature. Everyone's had a chance to cogitate. Let's start with the most pressing issues facing Texas today."

Matt opened his mouth to speak, but Tom's large head and shoulders (his neck conspicuous in its absence) were suddenly looming in front of Rebecca. "Rebecca? What do you think?"

What did she think? Why? Why did he want to know what she thought? "I, uh...I—"

"The economy," Matt interjected, his focus on Tom now. "Either we propose something to stimulate the economy or start gearing up for a debate on the merits of a state income tax."

"What about health insurance?" Gilbert said, looking unexpectedly smart. "Texas has an unusually high percentage of uninsured persons that are eating away at state coffers."

"Sorry, but I think education is going to be the biggest battleground," Pat chimed in. "Teachers in Texas have one of the lowest starting salaries of any state, and the school funding mechanism is a piece of junk."

"All important issues," Tom said, nodding thoughtfully. "And as you know, education and insurance have certainly been the basis for several of my bills this session," he added. Everyone nodded. Tom glanced at Rebecca from the corner of his eye. "Anything you want to add, Rebecca?"

"I, ah, I don't really—"

"Don't be shy! There are no stupid questions or comments in this room!" Tom urged her.

"Well, okay," she said, frantically racking her brain. "Umm...this is for the campaign?"

Tom laughed. "Well now, that question was a little on the stupid side."

Rebecca blinked.

Tom punched her lightly on the shoulder. "Just kidding! Yes, this is for the campaign. So what do you think?"

Okay, God, just go ahead and open up the floor now, please.
She glanced at the others sitting around the table, looking
at her so expectantly, as if she knew something, as if she had
something to offer! *Come on, it's not rocket science! Just think
of what you've read in* Texas Monthly*!* her new, improved self
chastised her. *Be bold!* "Well…"

Across from her, Matt Parrish sighed impatiently. It
wasn't a very loud sigh, but the sound of it, so goddamn
familiar, kicked her square in the butt and made her sit up.
Perhaps she had heard that sigh one too many times in her
life from her father and her ex-husband for all the wrong
reasons. Who knew? The only thing she knew for certain
was that it made her blood boil. BOIL. She shifted her gaze
to the litigator, and damn him, *that* was a smirk if ever she'd
seen one.

"The environment," she said clearly and distinctly, surprising the holy hell out of herself. "Protecting the beauty of
Texas land, indigenous wildlife, and natural habitats."

No one uttered a word; Rebecca panicked, fearing that
she'd said something completely ridiculous. But then Tom
grinned proudly. "Hey, that's good!" Rebecca instantly felt
the panic begin to ebb, and a new sense of emboldened self
began to creep in.

Mr. Hotshot Litigator looked unimpressed. "Do you
really think that issue is important around the state, outside
of Austin?"

She nodded resolutely in spite of having not even the
slightest clue how important it was anywhere, much less in
or out of Austin.

"Everyone is concerned about the environment," Gilbert
said.

"It's a death knell outside Central Texas," Matt said, frowning. "It's a regional issue, not a statewide one."

"I don't think it's just regional," Rebecca heard herself say, surprising herself yet again with her sudden, newfound, based-on-one-short-article knowledge of the environment. "I think it's something all Texans are concerned about, from the panhandle to the coast."

"Really? So let me ask—is everyone in your social circle living in fear of global warming and the destruction of the rain forests, or is it just the endangered salamanders that keep y'all awake at night?"

Smart-ass. Definitely the type that had to have all the ideas, and therefore, all the attention. "Well, certainly the salamanders," she said in her best I'm-just-a-stupid-beauty-queen voice. "But also strip mining. You know about strip mining, don't you? Surely someone has sued over it," she said sweetly, putting aside that she knew nothing about strip mining, other than the article in *Texas Monthly* she read: *Golden Cheek Warbler Habitat Destroyed by Strip Mining; Other Habitats Threatened.* Nevertheless, Rebecca was prepared to fake her way through it and flashed Mr. Big-Ass Lawyer a very definite, very unperfect Rebecca-like smirk.

Matt clearly didn't like that, but before he could speak, Pat said, "She's absolutely right," which instantly cemented Rebecca's undying friendship for life. Even more incredibly, Gilbert asked, "Aren't there a lot of federal dollars for preserving natural habitats? Isn't that something we ought to look into?"

"What does this campaign have to do with a bunch of birds or salamanders?" Matt asked.

"It's not about birds or salamanders, Matt," Pat said with a hint of snippiness in her voice. "Strip mining is devastating to the environment, destroys natural habitats and threatens our groundwater. It's about *our* environment."

"What about heat? Don't you think we need coal? Or uranium? What about all the jobs the strip mining industry provides to Texas? Look," Matt said, holding up a hand before Pat could argue, "Don't get me wrong. I'm not anti-environment. I'm just saying it's not a huge issue in Texas, and it's a topic I think we should avoid altogether. Trust me, in a statewide campaign, no one is going to want to talk about a bunch of pits."

"But what if they do?" Rebecca heard herself ask. "People feel strongly about it. There are some pretty passionate feelings just here in this room."

Matt's narrow gaze zeroed in on her as Tom quickly agreed, "You're right, Rebecca. We should at least have a position in case it comes up on the campaign trail. Can't hurt, right?"

Now Matt looked as if his head might blow off his shoulders into tiny pieces. "Can't hurt," he said tightly, dragging his gaze from Rebecca to Tom, "but we've *got* to focus on the economy. The jobless rate is the highest it's been in two decades, the Homeland Security initiative is putting the urban counties into fiscal straits like they haven't seen in a century, and minimum wage is not keeping pace with inflation."

"Dude, you're so rad!" Angie laughed. "You really know your stuff!"

"Yes, you're absolutely right, Matt," Tom agreed, but grinned at Rebecca. "And so is Rebecca! You seem to have a sense of what's important around the state—I knew I was right about you. Folks, meet our new campaign strategist!"

Campaign strategist? Rebecca let out a little cry of happy surprise at that unexpected announcement—it even sounded like a real position.

Popinjay blinked at Tom in total, unfettered, disbelief.

"Tom, are you sure?" Rebecca asked, smiling so broadly that her cheeks hurt.

"I am very sure," he said, nodding emphatically. "You bring just the right touch of empathy to this crew," he declared. "Say, where's that pizza'? I'm starving! Rebecca, you like pizza?"

"Love it!" she lied, and as Smarty-Pants glared at her from across the table, she shrugged out of her Chanel jacket and rolled up her sleeves to get down to work.

CHAPTER SEVEN

Stubbornness is also determination. It's simply a matter of shifting from "won't power" to "will power."

PETER McWILLIAMS, LIFE 101

Campaign strategist?

Matt tossed his briefcase onto one of several over-stuffed leather armchairs gracing his law offices, punched his fists to his waist, and glared out the plate glass windows at the shining dome of the state capitol. Campaign *strategist...* implying, naturally, that the person *knew* a little something about campaign strategy. Which she obviously didn't. Strip mining. A fork in his eye would have been better than that.

That little scene yesterday was exactly the sort of thing Matt couldn't abide, the very thing that made him want to drink himself into a catatonic stupor. If he'd had a brain in his head, he would have said not just no, but hell no, the night Tom and his pals cornered him at Stetson's. He should have known that involvement in this project was going to aggravate him. And it already had, ten times over. Which was really a pity, because Matt actually liked the work. Honest to God, he did. He found the range of political issues intriguing, the challenges facing the state invigorating. He liked the men and women he had met since signing on, the ones who were affiliated with the party and liked to joke he had the potential of being the next John Kennedy. The ones who kept whispering words in his ear, like district attorney. He had to admit he sort of liked the sound of that... Matthew Parrish, District Attorney.

But Matt was beginning to believe that Tom didn't have a stance on any issue that didn't further his personal agenda in some way. He had yet to hear Tom speak or act in a manner that would indicate that he didn't ultimately have his own interests at heart. He hoped he was wrong, and had stood silently by when Tom had hired Gilbert, a grad student with one pair of black jeans, some computer skills, and a dubious background in speechwriting (the son of an old friend and cheap, Tom said). Then Angie, the waitress from Tom's favorite Fourth Street haunt who had just graduated from tech school and was going to set up a phone bank for him (also cheap with the added bonus of a nice pair of ta-tas, which was, apparently, the most important consideration for Senator Masters). And when Matt had tried to add people to the team who knew something about statewide issues, like Pat, a former state attorney for the education department who knew everything there was to know about education and the goings-on at the capitol, Tom shrugged and said, "She's kind of old, isn't she?"

Fortunately, together, Tom and Matt had miraculously formed a decent crew. But Rebecca Lear? The woman who thought she was God's gift? Disgusted, Matt walked to his desk, fell into his chair, and propped his feet on the corner of his extra-long mahogany desk. He pressed the tips of his fingers together, stared at a painting on his wall of a bunch of cowboys around a chuck wagon.

Matt was still fuming about her hire. In fact, he couldn't get it off his mind. Not that he couldn't see why a philanderer like Tom would want a woman like Rebecca Lear hanging around—she was drop-dead gorgeous, had practically knocked him out of his socks when he'd first clapped eyes on her in the park. He would never admit it aloud in a million years, but for a brief moment (before she had opened her mouth and called him cheap), he was amazed that a woman who looked like that was actually about to speak to him.

Yeah, he could definitely understand how Tom would be captivated. He was a married man and had his dalliances from time to time, and Matt had considered the possibility that this was all about getting laid. But as he recalled Rebecca's curves in that tight white suit and the long shiny black hair and those eyes, he was pretty amazed that Tom could even know someone like Rebecca. She damn sure didn't seem the type to hang out with an old lineman like Tom.

So then what was she doing on his campaign? As a campaign strategist, the highest position to be held in this campaign? The very same position he held, a position for which there was only *one* slot before she came along and Tom created another out of thin air?

That was the reason why Matt had pulled Tom aside. "I thought this was a serious strategy session, Tom," he had said. "So what's with Miss Texas?"

Tom had laughed, cuffed Matt on the arm. "Nice ass, huh?" When Matt did not respond to that, and wondered if Tom ever heard of sexual harassment, Tom sighed. "Okay, do you have any idea who her father is? Ever hear of Lear Transport Industries?"

Of course Matt had heard of LTI. A person couldn't live in Texas without knowing about LTI—it was one of the biggest homegrown companies around. But what that had to do with the running of a campaign had gone right over Matt's head, and he had demanded, "So?"

"*So?* So she's got a list of contacts a mile long. She was married to Bud Reynolds—you know, the guy with all the car dealerships? We could really cover some ground with her."

"Okay. Take her money. Wine her, dine her, and get her to make some calls. But what is she doing here? What does she know about political campaigns?"

"I guess we'll find out, won't we?" Tom had said cheerfully, and when he saw that did not please Matt, had added congenially, "Hey, if it turns out she has shit for brains, we'll lose her. But it seems worth a little ass-kissing to corner some of the biggest contributors in the state, and let me just go on record here saying that I, for one, wouldn't mind kissing *that* ass one bit."

Matt could only hope that she'd get tired of it and disappear. And really, what did he care, anyway? It wasn't like it was his campaign. He should focus on his most pressing issue at the moment, which was getting prepared for an important hearing on the Kiker case. With a sigh, Matt shoved a hand through his hair, switched on his computer, and punched the intercom, asking Harold to bring him some coffee.

A moment later, as he pulled files out of his briefcase, Harold came striding in, steaming cup of coffee in hand. "Here you are, Mr. Parrish. Exactly as you like it. Black."

"Thanks, Harold," he said absently.

Harold placed it on a coaster—the little bluebonnet design facing Matt, of course—and pushed it carefully toward him. "Will there be anything else, Mr. Parrish?"

"Yeah, you can bring me the Kiker briefs."

Harold wrinkled his nose. "Such sordid business," he said as he marched from the room.

Harold couldn't even begin to imagine how sordid. Kelly Kiker was a hard, chain-smoking woman who looked like she'd been rode hard and put up wet too many times to count in her forty-two years. She'd been in and out of the court system for most of those years, but she had finally gotten her act together, was living in her father's trailer, and had landed a clerical job collecting fees. Kelly Kiker might have made some bad choices in her life, but she wasn't stupid, and she quickly figured out that her boss was siphoning a little extra pocket money for himself from those fees. When she confronted her boss about it, he fired her. Kelly was going to let it go—she was used to letting stuff go—but the more she thought about it, the more she thought it wasn't right, and went to the trouble to get Matt's name from her probation officer (who happened to be another woman he'd once dated).

Matt had been doing litigation so long that nothing really surprised him anymore. But there was still occasions where a case would cross his desk and make him question his decision to become a high-flying lawyer. Cases that left him so bewildered that he would literally lie awake at night wondering what the hell had happened to mankind. Where was the good?

Kelly Kiker was definitely one of those cases. She was trying to do right and had been kicked in the teeth for it.

Why Tom's campaign had all the feel of being another one of those things to keep him awake at night, he didn't know—but it sure made the image of Rebecca Lear that kept flashing by his mind's eye all the more irritating.

While Matt was trying to craft a legal argument for getting Kelly Kiker justice, Rebecca had come back from a Transformations Seminar (Track Four) where she had learned how to self-visualize her alter ego (*Visualize success! Visualize your future!*). Currently, she was visualizing herself as a campaign strategist, and was trying to figure out how to surf the Internet for any information on strip mining.

Fortunately, she had Jo Lynn to keep Grayson occupied. Jo Lynn was her seventy-year-old neighbor who lived alone just the other side of six acres of blackjack oak, cottonwoods, and mesquite trees. Jo Lynn had posted a note on the bulletin board at Sam's Corner Grocery in Ruby Falls: *Looking for something to do a few hours each week.* Rebecca had called her; they'd had a lovely chat, and Rebecca hired her to watch Grayson a few hours a week.

Grayson had been resistant at first—"*I want Lucy!*" he'd screamed. When Rebecca told him he couldn't have Lucy, he had run into his room and slammed the door shut, crying, "You're MEEEEEEEEEEEEEAN, Mommy!" But then Jo Lynn had come over with a bucket of homemade ice cream and her pet goat, and Grayson had stopped crying for Lucy. Jo Lynn was a spry, "practically widowed" woman (practically, she said, because her husband, who was in a home for Alzheimer's patients, did not know her) who loved life. She had skin that looked like buttery leather, and laugh lines that seemed to have been hand-tooled onto her face. The sun had yellowed her gray hair, too, which she wore in a girlish ponytail. And oddly, practically everything Jo Lynn wore was tie-dyed—which gave the impression of some horrific laundry accident.

Jo Lynn loved Grayson, spoiled him rotten, and was doing so this very moment, down at the river.

Which left Rebecca with some time to hone her Internet skills. Heretofore, her forays onto the World Wide Web hadn't been many. Not that she was completely isolated from it—she used it for e-mail like the rest of the world, and she shopped online from Neiman Marcus (God, did she miss that store). She was determined to find some coherent information about strip mining and politics before tomorrow. Because tomorrow, Tom was having a meeting in his new campaign offices, and she'd be damned if she was going to show up without giving Matt Parrish a little something to think about.

Rebecca would bet her entire net worth that she'd met all the exasperatingly arrogant men she could possibly meet in a lifetime, but *that* guy had to take the cake. She was determined to find a way to rub that smirk right off his face, and visualized, per Track Four, doing just that. With her bare hands. Rambo-style.

Seated in her big square kitchen, she glanced up over her laptop and saw Jo Lynn marching across the lawn, Grayson and the dogs trailing earnestly behind. They clomped up the back porch steps and into the kitchen; Grayson immediately headed for the refrigerator and a box of juice. Jo Lynn helped him climb onto a stool at the kitchen island before wandering over to where Rebecca was working. She peered over her shoulder at the computer screen. "Whatcha doing?"

"Looking for some information about strip mining and environmental concerns."

"Sounds like something my mama would do. She always had a curiosity about things, you know? She was so curious, you know, she ran off with the circus."

"Your mom is in the *circus*?" Grayson gasped.

"No, honey," Rebecca laughed. "Jo Lynn's mom didn't run away with a circus," she said with all authority, then looked uncertainly at Jo Lynn. "Did she?"

"Of course not!" Jo Lynn grinned, her dentures stark white against her leathery skin. "That's just what my grandma used to tell us kids to make us feel better," she explained as she walked toward the back door, where she paused, looking absently out the screen door. "I suspect she was trying to put a little lipstick on that pig, 'cause I know for a fact it was just a carnival—you think Barnum and Bailey ever came to Ruby Falls?" She laughed, shook her head as she pushed the screen door open and marched through it. "Grayson, you take good care of them dogs, now!" she called as she bounded down the steps, leaving Grayson and Rebecca to gape at her as she cranked up the golf cart she used to travel the thatch of blackjack oak between their houses.

A half hour later, with Grayson napping in his race car bed, Rebecca was on page sixteen of the seemingly endless list of websites devoted to either the benefits or detriments of strip mining. Yet in pages and pages of websites and reference links, there was one thing that was so conspicuous that it might as well have been an elephant standing in her kitchen. Strip mining was not, apparently, a major problem in Texas. It was a problem in one spot near Austin about which *Texas Monthly* had reported.

How big of a moron could one person be? She'd have to say about five feet ten inches and one hundred and thirty divorce-skinny pounds, because that horrible devil of a man was *right*. So much for her inarguable stance on protecting natural habitats. Rebecca buried her face in her hands: she had no business being in this group of campaign people, absolutely none. But no way was she turning back now— she'd turned back all her life, and *this* time, she was pushing forward, because this gig had too much riding on it for her.

Rebecca went to the fridge, opened it wide, and stood, staring blindly at the contents. She could not erase the image of one supreme, holier-than-thou, smiling Matt Popinjay when she reported back that maybe strip mining wasn't such a big deal after all. Frankly, she'd rather be tossed into a murky hole of water and eaten by piranhas, or whatever it was they did on those reality TV shows, but she was not going to let that pompous ass intimidate her.

Rebecca slammed the fridge door shut without taking anything out and marched back to her computer, sat hard, glaring at Google as if it was that thing's fault, and punched in TEXAS POLITICS.

Unqualified Applicant Rule 8: Never let them see you cry.

CHAPTER EIGHT

Ignoramus, n. A person unacquainted with certain kinds of knowledge familiar to yourself, and having certain other kinds that you know nothing about...

THE DEVIL'S DICTIONARY

Positive Affirmations of My Life:
1. Google.com
2. Jo Lynn
3. I am not, nor have I ever been, as pompous as Mr. Big Pants (must find alternative source for insult vocab other than Cartoon Network)

As it turned out, the next day dawned gloriously brilliant, and Rebecca happily sucked the early spring air into her lungs during her predawn moment of becoming one with nature. This day was exactly the type the book, *A Brand-New Day: Starting Up and Starting Over,* said was perfect for fostering attacks on new challenges.

Later that afternoon, with the newly named Frank lying at the foot of her bed and Bean lying half under it, she dressed in black slacks, a sleeveless sky-blue sweater, and matching black-and-blue-checkered sandals (having determined that in Austin, Chanel suits were perhaps a bit overstated, unless one was someone really important, like

Sandra Bullock). After ushering the dogs outside, Rebecca popped into her Range Rover and hummed cheerfully along to her *Modern Mozart* as she sped down the two-lane road. Beside her was a brand-new ultra-chic briefcase, which was, for once, holding something besides a lipstick, a pen, and a blank notebook. In the back was a cardboard box stuffed with some surprises for the campaign staff and the new campaign offices.

She pulled into the parking lot of the Little Maverick Preschool just as Grayson appeared with his enormous backpack. Head down, he walked in that determined way of his to the Range Rover and climbed inside to his car seat.

"Hey, kiddo," Rebecca said, reaching back to help him with his seat belt. "How was your day?"

"Okay." He looked out the window.

"So what did you do today?"

"I pushed Taylor down," he said, as if that was as commonplace as nap time; which, alarmingly, it was fast becoming.

"Grayson!" she exclaimed. "I told you not to push him down!"

"I know," Grayson said, shrugging. "But he said my dad isn't really my dad."

"What do you mean, your dad isn't really your dad?"

"Taylor said that isn't my dad on the radio," Grayson repeated, looking up at her with Bud's hazel eyes.

Unfortunately, having handed the first three or four years of his life to a nanny, her maternal skills were far less honed than her maternal instincts, but her instincts said this squabble with Taylor was growing into something much bigger than a playground thing. "I don't care *what* Taylor says about anything, Grayson Andrew. If you push him down again, I will bend you over my knee and spank you like I've never spanked you before, do you understand?"

"But you've never spanked me, Mom."

"That is beside the point, young man! Do you understand what I am telling you?"

He nodded, rubbed his hand across his nose. "He *is* my dad," he muttered.

"Of course he is your dad. You know it, I know it. It doesn't matter what Taylor thinks, okay?"

Grayson lolled his head against the car seat.

She glared at him a second longer (fat lot of good glaring did in the bigger scheme of things, really), and handed him a pack of Batman Gummy Bears. Grayson eagerly worked the package open as she pulled out of the parking lot bound for Austin, reminding Grayson, in her most authoritative voice, that they were going to a grown-up meeting and he would have to remain very quiet while Mom worked.

"*Mom!* You don't work!" he laughed.

Rebecca judiciously ignored that remark.

She arrived far too early. "We're just going to have to turn down the enthusiasm a notch or two," she announced to Grayson. Fortunately, the leasing agent was early, too, and was more than happy to hand the key to Rebecca, seeing as how it was almost five o'clock and he had other places to be like everyone else in the free world, which left them with a half hour before the meeting. That was perfect. Rebecca was going to do some pre-meeting decorating. With Grayson in hand, they walked into the entry of what was the new campaign headquarters. It was the size of a postage stamp.

"Is this the doctor's?" Grayson asked.

"No, it's a campaign office."

"What's that?"

"It's where people like the president work to get elected."

"Like Batman?"

"Yep. Just like."

They wandered down the narrow corridor, looking into various rooms (well, *she* wandered—Gray took each room as a new opportunity to be shot and killed by a new assailant). Rebecca was, truthfully, a little disappointed that the new campaign offices were the exact opposite of Tom's posh capitol suite. This rental property was definitely government-issue, with drab gray walls and linoleum floors, and big metal desks and chairs. There was one big room that she presumed would host the phone bank, another large meeting room near the entry, and squeezed between were a handful of small, bleak, and windowless offices. At the end of the hallway, flanked by his and hers bathrooms, was a larger office with a window overlooking the parking lot for Tom to meet constituents and campaign contributors.

Having completed their tour, Rebecca and Grayson got the big box out of the back of the Rover. As Rebecca hung a few items to give the place a more lived-in, viable-campaign-office feel, Grayson amused himself on the floor with a Hot Wheels, which he repeatedly slammed into the wall, accompanying the car's collision with crash sounds of his own.

Mother and son both jumped when they heard the front door bang open and someone come striding in. That someone rounded the corner into the large room with conviction, and damn it if his eyes didn't seem to narrow and the corner of his mouth just barely quirk up when he saw Rebecca. But he had not seen Grayson on the floor until it was almost too late, and had to skid awkwardly to his left to avoid tripping right over him. He stopped dead in his tracks, stared down at Grayson, then looked at Rebecca.

"Hello *Matt*," she said, her hands finding her hips.

"Hello, Rebecca," he answered, mimicking her with a smile.

"This is my son, Grayson."

Grayson stood, big dusty patches on his knees, and blinked up at the man towering over him.

For a moment, Matt didn't seem quite so arrogant—he smiled warmly. "Hey, buddy, how's it hanging?" he asked, and held out his hand, palm up. Grayson looked at his big hand for a moment, then suddenly reared back and slapped Matt's hand as hard as he could.

"Good job," Matt said with a chuckle, then stepped around him and walked into the middle of the room.

"Cute kid," he said to Rebecca.

"Thanks. Do you have kids?"

"Me? *Nah*," he said, like it was unthinkable, and put his hands on his waist as he looked around.

Probably one of those guys afraid to commit to anything more than his morning jog, which, by the way, judging by his physique, he obviously managed to do on a fairly regular basis.

"But I hope to have a whole houseful someday," he added casually.

Ooh...Rebecca had not expected that response. Particularly and most especially because she had once dreamed of the same thing. She peered closely at Matt, prepared for the possibility that he was messing with her.

"You're early," he said.

"So are you."

He paused, nodding thoughtfully at her. He was, Rebecca hated to acknowledge, awfully good-looking.

"Anyone else here?"

"Ah…no, just us." Rebecca folded her arms, looked out the window, feeling suddenly very self-conscious under his casual perusal as her previous, self-visualized kick-ass campaign strategist evaporated into thin air. What was the matter with her, anyway? Men looked at her all the time—well, not precisely like *that*, really. Actually, they never looked at her like *that*. Men ogled her. But Matt wasn't ogling, he was just…*looking*. And that, for some odd reason, put butterflies in Rebecca's stomach. He had a certain way about him, an air or something. It was what her book *Friends and Lovers, and How to Tell the Difference* called brooding. Yeah, *brooding*, that mysterious thing going on, like he knew something she didn't.

At the moment, he was smiling. An amused little smile. "Love what you've done with the place," he said, looking around at the small American and Texas flags and the motivational poster promoting teamwork.

"Really?"

Matt looked around again. "Honestly? I think this is about the ugliest place Tom could have found."

"I thought the same thing," she admitted, mildly disappointed he hadn't commented on the personal touches. "But I guess looks don't matter when you're on a campaign budget, right?"

Matt glanced at her as if she were completely out of her mind (which she probably was—evidence: she was here).

"Image is everything in a campaign. You have to look and act the part if people are going to believe you can do the part. Candidates spend thousands and thousands on getting just the right image across. I'd think you of all people would know how important image is."

Her of all people? And what was that supposed to mean? "Yes," she said, nodding thoughtfully. "I think I see what you mean...sort of like, if you really want to be a smart-ass, it helps if you look like one, too."

"Or," he said, not missing a beat, "if you want to be gorgeous, you pretty much have to look gorgeous." And then he smiled that dimply, heart-sinking smile, and no amount of racking her brain was going to come up with a pithy comeback for that one. Not that Matt cared—he was too busy looking at one of her motivational posters. "I sure hope you didn't spend a lot of money on this shi...stuff."

"Mom always spends lots of money," Grayson said.

"Gray!" Rebecca said quickly, but Matt's dark brows had arched above his gray eyes, and dammit if she didn't feel a little warmth in her cheeks. *Warmth?* Oh *nooooo,* she wasn't having any of that! Self-consciously, she lifted her hand to her nape and rubbed.

"So, what did you do before this?" Matt asked, having lost interest in the motivational poster as he walked closer to where she stood, still wearing that lopsided smile.

"I was at home doing some research," she said, wondering frantically now if her cheeks were actually *showing* any sign of this absurd warmth she was not going to have.

His smile broadened. "I meant before this campaign."

Now her cheeks were flaming. "I, ah...I was living in Dallas until a few months ago, and since I've been in Austin, and…hmm…well, I've been settling in." Grayson chose that moment to poke his head under her arm. She pulled him around to stand in front of her and tried to smooth his hair as Matt stood there, hands on waist, being very cool and curious in his silk blue suit.

"So what did you in Dallas?"

Why did everyone *ask* her that? What, was she the only person in all of America who had not worked before the age of thirty? "I suppose you want to know if I have any campaign experience," she said, trying to sound pleasantly unconcerned. "Well, no, I don't."

"Ouch, Mom!" Grayson cried, swatting at her hand on the top of his head; Rebecca realized she was unconsciously twisting his unruly hair and immediately let go. "Sorry," she murmured, and quickly added, "In Dallas, I was a stay-at-home mom to Grayson."

"Uh-uh," Grayson piped up. "*Lucy* was my mom in Dallas."

Well, didn't that just shoot a little dagger through her heart, thank you, child of her womb. Even Matt looked a little nonplussed; now he probably thought she boozed it up all day. Which she might have done on rare occasion, thanks to Ruth, her former best friend and consummate socialite booze hound. Rebecca forced a laugh. "Nanny," she said above Grayson's head, patting it a little too hard as she forced a smile.

"Ah," said Matt. "So you didn't run a natural habitat for birds and dogs and salamanders?"

Of all the—

"Joke," he said, lifting a hand in response to her expression. "Just a joke."

Well, well, perhaps Mr. Big Pants had what might almost pass for a sense of humor. "Very funny," she said, unable to keep a small smile from her lips. "As a matter of fact, I'm sure you'll be ecstatic to know that I have reconsidered my position on strip mining."

"*Have* you?" he asked, nodding approvingly.

"It doesn't appear to be the best campaign topic."

"No? The team will be so disappointed."

"Not to worry. I have another idea." What was with her sweaty palms all of a sudden?

"Fantastic! So I am waiting with bated breath—what's the idea?" he asked as she surreptitiously wiped her palms on Grayson's shoulders.

"I'm not going to tell you. It's a surprise." Since when, she wondered?

"I don't think I can take another of your surprises," he said amicably, taking one last step so that he was standing just before her and Grayson, his gray eyes gleaming.

"Really? How interesting—I would think you could take quite a lot. I mean, any lawyer worth his tort claims should be able to handle a surprise now and then."

"True. But even lawyers have a limit of how many surprises per person they can take." Now that he was standing so close, too close—that gleam in his eye looked almost devilish, and it made her wonder, insanely, how many women must have looked into those eyes and felt as warm as she did. Matt's gaze dipped to her lips. "So I guess it depends on what you have up your...sleeve," he said as his eyes dropped lower.

"You'll have to wait and see," she said with a stiff shrug, and toyed with the idea of hurling herself through the window just to get some air.

"Promises, promises," he said with a sly wink.

Rebecca suddenly wanted someone, anyone—janitor, delivery guy, policeman—to join them, and looked away, pushed her hair behind her ears, cleared her throat, and asked, "So where is the meeting?"

"Back room. You might want to wait up here until someone comes to get your son. Grayson, right?" he asked, flashing a smile at Gray.

The deep flush beneath her skin began to recede as Rebecca looked at Grayson, then at Matt. "No one is coming to get him. He's here with me."

A look of confusion passed over Matt's face. "We're working."

"Yes. But he's very well-mannered."

"My teacher says I have good cizinship," Grayson reported.

"That's great!" Matt said to him, but then to Rebecca, "It's really not a good idea. We've got a lot of ground to cover today."

Well, here was a shocker—Matt didn't think her idea was a good one. "Yes, I understand why you might be concerned. I mean, he's only five," she said, and Grayson helpfully held up five fingers. "But the thing is, I'm a volunteer. Which means no one is paying me. So there's no one paying a babysitter, either, and I'm spending time here that I would normally spend with my son. Therefore, he's here with me."

Matt opened his mouth to say something, but they both heard the front door open at that moment and turned expectantly toward the door. Grayson took the opportunity to wriggle from Rebecca's grip on his shoulders.

"Rebecca!" Tom boomed the moment he laid eyes on her from the doorway. Behind him was Gilbert, crowding in to peek over Tom's shoulder. "Who is *this* young man?" Tom exclaimed, walking into the room with Gilbert practically on his back. "No, don't tell me—he looks *exactly* like Bud!"

Rebecca felt that inward wince. "This is Grayson," she said. "Grayson, say hello to Senator Masters."

"Hello," Grayson repeated, the darling little cherub.

"*Dude!*" Gilbert said. "Give me five!" He squatted down, held up his hand; Grayson happily wound up and shot across the floor to slap Gilbert's hand with all the strength in his stocky little body. Gilbert rocked back on his sandals for a moment, and then rolled over onto his back, playing dead, much to Grayson's delight, and that, of course, was all Gilbert had to do to make a friend. Grayson was instantly laughing and climbing over his dead body, until Gilbert suddenly shot up and hoisted Grayson onto his shoulders to take him for a ride.

In the meantime, Tom looked around at the things Rebecca had put on the walls. "The place looks *great!*" he exclaimed. "Did you do this, Matt?" he asked, and paused to laugh at his own jest before throwing his arm around Rebecca's shoulder and squeezing tight. "Rebecca, you are perfect for this team. This is great," he said, gesturing to the wall adornments. And then he abruptly let go, pivoted about, and started for the back room. "I want flags like these in every office," he boomed.

His enthusiastic response had put some wind back into her alter ego sails, and Rebecca followed him, walking past Matt, chin lifted. "Already done," she said pertly.

"I am so not surprised," Matt said behind her.

They gathered in the back when Angie (in gold streaks) and Pat (in standard-issue gay) arrived, laden with paper bags full of sodas, chips, and salsa, around which they all gathered in the back room. "I love chips and salsa," Tom said. "They ought to make it a law or something."

"You *are* they," Pat reminded him, to which Tom nodded thoughtfully, as if that notion had just occurred to him.

Matt (who had taken a seat right next to Rebecca, naturally, for what better place from which to torment her?) did not partake of the chips and salsa. He sat so close that she could smell his cologne, absently drumming his hand on the table in front of her. While the others chatted about unfamiliar people and events, Rebecca couldn't help noticing his strong, capable hand. It was huge. Which naturally reminded her of what Robin often said—"Big hands, big dick. They've done scientific studies, you know." And that Rachel often disputed that fact. "It's the *feet*, not the hands. Always check the feet first!" A surreptitious peek below the table confirmed that Matt had it covered on both fronts.

Too heavy on the visualization front had Rebecca's face flushing hot again, but damn it, she could not stop looking at his hand.

Fortunately, Matt didn't notice; he was too busy leaning across her to squint at the motivational poster she had pinned up on the wall. "*Building the Perfect Team: No one person can perform a task to the highest standards,*" he thoughtfully read aloud, then glanced around the table. "I'd say we've pretty much proven that in spades." He looked back at the poster. "*Yet a team can contain experts in many fields.*" He looked at Rebecca. "Like decorating?"

"Jealous," she muttered, looking straight ahead.

"Oh, I don't think so," he said. "I'm a lot of things right now, but jealous isn't one of them. Would you like to know what I am?" He smiled that deadly lopsided smile again.

Fortunately, Pat saved any conversation about which things, exactly, he was, by asking Tom, "Can we get started? I've got a school board meeting tonight."

Rebecca was grateful for Pat's intervention—Grayson was beginning to tire, and was, at present, hanging over her lap like a limp rag. Juggling his weight, she pulled from her new briefcase the papers she had printed from her computer, spread them neatly before her, lined them up in proper order, fished out a pen, and placed it carefully to the side, in case she needed to take notes.

"Okay," Tom sighed, clearly unhappy that Pat had ended the good time. "I'd like to get a list together of what groups we need to target immediately. I also need to get reports on where we are with the mailers."

Rebecca raised her hand. Pat did not; Pat just started to rattle off a number of the groups Rebecca had so carefully researched. "Young Democrats in the metro areas, Junior League in Dallas and Houston, and maybe most importantly," she said, "the Texas Democrats for Change."

"Let's start with TDC," Tom said as Rebecca frantically looked at her list. "So, let's think of—"

Be aggressive! Rebecca's alter ego shouted at her. "Ah, Tom, excuse me?" Rebecca blurted, hand up high. "There is one other group I'd like to put on the table."

"Okay, let's hear it."

She cleared her throat. "Well, ah...Pat covered most of them," she said, flashing a smile at Pat, "but there is one other that might be worth a look. The Silver Panthers."

Next to her, Matt sat back, folded his arms loosely across his chest and grinned.

"They are a grassroots organization of senior citizens," she explained.

"Oh, we know who they are," Tom said. "And thank you for mentioning them. We inadvertently forgot them." He smiled. "They are a tough nut to crack...but I'm sure you know that, right?"

"*Ooh*...well, they are having their state convention at Lakeway at the end of the month. And I...I was thinking it might be a good opportunity to introduce you to them."

"Rebecca, that's a great idea," Tom declared.

She smiled, relaxing a little. "I don't know for a fact if we can get their attention at this late date—"

"Here's a surprise: we can't," Matt interjected amicably.

Without sparing him a glance, Rebecca continued, "But I thought, maybe, we could host like a little party or something, and invite as many conference attendees as we could get."

"Perfect! Line it up!" Tom said.

"Ah, Tom..." Matt interrupted. "Nothing against a good early fund-raiser. But it's really a little early to do more than a 'friends of Tom' deal, don't you think? I mean, don't you want to finish getting your platform together before we meet with any significant groups? We skated through the March primary with the bare bones, but now is the time to focus on getting your message out there. The Panthers might want to hear your stance on any number of issues."

"Ah hell, Matt, they're just a bunch of old folks!" Tom said cheerfully.

"That might be a little shortsighted," Matt easily continued. "These are active folks who will care about more than just health care."

"Dude—don't worry, be happy," Tom insisted with a winsome grin. "Look, we've got plenty of time. I am already working out the last platform issues with the party folks," he assured Matt. "So, Rebecca, if you can get us in front of the Silver Panthers, you'll be the shining star of this campaign. Okay, let's see what else—Angie, I want the phone bank up so we can start making some cold calls next week."

And as Tom began to rattle off a list of tasks for the group to tackle, Rebecca risked a look at Popinjay. He was looking at her, too, calm and expressionless. She smiled tightly, turned back to her papers. Matt slowly leaned over, so close that when he whispered, she felt his breath in her hair. "Don't set it up," he said. "We need to chat with the party folks first."

"He just asked me to," she whispered back.

Matt scooted closer, leaned over again. "I'm telling you that it's premature. He doesn't have enough of the right things to say just yet, and the party will want to orchestrate it. Don't worry; I'll talk to him when we're through here."

Rebecca wondered if Matt knew so much, why he wasn't running for office himself. "FYI," she whispered, "you are not the candidate. Tom is."

"Now, why am I not surprised to hear you say that?" he cheerfully remarked, and straightened in his seat. But then he leaned over again, his eyes on Tom. "By the way...do you always smell so good?" he whispered.

There was that bothersome flush again.

"The March primaries are over, folks!" Tom was bellowing, moving into his pep talk. "We've got our work cut out for us and we need to gear up for the big fight!" He slapped both hands down on the scarred metal table. "The Republicans are going to try to chew us up and spit us out, so come in each day ready to do the work of two people. Fair enough? Angie will get the offices set up tomorrow and man the front. Parrish, we'll fine-tune that platform soon," he said with a wink, and abruptly stood up. "Okay, gotta roll! Thanks for dropping in, folks. Come on, Angie, let's go check out my office."

Angie immediately jumped up to follow Tom, as did Gilbert, which left only Pat and Matt behind with Rebecca, who was busy getting Grayson off her lap, who was pretending he was dead and was not cooperating.

Pat turned and looked at Matt. "Another productive meeting, huh?" she asked sarcastically.

Rebecca had no clue what Pat meant—she thought the meeting had been very productive.

Grayson slid off her lap, stood, and shoved his hands into his jeans. "Mom, when can we go home?" he whined.

"Now, honey," she said, and gathered her papers, stacking them properly (all facing the same direction and in numeric order. She had, of course, numbered them) before sliding them carefully into the color-coded file in her new briefcase.

"Good idea about the Silver Panthers, Rebecca," Pat said. "But...getting something together so soon by the end of the month is kind of stretching it, don't you think?" she asked, exchanging a look with Matt. "I mean, if you want to do it right."

Now, those were fighting words. Right was the only way Rebecca ever did anything, and if there was one thing on this earth she did to perfection, it was host a party. She pasted a pageant smile on her face. "It's really not so hard. I've got some ideas."

"I'm just saying, don't be too disappointed if you can't do it, honey," Pat said in such a condescending way that it made Rebecca's alter ego campaign strategist rear her ugly head and growl.

"I can do it," she repeated.

"Look, Rebecca," Matt said, "no offense, but seeing as how you're really new to the political scene, what Pat is saying is that it's really not doable. You're hitting the start of the campaign season, and if you aren't already on their agenda, you're not going to get on it at this late date. And besides, the Panthers are notorious for keeping their meetings closed."

Rebecca did not care to be lectured to, particularly in a tone that made her feel stupid, and particularly with Grayson hanging, dead weight, off one hand. All it took was knowing the right people, which, okay, she didn't know, really. But she knew how to find them. "Thanks for your concern," she said, trying to make Grayson stand. "But I'm not trying to get on their agenda. I'm just talking about a little preconvention party."

Matt sighed in a way that made Rebecca want to punch him square in the nose. "Well, whatever," he said, dragging a hand through his hair. "It won't hurt you to try, I suppose. It will probably be good experience for you."

Rebecca smiled, shoved a limp Grayson in the direction of the door, and heard herself ask, incredibly, "Would you like to put a little wager on it?"

That certainly got his attention. "*What?*" he asked, choking on a laugh.

What was she doing? But Rebecca looked at Matt and realized she meant what she'd said. She hadn't been married to Bud for nothing—if there was one thing she knew how to do, it was throw a bash that would leave people talking. She smiled, slung her briefcase over her shoulder. "I said, do you want to bet?"

Pat's mouth dropped open, but Matt smiled very darkly as he turned toward her. "I'll definitely take that bet," he said, his gray eyes piercing hers with the challenge. "So what's the wager, Miss Texas?"

"Come *on*, Mom!" Grayson moaned, tugging on her hand.

Matt's dark smile deepened, and Rebecca felt a curious shiver race down her spine. "I'll make it easy," he said, and honest to God, that cool, steady voice made her weak in the knees. "The winner gets to choose a favor of his or her choice," he said. "You get Tom in front of the Panthers, and you can make me do whatever you want." He lifted his gaze from his casual perusal of her, and she could have sworn she saw smoke in his eyes. "Deal?"

No, Rebecca! Don't be stupid! Nononono… "You're on," she said, and let Grayson drag her out of the room with him.

CHAPTER NINE

From the age of six, I have known that I was sexy. And let me tell you it has been hell, sheer hell, waiting to do something about it...

BETTE DAVIS

In an old Victorian house in the Heights of Houston, Robin Lear was lying on the couch, dressed in her preferred style of jeans and a boy's T-shirt, her bare feet propped on the arm. She held the phone to one ear as she squinted at the crown molding along the ten-foot ceiling and absently played with the silk fringe of a pillow. "I haven't talked to her," she repeated to her father, who was, and had been for the last month, trying to get hold of Mom.

"Are you telling me your mother hasn't called you in a whole goddamn *month?*" Dad demanded in his typically subtle, kid-glove fashion.

"No, I'm saying I haven't talked to her since the last time you called me and interrogated me about it. Mom is in LA." Exactly where she'd been for the last few months since Dad's cancer had gone into remission and he'd gotten impossible to deal with again. For all his jaw-boning about how his three daughters needed to learn to stand on their own two feet and appreciate the important things in life, *he* could certainly use a lesson or two in that very thing.

"I know she's in LA!" he barked in her ear. "I want to know if you've talked to her!"

"No!" Robin shouted back, drawing a look from her significant other, Jake Manning, who was at his drafting table, busy with their latest renovation project and trying very hard to tune Robin out. But he looked at her now, one brow lifted in silent question. She waved a hand at him, indicating it was nothing out of the ordinary. "Try Rebecca," she suggested. "She might—"

"I can't get her on the phone, either!" Dad pouted.

Hmm, go figure. "She's really busy."

"She doesn't need to be so damn busy! You tell me— why can't she just relax and take good care of Grayson and stop trying to one-up Bud?"

"One-up Bud? She is not trying to one-up Bud."

"Like hell she isn't. She—"

Fortunately (for Robin anyway, who didn't want to hear whatever Dad was going to say about Rebecca's life, because it was Rebecca's life, a fact he seemed to have forgotten in his determination to make Rebecca lead her own life) was lost behind the beep of an incoming call.

"—that she was wasting time, but she won't listen to me."

"Dad, I'm getting another call."

"I'll wait," he said gruffly.

With a groan, Robin sat up, punched the second line. "Hello?"

"Robin, thank God," Rebecca said breathlessly into the phone. "Listen, you keep up with politics, right? Have you ever heard of the Silver Panthers?"

"The who?"

"*The Silver Panthers!*" her usually calm, rock-solid sister cried impatiently.

"No. Should I?"

"Why shouldn't you? Don't you pay attention to anything except Jake?"

"Hey, watch it," Robin said. "Listen, Dad's on the other line—"

"*Shit!*" Rebecca moaned. "Don't tell him it's me, okay?"

"I won't, just let me get him off the phone," Robin said, clicking over Rebecca's moan. "Dad? I need to go."

"Who is it?"

"It is someone for me," she said primly. "I really have to go, but listen, call Rachel. She was talking to Mom a couple of weeks ago, even thinking of going to LA." Rachel would be pissed that Robin was sharing the love.

"She was?" Dad asked, his voice hopeful.

Robin bit her lip; Rachel was going to kill her for sure.

"All right, I'll call her. But when you next talk to your mother, you tell her I'd appreciate a phone call."

"Okay. I'll talk to you soon. Bye, Dad." She clicked over. "Rebecca?"

"I'm here. Is he gone?"

"Yep. Listen, the next time you talk to Mom, will you please ask her to call him before he drives us all to jump off a cliff?"

"Okay…but she is not going to call him."

"I know." Robin sighed.

"Listen Robbie, I need your help." Rebecca said. "I've gotten myself into a big mess."

Rebecca in a mess? Impossible. She was too perfect to get in anything even remotely resembling a mess. Robin and Rachel, on the other hand, could, and often did. But not Rebecca. *Never* Rebecca. "Really?" Robin asked excitedly, causing Jake to look up again. "So *tell* me!"

"Okay. It's sort of a long story, but you know I signed up to work on Tom Masters's campaign, right? I went to my first meeting, but it was so obvious that I didn't know anything, and there was this...this guy who pretty much thought he knew every little thing, and I got mad, and I sort of mouthed off about strip mining, for Chrissakes, and—"

"*Strip* mining?" Robin couldn't help it; she laughed out loud.

"Do you mind?" Rebecca said testily. "So anyway, at the next meeting I had done my homework, and I came ready to tackle all the campaign issues." She paused there to draw an unusually long and tortured breath, which Robin found fascinating. Of the three of them, Rebecca was the one Robin and Rachel always clung to in a crisis, because she was always so calm and cool and collected. "Well, I said, the Silver Panthers—they're a group of politically active senior citizens and they're having their annual convention this month, and why don't we do some early fund-raising?" Rebecca continued.

"Okay...so? That sounds like a good idea."

"Yes, it does. In theory! But practically speaking, it's a ridiculous idea!"

"Why?"

"Because I can't get *in*!" Rebecca exclaimed angrily. "Can you believe that? I can't get in!"

Robin stood, began to roam the room. "Well...if you can't get in, can't you just put it off for a while? I mean, the election isn't until November, right? It can't be *that* critical—"

"Yes! YES. IT IS. THAT CRITICAL!" Rebecca shouted.

"Jesus," Robin exclaimed.

"Oh...just fuck it," Rebecca muttered.

Just *what?* Robin gasped out loud, pulled the phone away and gaped at it. Rebecca never, *ever* cursed—it was not befitting her spun-gold aura. "Rebecca! Why is this such a huge deal? I mean, are you going to get fired or something?"

"No, no, nothing like that. I'm only a volunteer."

"Then what is the big deal?" Robin asked again.

There was a long, silent pause on the other end.

"Hello?"

Rebecca sighed loudly. "Okay. This is going to sound really stupid. Just really...*stupid.* But, Robin, I have sent out résumé after résumé, and no one wants me for anything, not even to clean toilets. I can't convince them to even let me answer the phones. I'm about as employable as a doorknob, and then, I just stumble into this thing with sheer dumb luck, and it's really a great opportunity for me! I might be able to turn this into a job somewhere, at least use it as real experience. But I have to do it right, and I already sort of blew it with the strip mining thing, and so the Silver Panthers event was something I was sure I could do. But I *can't!*" She paused again, sighed with much exasperation. "And there is this *guy*..."

A guy she had mentioned twice now, thank you. "You mean...a guy you like?" Robin asked carefully.

"Like? Come on, Robin, you know me better than that. I'm off guys, especially guys with huge egos."

Right. Rebecca might believe she was off guys, but it sure sounded like she liked *this* guy. "So what is it about him you don't like?" Robin asked, grinning.

"I really don't have the time to list everything, but here's one thing…I mean, he hasn't come right out and said it, but it's pretty clear that he doesn't think I should be working on this campaign. Like I'm not good enough or something. And when I said I'd do this party with the Silver Panthers, he said there was no way, they wouldn't let me in, I couldn't pull it off, blah blah blah. And then I said, in so many words, just hide and watch, asshole."

Robin grinned proudly. "You actually said that?"

"No, of course not! But I bet him I could do it. And the loser has to do whatever the winner wants, and now, well…I have to do this even if it kills me."

Aha. It was all becoming crystal clear. Robin whirled around and winked at Jake, who was staring at her with concern. "You know what your problem is, Rebecca?" Robin asked with great authority, and without waiting to see if Rebecca knew or not, she blurted, "You need to get laid."

"Oh my God."

"You need to get *laaaaaid,*" Robin repeated slowly and articulately.

"*Robin!*" Rebecca shouted at the very same moment Jake shouted, "*Robin!*"

"You *do,*" she said, shrugging helplessly at Jake. "It's been way too long—what, four years?—that's why this guy is bothering you so much."

"Well thanks for broadcasting that to all of Houston! And this is not about that. This is about proving that I can do something. It just so happens that Matt is so full of himself that he thinks he is the only one who ever has any good ideas, and God forbid anyone *else* should suggest anything—"

"Is he cute?" Robin interrupted.

Rebecca groaned. "Movie star gorgeous."

"You definitely need to get laid, sister," Robin cheerfully concluded.

Jake moved so quickly she could hardly react before he jerked the phone from her hand. "Rebecca? Hey, how are you doing?" he asked, and motioned for Robin to go away, which she refused to do, and crowded in next to him so she could hear, too.

"Hi, Jake. I'm doing okay—I just have this little problem and I'm not getting a whole lot of help from my big sister, but what else is new?"

"Hey!" Robin protested.

"What is it you need?" Jake asked, frowning darkly at Robin. "Maybe I can help."

Robin stuck her tongue out at him and walked away.

Jake turned his back to her and said, "No, I've never heard of them…Uh-huh…Oh…Okay, I see. Listen, call El. Your grandpa knows everyone in this state, I think. I bet he can hook you up…No problem. Hey, how's Grayson?" Whatever she said made him sigh and shake his head. "Poor kid. But we're still gonna meet up at the ranch in a few weeks, right? I'll take him fishing, how's that?…Okay…Talk to you soon."

Jake clicked off, lowered his head, and frowned at Robin.

"What's wrong with Grayson?" she asked.

"Oh…his dad keeps bowing out of visitation, and the poor kid is missing him."

"Once an asshole, always an asshole," Robin said with disgust.

"As for *you*," Jake said, pointing at her with the cordless phone before tossing it onto the table, "that is no way to talk to your sister."

"Why? It's exactly her problem and she knows it."

"At the moment, it's your problem," he said, and started walking toward her.

Robin laughed, fell back onto the couch with a bounce. "Bring it on, big guy," she said, and laughed again when Jake jumped on top of her.

Grandpa! Why the hell hadn't she thought of that?

Rebecca pressed a hand to her cheek. She really needed to chill out. This was no big deal; a minor setback, nothing more. She had the Elks Lodge lined up, the use of their charity bingo equipment, and she had even finagled the refreshments for a pittance. All she needed was a list of conference attendees to send invitations to and she'd be home free. That wasn't an impossible task; it was just a matter of finding the right person.

Unqualified Applicant Rule 9: The glass is always half full.

Rebecca picked up the phone and called her grandparents.

"*Hel-*LO-*oh!*" Lil Stanton trilled loudly when she picked up.

"Hi, Grandma. It's Rebecca."

"Becky!" Grandma cried. "Ooh, how's my adorable precious little boo-boo of a great-grandson?"

"He's great. He's taking a nap right now."

"You mean I don't get to talk to him?" Grandma was clearly disappointed.

"Sorry, Grandma. Next time, okay?"

"Oh honey, are you looking for your mother, too? Aaron called here this afternoon. You know how he is, one minute he's so sweet, then the next minute he's about as ornery as—"

"Actually," Rebecca said, interrupting her grandmother before she could go off on a tangent, "I was calling to ask Grandpa an important question. Is he home?"

"Well, good night, where else would he be?" Grandma snorted. "Jake won't let him on the job site anymore since he took down all the trim the boys had just put up on the last job. I swear, you cannot let that man out of your sight for even a min—"

"Could I please speak to him, Grandma?" Rebecca asked sweetly.

"Well of course you can, sweetheart. You just wait one minute."

Grandma put the phone down on the phone table and bellowed, "*Elmer! Your granddaughter wants a word with you!*" A moment passed, then another, before Grandma shouted, "*I Say-Yed, Your Granddaughter Wants A Woooord With You!!*"

A moment later, Grandpa picked up in another part of the house. "Robbie-girl?"

"No, Grandpa, its Rebecca."

"Becky! How's my sweet girl?"

"I'm doing great, Grandpa. But I'm working on a little project, and I need your help."

"I'll do what I can, honey. Just a minute," he said, and put his hand over the receiver. That did not, however, muffle the sound of his shouting. "*LIL! Hang up the gosh-dern phone!*"

Grandma picked up the phone. "You take care, sweetie, and you give my sweet Graybie-baby a big hug from Grandma Lil."

"I will."

"So what do you need, Becky?" Grandpa asked.

"Have you ever heard of the Silver Panthers?"

"Heard of 'em? Why, I practically invented 'em!" Grandpa cheerfully claimed, and launched into a long and extremely circuitous tale of how exactly he had invented them, during the course of which Rebecca had to remind him twice what he was talking about (Grandpa liked to talk). But from his discourse, Rebecca gathered he had been a member of the Silver Panthers at some point in time, and at the end of his lengthy little tale, when Rebecca could get a word in edgewise and could tell him what she needed, he snapped his fingers. "Piece of cake," he said, and told her he'd have that list of attendees by Monday or there would be some butt kicking across Texas.

Rebecca visualized him doing just that in his enormous white support shoes, and thanked him profusely.

Later that afternoon, when she and Grayson wandered down to the bank of the river—her to sit in her Adirondack and chill out with a margarita courtesy of Jo Lynn, and Grayson to throw a stick in the river so that the dogs could refuse to go in after it, Rebecca closed her eyes and dreamily imagined the look on Big Pants Popinjay's face when she announced at the next campaign meeting that a little fundraising with the Q-tips was not only doable, but on.

That night, when she had at last turned out the light (having read the first half of *Please Understand Me—Character and Temperament Types*), she lay there for a very long time staring into the dark, thinking about what Robin had said.

The part about needing to get laid.

CHAPTER TEN

How's that working for you?

DR. PHIL

In Austin, Matt was having thoughts of Rebecca, too—there was definitely a love-hate thing going on there, for sure. At least he had figured out the root of his problem with her: she reminded him of Tanya Kwitokowsky, a vicious, mean-spirited Nazi commando and his archenemy in the second grade.

Yep, back then, he was always standing in the corner for some alleged but totally unfounded schoolhouse infraction, and Tanya was sitting in the front row, directly in front of Mrs. Keller, her papers nice and neatly arranged, her fat pencils carefully lined up and awaiting the next assignment. She had been the most infuriating teacher's pet he would ever know in his many years of schooling—a girl who was quick to point out when he was doing something wrong and beamed like sunshine when he was sent to the corner. And the most infuriating thing of all? He had wanted nothing more, even at that tender age, than to look up her skirt.

Same as he wanted to look up Rebecca's skirt in a major way.

Which made the fact that she really had no business on this campaign (with the exception of patriotic office decorations) all the more exasperating. Nothing against Rebecca—she was charming in a not-of-this-earth way. And she wasn't stupid. Matt suspected she was stupid like a fox, really. And okay, he did marvel at how prepared she seemed to be for the fly-by-the-seat-of-your-pants gig this campaign had a tendency to be.

But she was ridiculously uninformed about everything. It really was like she had just landed here from another planet. At least, he thought wryly, if she was an alien, that would explain a few things. However, the most annoying thing about Rebecca Lear was that he couldn't figure out why he was thinking of her all the damn time.

Not that he didn't appreciate the package—he'd have to have a bona fide case of numb nuts if he didn't. Hers was actually a pretty astounding case of beauty, the sort that made a man wonder why the hell she wasn't in Hollywood instead of hanging around a boring state campaign.

Honestly, he was sick of thinking about it, didn't want to think about it anymore, and as the weekend was upon him, he let thoughts of the alien beauty queen evaporate in the whirl of activities, beginning with his Friday night date with Debbie Seaforth, one of the county's top prosecutors. When he took her home, she invited him in, even though it was only their second date. But he was a guy, and when a woman offered, well…Matt left Saturday morning after naked pancakes, rushed by his loft to change and get rid of the electric-green condoms she had stuffed in his pocket on his way to a golf date with Judge Halliburton.

After golf, it was off to Lake Travis, where he met up with Ben's brother Alan, a self-styled entrepreneur who was having another party on his houseboat. How Alan, a forty-year-old, could know so many luscious university students was something of a mystery to Matt, but who was he to question it? Even though at the age of thirty-six he tended to think of them as kids, he liked their (barely bikini) company.

On Sunday, it was the obligatory monthly dinner at his parents' house in nearby Dripping Springs. This Sunday, Dad was barbecuing for the fam—sister Bella and her husband, Bill, and their six-month-old daughter, Cameron; and Matt's two younger brothers, Mark and his wife, Nancy, and Danny, whose fiancée, Karen, was missing in action for the evening.

In the course of his work, Matt saw a lot of family dysfunction that could fry his brain if he let it, so he considered himself fortunate to have one of those families where everyone genuinely got along and enjoyed one another's company. The only drawback (and this a fairly recent one) was that Mom was in her sixties now and was beginning to harp on Mark and Danny about grandkids. "Your father and I aren't getting any younger, you know," she lectured them. But Matt, the oldest, had had much tougher opponents than Mom, and when she brought up the subject with him, he'd kiss her on the cheek and say, "Have another glass of wine, Mom. It will take the edge off." That one was always guaranteed to draw a snort of laughter from Dad.

Mom was a good sport. She chalked up his remarks to her stated belief that her oldest son was not the settling down type (Matt wasn't sure if that was true, really, but he honestly just hadn't met The One).

That evening, the conversation was pleasantly unguarded and focused on Danny's upcoming nuptials (*nine* bridesmaids, poor sap). By the time Matt turned in late Sunday evening, he had successfully put Looney Tunes Rebecca out of his mind.

Monday was quiet. Tuesday morning, he appeared in court for a hearing. As the docket was called, he and the opposing counsel, Ricardo Ruiz, who happened to be a basketball buddy of his, were waiting in the corridor when another prosecutor and ex-girlfriend, Melissa Samuelson, went sailing by, pausing briefly to sneer at Matt.

Ricardo looked at Matt; Matt shrugged. "Wassup—are you working your way through the roster?" he asked, laughing.

"Yeah, right—I've almost made it through the *R*s," Matt said with a wink.

Ricardo, being the jovial type, laughed appreciatively, then asked Matt if the rumors were true.

Still thinking of female prosecutors, Matt asked with a devilish grin, "Which rumors?"

"District attorney. Everyone was talking about it at the bar association meeting last night."

That surprised the hell out of Matt—there had been talk of it around the party bigwigs, but he hadn't breathed a word to anyone, not even his father, the retired US Court of Appeals Judge Winston Parrish.

"So?" pressed Ricardo, grinning. "You gonna be our next DA? You know Hilliard is on her last legs," he added, stating what everyone knew to be true of the current DA.

"Oh man, is that going around?" Matt asked, trying to laugh it off with a shake of his head. "It's just a rumor. Don't believe everything you hear."

Judging by the way Ricardo clapped Matt on the shoulder and laughed like they had a little secret, it was obvious he didn't believe what he was hearing at that very moment.

Still, Matt blew it off. Austin was a small town in some respects, and around the courthouse, rumors like that took on a life of their own. By the end of the week, he and Debbie Seaforth would be getting married. But when the hearing resumed (and Matt's request for a summary judgment was denied), the sparkle had not quite left Ricardo's eye. "See you in court," he said with a wink, and strutted out.

That afternoon, Doug Balinger, the Democratic Big Cheese from Stetson's, called to tell Matt that some of their early work was getting good press around the state. "It's nothing short of a miracle, after what Tom said about that insurance bill," Doug remarked.

Matt knew exactly what he was talking about. Last week, Tom had made an off-the-cuff remark about uninsured people, which had, unfortunately, come across like a rich white guy dissing the poor. Matt had worked an entire afternoon on damage control, and fortunately, as a result of his efforts, it had turned up as nothing more than a blip in the papers. But Doug was concerned—and rightly so, in Matt's opinion—that slips like that would come back to haunt Tom as the election grew nearer.

"He needs to firm up his platform on health care and insurance. He's too dangerous when he just shoots from the hip," Matt said.

"We're working with him," Doug assured him. "Just be patient. In the meantime, let me tell you what we've talked about," he said, and proceeded to give Matt a rundown of the platform issues.

When at last Matt hung up, he glanced at the clock—he was going to be late for the campaign meeting, and debated going. But they had started up the phone bank, which interested him, and supposedly, they had begun the roll-out of thousands of yard signs across the state.

There was, he supposed, one other little reason for going, and that was to learn the status of his wager.

Matt buzzed Harold, who almost instantaneously appeared at Matt's door. He strode through, his hand extended for the files Matt was holding. "Pass these on to staff, will you? And I need this brief finished by the end of the week."

Harold took the files, cocked his head to one side. "If you don't mind me saying, sir, you look exhausted. You might want to try a cucumber press for your eyes," he added as he pivoted sharply. "If that doesn't work, do what the pageant contestants do and try a little hemorrhoid cream under the eyes to take the puffiness out."

Matt raised his head as Harold moved briskly for the door. "You're kidding."

"Of course I'm not."

"But that's disgusting!"

"Perhaps. But it works!" Harold sang as he sailed out the door.

Hemorrhoid cream? Still shaking his head, Matt gathered up his things, loosened his tie, and left, headed for the campaign offices.

On his way over, he got caught in a little traffic and tuned in the radio to catch some news. "*If you want the best value for your money, then bring any deal over to Reynolds Cadillac and Chevrolet and we'll meet it or beat it! We're right here on the motor mile...*"

Damn ads. Was it his imagination, or did they pump the volume up on those things? He punched to an AM station. "*Reynolds Cadillac and Chevrolet cannot be beat! We'll meet or beat any deal you find in Texas…*"

He switched to a jazz CD.

Traffic was moving at a snail's pace: a wreck or something ahead had mucked up the works, so Matt veered off, took the neighborhood route. Only when he turned down a well-traveled side street in West Austin—a notoriously political side street—he noticed several of Tom's yard signs (*Vote for Tom Masters…*now there was a brilliantly snappy little slogan) were stuck up against the houses and complexes. Stuck up so close that he literally had to turn his head away from the road to see them. Honestly, sometimes it seemed if he didn't do it, it didn't get done right. Matt pulled over into an apartment parking lot, rolled up his shirt sleeves, and fished in his trunk for something to pound with, found a golf club, and jogged up the street, pausing in each of the twelve yards to pull up the signs and put them out by the street where they would be seen. Facing oncoming traffic. Who could not *know* that?

When he reached the campaign offices, he strode quickly through the front door and almost collided with a desk someone had put there that all but consumed the little entry. On top of the desk were several stacks of hand-addressed envelopes, the handwriting flourished and cursive, and it struck him as a waste of free manpower—a simple keystroke would have produced labels in a fraction of someone's time.

He stepped around the desk, made his way to the back, noticing the new additions to the walls (springlike things, along with some new campaign banners—*Vote for Tom Masters for Lt. Governor,* which, incidentally, looked like they had been finger-painted). He could hear several voices coming from the conference room—it didn't sound as if anything had started up yet, save another bashing of the Republican Phil Harbaugh—but somewhere, a phone was ringing. Gilbert stuck his head out the door, saw Matt. "Oh hey, we're getting started. Would you mind getting that?" he asked, and Matt nodded, headed on back to the phone bank.

He walked into a room full of gunmetal gray desks, on top of which were legal pads and pencils, phone books, and the old-style putty-colored hard-wired phones.

The phone had stopped ringing. No one was in the room, except, surprisingly, Rebecca, who, not surprisingly, looked lovely in a dove-gray blouse and skirt. Her hair was bound up at her nape; two small diamond earrings glistened from her earlobes. She hadn't yet noticed Matt; her brow was creased with concentration as she listened intently to someone on the phone.

Matt moved farther into the room; his movement startled her, and she jerked her head up, her wide blue eyes arresting him and unexpectedly pinning him to the wall with their brilliance. She lifted her hand, waved stiffly at him.

He nodded, thought he was intruding and should go back to the meeting, but couldn't quite bring himself to do it. He couldn't break free of the mesmerizing hold her eyes had on him.

"Yes, I understand, it's really awful," she was saying.

Matt lifted a questioning brow, but she glanced away.

"I know, I can't bear to think of it, either—it's appalling. I will do whatever I can, I promise. Yes, I'll do just that and call you first thing," she said, and was suddenly looking around for a pencil. "I am sure Senator Masters will want to know about it."

Matt quickly moved forward, pulling a pen from his breast pocket and holding it out to her. Rebecca glanced up with surprise, smiled as she took it. That smile trickled right down to Matt's toes, and he realized, a little numbly, that he was standing there staring at the slender curve of her neck like an awestruck kid as she jotted down a number and a name. "Thank you for calling," she said. "I'll speak with you soon. Take care." She put the phone down and stood a moment, staring morosely at the legal pad.

"Is everything all right?" Matt asked.

"Not really," she said sadly as an elegant hand fluttered to her collarbone. "Actually, it's horrible."

"So what is it? Can I help?" he asked, now truly concerned.

"Oh Matt…" She glanced up, smiled sadly. "There's nothing you can do. I just need to set something up with Tom as soon as possible. He'll know what to do."

What was that he detected—the faint smell of a big fat rat? Matt slowly folded his arms across his chest. "So who is it that Tom will be meeting with?"

"The Citizens for the Humane Dispensation of Hill Country Deer."

Matt waited for the punch line. But Rebecca just stood there, her gorgeous eyes blinking up at him. She was not kidding. Nope, there wasn't even the slightest hint of a joke on her pretty face. She really, truly was an alien. "The humane dispensation of deer," he echoed aloud, just to hear that fatuous term spoken out loud.

Rebecca nodded. "They are shooting them in the hill country to reduce the population. These folks would rather see them moved somewhere and they want to talk to Tom about it."

Matt could not believe what he was hearing. On a cold call, she had picked up a clan of bark-eaters who wanted to save a bunch of deer? He stared at her; but oblivious, Rebecca leaned over, picked up her briefcase, and slung it over her shoulder. "I guess we should join the others. Here's your pen." She held it out to him with a sunny smile. "Thanks so much."

"Are you nuts?" Matt asked as he took the pen and shoved it into his breast pocket.

Rebecca's thick lashes fluttered. "I beg your pardon?"

"Nuts. Or do you just do this sort of thing for fun?"

Dark, perfectly sculpted brows dipped crossly over blue eyes. "Do what for fun?"

"Seriously, now…all kidding aside. Did you just have an emotional conversation about deer, or are you jerking my chain?"

"Do you honestly have something against deer?" she asked, her voice full of a woman's indignation.

"As a matter of fact, I do, and here's what: they aren't a problem for *Texas*. They're a problem in a couple of counties where big houses back up to golf courses, but they are really not a problem for the state as a whole."

"So?" she demanded, her eyes flashing.

"So, why should Tom waste one second of his valuable time on deer?"

"Because," she said, marching around the desk, "Tom is a humanitarian. I know that's not something maybe *you* aspire to be, but Tom is a nice guy, and it's obvious there are a lot of people in Texas who think animal rights are important."

"God no, tell me it's not so," Matt groaned to the ceiling. "Is this the dog thing again? Or are you seriously thinking about making a pitch to take up animal rights in this campaign?"

Rebecca glared at him. "FYI, Mr. Big Pants, all these people want is a resolution against killing deer and for relocating them. I don't think that is outside the realm of Tom's influence." She began marching from the room, the heels of her flimsy little sandals making a staccato *click click click* across the linoleum floor.

"Yes, but is it practical?" Matt asked, following close behind, even more irritated that in spite of his frustration, he could not help but watch the jiggle of her magnificent tush. "You don't think that it's asking a little too much to take up Tom's time with something that has absolutely no bearing on his candidacy or running this state, just because you feel sorry for a bunch of deer?"

That got her—she gasped, stopped in her march, and whirled around so quickly to retort that Matt almost collided with her. "What sort of man *are* you?"

"The sort of man who would like to help Tom get elected and not become the poster child of Save Bambi."

"Oh. My. *God*," she muttered, whirling about and marching again. She made it three whole steps before she stopped and pivoted again, forcing him back on his heels. "You know what you are? You are...you are...I can't even say it!" she snapped with a wave of her hand, and abruptly whirled about again with a little too much force. Matt stopped her from banging into the wall by catching her arm, but blocked her exit by planting his arm against the wall, just next to her head. Rebecca was effectively trapped. And he liked that.

She folded her arms across her middle and glared at him. "What do you think you are doing?"

Matt's gaze dipped to her pouty lips while his head filled with the scent of Chanel. "Giving you the opportunity to say it," he said. "Speak your mind, Rebecca; let's hear it."

"Okay. You're infuriating."

"*I'm* infuriating?" he snorted. "You're playing a little fast and loose with that word, aren't you, Miss Priss?"

"You know, you're right, Popinjay, I meant to say that you are impossibly arrogant—"

"That's nice, coming from someone all puffed up over a couple of flags," he interjected, smiling a little now, because the woman was really stunning when she was all charged up.

"And you're overbearing."

"Determined," he corrected her with a lazy grin as his gaze drifted to her lips again.

Rebecca didn't say anything for a moment, but then surprised him by laughing low and lifting up, so that her face was just below his, so close that he could have, were he insane, kissed her without much effort. What alarmed him a little was that he was sorely tempted to do so. "I know what you are doing," she said, her voice barely above a whisper.

"Oh, yeah?"

"*Yeah.*"

"So what am I doing?" he asked, actually a little curious as to what he was doing, because he was feeling just on the edge of out of control.

"You," she said, poking a finger at the knot of his tie, "are trying to get to me." She smiled softly, inched up on her toes so that her lips were even closer to his. One teeny-tiny millimeter away. "You don't think I belong here, and you think you can scare me away," she murmured, her breath warm and sweet.

Those lips, those smiling, full and lush lips...Matt's smile deepened. "I'd be a fool to try and scare you away. But I am trying to put a little sense in that pretty head of yours."

"Well, guess what, Matt?" she asked, her gaze languidly wandering his face. "*It's not working.*" And he suddenly felt a sharp pain on the top of his foot at the precise point where her heel had come down on it. Matt instantly dropped his arm and fell back, wincing. "And I'm not going *any*where," she added pertly, walking on.

"I was afraid of that," he muttered, and still grimacing from the pain, he followed her.

They burst through the door where the others were meeting so that everyone looked up in surprise. "Sorry we're late," Rebecca said, striding forward, and sat down hard at the table. Matt sat down hard next to her. Both of them looked expectantly at Tom, and both of them made a concerted effort not to look at each other.

Tom looked at Pat, then at Matt and Rebecca. "Okay... well, then! We've got a lot to cover, folks. So! Let's hear some reports! Angie? That's some nice red hair you have today. What else have you got?"

"The phone bank went well today," Angie reported. "We had five volunteers from the university, me, Gilbert, and Rebecca. We made a little over one hundred calls in two hours."

Pat and Gilbert cheered and clapped. "That's great!" Tom exclaimed. "Gilbert? What about the yard signs?"

"Teams in Dallas, Houston, and San Antonio went to work this weekend and placed eighteen hundred signs. Pat and Rebecca and I split up into three sectors and placed three hundred and fifty signs just in Austin."

At least now Matt knew which Chanel-scented beauty queen had put the yard signs in West Austin.

"Great work!" Tom exclaimed.

"Might I make a suggestion here, Tom?" Matt asked "Can we all agree to put yard signs in an area of the yard where traffic might actually *see* them as opposed to making them into a decorative feature of the whole landscape?" he asked, and felt Miss Priss go stiff next to him.

"Sure!" Tom said. "Everyone take note of that. Okay, Rebecca, what about our Silver Panthers?"

"Yeah, I am dying to know about the Panthers," Matt said, turning to look at Rebecca, already imagining what he would do with the favor she owed him, and it was, after that heel to the foot thing, a deliciously nasty idea.

Rebecca sat ramrod straight on the edge of her chair, hands folded primly on the table, just like Tanya Kwitokowsky. She probably even had an apple for Tom in that bag of hers. "We're on," she said proudly, and beamed a big *told-you-so* smile at Matt. "We've got a hall, we've got entertainment, and we've got refreshments the night before the convention kick-off. But more importantly, we have the coveted list of attendees," she said. "So all I need is the word go, and I'll mail out five hundred invitations to come meet Senator Masters."

Matt could not believe his ears. That group was as tight as a drum, and *no* one—certainly not a former beauty queen—could break that attendance list.

"That's *fantastic!*" Tom shouted, slapping the table. "Well, now, Rebecca, aren't *you* just the cream in our coffee? Folks, this is the kind of drive I'm looking for. The desire to accomplish goals, just like that poster says." He paused, squinted at the motivational poster on the wall. "Well, I can't read it from here, but you get the gist of what I'm saying. So Gilbert, work something up for me to say. Pat, will you get some campaign literature together? And Rebecca, if you've got a minute after we're through here, there are some people I think I'd like you to meet."

Miss Priss's spine got, impossibly, even straighter, and she gushed, "I'd love to help in any way I can."

If this went on much longer, Matt half expected Burt Parks would pop through the window singing "*Here She Is…*" while she took a little walk around the conference room, blowing kisses to them all.

"Is it Matt's turn?" she asked with feigned innocence, and turned in her seat to face him, a smart little smirk glittering in her eyes.

"Yep. Matt, you're on," Tom said. "What did *you* do since our last meeting?"

Matt frowned; Rebecca actually had the nerve to turn the smirk up a notch. Man oh man, the poor little alien had no idea what she was up against, but if that's the way she wanted to play it, he'd be happy to engage. Just as long as she understood that if she played with fire, she definitely would get burned.

"Talked to Doug today," he said, turning back to the group, and began to lay out the finer points of a plausible stance on health care.

CHAPTER ELEVEN

All you need in life is ignorance and confidence; then success is sure...

MARK TWAIN

It was nothing short of a miracle that Bud actually picked up Grayson in Austin that Friday, because he'd dumped his son the last four weekends he was supposed to have had him, and because the people Tom wanted Rebecca to meet were the new media people, hired out of Los Angeles. They were going to transform Tom's image into someone who looked like he *owned* the lieutenant governor's office (Tom's exact words).

After dropping Grayson off, Rebecca spent the day preparing herself for the happy hour meeting at the Four Seasons Hotel. The best news was that Popinjay would not be there to discombobulate her as only he could do with that body and that face and that rapacious smile.

"I really need *you* to come," Tom had told her in confidence. "These are media people with offices in LA. They know what they are doing, and I mean, Pat's nice and all, but she's, well...you know."

Rebecca didn't know.

"And Gilbert and Angie," he added with a roll of his eyes. "Now there's a pair, huh? Don't get me wrong...they're great and all that, but they just aren't the right type. I really need you, Rebecca. You know how important appearances are," he said with a wink. "You're perfect for this!"

That was the second time someone had insinuated she was all about appearances. On the one hand, it thrilled Rebecca to know that Tom thought highly of her, particularly after a drought of anyone thinking of her at all. But on the other hand, it wasn't as if she had any experience with the media. What few media encounters she'd had had been more than ten years ago after winning the Miss Texas crown. Nevertheless, she knew she could do it, just like she knew she could do the Silver Panthers. How hard could this be? All she had to do was have confidence (*A Woman's Guide to Meaningful Employment*); visualize herself in the role; and give off an appearance of self-assurance and capability (*Unqualified Applicant Rule 11: Never wear pink and never go sleeveless*).

It was obvious that Uranus and karma were making plans for the permanent renovation of her house! *Yeah bay-by*, her life was finally about to turn around. And to keep it on track, Rebecca made time to practice her self-visualization techniques, and jotted down her three daily positive affirmations:

1. Nice clothes
2. Good phone presence (phone bank) with a HEART, unlike some people
3. Hard worker (yard signs) when some people think their lame ideas are all the work they need to do. PS: there is nothing wrong with placing yard signs where they are aesthetically pleasing to the eye!

And thereby being fully prepared, Rebecca arrived at the Four Seasons in a tastefully low cut, sheer lavender blouse with full sleeves, a knee-length black skirt, and black knee-high boots. She spotted Tom in the very crowded bar, noticed he'd even managed to snag a table in the center of the room, where he was flanked by two twentysomethings. That surprised Rebecca—for some reason, she had pictured *"media types"* as looking generally like Tom Brokaw Mini-Mes.

When Tom caught sight of her, he came instantly to his feet. His companions—a male and female, both thin and wiry and dressed in black, both sporting black-rimmed matchbox glasses, and both with the bed-head look, only hers a little longer—swiveled in their seats to have a look.

"Rebecca!" Tom called, as if she hadn't seen him, which of course she had, since they were looking directly at each other and waving.

Visualizing *Rebecca, campaign strategist,* she marched forward to greet them. "Hi, Tom. How are you?" she asked as she reached the table, confidently extending her hand.

"Great! I'd like you to meet Gunter Falk and Heather Hill. They are with DGM and Associates, our new media consultants. Gunter, Heather, this is an old and dear friend of mine, Rebecca Reynolds."

"Umm...*Lear,*" Rebecca politely corrected him as Heather shifted, folding her arms on the table as she had a look at Rebecca from the top of her head to the tips of her boots.

"Yo," said Gunter, giving her a two-finger salute as he slid down in his chair so deep that he was practically prone, looking a little like an elongated semicolon. "You work with

Tom's campaign?" he asked, as he, too, eyed her critically—so critically that Rebecca was beginning to feel just a smidge self-conscious.

"Ah, yes," she said, feeling, all of a sudden, that she looked like some souped-up soccer mom, and definitely not a player. *Unqualified Applicant Rule 7: Be confident! If you aren't confident in yourself no one else will be confident in you, either.*

"Rebecca, would you like something to drink?" Tom was asking her.

"I'd love a glass of wine." *Like an entire barrel.*

He smiled reassuringly as he held out a chair for her. "We were just talking about a look for the campaign."

"*Masters!*" someone shouted. Tom jerked his head up, saw whoever it was and waved. He then leaned down, patted Rebecca on the shoulder. "Rebecca, tell them what activities we have planned, okay? I'll be back in a sec. Oh, hey! If you didn't know it, Rebecca was Miss Texas!" he announced in what was becoming a really annoying habit of his, and stepped away from the table before Rebecca could frantically grab his coattail and pull him back.

"*Really?*" asked Gunter, outwardly amazed, as Tom strutted away.

"Well," Rebecca said, laughing nervously. "That was more than ten years ago."

"But that's so *cool*," Heather said, nodding in unison with Gunter. "But probably way too old for us to use," she added thoughtfully.

Well, thanks, Heather! Want to borrow my comb? "Fortunately, I'm not the one running," Rebecca reminded her with a sheepish laugh.

"Right," Gunter said, nodding again. "Let's get a drink. And then you can tell us what all the campaign has going on."

What all the campaign had going on? All she knew was that Tom wanted her to meet some people! Heather and Gunter were discussing what they would order from the bar, so Rebecca tried to think. Here she was with media types, talking about...*what?* She had no idea what Tom had in store.

The waitress appeared with two martinis and a glass of wine. White wine. Rebecca despised white wine; it made her silly. But she took a good, fortifying sip all the same and looked at her new companions, Frick and Frack, who blinked back at her. Okay. She'd been at the top of Dallas's social scene, which meant she had swum in shark-infested waters many times. A couple of kids from LA shouldn't be a challenge. Where the hell was her alter ego, anyway?

"So. We're looking for some of your upcoming events and how we can weave those into a couple of TV spots about Tom," Heather said. "You know, Tom Masters doing good things and meeting people, that sort of thing."

"Oh," Rebecca answered brilliantly.

"Yeah...so what have you got?" Gunter pressed her.

"Let me think," she said, and hid behind a sip of wine as she looked to where Tom was standing, between two chunky gray-haired dudes, and thought, in answer to Gunter's question, that what she had was a good swift kick in the ass for Tom. In fact, she visualized it, which caused her to smile.

"Something good, huh?" Gunter asked.

Be confident. Be strong. Be assertive! "*Yyyess!*" she said, perhaps just a tad too enthusiastically. "We have an appearance at the Silver Panthers lined up. We're throwing a little party the night before their conference begins."

Neither Frick nor Frack said anything for a moment; they seemed to be mulling it over. But slowly, Gunter began to nod. "No, that's good—we can actually use that in a couple of spots." He suddenly sat up, intent on Heather. "I'm thinking of something like those arthritis pill commercials. You know the one that has all the old people dancing and looking hip?"

"Yeah, yeah...and there's the old guy who gets into a rocket and decides to check out the universe?" Heather reminded him.

"*Sweet*," said Gunter. "We can get some shots of old dudes like that at the party." Frick and Frack smiled thinly at each other, then at Rebecca. "So when is this deal?"

"This Thursday evening."

"We'll get a photographer out to get some shots of Tom dancing with an old lady," Gunter said.

Never mind the fact that Rebecca was fairly certain that *old lady* was not a politically correct term, but they had the wrong idea if they thought there would be any dancing. "I'm sorry if I gave you the wrong impression, but there won't be any dancing—"

"You said party!" Heather said accusingly.

"Yes, but not dancing—"

"Then what?" asked Gunter.

"Then bingo."

"*Bin*-go?" Gunter shouted, sounding more clueless than upset.

"Lots of senior citizens play bingo."

"I know seniors *play* it. But I didn't think that was what Tom had in mind." He looked hopeful that Rebecca might, perhaps, be kidding.

She was so not kidding. She had thought long and hard about how to engage the Silver Panthers, had even consulted Jo Lynn (who thought her idea was *genius*, thank you very much, Frick and Frack). Tom could mingle a little between games and even take one of the breaks to deliver some sort of speech. "Think of how good Tom will look, hanging out with seniors," she said. "It will be a great way to get their attention."

"It *is* a great venue," Heather reluctantly conceded. "Don't get me wrong. I mean, the object is to get Tom and voters in the same place at the same time, right? In a place that feels comfortable to them."

Okay! Heather and her hair were coming around!

"I suppose we could shoot something there. Actually, it might be kind of cool." She looked at Gunter. "A sort of hip throwback, something like that."

"Right!" Rebecca brightly agreed, having absolutely no idea what Heather meant.

"Talk to me," Gunter said, and the two of them proceeded to brainstorm as if she wasn't sitting right there between them. The one time she tried to interject, Frick flashed a thin, go-over-there-and-leave-us-alone smile, which had unhinged her so completely that she could do nothing but down her wine.

So Rebecca looked around for Tom. While she was drinking that godawfully sweet white wine and doing his business with Frick and Frack, he and his pals had pulled up another table and chairs. Apparently, Tom meant to have a little party. She imagined herself dropping a potted plant on Tom's fat head. In the course of visualizing that, she noticed that one of his pals—the one with the duck lips and bald pate—was smiling at her.

Ugh.

Unbeknownst to Rebecca, Ben was smiling at her, too. "*Jesus, who the hell is that?*" he asked, motioning toward Rebecca's back with his bourbon.

Matt looked up; his heart did some strange, annoying little flip that he paid no heed. "You don't want to know, trust me." He noticed that Tom was there, too, along with Representative Jeffers and Fred Davis. *Hello, what is this?*

"Like hell I don't. What are you saying—you *know* her?" Ben demanded.

"Yeah. She's working on Tom's campaign. But she's a beauty queen from outer space and believe me, you don't want to get within a ten-mile radius. What I want to know is what the hell is she doing here with Tom."

"Jealous?" Ben scoffed.

"Hell no," Matt said as he stood up.

"Let's talk about slogans a moment," Gunter was saying, drawing Rebecca's attention back to him. "Maybe you can help us out."

And maybe I'll just have another glass of wine.

"I'm sorry, did you say something?" Gunter asked.

"Me?" Rebecca asked, just as one of the men who had joined Tom lunged across the table, hand extended, and shouted, as if anyone could have possibly cared. "Hey! Fred Davis is the name!"

Rebecca looked at his hand. Was that his cologne she smelled? Because it smelled like—

"Matt Parrish," she heard behind her, and saw that French-cuffed hand intercept Fred's, sliding in dangerously close to her head.

"Oh *great*," Rebecca muttered into her glass.

Matt had startled Gunter so badly that he'd almost slumped right off his chair. Fred Davis did not seem surprised, but neither did he seem particularly happy. He frowned, extracted his hand, and melted back into his seat next to Tom. Heather, however, lit up with a smile so sudden and blinding that Rebecca was tempted to get her shades out. Instead, she signaled the waitress for another glass of wine. Then she turned and looked at Matt just to make sure she wasn't a little tipsy and had imagined the whole thing.

Nope. That was him all right, looking too cool, the old cucumber in a suit routine, smiling that terribly charming, lopsided smile at Heather. *Barf.*

He shifted his charming lopsided smile from Heather to Rebecca, and damn it if she didn't see a little sparkle in his eye that made her belly flutter. "Having a little campaign strategy meeting?" he asked with a sly wink.

Rebecca rolled her eyes.

"Matt!" Tom boomed. "Hey, what brings you here?"

"A client," Matt said, reaching across the table to shake Tom's hand. "Mind if I join you?"

"The more the merrier," Tom said.

"That's. Just. *Grrrreat*," Matt said, smiling fiendishly at Rebecca. Then he disappeared to find a chair.

Heather—*Frack*—took the opportunity to nudge Rebecca. "*Who?* Who, who, who?"

"Him?" Rebecca asked, jerking a thumb at Matt's back. Heather nodded and even Gunter seemed to inch up a vertebra or two to hear the answer.

"Matt Parrish. I think he's a junior lawyer somewhere."

Heather nodded again, anxiously awaiting more information, which Rebecca was not inclined to give until Heather put her eyes back in their sockets.

"That's pretty much it. Just one of those dime a dozen lawyers."

Ah, what a shame—Heather looked so disappointed. Until Matt pulled a chair up to sit between Heather and Rebecca, which was, of course, the placement God's gift to women *would* take. Rebecca spared him a glance, noticed the handsome man behind him, and perked up a little. Now who would have thought Matt would have a friend? But there he was, standing behind Matt's chair, just as handsome (okay, not *quite* as handsome), and decidedly less smug-looking.

Matt planted his elbows on the table as the waitress delivered a glass of wine to Rebecca. "How you doing?" he said to the waitress, shooting what was obviously his trademark, I'm-gonna-get-lucky smile at her. "How about bourbon on the rocks?"

"Sure," she said, smiling for the first time since Rebecca had seen her. And behind her, Heather was smiling. Hell, even Gunter was smiling. But Matt was looking at Rebecca. "So—"

"Excuse me!" Rebecca suddenly called, catching the waitress before she took Heather's and Gunter's orders. "One more, please?" Wouldn't want to be caught with nothing to numb her into oblivion if *he* was going to stay very long, would she?

The man behind Matt was jostling him; Matt groaned, said to Rebecca, "Meet Ben Townsend, my partner."

Beaming, Ben Townsend stuck out his hand, knocking Matt back out of the way as he did so.

"Ah…hi, I'm Rebecca," she said, shaking his hand.

"*Hiii,*" he said, and angled himself so that he was standing between Matt and Rebecca. Only the room was packed, and he really couldn't do much but stand between them, smiling down at her. "So…Matt says you're new in town?"

"I've been here a couple of months."

"Great, great. Matt says you're doing fabulous work for Tom's campaign."

No way! Rebecca leaned forward and peered around Ben's thigh at Matt. "He *does*?"

With a roll of his eyes, Matt said, "Actually, Ben, I hadn't mentioned it." Then to her, he said, "Pardon Townsend—he has to go prepare for a trial we can't afford to lose. Right, Ben?"

"Yeah, yeah," Ben said dismissively, without bothering to look at Matt, still grinning like a neon sign. "It's a big *profitable* case. Not the kind Matt's used to bringing in. But hey, it was really great meeting you, Rebecca."

"Thanks," she said, wishing *this* partner had signed on to the campaign. "A pleasure meeting you, too."

Ben turned up the wattage on his smile. "You know, maybe we could get together sometime, and—"

"Ben, the trial?" Matt interrupted.

"I guess that's my cue," Ben said laughing. "Bye for now." He winked at Rebecca as he walked away.

"*He's* nice," Rebecca said with a scowl for Matt.

"No, he's not. Trust me," Matt said smugly, folding his arms on the table in front of him. "So, what have we got here? Spending a little quality time with Tom?"

Rebecca smiled sweetly and shrugged.

"So? What's going on?" he asked, looking and sounding a little too impatient to suit her.

"Oh, *big* doings," she said low, and with her finger, beckoned him closer. Matt leaned in, all ears. She glanced around, whispered, "We got some new mouse pads for the computers today—they're Texas flags."

With a loud groan of exasperation, Matt sat up.

"*Parrish!*" Tom shouted from the other table. "Did you meet our new media folks?"

Heather was smiling pathetically at the back of Matt's head, anxious for her introduction. God, did women drool over him like this all the time?

"Media folks. That's interesting, isn't it, Rebecca? Sounds like a meeting *all* campaign strategists would want to attend," he said. "Well? Aren't you going to introduce me?"

Rebecca looked to Tom, but he was in the middle of some howling joke he was telling yet another new arrival to join the group. "This is Gunter Falk and Heather Hill. Matt," she said, "is working on Tom's campaign, too."

"Ooh, *really?*" Heather asked, sitting up a little straighter.

"Yes. *Really,*" Matt said with a wink that wound Frack up all over again. "So what are y'all talking about here?" he asked as someone else squeezed in next to Rebecca, jostling her, and pushing her into Matt, so that she was all but sitting on his lap, an extremely uncomfortable situation, And hard. *Matt* was hard. His body—leg, arm, torso—was solid as a rock. The horrible thing about it was that she kind of *liked* that hard feel, liked it enough that she felt compelled to fortify herself with a nice big gulp of white wine.

"Just trying to develop some good campaign jingles," Heather interjected before Gunter could open his mouth. "Something we can turn into radio spots. You know, attention getters, something really sweet that will click in the minds of listeners around the state and stick with them."

While Heather droned on and on about that, Rebecca noticed that Tom was glad-handing two more men who had stopped by to join the party. This was insane—they wanted to come up with campaign slogans in the middle of Tom's happy hour party? Ah well, when in Rome...and she *was* feeling a little warm and creative now. Rebecca picked up her glass of wine and said, "Well, *Masters* seems pretty usable," as the two new guys found chairs and pulled them up to the table to join Tom.

"Okay," said Gunter. "Masters...Masters..."

"Like...'Why settle for a bachelor when you can have a Masters?'"

"Oh God," Big Pants groaned.

"What?"

"For starters, our opponent, Phil Harbaugh, has a PhD," he said. Gunter nodded.

"I *meant*, he's a *bachelor*," Rebecca said. All three of them looked at her blankly. Seriously, what did it take to get a glass of wine around here? "Okay, what have you got?" she asked Matt.

He pondered that for a moment. "How about this... 'Elect a Masters for the job.'"

Frick and Frack gasped at each other. "That's *great!*" Heather cried.

Rebecca all but choked. *That* was great?

"You think?" Matt asked Heather, obviously pleased with himself.

Rebecca closed her eyes, suppressed a groan. Fortunately, the waitress reappeared in what was record time for her. Matt accepted the bourbon, chuckled quietly when the waitress put another glass of wine in front of Rebecca, and then winked as he tossed a ten onto the girl's tray. The waitress fell over herself and Heather's hair trying to get his attention long enough to smile back at him.

"So, Matt, we've been tossing around some ideas about where to get some shots of Tom for some TV spots. Any ideas?" Heather asked, not wanting to relinquish his attention to the waitress, who turned and flounced off when she did not receive it.

"Hmm...Rebecca, do you have any Save Bambi meetings lined up? Maybe we could get some shots of Tom nursing a Bambi, then releasing him to the wilds. What do you think?"

"Shut up," she murmured (and what a witty comeback *that* was), then visualized twisting his arm around his back and flipping him out the window. Okay, *that* was funny—visualizing, she was learning, was *fun*. And one other thing, she thought as she picked up her fresh glass of wine, was that she had sorely underestimated a good Chablis. Or Chardonnay. Whatever.

"Just kidding," Matt said for the benefit of Frick and Frack, who, between the two of them, had about as much sense of humor as the ashtray on the table. "What about the Silver Panthers?"

"Yeah, we covered that," Gunter said. Matt nodded, thought a minute longer. "There are some important bills coming up for a vote; we could give you a call a couple of days ahead of time and you could get sonic shots of him in a legislative setting. There is a candidate debate next month in front of the state conference of the League of Women Voters…that usually draws a huge crowd. How's that for getting started?"

Either Gunter's martini was better than he was letting on, or he had finally found his reason for living. "This is *great!*" he said, nodding furiously and slapping the table, which drew the attention of the five men and two women who were now sitting around three tables Tom had daisy-chained together. "That is *exactly* the sort of thing we need!" He paused long enough to look at his watch. "Listen, we need to split if we're going to catch our plane." He stood up. "We'll call early next week to set these things up. Don't worry about the tab. We've got it," Gunter said, and started slinking off toward Tom's end of the tables.

"Thanks!" Matt said, and smiled as Heather rose much more reluctantly to her feet.

"Well, it was nice meeting you," she said, smiling at Matt. "I'm sure we'll be seeing you around."

"Right," Matt said.

"Well…okay. Later." Heather tore her gaze away from Matt the Stud and looked at Rebecca. "Later."

Yeah, later. Way later. Maybe so later that it's never, how about that? "Bye-bye now!" Rebecca called after Heather. Next to her, Big Pants chuckled. She took another drink as Heather disappeared into the crowd, tried to ignore him, and when she couldn't do that, forced herself to focus on him. "*What?*"

"You. You're surprisingly interesting, you know that? Not all uptight like I originally thought."

"*Uptight?*"

"That's what I said," he agreed with a chuckle. "I had you pegged as a little too uptight for your own good. But now I see you're much more than that. I mean, either you're accusing people of stealing your quesadilla, or lining up your pencils, or having secret meetings. I'd call that pretty feisty, wouldn't you?"

What's that, your best line? "I am not *feisty*."

"Feisty is not a line," Matt said pleasantly. "It's an observation."

Crap, had she actually said that out loud? Wow...she was going to have to be more careful with her thoughts. *And* visualizations, because she really couldn't look at him without visualizing...*yikes*. Definitely didn't want to go there, she thought fuzzily, stealing a glimpse of his hand. Rebecca looked at her wineglass(es). And was duly alarmed by how many empty ones there were carefully arranged in front of her, lined up like little soldiers. Where had all those come from?

"And furthermore, for the record, if it *was* a line, I wouldn't waste it on you, Miss Priss."

"Why not?" she demanded, strangely incensed. But before he could answer, she blurted, "If you *tried* a line on me, I'd just laugh. Ha. *Haaaa.*" She slapped her wineglass down, and felt, all of a sudden, warm and very mushy inside. Not good mushy. Sick mushy.

Matt was looking at the pile of empty glasses in front of her. "So tell me...are those all your wineglasses? Or did you just walk around the room and take them?"

That did it. Indignant, she glared at him. "I. Don't. *Know.*"

Matt laughed; the sound of it gained the attention of the men on the other end of the table, including Tom, who waved at Rebecca. At least she thought he did; she looked over her shoulder and didn't see anyone else she knew, other than the waitress. *At last!* She held up one finger—and could have sworn the waitress rolled her eyes.

When she looked around again, Tom's big flaccid face was looming in front of her. "Hey, let me ask you something, Rebecca," he said, bracing himself against the table. "I got a friend over there. Fred Davis is his name. Owns KTXT television."

Big fat deal. "How nice for him," she said plastering a woozy smile on her face.

"He'd really like to come over and say hi. You know... maybe see what you are doing later?"

"Later?"

"Yeah, later. *You* know." He winked, ignored Matt's groan. "Like maybe y'all could get a drink or something."

Rebecca blinked. Tom smiled. Dear God, was he..."Are you...are you setting me *up*?"

Tom shrugged, looked over his shoulder. She peeked around him, saw Fred and a very oily smile that sent a shiver of revulsion down her spine. "Come on, Rebecca. You're divorced, and there's no evidence of any guy hanging around. Hey, I'm just doing a pal a favor, that's all."

"Sorry, Tom, you're too late," Matt said cheerfully.

Both Tom and Rebecca looked at him and said, at the same moment, "Huh?"

Matt stretched his arm across the back of Rebecca's chair, which she was half tempted to kick, but that didn't seem feasible with Tom looming over her. Matt leaned slightly forward, so he was just inches from Tom, and whispered, "Rebecca is having dinner with me."

The bark of hiccupped laughter, Rebecca realized, was hers.

CHAPTER TWELVE

'Tis the privilege of friendship to talk nonsense, and have her nonsense respected...

CHARLES LAMB

He had in mind to take her to Stetson's, where else? Nothing like a half pound of good, quality beef to sober up a skinny, wacko woman.

Naturally, they weren't going anywhere without some wrangling, because, not surprisingly, Miss High and Mighty wasn't in the mood to dine with him. Actually, she wasn't in the mood to dine at all, and seemed rather intent on drinking her way through the evening, while at the very same time proclaiming, emphatically, that she didn't drink. There was, Matt supposed, a gentleman buried somewhere in him, because he could not sit there and look at such a beautiful lush and leave her for the likes of Fred Davis. Nor could he possibly allow her to drive anywhere, so he figured that he was honor-bound to see her safely somewhere.

"Where do you live?" he asked her, once he had managed to send Tom tottering away with the bad news for Fred.

"Ruby Falls," she said, leaning over so far that she almost tipped out of her seat.

"Great. That's way the hell out there."

"Forty-five minutes driving eighty miles an hour," she stoically informed him.

He didn't even want to think about her driving on those curving hill country roads. "Where is your son?" he asked.

"In South Padre with his dad!" she exclaimed, hitting him playfully on the arm as if he somehow should have known that.

"Any family or friends in town?"

"Nope."

"An apartment?"

"Uh-uh," she said, giggling as if they were playing a game.

"Is there *anywhere* I could take you?"

She thought about that a moment, tapping a manicured nail against a full bottom lip. "Nope," she said at last.

"Then you'll just have to go with me," he sighed.

Rebecca snorted like a dock worker at that suggestion. "I don't think so. I'm not interested," she said haughtily.

"Trust me, I'm not interested, either," he quickly and decisively informed her, and started looking around for her purse.

Fortunately, Rebecca's tipsy state of mind made her easy to maneuver, and in spite of the heated discussion that ensued, Matt managed to convince Miss Texas that she was too inebriated to drive (*Am not! Well, I can't drive right this very second, but give me a little bit!*), and furthermore, she'd only make herself sick drinking that much Chablis on an empty stomach (*I* hate *Chablis!*). Finally, he got her by pointing to Fred Davis, who, having tossed a few back himself, was doing the sloppy duck lip thing at her.

"You can't drive, agreed?"

"Agreed," she said, nodding resolutely.

"So if you don't go with me, you're looking at *that* guy. Choose your poison."

She squinted at Fred. "Okay," she said instantly, then slid out of her chair, sighing resolutely as if she were teetering off to hell. And away she went, sloshing her way into the parking garage and managing to pour herself into his Jag. That was the point at which Matt eighty-sixed the Stetson's idea. So where? Sitting in the car in the parking garage while he was trying to figure out what to do with her, Rebecca chattered on about campaign slogans and some nonsense about kicking Gunter's ass, the reason for which, Matt did not quite catch. The woman needed food, and quickly.

He hit on a brilliant idea. "You like steak?" he asked, reaching for his cell phone.

She snorted. "Don't you know? You have *all* the answers, don't you?"

"Oh, come on, Rebecca," he scoffed. "I just have most of the answers. And for your information, smart-ass is not going to work on me. First of all, I've had a bossy sister all my life, and on her best day, she can't get under my skin. Second, I am frequently in family court, which means I have seen the best smart-asses the world has to offer, and you are no competition. I am going to call in some filets, okay?"

"O-*kay!*" she shot back, swaying a little with the force of it.

"And a gallon of strong coffee," he added, more to himself.

"Don't start," Rebecca warned him, folding her arms across her middle to steady herself. "You always *start.*"

Whatever that meant. Matt couldn't help noticing that the bucket of wine she had imbibed had given her a bit of a flush that made her look...well, gorgeous. Man. He was a sick bastard.

"What are you looking at?" she demanded.

"Oh, for the love of—Rebecca, listen very carefully and let's see if we can't get at least *some* of what I'm about to say into that thick skull of yours. I *am not* looking at you. I *do not want* in your pants," he said, even as the thought that it wouldn't be *all* bad zoomed across his mind. "I'm not doing anything but trying to sober you up because you are three sheets to the wind. That's all."

Her frown crumbled, and she unexpectedly admitted, "I know. It's so *weird.* It just sort of happened without me knowing it." She groaned; her head dropped back against the seat. Matt dialed Stetson's. "How did this happen?" she sniffed, suddenly maudlin. Matt shrugged. "I mean, I was just sitting there—"

"Just sitting there with your own little vineyard, you mean...Hello! Yes, an order to go..."

"I was trying to do a good job! That's all I ever wanted to do, a good job. And then *you* came along," she pouted as he ordered the steaks.

"And saved you," he added, clicking the phone off. "Don't forget that. Now quit looking at me like I'm some sort of molester. Just relax. I won't even mention strip mining or deer."

"Or stupid campaign slogans, either," she added, wagging a finger at him.

"I won't mention the campaign at all if you won't."

"Then..." She cocked her head to one side as she tried to focus on him. "What in God's name will we talk about?"

"Excellent question," he agreed. "But we'll think of something." In fact, he was already racking his brain. "First, let's get you sober." He started the car, pulled out of the parking garage, and drove a couple of blocks to a convenience store, where he bought her some water. Rebecca gratefully took the bottle and drank the entire contents in one gulp, then dragged the back of her hand across her mouth.

"Are you all right?" he asked, chuckling.

"Right as rain," she said cheerfully, beaming that knockout grin at him again.

They continued on, Rebecca now rambling about how she never drank and Heather's need of a comb until he pulled up in front of Stetson's. The valet went in to check on the food, returned and said it would be a bit. So Matt pulled into a metered spot.

They sat there in silence for all of four seconds before Rebecca blurted, "See? There is nothing to talk about."

"Sure there is."

"Name one thing," she challenged him.

"Okay," he said, and not able to think of even one thing he could possibly have in common with her, he blurted, "How come you're always mad at me?" Where, exactly, *that* had come from, he had no earthly idea, and it surprised him, because honestly, he didn't care what she thought or didn't think about him.

Much to his indignation, however, Rebecca responded with another very unladylike snort of laughter. "Are you kidding?"

"Well, no. No, I'm not kidding."

Rebecca's head lolled back against the seat, and when she lifted it again, her blue eyes (*damn those eyes*) were shining with amusement. "You've got it *aaaall* wrong, Mattie," she said, tapping the console with her finger to emphasize each word. "I'm not mad at you. I just don't like you." And she flashed a charmingly crooked little smile.

But it flabbergasted Matt—what was not to like? Everyone liked him! Even the judges who hated him liked him! "How could you not *like* me?" he asked, aghast.

"Oh, it's easy!" she said, nodding enthusiastically. "But I do think you're very cute."

But Matt's head flew right past the *cute* thing and went straight to the *not like* thing.

"No, no, it's *not* easy. I'm a pretty likable guy," he insisted. "Ask anyone."

She laughed loudly. "You're not likable at *all!* You're just really cute. And that is as far as I can go," she said, swinging one arm out wide to demonstrate just how far she could go and barely missing his chin.

"Well," he said, more than a little miffed that she would not *like* him, like *she* was such a piece of cake to like or something, "you're not exactly the easiest person in the world to get along with, either, Miss Priss."

"Why not? I am very *polite*," she said, with an emphatic nod.

"No, sweetheart, you're actually a little on the stuck-up side." Had to be, or else she'd like him.

"I am *not* stuck-up. I am very *nice*," she said, now punching the dash with her finger. "In fact, everyone says I am *too* nice!"

"No one on this planet," he muttered, looking around for the valet. What had possessed him to appoint himself her protector and bring her here? Miss Priss probably thought if a guy didn't fall on his knees the moment he saw her, there was something wrong with him. "You know, that Miss Texas thing you have going on is a little too much," he added irritably, if only to make himself feel better.

Rebecca groaned. "You don't know what you are talking about, Mattie! I didn't even want to *be* Miss Texas!"

"Please! All girls want to be a beauty queen when they grow up."

"Not all girls want to be a beauty queen when they grow up, you...you *moron*," she said, and inexplicably, the moment the words were out of her mouth, she made a soft little gasp and smiled, a beautiful, radiant smile, as if she were proud of herself.

"So now I'm a moron?" Matt echoed, incredulous. "I didn't know we were adopting the fourth-grade rules of name-calling. Look, I'm just saying that it is pretty hard to believe you didn't want to be Miss Texas. I mean, you give off the impression that you need a lot of attention...a *lot* of attention."

"See why I don't like you?" she asked, poking her finger into his shoulder. "And I didn't mean that it wasn't anything. Wait...no, that's not right. I mean, it was *something*," she said, leaning forward, so far forward that he glimpsed a tantalizing flash of the lacy black bra (which, truthfully, he had noticed beneath her filmy blouse more than once this evening). "It was *great*!" she declared. "It's just...I mean, I never really saw myself as...*that*."

"As what?"

"As a beauty queen! *Duh!*"

Well, good God, who could understand her? And how could she not see herself as a beauty queen? As far as he knew, the one requirement for a beauty queen was to be beautiful, and Rebecca Lear was definitely one of the most beautiful woman he'd ever seen. Even when she was shit-faced.

The beauty queen was now sliding down in her seat and planting an elbow on the console to steady herself. "Lemme ask you something, Mattie. Have you ever thought that?"

"Thought what?" he asked, confused, and all right, a little lost in the lush pout of her lips again.

"Did you ever think that you didn't really think that you'd *be* something?"

That gave him pause—primarily because he had to repeat the question in his head to decipher it. But then he said honestly, "I don't think so."

"*Oh,*" she uttered softly, clearly disappointed

He hadn't thought that, had he? He'd always imagined himself a lawyer. His grandfather had been one, his dad was one. And didn't he believe that he'd follow in his dad's footsteps and be a judge one day, too? So why, then, did he feel so uncomfortable and have that vague notion he ought to be doing something good with his life instead of chasing a buck? Because he was hungry. He honked for the damn valet. When none appeared, he sighed and looked at Rebecca. "How exactly did you end up as Miss Texas if you didn't really want to be Miss Texas?"

Rebecca looked up from her study of the radio and pierced him clean through with those blue eyes without even trying. How she did that was really starting to unnerve him

"I guess because...because everyone wanted me to."

"Who, your parents?"

"Yeah, my dad. And my boyfriend. Or husband. Well, he was both," she said, and dropped her gaze to the radio again. "Bud. He was both." She made a whirling motion with her hand. "Boyfriend. Then husband. Oh…and jerk." She laughed at her little joke.

This was not exactly territory Matt wanted to enter—not that he wasn't mildly curious about the dolt who was stupid enough to let go of a woman like Rebecca. But then again, she did raise big red flags on a routine basis.

"But it wasn't just *them*," she continued, sounding almost as if she were arguing with herself. "It was me, too. I mean, I didn't enter the pageant at gunpoint, did I?"

"I would guess not."

"And I went through all that stuff to get there, didn't I?"

"I would assume," he said, and tried to imagine Rebecca putting hemorrhoid cream under her eyes. Nope, couldn't see it.

"No, *I* did it. But still…" she sighed, swung a hooded gaze to him. "Hey, Mattie, do you remember when you were young and full of…of…"

"Piss?" he offered, noticing how elegant her hands were.

She smiled; her eyes were now an incredible smoky blue. "*Hope*. You know, hope about life. The future and who little Mattie was going to be. Remember?"

"I suppose so." Although it was near to impossible to conjure up the young Matt anymore. That was such ancient history.

Rebecca nodded slowly and looked down, and he wondered if she was having A Moment. "Sometimes, I wonder if the young Rebecca would have liked me very much," she said, and propped her head on her fist, slanting toward him. "I wonder if she would have liked me at all."

The hair on Matt's neck rose; *danger, danger Will Robinson!* He cocked his head to one side, tried to see if she was crying. He couldn't tell, but in a valiant effort to stave off any tears (Over what again, exactly? Having won the Miss Texas title?), he said, "Everyone wonders, don't they? Don't we all wonder if we have achieved what we set out to achieve? Or if we became the man—or woman—that we'd always believed we could be?"

Rebecca didn't say anything.

Damn it, where the hell were those steaks? "Look, let's talk about something else, okay? Let's talk about...hey, what about your son? So what is he, like seven? Eight? In school? What does he like to do?" Against his better judgment, Matt dipped his head a little lower to see if she was crying. "Rebecca?"

But instead of answering, Rebecca's head slid off her fist, and landed, facedown, smack in the middle of his crotch.

CHAPTER THIRTEEN

One reason I don't drink is that I want to know when I am having a good time...

NANCY ASTOR

Just as that mushy spot on his body registered in Rebecca's brain, Matt had her by the shoulders and was propping her up in her seat.

"Whoa!" she exclaimed, mortified, and gaped at Matt, who was likewise gaping at her, apparently just as mortified. Oh, for the love of Pete, how did that happen? Rebecca blinked several times to clear her vision, and noticed that Matt was staring at her so intently that she began to worry how long she had actually been lying facedown in his crotch. And to make matters worse, there was a guy at Matt's window, tapping on the window. Only Matt didn't seem to hear it. He didn't seem to be even breathing.

"Ah..." She gulped, wide-eyed.

"You have my undivided attention," he said.

Rebecca pointed at the window.

Matt slowly turned his head, at which point Rebecca covered her face with her hands. Humiliation aside (not possible)—she couldn't remember the last time she had drunk too much, and really, at the moment, she couldn't remember where she'd left her *car*. She took a breath and reminded herself that all of her books said there was always more than one way to look at a bad situation. So what if she'd just made a huge and enormous jackass of herself? Maybe she was just being the *new* Rebecca, the carefree let's-have-a-little-fun Rebecca, who could let her hair down every once in a while instead of just dreaming about it.

Rebecca lowered her hands as Matt handed the guy a wad of cash "Keep it," he said, and took the Styrofoam containers the guy handed him, rolled up the window, and turned and deposited the containers on her lap. "Try not to pass out on those, will you?"

Rebecca blinked at the white containers and laughed desperately. "This is not what you think!"

"What I think is that you need a steak and a bed."

"I just slipped. Haven't you ever slipped?"

"Yes. In fact, I think I might have slipped right off my rocker," he said and smiled a little. "But either you have a strange way of trying to get in my pants, or you're seriously inebriated," he said as he put the car in drive and pulled away from the curb.

"I am not *seriously* inebriated, only a little," she said, holding up thumb and forefinger together to show him just how little. "And if I wanted in your pants, I'd be a whole lot more...more..."

"Careful?" he suggested.

"Interested," she said, pleased that she'd actually thought of a word.

Matt laughed at that. "Admit it. You don't even know what you're talking about."

"I *know*," she insisted. "I am talking about never wanting sex from you, so…read something else into it," she said, fluttering her fingers at him.

Matt was still grinning as the light changed. "Hey, sex with me is not half bad, if I do say so myself. But okay, let's just pretend that you *did* want in my pants. How would you get there?"

A better question was, how were they having this conversation? Rebecca felt pretty certain that the words *sex* and *Matt* were a dangerous combination. "Come on," she said, shaking her head.

"You know what I think?" Matt continued, clearly ignoring her. "I think you'd smile that little smile of yours," he said, glancing at her from the corner of his eye. "You know, that pretty little *come hither* smile you have."

"*Puh-leez*," Rebecca said, swaying too far and bumping into him when he turned a corner. "I don't have a *come hither* smile."

"You do," he insisted as he turned into a parking garage. "You've even shot it at me a couple of times, and don't lie," he said as he coasted into a reserved spot.

"You honestly believe that?" she exclaimed, almost dumping the containers in her determination to set him straight. What was he talking about? When had she ever smiled at him, much less in a suggestive way? "Whatever I flashed at you was not a *come hither* smile, Popinjay," she said heatedly. "Because I smile *all* the time and I haven't had sex in *four years*—" Something in her Chablis-soaked brain stopped her—she sure hadn't meant to say that out loud.

For his part, Matt didn't even move, just stared at the concrete wall in front of them. "Did you…did you just say what I *think* you said?" he asked at last, his voice full of awe. "I mean, *I* was just kidding around. So you were kidding, right? Right, Rebecca?"

"Where arc we?" she asked, trying to change the subject.

"Ohmigod, how is that *possible*?" He turned to look at her now with the same morbid fascination of viewing a wreck on the highway. "How can someone go four years without sex?"

"Well, it's not easy!" she snapped, fumbling to open the car door, which she could not, for the life of her, figure out.

"Not easy? I'd say it was goddamn near impossible," he said, shaking his head, and got out of the car. He ducked his head back inside. "You really are an alien, aren't you?" he asked, and then disappeared. But before Rebecca had a chance to collect her many wild and loose thoughts, Matt was at the passenger door, relieving her of the Styrofoam containers as he simultaneously grabbed her elbow to pull her out.

She stumbled out of the car, but as everything was sort of swimming around her, she caught the door to steady herself and very cautiously dipped down to retrieve her bag.

"Are you all right? I mean, besides...you know...*that*?" he asked, gesturing vaguely at her. His question didn't really sink in, however, because Rebecca had noticed his face was looming large in front of her, still smiling, and he seemed a little softer now, not all hard edges, and she was a little taken aback by how handsome he was. So handsome that she unthinkingly reached up and touched his cheek to feel his five o'clock shadow. "You know, you really are cute."

With a roll of his eyes, he shut the door behind her. "So you said." He put an arm around her waist, and pulled her into his side as he balanced the steak containers. "Okay, one foot in front of the next."

"I *know*," she said, even though she was stumbling along beside him. And she was concentrating so hard on walking straight that she didn't even notice where they were until they were in an elevator and he punched the *P*. She hiccupped. Tried to think of what *Peeeeeee* stood for. "Where are we again?" she asked.

Matt sighed loud and long.

When the elevator door opened onto a carpeted corridor, Matt grabbed her hand and stepped out, pulling her along with him, and causing her very large bag to bang against him and almost topple the containers. There were no doors in the hallway, just one on either end of the long, long corridor. Matt pulled her along to one at the far end, stuck a key into it, and pushed the door open. Then he pushed Rebecca through it.

She stumbled into a large room painted white, with gray tile floors covered with Pottery Barn rugs (she had studied the catalogs at length during periods of raging insomnia). The furniture was black and chrome; the light fixtures were chrome, too. It was like walking into a page from *Architectural Digest*. Clean. Stark. Uninhabitable. "Wait a minute...what is this place?" she asked, turning around slowly so as not to make her head swim any more than it already was.

"My place," Matt said, depositing the Styrofoam containers on a granite bar. "Welcome to Chez Parrish," he said, shrugging out of his coat.

Chez Parrish. Whoa. How had they ended up here? "Wait a minute, *bucko*—"

"Ach!" Matt said, throwing up a hand and stopping her before she could begin. "Not getting in your pants, remember? But you're too intoxicated to drive, and I am sure as hell not driving you all the way out to Ruby Falls. Why the hell are you living in a retirement community anyway?"

"Why are you living in a...a sanitary penthouse?" she shot back.

Matt put his hands on his waist and frowned at her. "Okay, Mork, time to put some steak in there and soak up that barrel of Chablis."

"I'm not hungry!" she stubbornly protested, and lurched toward the full plate glass windows that formed one wall of his apartment.

"At least now I understand what it is with you," he said, loosening his tie as he followed her to the windows. "I'd be a little uptight, too, if I'd been in the desert for four years. Judas *Priest*," he said, shaking his head again with that bewildered look as they stood, side by side, looking out over the lights of the city. Or the huge blurry blob of light, as it were. "Why haven't you?" he asked after a long moment.

"Huh?"

With a chuckle, Matt looked at her. "You know what, Rebecca Lear? You're a mess." He smiled and tucked her hair behind her ear. "I'm asking why someone as beautiful as you hasn't had sex in four years."

Dear God, was that her heart thumping in her ears? "Because," she said, folding her arms across her middle to steady herself, "I was married to a jerk, and then I wasn't. You can't just order sex up from the yellow pages, you know."

"Actually, you can," he responded, and flashed a sexy, George Clooney smile as his eyes wandered the length of her, from the top of her hair, down to the tips of her toes. "That's really a shame," he uttered, lifting his gaze to hers, his smile now shining through his smoky gray eyes. "I would think the vast majority of men on this planet would think they had died and gone to heaven if they had a chance to be with you."

The unexpected sentiment unhinged her. She wanted to say that Bud sure hadn't wanted to be with her, and at present, she wasn't exactly turning them away from her door and that really, in spite of what everyone seemed to think, men rarely approached her. But Matt was standing there looking so handsome, so...manly man, that for a moment, Rebecca couldn't remember why she didn't like him. And to make matters worse, the new Rebecca—the saucy drunk one—reminded the old Rebecca that it had indeed been FOUR YEARS. Four *long* years. Boring years. *Achy* years.

"What?" he demanded of her casual perusal, still grinning.

"Would *you?*" she asked in a whisper, and through no conscious thought, stepped forward, stepped into him, stepped so close that her breasts brushed against his chest, and she lifted her hand, laid it against the hard wall of his chest. "Would you want to be with me?"

Matt's gaze drifted to her hand on his chest, her breasts. "I don't know," he said softly. "I've never made love to an alien before. And besides," he added as he lifted his hand to brush hair from her eyes again, "you're drunk."

"I'm *free,*" she corrected him, amazed at how free she *did* suddenly feel. "Come on, Mattie...you owe me a favor, remember?" she murmured, and closed her eyes.

Nothing happened.

She felt a tug of disappointment and the world spinning furiously beneath her, and just as she was about to let go and fall into the vortex, she felt the slightest whisper of breath against her lips.

Rebecca froze; the feel of it was shockingly raw. *Come back,* her heart whispered. *Come back, come back.* For all she knew, she said it out loud, because the next thing she knew was the pressure of his lips on the skin of her neck, a pressure so softly demanding that it immediately fired down to her groin.

The sensation of it rocked her; it was a thousand-watt, searing jolt of life through her body, a sensation as deeply familiar and buried as it was new and fresh. Like silk against her skin, his lips slid to her mouth. Her heart and her body were instantly on fire, a raging inferno. Rebecca opened her mouth, and the pressure of his lips intensified as his tongue dipped into her mouth. Matt's fingers tangled in her hair as he pulled her closer, lifting her to him. Held tightly against his chest, his scent filling her nostrils, his taste filling her mouth, she wondered if he could feel her heart pounding, because this was, she realized, the most exquisite feeling. She'd forgotten how exquisite, how exhilarating.

That feeling quickly turned to fever that built in her chest, filling the space her pounding heart did not, then traveling fast and furious to her groin. Matt shifted, pressed his body tightly against hers, and Rebecca realized in that sensual fog that her body was eagerly curving into him, melting against the hard ridge of his desire. Matt's hand drifted from her face to her breast, brushing his palm lightly across it, then cupping it, feeling the swell of it in his palm.

She felt herself melting away when his lips sought her neck again, and she let her head fall back, let her entire body melt into that oblivion of pure sensation, until she was floating and spinning below the weightlessness of his kiss.

They were moving, waltzing backward, Matt moving her, Matt's hands on her back, lifting her, moving her. Her body was shimmering, pulsing around him, absolutely alive, and she drifted onto the leather couch when he gently pushed her into a sitting position. Smiling, her head lolling along the top of the couch, she felt him go down one knee before her, unbutton her blouse, his hand on her breast.

"It's unnatural, four years," he murmured. "No one should have to go so long as that."

"I should stop," she said breathlessly to the ceiling. "Make me stop."

"You want to stop? Or do you want to end the drought?" he asked, his voice deep and soft. "Rebecca...do you want me to make you come?"

"*Ooooh*," she breathed. She could feel the dampness between her legs, and felt her alter ego, the new Rebecca, take firm control. "*Yes!*" she whispered, and lifted her head through the fog to smile dreamily at the man on his knees between her legs.

Matt did not hesitate; he surged upward so that his mouth was on hers, devouring hers, as his hands slipped into her filmy blouse, pulling her forward until he could slip it off her. She felt a cool burst of air on her back, felt the heat of him on her chest as his fingers sought the hook of her bra and released it. Her bra went slack and slid down one arm. She grabbed it, fumbled out of it, and tossed it somewhere, who knew, because Matt's mouth was on her breast, devouring first one, then the other, and she couldn't move, couldn't think. Every flick of his tongue, every nip of his teeth shot down to the apex of her thighs. The sensation of his mouth and hands washed over her in one hot tide, pulsing between her legs.

He pushed her skirt up, pushed her legs apart, while she just sat there, the pulse racing between her legs now, beating out a desperate rhythm toward a climax her body had been denied for four years.

And then she felt his mouth over her panties, heard his strangled moan, and then the cry of pleasure that was hers. He moved against her, and she realized she was panting. The fabric of her panties suddenly disappeared, and she was shaken by the flawless and intense pressure of his tongue between the slick folds of her sex.

Rebecca cried out to the ceiling as her body seized around his head, quivering uncontrollably with the pleasure. With his hands, Matt pulled her farther down, then held her hips steady as he slowly and deliberately licked the valley. Her panting turned to groans of pure bliss as the pressure in her groin built to an intolerable pulse. "Make. Me. *Come!*" she said through gritted teeth, grabbing onto his shoulders, his head, his hair, whatever she could grasp in the fog that surrounded her, unable to endure the torture of his lips or his tongue another moment. And suddenly, so suddenly she could not catch her breath, his lips closed around her flesh and he sucked it into his mouth.

The climax was deafening in her mind, a heart-stopping release of four years of pent-up frustration, spilling out of her like water over a dam, spilling onto his mouth, his hands, his couch. Her cry sounded garbled and raw, a primal voice in the hot air around her, and she felt herself sinking fast, sinking and sinking...

The next thing she knew, she was lying on the couch. Alone. And everything was spinning. Rebecca opened one eye. Then the other. Matt was standing above her—both of him, their hands on their hips, their eyes peering down at her. She tried to smile, and the Matts came down on their haunches next to her, put their hands on her damp forehead. "I think I'm going to be sick," she whispered.

"I have that effect on women," he said, and picked her up, carried her to the guest bath.

That night, Rebecca dreamed of the person she might have been. Her father had died and she was the head of LTI Enterprises. And she wasn't an inexperienced fool, but a terribly competent executive, and the members of the board of directors were all looking at her with great approval.

The only problem was that she was naked.

That caused her to sit up with a start...to discover that her head was aching something fierce, it was pitch-black, and she had no idea where she was. She blinked against the darkness as her memory began to return in little pieces, and it at last seeped into her brain—she was at Matt's place.

Oh. *Hell.*

Not only had she *kissed* Big Pants, she had let him do things to her that had never been done to her quite that well. Oh yeah, it was all coming back to her, tumbling in her brain like so much debris, bits and pieces of a night—and while it was, best to her fuzzy recollection, *spectacular,* she had not intended this to happen, ever! *Never!*

Rebecca promptly fell back on the bed, slung an arm over her eyes. Still…it had been outstanding. So outstanding that she felt it now, a shiver of it coursing her body and landing in the pit of her groin. Or maybe, because it had been four years, she was just all giddy with the excitement of having been freed…but she could remember the strength of his hands on her hips, holding her still while he sent her into an oblivion of pleasure, where she knew nothing but the feel of her body pressed against his, every rock hard inch of him, the sensation of his mouth on her, the sound of his breathing, the moans, the *release…*

And *then* what? Rebecca suddenly sat up, looked to the rest of the bed, felt it with her hands. Empty. Okay. But what did it mean?

It meant, she suddenly remembered as her stomach rebelled, that she had had too much to drink, and with a start, she forced her legs over the side of the bed, felt the spin in her head spiral down to her stomach with violent force, and lurched forward, groping along the wall until she found the bathroom.

Afterward, she lay on the cold tile floor until she was certain that she was going to live. Not that she particularly wanted to at this point, but if she was going to be lucky enough to die, she at least hoped it would be somewhere other than his bathroom floor, please God.

When she was able to sit up at last, she realized she was wearing nothing but a skirt and a bra (that was on her very crookedly), and couldn't even begin to guess where blouse, boots and, hell, her panties might be. This was not good.

While she was all for loosening up a little bit, she could clearly see that the new, alter ego Rebecca was going to have to be lassoed and hog-tied.

Planting her hands on the bathroom counter, she hoisted herself up and had a good long look in the mirror. *Just take me now, Lord. Please.*

At the end of the long vanity was a medicine cabinet, and she lurched toward it. Much to her considerable relief, she hit pay dirt. Obviously, Matt often had female visitors, as there was a toothbrush. And toothpaste. And tampons, facial moisturizer, shampoo, conditioner, aspirin. *And* a bottle of Maalox? Priceless.

Rebecca took the toothbrush and toothpaste, the aspirin and Maalox. When she was done, she dragged her fingers through her hair, determined she was going to have to find her bag with the comb and little makeup kit before she could even begin to think how to get herself out of this mess. Very cautiously, she stepped into the bedroom again, made her way to the window, drew the drapes aside, and instantly staggered back, blinded by the sun. Damn, what time was it?

"Definitely time for you to go, you little four-year idiot," she muttered hoarsely. "You could be the poster child for why people shouldn't drink. Ah, but you did, and then you just had to go *there*, didn't you?" she angrily chastised herself as she turned away from the window and went in search of her boots. "Why stop there? Why not just go ahead and tell him everything? Like how you hoard Häagen-Dazs ice cream, and how you've never had a job, and Bud never ever, not *once*, gave you an orgasm all by himself."

She found her blouse at the end of the bed. How thoughtful. No panties, she noticed as she snatched up her blouse and struggled into it. And no boots. It would be hard to escape without boots.

She harkened back to her bazillion books that would advise her how to cope with *this*. "How about Rule Five?" she asked herself. "When mistakes happen, step out of the batter's box, regroup, and then step right up to the plate again. There you go, Rebecca, just step back—like all the way to China. And by the way, your boots are obviously not in this room."

She made for the door, turning the handle very slowly and cautiously so as not to wake anyone she did not want to see ever again in her lifetime, then quickly pulled the door open—and shrieked bloody murder.

"*Jesus!*" Matt yelped, as Rebecca stumbled back, slapping her hand over her pounding heart. She was having a heart attack. It served her right!

Matt gripped the doorjamb and stood there, muscular arms, bare chest tapering to a trim waist, pajama pants that rode low on his hips. His feet were bare and his thick hair looked slept in, and that being said, he looked about as fine as any man Rebecca had ever seen. Better. Man, this guy was *hot*.

"I thought I heard voices," he said apologetically, looking past her into the room.

"No one but us chickens," she muttered, self-consciously pushing her hair behind her ears. In that instant, she realized that if she didn't get out of that room right that very minute, she'd explode, and moved so quickly that he sort of jumped as she slipped past him and hurried down the hall, past two doors, one closed, one open (through which she could see a huge platform bed, the sheets all messed up, which made her heart flutter wildly), and into the big, sterile expanse of chrome and black he liked to call home. And there she stood, staring at the couch and trying to gather what was left of her obliterated wits.

She heard his sigh then, and wincing, risked a glance over her shoulder. Matt had followed her; he was leaning against the bar on one arm, his legs crossed at the ankles as he watched her. He pushed a hand through his hair and made it stand up even more. "I assume that as you are hurtling through the house like a rocket that you're going to live after all. You want some coffee?"

Dizzy. She was so dizzy. Maybe because she wasn't breathing. "*Yes,*" she said in a *whoosh* of breath.

Matt walked into a kitchen that was separated from the room by a long granite bar, on top of which sat her bag. Her boots were just beneath it, tucked neatly side by side against the bar. She quickly made her way over and looked around for her panties. Unfortunately, those puppies were still MIA.

Matt glanced up as he poured a cup of coffee and slid it across the bar to her. "So...are you all right?"

She nodded.

"Need anything?"

She shook her head.

"Hungry?"

"Ah, *no,*" she said, holding a hand up to protest even the mention of food. Matt smiled. "Don't," she warned him, finding her voice at last. "I'm mortified enough as it is. In case you didn't notice, I'm not much of a drinker."

"Really?" He poured himself a cup of joe. "You seemed to be doing a pretty good job of it last night."

Rebecca winced, took a sip of coffee, immediately determined coffee was *not* a good idea and carefully pushed the cup away so she wouldn't have to smell it. Matt watched her curiously; she put her fingers to her temples and rubbed them. "Matt...I'm...really sorry. I'm really very...*sorry*."

"Don't sweat it," he said easily. "I figured out that day on the capitol grounds that you were dangerous."

"I'm really not," she said, and looked at the curve of his mouth, felt a sudden shiver as she remembered, with surprisingly clarity, everything that mouth had done to her last night. "God," she muttered helplessly.

"What's wrong?"

"Ah, well...as much as I, ah...*enjoyed* our...encounter," she stammered, avoiding his gaze and the couch where IT had happened, "I'm really not the type to come on to a guy like that."

"Somehow, I knew that," he said amicably as he walked around to her side of the bar, which she was gripping with all her might. He moved closer—very close. Rebecca risked a glance at him, saw the warm light in his gray eyes, and remembered those same eyes looking down at her last night with compassion. Even now, he was smiling sympathetically. Remembering him as he had been before her just a few hours before, she couldn't help herself—she dared let go of the bar to touch his bare chest, tracing a line down the center to the top of his pajama pants and back again. "I had too much to drink. I'm really sorry."

Matt covered her hand with his own; the warmth of his fingers spread up her arm, to her heart. "One apology is okay. Two could give a guy a complex," he said softly. "But don't worry about it, Rebecca. I'm not the kind of guy to take advantage of a sot. We messed around a little, okay? I mean, look at it—a drunk, sexually repressed woman sees her opening and—"

"I am not sexually repressed!"

"No? Well, that was one helluva it's-been-four-years kiss you laid on me last night. And I believe all that wailing was you, too—not that I'm complaining, mind you," he added with a wolfish wink.

Her alter ego, who was, apparently, as hungover as she was, was dying to ask him if there were really no complaints, but she laughed sheepishly and muttered, "I didn't wail that loud."

"Are you sure?"

"No," she said, her smile broadening.

Matt didn't say anything, just looked at her, then murmured, "It was *great.*" He bent his head, tenderly kissed the corner of her mouth. "We had fun. Let's just leave it at that, okay?"

"Oh, thank God," she said with relief. "I hoped you didn't think that I…that I am *wanting* anything."

Matt let go of her hand and stepped away. "Who, me? Nah. Listen, why don't you grab a shower? You'll feel a lot better. I'm sure I've got something you can wear," he said, and indicated she should follow him.

"You're going to make me wear girlfriend clothes?" she whined as she grabbed her boots, her bag, and followed him back to the room she had slept in.

"Sister clothes," he corrected her as they walked into the room. "My sister lives almost to the middle of nowhere like you, and she crashes here sometimes when she is in town." At the closet, Matt pulled out a T-shirt and pair of tennis shoes. "Here, try these on." At the sight of her frown, he put them in her hand. "*Try* them."

Rebecca donned tennis shoes a size too big, and a T-shirt that said *Stubbs Bar-B-Q* across the front. As she checked herself in the mirror, Matt opened a drawer and pulled out a pair of panties.

"Oh no," Rebecca said. "I have to draw the line somewhere. Which, ah, reminds me…"

"You know, I'm not really sure," he calmly answered.

"Oh. Well." She could feel her face go full throttle red. "That's okay—you can keep those."

"Then—?"

"Don't worry," she muttered.

Something passed over Matt's nonchalant expression. "Oh, I'm not going to worry. But I'm damn sure going to think about it." He walked to the door again. "Shower's in there. You'll find all the stuff you need in the medicine cabinet or the linen closet." And he flashed a smile and walked out so collected that Rebecca could imagine he had done this very thing a thousand times before. Nevertheless, she fell back onto the bed for a moment and closed her eyes, wanting to remember it all just one more time.

In Los Angeles, Bonnie Lear had just emerged from the shower herself when the phone started to ring again. She padded across the carpet to look at the caller ID. Dammit! Aaron *again.*

She stood there, debating. If she answered it, she'd be drawn back into his bullshit, and she was so sick of his bullshit. But if she ignored it, he'd just keep calling because the man had the tenacity of a deranged goat. Bonnie irritably snatched the phone up. "Yes, Aaron?" she snapped. "What do you want?"

"Christ! Have you moved? Been out of the country? Lose your phone?"

"Aaron!" she said sharply. "Are you stalking me?"

"Of course not!" he said angrily, then sighed. "Ah, Bonnie, what you must think of me. I'm sorry."

No, he wasn't. The word *sorry* came off his tongue like so many watermelon seeds—he constantly spit it out without even thinking. "What do you want?" she demanded.

He sighed again. But it wasn't a tedious sigh, it was a *sad* sigh, a sigh totally unlike anything she had ever heard from Aaron in the more than thirty years they had been married, separated, or whatever they were. "What I want…what I want is not easy to put into words," he said softly. "That's always been my problem, you know. The ugly stuff comes right out, but what's really inside me gets stuck there."

"Don't start," Bonnie groaned. "You're always saying shit like that and you don't mean it. You grovel for a while, and I come back, then you forget all your promises and I leave. I'm *sick* of it. I am sick of your promises and I am sick of leaving. I don't want to do this anymore."

"Please don't say that!" he exclaimed. "I called to tell you that I want you back, Bon-bon. I'll do anything if you'll just come back."

Bonnie didn't say anything at first, just sank onto the edge of the bed, staring blindly at the brightly patterned wall.

"Let me say first that I am sorry," he said quickly, filling the silence. "I mean it this time, Bon-bon. I am sorry for *everything.* For all the years, all the heartaches, just like you said. And then, when I found out I was sick, you came when you didn't have to, and I know how hard you tried, and what did I do? I just pushed you away again, I know I did. The girls, too. But I've thought long and hard about it, Bonnie, and I *see* the mistakes I made. I don't know why I didn't before, but I do now. *Please* give me one last chance. Please come back one last time! I swear you won't regret it, I swear on my life you won't."

Bonnie sucked in her breath, closed her eyes, and squeezed them shut. What was this, the hundredth, maybe thousandth time they had had this conversation? How did he do it time and time again? How did he keep drawing her back in with his promises? But more importantly, how was it possible that after all they had been through, she could still love him so?

"Come on, Bon-bon...what do you say?" he asked.

Bonnie opened her eyes. "I say no, Aaron." And she hung up before he could draw her in again.

CHAPTER FOURTEEN

When your personal boundaries are stretched to new dimensions, you cannot return to the old dimensions. You will transform to fill your new boundaries...

TRANSFORMATION STRATEGIES SEMINAR, TRACK 2

Rebecca emerged a half hour later still a little pale but nonetheless remarkably improved, so Matt decided to call off the funeral after all. Nonetheless, now that he had held her, seen her up close and personal so to speak, he had decided she was too thin. And without the knee-high boots, her very shapely, long legs looked more like bird legs stuck into enormous sneakers. The *Stubbs Bar-B-Q* T-shirt, which she had tucked into her skirt, swallowed her whole. Probably the result of some stupid beauty queen diet. For the life of him, Matt couldn't figure out why women thought stalag-thin was attractive. *Flesh* was attractive. Soft, sweet-scented, succulent flesh like *her* flesh...flesh that was now forever seared into his memory, thankyouverymuch.

He'd grabbed a shower, too, and had whipped up some steak sandwiches. Rebecca blanched when he said so, but after her little wine binge last night, Matt wasn't about to let her walk out the door without eating something, and made her sit at the bar and try it.

Rebecca sat. She even ate a little. But she was not the same, dangerously appealing *you-owe-me-a-favor* Rebecca that she had been under the considerable influence of alcohol. That sexually repressed Rebecca had knocked his socks off, and truthfully, he couldn't get that unexpected kiss or its wake out of his head—the big head *or* the small head. In fact, the small one had awakened bright and early, remembering last night with some enthusiasm. What was a guy to do? From the moment she had said *four years*, every male fiber in him had kicked into testosterone overdrive.

It was funny what a person could make of a single word, a gesture, a look…but he'd known last night that she wanted him to end her four-year trek through the desert, and he could have sworn it was more than just a little fun between adults when it was all said and done. In fact, he'd felt something extraordinary—he had wanted to fall back and lie in that state of grace as long as he could, hold the emotion they had created in his hands. Maybe it was the raw release wrenched from her gut that did it to him. Maybe it was just the honesty of it all. Whatever it was, he'd never felt quite that way in his life, and it was a little weird.

Which was probably why he'd been so quick to throw in the towel and chalk it up to a Friday night shenanigan. But the moment he said that, she'd been so damn *relieved*, like she'd rather die than…

To hell with it—whatever the reason for her relief, it had annoyed him, and in the shower, he had tried to scrub the taste of her from his lips.

He couldn't do it.

Looking at her now, head down, trying to choke down a steak sandwich, he could not believe that of all the women he had ever known in his life (and had lost count of way back there), this wacko ex–beauty queen could unhinge him so completely with one, single, breathtaking question. Her whole body had lit up, had pulsed beneath his hands and his mouth. And that smile of hers, that little *smile* she had on her face when he was…well, doing her. *Christ.*

At the moment, he was wishing pretty hard that the passionate, free Rebecca would wake up, take a peek outside, say hi, say *something*—but instead of receiving the message telepathically like he hoped, she pushed her plate aside, leaving the better half of a delicious steak sandwich (even if he did say so himself). "Go on, eat it," he said, wolfing down the last of his. "You could stand to put on a little weight."

"Oh, *thanks*," Rebecca said, and with a groan, put her head in her hands. "Will you please take me to my car now?"

Great. Now he felt like some guy she might have picked up at a bar, when, at the same time, he was feeling all warm and fuzzy about her. "Sure. Okay." He tossed the dish towel onto the countertop. "Just give me a minute," he said, and walked out of the kitchen, to the master bedroom. As he banged around looking for shoes, his mind was racing and he was, incredibly, pissed off. After all, he was the one who was usually doing the morning-after regret thing. And furthermore, she had started it, not him, and she had jumped right in with both feet, lighting up like the University of Texas Tower from the moment he touched her. Hell, he'd just hung on for the ride. One would think Miss Four Years would appreciate all his efforts for her sake.

How could she *not?*

Alien. That was how.

Frankly, her everyday *I'm-above-this* attitude was really starting to grate. He didn't want her. Well, okay, yes he did—but only in a very base man-level way. He damn sure wasn't going to *do* anything about it. And if the earth should ever stop revolving, which it would have to do before he would even *consider* touching her again, no matter *how* long she'd been without, she just might have to crawl and beg. *Ha.* That would teach her.

Matt found loafers, shoved his feet into them, and went marching out of his bedroom to get rid of her.

But when he entered the living room, Rebecca was standing at the windows, wearing a very gentle smile that slowed him down a step or two. "You know what?" she asked immediately. "You were right."

Damn straight he was right. *She* had started this whole thing, not him.

"I feel so much better after that sandwich. I really can't thank you enough, Matt. I don't know what I would have done without you. I mean, I never drink too much—I'm usually very careful about that."

Usually very tightly wound was more like it.

"I really appreciate your help," she said with a grateful smile.

All right. Well *okay* then. This was more like it. "It wasn't anything," he lied, and picked up his keys. "Ready?" He gestured toward the door and followed her, pausing to pick up a couple of baseball caps.

"What's this for?" Rebecca asked as he handed her one.

"We ride with the top down." He opened the door. "After you, Mork."

She gave him an inquisitive look, shook her head, and walked out.

Matt had every intention of taking her directly to her car, do not pass Go…but in spite of her lack of attachment after last night's activities, she looked sort of cute with the baseball cap on, and it was a glorious early-spring day, with temps hovering around seventy.

The kicker was his mom's birthday, which he didn't really remember was next week until he saw the West Lynn Art Festival, a tony little two-street art show. His mom loved crap like that, filled her whole house with it. And then, a gift from heaven—a Chevy half-ton had pulled away from the curb right in front of him and opened up the greatest parking space in the history of mankind.

Matt instantly jerked his car into it.

"What are you doing?" Rebecca asked, gripping the door to keep from being tossed onto the sidewalk.

"My mom's birthday is next week."

Rebecca leaned forward, looked down the little street where the art festival was in full swing. "Won't you take me to my car first?"

"No way," he said, slapping the gear into park. "I will never get a parking space this good again in my lifetime and you owe me at least that much." That left her speechless. "I'm just going to pop in and find my mom something nice for her birthday. I won't be a minute. You can come with or you can sit, makes no difference to me."

She puffed her cheeks out, obviously debating, then huffed her disgruntlement as she opened the car door, swung her bag over her shoulder, and slammed the door shut before marching around to his side of the car. "Okay. Let's go," she said grimly.

"It's not like I am asking you to jump off a cliff, you know," he said as he unthinkingly grasped her elbow to shepherd her across the street.

"I just think it would be better if we went our separate ways and moved on," she said pertly.

What was he, the last guy on earth or something? "Why are you making this out to be such a big deal?"

"I'm not making it into anything," she said. "And FYI, you may think it's all well and good, but it is a big deal to me—"

"It would be to me, too, after four years," he grumbled, steering her down the path.

"Do you *mind?* I'm trying to say I am not the sort for casual sex."

Matt quirked a brow and glanced at her from the corner of his eye. "Like to really go at it, eh?"

"Matt."

He sighed. "Just trying to get you to lighten up, Rebecca. We agreed—a good time was had by all. That's it, nothing more," he said, noticing her cheeks were turning an appealing shade of pink. "And since it was agreed that I am not going to drop down on a knee and ask you to make it permanent, I think you could stand a little shopping."

She sighed. "Okay." She followed him into the first row of canvas-bound booths. "Are you an art enthusiast?" The tents were filled with original oil and watercolor paintings, colorful pottery, wrought iron yard art, woodworks, and metal sculptures.

"I don't know. I just like originality in anything."

"I wanted to be an artist," she said wistfully, and paused, looked at an oil painting of a field of bluebonnets. "When I was a girl, I never went anywhere without my sketch pad and pencils."

Honestly, Matt had her pegged as the cheerleader homecoming queen type, not the thoughtful artist type. "So what stopped you?"

"Life," she said with an indifferent shrug. "What else?" And she continued into the little booth, looking at more paintings of windmills and bluebonnets and dilapidated country barns.

But that sounded like a cop-out to Matt, and he followed her inside, asking, "Why would life stop you? Life happened to me, too, but I still went to law school."

"Of course. But you're a smart man." (Matt immediately chalked that up in her *pro* column). "But I wasn't smart enough to figure out how to be me. I tried to be who others wanted me to be."

"Now why on earth would you want to be who others wanted you to be?"

Rebecca flashed a funny, sad little smile that crinkled the corner of her eyes. "That is the million dollar question. I don't know. I was so young and so stupid and I gave up so much. I've only recently begun to realize how much." She moved away from him to look at a painting of a herd of cattle.

Her answer intrigued him—Rebecca didn't seem like a woman who had ever had to give up anything, but in fact, quite the opposite. "So you made some mistakes as a kid—everyone does," he said. "Can't you just get it back?"

"Get what back?"

"Your life. Whoever you were going to be."

Her laugh was pleasant and light, washing over him like some freaky cosmic rain. "I would if I could go back in time."

"I know you can't go back in time, but you can pick up where you left off," he insisted, suddenly wanting nothing more than to see the Rebecca that might have been.

"No, I can't. Too much time has passed since then, and besides, you should never look back, only forward, for tomorrow is where the future lies, not in your past."

Matt laughed. "Where did you get *that*? Out of some lame self-help book?"

That remark earned him a cool look. "I suppose you have something against people who try to improve themselves?"

"No. But I have something against people deciding they can't have the same desires and dreams they did when they were a kid. Do you still want to pick up a sketch book?"

Rebecca sort of rolled her shoulders.

"What's that?"

"What?

"That little thing you just did with your shoulders. Was it a yes or a no?"

"I didn't do anything with my shoulders. I just don't have anything else to say on the subject."

"Ah," he said as they paused at a potter's booth. "I hit a button."

"*Nooo*, you didn't hit a button, Matt," she said impatiently. "I'm just not the same person I was then."

"Or last night, for that matter," he muttered.

"I'm going to ignore that," she said, her eyes narrowing. "I will tell you, however, that most people go through at least seven stages of personal development before they are transformed into who they really are!"

Man, she *had* been reading self-help books. "That's a bunch of crap. We are all essentially the same person we were as a kid. And I think you still want to paint but that you've been trained to think it is some sort of childish wish."

"It is a childish wish. And besides, I have Grayson now."

"*That's* just a lousy excuse not to try."

She came to an abrupt halt in front of a glazed clay pitcher and matching cups. "Why should you care if I paint or not?" she demanded.

"I couldn't possibly care less," he assured her. "I just don't like adults copping out on their true desires. If I were you, I'd quit reading self-help books and follow what's in my heart, because you can be whoever or whatever you want to be, Rebecca. There is no limit, no rule, no childish fantasy if you really want it. Just *be*. And furthermore…" He glanced around them, leaned down to whisper in her ear. "It's okay to enjoy sex for the sake of sex now and again. It's good for you."

She jerked backward. "Thanks for the tip, Mr. Know-It-All—"

"Congratulate me; I've climbed up a notch from moron—"

"But I don't need any advice. I have a mom, a dad, two sisters, a grandmother and grandfather, *plus* an ex-husband who are more than happy to give me all the advice I could ever want without even being asked. I certainly don't need *you* to—"

"Mr. Parrish!"

Both Matt and Rebecca whirled about at the sound of his name; Matt immediately suppressed a groan. It was good ol' Harold, looking like a giant Pez dispenser in his festive weekend wear (seersucker shirt, white denim shorts, and sockless leather boat shoes), arm in arm with a man Matt presumed was his lover—a short, buff guy in shorty-shorts and a tank top, boots, and carefully scrunched socks. Judging by the grin on his face, Harold was much happier to see Matt than vice versa. He came galloping forward, pulling Arnold Schwarzenegger with him. "Mr. *Parrish*! How *are* you?" He beamed.

"Good, Harold."

"Have you met Gary?" he asked breathlessly.

Well, as he hadn't been to any gay bars lately... "Ah, no—"

"This is Gary," he said, letting Mr. Atlas go long enough to shake Matt's hand, then grabbing him right back as if he feared Gary might float away.

"Good to meet you, Mr. Parrish!" Gary said. "I've heard an awful lot about you."

"That right?" Matt asked, and looked at Harold, who avoided his gaze altogether by looking at Rebecca, at whom he cocked one well-groomed brow. "Oh ah...Harold and Gary, I'd like you to meet Rebecca Lear," Matt said. "She's working on Tom Masters's campaign with me."

"Hel-*loh*," Harold said, immediately floating over to offer his hand to her.

"Harold is my secretary," Matt said, trying not to wince.

"A pleasure to meet you, Harold. And Gary," Rebecca said with a winsome smile that would have felled lesser—certainly straighter—men.

"You know, you look really familiar," Gary said, cocking his head to one side, finger tapping against his cheek as he peered at Rebecca.

"Ohmigod, do you *know* each other?" Harold gasped, ecstatic over the prospect.

"I don't think we've met," Rebecca said politely, and took, Matt noticed, a small step backward.

"No, no—I'm sure I've seen you," Gary insisted, matching her backward step with a forward one.

"She was Miss Texas one year," Matt said helpfully.

Harold and Gary gasped at the exact same moment; Rebecca shot him a withering look. "You're kidding!" Harold exclaimed.

"I *knew* I knew you!" Gary cried. "This is *wonderful!* Wait until we tell Jim!" he said, and Matt suddenly feared that Harold and Gary were dangerously close to grabbing hands and dancing around in a circle. But Gary swirled back around to Rebecca, beaming from ear to ear. "Miss Lear, I can't tell you how thrilling it is to meet you! We have all the Miss Texas pageant tapes from the mid-eighties on!"

"You do?" Rebecca asked skeptically.

For the life of him, Matt couldn't figure out why anyone, save maybe teenage girls, would be interested in the pageant thing—well, except maybe the thing about hemorrhoid cream, which fascinated him on some morbid level he didn't want to explore too deeply—but it was painfully clear Rebecca wasn't too crazy about the recognition. "Listen, guys, we need to get going," he said, and grasped Rebecca's hand.

"Oh! Oh, oh, of course!" Harold said, and he and Gary turned twin beams to Rebecca. "It was great to meet you, Miss Lear!" he said, dipping a little at the knee to emphasize just how great. "I just can't believe we *did!*"

"Thanks," Rebecca said, inching closer to Matt. "A pleasure meeting you, too," she said, lifting her free hand and crowding into Matt with a not-so-subtle elbow to the ribs. Matt didn't need any encouragement; he pulled her away, into his side, and as they disappeared into the crowd; he had a final glimpse of Harold and Gary standing side by side, watching her with reverence.

"Thanks a lot," Rebecca said as they stepped into the middle of the throng, and pulled her hand free of his.

"He said he knew you," Matt reminded her. "What's wrong with you, anyway? It's not something to be embarrassed about."

"I'm not embarrassed."

"You act like you are. And you said as much last night."

"I did?" she asked weakly.

"Maybe not in so many words, but you definitely sounded like there were some regrets. I don't get it—why *not* be a former beauty queen?"

Rebecca paused in front of some iron sculptures, obviously pondering that question. "I guess it just doesn't seem very important," she muttered.

"Important?" Matt laughed. "We could all look back at our lives and say the same about any number of things. What's important, really?"

"Art," she said resolutely. "Art is important. For example, look at this piece," she said, pointing to a strange looking thing, explaining what she saw in the maniacally shaped vase with holes in it, while Matt quietly wondered how it held water. And when they moved on to the next booth of paper sculptures, shapes delicately molded and painted, Rebecca pointed out a bouquet of flowers that was truly exquisite with unusual colors and lines. Matt picked it up; she suggested that it was a nice gift for his mom. It *was* something that his mom would like.

He paid for it and found her outside at the next booth, admiring some pottery work. With the flower thing in the crook of his arm, he asked if she had dabbled in any other art besides painting. Pottery, she said, pausing to look at more pieces. And when he asked what her favorite art form was, Rebecca slowly began to talk about a life she once had as a teenager, the life of a budding artist, who had painted and made sculptures from clay, and had even sold a few pieces to friends of her parents who thought she was destined for greatness. She talked with such animation that Matt could see it really had been important to her. Still was, regardless of what she wanted him to believe—or what she was trying to make herself believe.

More importantly, by the time they reached the end of the booths, he realized he had glimpsed a woman behind the beauty queen, one who was far more interesting and vibrant and funny than he had originally thought, and he was fascinated. She was a challenge, too, as he imagined ways one might draw that vibrant woman out of her shell of suppressed perfection. The only problem was—and it was sort of a big one—she didn't particularly *like* him. For the first time in his life, Matt was looking at a woman who didn't like him. What had happened to the universe as he knew it?

They wandered out of the art festival, and he took her to her car, feeling more and more disturbed with each block as she chatted about art. He had the strange and unusual compulsion to prove to her that he was likable, that he could be more than a one-night stand, and when she got out of the car with his mom's gift that she had held in her lap, he got out too, grabbing her bag from behind the seat and walking around to her side of her car.

She looked up at him, lifted a brow in question.

How odd that he should feel so awkward—he held out her bag to her; she took it with a faint smile and slung it over her shoulder, then attempted to hand him his mother's gift.

"You know what? You really shouldn't be uptight about that Miss Texas thing. I mean, if ever there was a woman who was meant to be a beauty queen, it's you."

A strange expression washed over her face, and Rebecca looked down at the gift she was holding. Matt had the uneasy feeling that she had heard this a million times before, and it made him feel an even bigger fool as his brain groped the rusty parts for how to express his feelings. "I'm not...look, Rebecca, I'm a lawyer, not a poet. But there are some things I just know, and all I am trying to say is, you are so damn gorgeous that you probably steal into men's dreams all the time without even knowing it. You *are* a man's dream."

Rebecca said nothing, but slowly pushed the floral piece toward him.

Matt took it in one hand, and with the other, he impulsively reached up, touched her temple, unable to stop himself from feeling her skin beneath his fingertips once more. "If you ever want to finish off that drought," he muttered, listing forward to kiss her while she stood, paralyzed. Her lips, slightly parted, quivered beneath his, and as his hand drifted to her neck, he felt her pulse racing. And then she was responding, lifting up to him, kissing him deep, stepping closer, her hand on his neck, her tongue in his mouth, kissing him *deeper*. Every fiber, every cell in him was suddenly alive; he could feel a draw from his groin to his throat, and as he began to snake his arm around her waist, she broke the kiss.

Dazed, Matt just stood there.

Rebecca touched her finger to his lips, looked up at him through thick, dark lashes, her eyes crystal blue beneath. "Thank you, Matt. Thanks for last night and for saying what you did about me. But I think you should know, I'm not really in a place—"

She was about to give him the brush-off, and Matt's survival instincts kicked in. He pulled the floral thing between them, smiled lopsidedly. "*Whoa*—don't get me wrong," he said, forcing a laugh. "I was just saying thanks for the memories." He winked at her.

Rebecca smiled, but her eyes said she didn't believe him. "That's what I thought," she said softly, and stepped around him, walked to her car, opened the door, and tossed her bag inside. And then she started it up, throwing the thing in reverse and leaving the parking lot while he stood there like a dolt, holding some artsy-fartsy sculpture of paper flowers, quietly disturbed by the uncomfortable realization he had made that very same exit more times than he could count.

CHAPTER FIFTEEN

As with most things involving human emotion and sexual-
ity it may take some time getting through whatever holds
you back—but the outcome is certainly worthwhile!

AWOMANSTOUCH.COM

R ebecca couldn't get back to Ruby Falls fast enough.
Once she was safely ensconced in her refuge, Rebecca
fed her dogs, then treated herself to a long, soaking, bubble
bath. But the soothing eye compress was not cold enough to
chase his image from her mind's eye, and the water wasn't
hot enough to melt away the feel of his body against hers,
nor the lingering heat of the most sublime orgasm of her
life. Each time she thought of it, she felt an enticing shiver
snake down her spine. And when he had kissed her again
in the garage of the Four Seasons—or rather, when she had
kissed him—she had feared that she would melt again, like
she had the night before, right into his arms...

So what if she did? Was that so bad? *Yes! Yes, yes, yes...*

Okay, maybe it was, but she'd be a whole lot happier if
she could only say why.

Her head was pounding, so Rebecca turned in very
early, Frank at the foot of her bed, and Bean with his head

under the bed (the only part of his body that would fit) and dreamed a stupid, ridiculous, sensual dream in which she and Matt had mind-blowing sex, and he brought her to the very brink of what had all the markings of being the most stupendous orgasm ever. But she awoke, unfulfilled and miserable. The usual.

What worried her was that it didn't end there. She felt fearfully and mysteriously fantastic Sunday, as if there was something wild inside, something that had been awakened after years of paralysis, trying to claw its way free, and it scared her. It had been so long since she had been anything but perfect, never so much as a hair out of place, her manner and her life all carefully controlled. To think that something wildly imperfect was rumbling about inside and demanding to be set free seemed like... *anarchy.*

There was only one thing to be done for it—housecleaning. Top to bottom, scrubbing, scrubbing, and scrubbing to get rid of that earthy feeling and put everything back in its proper place, including Matt, who had become, much to her horror, someone she thought she could actually like. *Really* like.

Naturally, the housekeeping did no good. Exhausted, she tried a different tack, and after devouring a container of Häagen-Dazs for supper, she spent the evening in the midst of her growing library of self-help and Zen books, scouring them for any tips or advice that might help her move onward through the strange fog that had enveloped her sometime Friday and now refused to dissipate.

No luck, of course.

So she pored through *Friends and Lovers and How to Know the Difference* in minute detail, but found nothing to help her put Matt in his proper category. Stupid book. It could at least list some attributes or something.

A phone call from Rachel, all excited, was the topper of her excruciatingly raw day. "I've been charting your horoscope!" she said happily when Rebecca answered the phone.

"Why?"

"What a silly question. Bec, it's *fantastic*. Okay, you know Uranus is in Pisces, which is really great, I mean, you should really be prepared for something totally awesome. And then, guess what. Venus is in Pisces, too! So anyway, I was looking at your horoscope for the next year, and you will not believe what it says. Guess."

"I—"

"Okay, I'll tell you," she said breathlessly. "It says that Venus will orbit very closely to Uranus, and there will be a strong current of electricity in the air, and that a Pisces will have powers of magnetism they have not known in seventy *years*. And that there is someone very close to you, probably a Cancer, who will fulfill you in ways you never dreamed." Rachel paused there for dramatic effect, waiting for Rebecca to say something.

"Oh," Rebecca obliged her.

"*Bec!*" Rachel cried, distressed she was not made ecstatic by the news. "Have I steered you wrong yet? Don't you want to fall in love and—"

Rebecca's heart suddenly lurched. "*No!*" she said sharply. "No, Rachel, I don't. I just got a divorce, remember?"

"Come on, of course you do. Your divorce was months and months ago. So what, are you going to live alone all your life listening to sad songs on the radio? Listen, *Someone very close—*"

"I heard you. But there is no one very close to me, and I am not unfulfilled. I'm happy!"

"Being perfect does not necessarily equal happiness."

"What's that supposed to mean?" Rebecca demanded.

"What part did you not get? The perfect part or the happy part?"

Rebecca snorted. "Will someone please explain to me why everyone is so concerned about my life?"

"Well…because we love you," Rachel said, as if that were the most obvious thing in the world. "And Bud was a jerk. You deserve to be happy."

"I am happy," Rebecca insisted, feeling, inexplicably, close to tears.

"Whatever," Rachel said, clearly exasperated. "Listen, I have to go. I'm leaving for England Thursday and I have to finish Robin's horoscope. She's going to get a huge windfall in June!"

"She'll be thrilled," Rebecca said, and listened to Rachel's singsong good-bye as she hung up.

Honestly, she wished Rachel would stop calling with her bullshit because Rebecca could never shake it from her thoughts. She certainly tossed and turned her way through that night (*thanks, Rach!*), staring long and hard at the shadows of leaves dappled in the moonlight on the old limestone wall of her room. By morning, she had reached a few wobbly conclusions: one illicit encounter did not a romance make, and in fact, Matt's great looks aside, there really wasn't that much to like about him, except maybe his sense of humor, even though it tended toward the smarty-pants. Oh, and he seemed practical, which she liked. And smart. And there was the fact that he had been unexpectedly kind to her. But that was about it as far as she could see. He didn't seem that crazy about her, either, and they really had nothing in common and even if they did have something in common, which they did not, she really wasn't ready for anything like... *that.* Horoscopes notwithstanding.

Frankly, after years of marriage, she was just now beginning to find herself again. She did not want to risk losing herself all over again, and men had a way of making her lose herself. No, no, all that had happened was a sexy little— *okay, mind-blowing*—thing in the middle of a very bad drunk. It was not the end of the world, and neither was it the start of anything big. It was just...nothing.

She wasn't unhappy.

There was, however, one thing she could privately admit: Robin was right. She really needed to get laid.

Positive Affirmations of My Life:
1. Grayson coming home today!
2. Bingo bash this week, which means, at last, I can get that monkey off my back! Yippee!
3. Survived drunken stupor and bonus, broke the four-year dry spell. Which means I can do a couple more years no sweat until I am ready for a relationship. With sex. Because a person can do <u>anything</u> for a couple of years if they put their mind to it.

When Rebecca arrived to pick up her son at the designated rendezvous point (a Holiday Inn on the interstate),

Bud and Grayson and what's-her-face were already there. Grayson got out of the big Cadillac Escalade and waved, then darted around to the back of the vehicle. Bud met him there, opened up the hatch, lifted out his backpack. And while Grayson struggled to put it on, Bud reached into the back and handed Grayson a fat, wiggling, little black puppy with paws the size of Frisbees.

"Hey!" Rebecca shouted, marching across the parking lot as Bud gathered the leash and water bowl.

"Hi, Mom!" Grayson called cheerfully. "Look what Candace got me!"

Why, how thoughtful of Candy Ass! "Gray, honey, did you tell Candace that we already have two dogs?" she asked, leaning down to kiss his face, which was covered with something very sticky and sweet.

"What's one more?" Bud asked matter-of-factly, thrusting a box with biscuits and a water bowl at her. "And besides, he wanted the dog."

"Really? He wants a horse, too," she said over Grayson's head. "Are you going to pull one of those out of your truck?"

"Come on, Rebecca."

"Gray wants lots of things he can't have, Bud," she said calmly. "You might have at least asked. This means more food and more dog to take care of, and by the look of him, that will not be a cheap proposition, because that guy is not going to grow up to be a dainty little dog!"

"We named him Tater," Grayson announced. "Candace helped me think of it." The puppy reacted to his new name by licking the sticky stuff from Grayson's cheek.

"How helpful of her," Rebecca said, then glared at Bud.

"Would you please stop acting like a princess? What's one lousy dog? You got a big enough place, and Lord knows you have enough of my money to feed it."

Actually, in hindsight, she did not have nearly as much of his money as she should have gone for.

"So I hear you're with Masters?" he said, changing the subject and startling her.

"What? How did you know that—Robin?"

He shrugged. "That's a better move for you, really, instead of the work idea." He paused to get something out of the SUV, giving Rebecca time to visualize herself kicking him square in the nuts, martial arts style. "You know, Aaron would really like Tom."

"Who, Dad? He doesn't like politics or politicians."

"Masters is different. You should really talk to Aaron about Tom."

What was this? Bud's sudden interest in her dad's political leanings—*any* leanings—was certainly odd, and as he shut the back of the SUV, she had a sudden, sickening thought. "Did you have anything to do with Tom calling me in the first place?" she asked, eyeing him suspiciously.

"No, Rebecca. I just think it's a good move, that's all."

What a relief. She'd rather die than take something Bud had set up for her.

"Okay, buddy, I have to go," Bud said, running his hand over Grayson's unruly top. "Candy and I have a long drive to Dallas."

"But Dad, when can I come see you and Lucy?" Grayson asked, struggling to hold on to the monster puppy.

"I'll call you," Bud said, and then looked at Rebecca. "You doing okay? You look too skinny."

"Thanks."

"You sure you're handling all this okay?"

"All what?"

"You know, us. Our split."

"Bud, please don't patronize me," Rebecca said evenly. "We've been divorced almost a year." She grabbed the puppy by the scruff of the neck before it wriggled free of Grayson's grip.

"Don't, Mom! I got him," he complained, and twisted away from her. "Tater is *my* dog!"

"Okay, see you," said Bud, already striding toward the driver's seat.

Grayson whipped around. *"Dad! Dad!"* he screamed. *"Byyyyyye, Dad!"*

Bud waved, then disappeared into the Escalade. Grayson stood there, watching Bud take off, speeding out of the parking lot without so much as a backward glance. When the Escalade had disappeared into traffic, Rebecca put her hand on his shoulder. "Come on, sweetie."

Grayson jerked away from her. "I'm *coming*," he said, and began stalking toward the Rover as well as he could with the squiggling puppy.

Rebecca tried to talk to him on the way home, but Grayson was in a foul mood, as he usually was after seeing Bud. "I had *fun* with Dad," was the only thing she could get out of him about his weekend at the coast. "I wish Dad had married *Lucy*," he added petulantly, and Rebecca figured the kid was determined to find a way to hurt her.

His disposition did not improve that evening, either. While Bean took the new addition to their family in stride (if he even noticed), Frank wasn't too pleased, and snapped twice at a very playful Tater. That infuriated Grayson, who, after throwing a tantrum and insisting that Rebecca put Frank out, which she would not, scooped up Tater and marched off to his room, slamming the door behind him.

A half hour later, Rebecca peeked into his room. Grayson was sprawled on his race car bed, snotty-nosed and red-faced from having cried himself to sleep. Her heart went out to him; what could possibly be so troubling to a little kid? She didn't know, but at the moment, Tater, who had already shredded one of Grayson's books, was working on a shoe.

Rebecca trotted the pup out into the backyard and handed him over to Frank and Bean for proper training. Well. To Frank, anyway.

With the help of Grayson's cranky return, Rebecca was able to push Matt from her mind and focus what was left of her brain on Tom Masters's Bingo Bash. She exchanged what seemed like no less than a thousand e-mails with Francine McDonough, the Silver Panthers' president. The plan was simple: the pots would be split between the Silver Panthers Charity Drive (the proceeds to be donated to the charity of the winner's choice), and reimbursing the Elks Lodge the expense of the room and food. As the Elks Lodge frequently held their own charitable bingo nights, Rebecca had all the bingo stuff lined up—bingo sheets, bingo balls, a bingo ball mixer-upper thing, as well as extra "dabbers." And as Grandma was an avid bingo fan, she helped Rebecca line up the most important feature: the bingo caller, who, Grandma said, was the best this side of Louisiana.

Rebecca paid a couple of visits to the Elks Lodge to review the setup, making sure the refreshments and decorations were all in order. She even coaxed Grayson into helping her finger-paint some cute signs to be placed around the bingo room (*Tom Masters for Lt. Governor!*). She called Tom three times to make sure he understood where and when he should be in attendance, but could only get Gilbert, who assured her Tom was on board and would be where he needed to be at the appropriate time. She did not, however, make or receive a single call from Big Pants, and frankly, wasn't quite sure what to make of that. On the one hand, she had told him—sort of—that she did not want it to go any further. But after he said what he did, she had thought...maybe even hoped a little...that he might call. Not that she wanted him to call, because she didn't. Really.

So when he did call late the night before the bingo bash—when she was in her silk pajamas, curled up with *Surviving Divorce: A Woman's Path to Starting Over*—she wasn't sure if she should be put out with how long it had taken him or just politely pleased that he had called.

"Hey, Mork," he said when she answered.

"Matt Parrish. Is there a problem?" she asked evenly, and God help him if he had really called at this hour about the campaign.

But with a chuckle that was surprisingly reassuring, he said, "I was going to ask the same of you."

"Why would I have a problem?" she asked, pushing her book aside and pulling her knees up under her chin.

"God, where do I start?" he asked with a laugh as smooth as silk, and Rebecca smiled in spite of herself. "Actually," he said, "I was just calling to see if you're okay."

"I'm fine! Why do you ask?"

"I don't know—I guess it's just that the last time I saw you, you seemed a little...befuddled."

"Be*fuddled?*" Rebecca laughed. "What sort of word is that?"

"The best I could think of."

"And I suppose you thought I must be befuddled because I left you holding the bag, right?"

"*No,* Miss Priss," Matt drawled. "Because you lost your panties."

An intoxicating heat flooded her face and neck; grinning, Rebecca pushed her hair behind her ear and slid down into the pillows. "So...this is like a panties check?" she asked softly.

"Yeah. Wearing any?"

"Wouldn't you like to know?"

Matt made some sort of guttural sound that was half laugh, half groan. "I would. But don't tell me—let me imagine. Come on, Mork, imagine with me."

"Matt..."

"Okay, I'll go first. I am imagining you lying there with some pretty and skimpy little thing on, and I imagine you're completely naked underneath—"

"*Matt!*" she exclaimed, laughing.

"And you're getting all hot and bothered thinking about me—"

"I am *so* not doing that," she insisted gaily, and hugged her knees tighter, lest she get too hot and bothered.

"And now your skin is flushed and you feel all warm inside, and you're squirming a little, because all you can think about is when I was kissing you down—"

"MATT!" she cried, instantly pushing herself up.

"Okay," he said, and added a long and exaggerated sigh. "I'll just have to imagine by myself."

"Do *you* have some pretty little thing on?" she asked.

"Darlin', I'm just plain ol' buck naked," he said confidently. "Just me and my enormous and hard—"

"Okay, okay!" she said as the heat spread down to her toes.

Matt laughed low and knowingly. "I can take a hint, believe it or not. So you're okay?" he asked once more. "Haven't signed up for rehab or anything rash like that, right?"

Rebecca laughed. "I'm fine. But thank you for checking."

"Sweet dreams, Rebecca," he said softly, and clicked off.

But with an image of naked Matt dancing about her brain, it was a while before Rebecca could sleep.

Early the next afternoon, on the day of the Tom Masters Bingo Bash for Charity, Grandma and Grandpa, who had invited themselves to the event, arrived at the lake house in a huge RV.

Grayson, Rebecca, Jo Lynn, and of course, Bean, Frank, and Tater, all came out onto the front porch to watch as the monster bus rumbled down the gravel road to her house. Grandpa was the first out, clumping off-kilter around the front of the RV in his haste to get at his great-grandson, in tan Sansabelt slacks and a Players polo shirt with a single red stripe across the breast pocket, which, Rebecca thought, was spruced up for Grandpa. Grandma wasn't far behind, wearing tan pants with elastic in the waist that matched her taupe shoes, a pink knit henley top, and a denim vest that said *LET'S BINGO!* across the back. In addition, Grandma was carrying her bingo bag, which was really a beach bag lined with compartments that looked as if they might hold water bottles to the average Joe, but were actually intended for the brightly colored bingo dabbers. Inside the bag were a variety of tiny stuffed animals that Grandma swore brought her luck while at the very same time complaining that she never won.

When they were through smothering poor Grayson, Grandma and Grandpa came forward to smother Rebecca. She managed to introduce Jo Lynn in spite of the usual Inquisition (Grandma: *You're too skinny, honey, don't you ever eat? Is that the way you are wearing your hair now?* Grandpa: *How much did this place set you back? How much did they want for that Range Rover? What the hell is the matter with that big yellow dog? He damn near walked into the porch.*)

"Why the RV?" Rebecca asked.

Grandma and Grandpa simultaneously turned and looked at the huge RV, perhaps already having forgotten that they had driven it all the way from Houston. Grandma shrugged. "You just never know, do you?" she said, as if that explained everything, and smiled at Rebecca, her octagonal pink-rimmed glasses making her blue eyes look like enormous fish eyes. "When are we going to get over to the bingo hall? I want to make sure I get a good spot."

"It's two o'clock in the afternoon, Grandma," Rebecca said. "The event doesn't start until seven."

"Well then, I need to fix you something to eat," she said, pushing past Rebecca into the house while Grayson took Grandpa around back to see where the dogs slept.

The rest of the afternoon was spent on phone calls to Gunter (what a shame Heather couldn't make it tonight!), who required several directions from the airport, then barking dogs and trying to keep Grandma from rearranging her kitchen (or Grandpa from rearranging her toolshed), and of course, avoiding the continuing Inquisition. Rebecca loved her grandma, but if she gave her an inch, she'd demand all the details of her life. Fortunately, as Rebecca was on and off the phone, Grandma had to limit herself to quick, short observations about Mom. "She's just running away from her problems out there in Los Angeles, if you ask me," she said, shaking her head. "She needs to poop or get off the pot, and decide if she's going to leave him or come on home." This, with an emphatic nod of her blue-tinted head.

When it came time to go, Rebecca emerged from her bedroom dressed in a conservative gray Ralph Lauren pantsuit. Grandma took one look at her and shook her head. "You don't play a lot of bingo, do you honey?" Rebecca changed to a slinky long black skirt, black cowboy boots, and a brown suede jacket with fringe, which Grandma said was a little too dressy, but Grandpa said was perfect.

They drove over to pick up Jo Lynn, then on to the Elks Lodge, whose parking lot was full when they arrived a half hour before the scheduled time. "I *knew* we were going to be late," Grandma moaned, and was the first one out of Rebecca's Range Rover, Jo Lynn close on her heels. The two of them rushed forward, their bingo bags knocking into each other as Grandpa, Rebecca, and Grayson hurried behind.

The smell of brisket and beans blasted them as they walked into the lodge, where they were greeted by a veritable sea of nylon and polyester, all beneath cotton-ball heads. A heavyset woman with a pink cotton ball spotted them, broke away from a group, and came racing toward them astride a motorized scooter at such a speed that Grayson fearfully ducked behind Rebecca. The woman slammed her scooter to an abrupt halt, her dentures gleaming pearly white in a broad smile. "Welcome to the Senator Masters Bingo Bash for Charity!" she exclaimed. "I'm Francine McDonough, the president of the Silver Panthers."

"Ms. McDonough, I'm Rebecca Lear."

"Well, I'll be a monkey's uncle!" the woman cried, slapping her handlebar. "E-mail just doesn't tell you what a person looks like, does it? Honey, I thought you were some old-timer from Lakeway." She laughed uproariously.

Ignoring the fact that she came across as an old lady on e-mail, Rebecca pulled Grayson from out behind her. "This is my son, Grayson."

"*Oooh*, what a cutie!" Francine exclaimed. "Come here, sweetpea, and let ol' Francine have a look at you!" Rebecca pushed a reluctant Grayson forward. Francine leaned over her handlebars in a gravity-defying move and pinched his cheek. "You are such a *cutie*," she said through clenched teeth, and abruptly let go.

"And this is my grandfather, Elmer Stanton."

"I practically started the Silver Panthers," he said.

"Did you?" Francine asked, clearly skeptical. "The place looks good, doesn't it?" she said to Rebecca before Grandpa could continue. "You know, when you wrote me about this party, I thought you were out of your mind. Ask a bunch of Silver Panthers to a bingo party, and you are asking for trouble!" Francine laughed, braced her pudgy hands on her pudgier thighs. "But here we are, ready to go! Now all we've got to worry about is that the caller had to cancel."

Rebecca was with her right up until her last statement. "What?"

"That boy you had lined up called here not a half hour ago and said some emergency had come up, so he ain't gonna be here."

She said it so cheerfully that Rebecca wondered if she'd heard her correctly. "Then who is going to call the bingo?"

"Hell if I know," Francine said with a jolly laugh, then suddenly craned her neck to see behind Rebecca. "Well, will you lookie here, there's my old friend Mary Zamburger! Pardon me, sugar!" She hit the accelerator of her scooter so hard that Grayson knocked into Rebecca trying to get out of the way.

"But…" Rebecca said, her voice trailing off as she whirled around to say something more to Francine—and saw Gunter and his photographer cowering near the entry.

"Now don't you worry, Becky," Grandpa said, patting her arm. "*I'll* call the bingo."

CHAPTER SIXTEEN

*If you can find a path with no obstacles, it probably doesn't
lead anywhere...*

FRANK A. CLARK

Chips and salsa were now the official state snack of Texas,
thanks to the diligent efforts of Senator Masters.

Tom was really beginning to confuse the hell out of Matt.
He had shepherded some good, decent legislation through
the senate this session, but unfortunately, the only item to
hit the papers was that stupid chips and salsa bit, and it made
Tom look like a redneck. Matt's opinion which was shared by
Doug, and the two of them had plotted how to undo Tom's
damage that afternoon, with no help from Tom, who argued
that he would get mileage out of any bill. "If you send a
press release on anything that matters, there's always a loser,
which means someone to get bent out of shape. You know
what happened to me on the campaign finance reform bill
I authored—they might as well have nailed me to a cross on
the capitol lawn. And besides, you can't deny that every red-
blooded Texan loves his chips and salsa. I know I do."

"But they don't love candidates who have nothing better to do with their tax dollars then sit around making up
meaningless legislation," Matt responded.

"Well, good God, Parrish, you sound like a damn Yankee!" Tom had laughed, clapping him on the back.

The whole thing had made Matt question his motives again, and what it was he hoped to achieve on this campaign. He was dreading the Silver Panthers event that evening, and probably would have skipped it altogether, taken some time to get his head on straight, had it not been but for one tiny little thing. Yep. Her again. The sexually repressed wacko.

He was, for reasons that could not possibly be less clear to him, feeling discouragingly protective of her. Or maybe it was possessive. Whatever it was, he didn't like feeling it, particularly since, for all intents and purposes, she'd essentially had given him the ol' heave-ho. In the aftermath of that, his assessment of what had happened (a full twenty minutes, a new personal best) between him and Miss Priss last week was that it had been an aberration in the space and time continuum. Nothing else would explain it. He knew she was trouble, that he was better off with women who actually liked him. So what if Rebecca was beautiful and sexy and just this side of odd? There were lots of intriguing women out there. There *were*.

Just as he never took a case with too many screwy twists, he never took on a woman with too many screwy twists, either. He was quite comfortable doing the casual dating thing, and frankly, not since his college days had he engaged in a relationship that wasn't based primarily on fucking, to put it bluntly. Rebecca wasn't like that, and she'd made it perfectly clear that she definitely was not his type. So why, then, had he given in to the senseless urge to call her? He might as well paint a big giant red *F* on his chest for *FOOL*. It was that four-year thing, he decided. He just couldn't forget it. There was something very alluring about it, on many, dusty and precarious Matt levels…not to mention the silk panties he'd found that were still on his dresser.

So it was with a great deal of uncertainty and reservation that he said good night to Harold and told him he'd be out at the Lakeway gig. Harold (whose fingers were flying across the computer keyboard at a perfect 120 words a minute) said, "Tell Miss Lear hi for me," without so much as a pause in his maniacal typing.

When Matt walked into the Elks Lodge an hour later, the room was packed with what looked like so many plain sno-cones. Row upon row of white heads (interspersed with the occasional jet black or reddish purple) were bent over big white sheets, marking with fat, bright neon markers. Some of them were manning more than one sheet, and some of them had surrounded their sheets with a variety of stuffed animals.

In a smaller room to his right, another dozen or more sno-cones were seated around tables gnawing on some sort of meat amid a littering of pink TaB cans.

Cautiously, Matt stepped deeper into the lodge and noticed two elderly women, wearing identical green vests, seated behind a stack of big white sheets and colored markers. One of them eagerly waved him over, but Matt was too stunned to move, because the bizarre scene hadn't quite registered. He had expected some sort of meeting, a solemn, serious event, but this looked like…except that it couldn't be, could it? Nah…it would be next to impossible to pull *this* off.

"N-45! We all remember '45! N-45!"

"Bin-go!" A woman shouted, and popped up like a jack-in-the-box, her paper skin swinging loosely under her arms as she *woo-hooed* to everyone's applause.

"We have a winner!" The announcer was sitting with one extra-large hip half cocked onto a bar stool, looking like some senior citizen lounge lizard. Next to him, a machine popped white bingo balls like a giant snow globe. "Come on up here, honey, and let's make sure you won that twenty-five-dollar pot!"

"I'm definitely in the wrong place," Matt muttered to himself, and pivoted around, only to be stopped cold by a huge banner sagging across the door:

Welcome to the Masters Bingo Bash for Charity!
Thank you Senator Masters!

"What the hell?" he breathed as the winner did a little cha-cha through the tables on her way to the dais to claim her prize.

"Matt, right?" a male voice asked, causing him to jump a good foot in the air as the announcer asked for the winner's sheet to double-check the numbers. It was Gunter, dressed in all black again.

"Gunter," Matt said with a sigh of relief, extending his hand.

"That's a bingo, all right," the announcer said. "Okay, doll, what charity are you going to donate to?"

"I'm going to donate it to the Arthritis Foundation."

"That's a good one! I could use a little of their help myself. Okay, folks, line 'em up, we got us a forty-dollar pot coming up!"

"They're really into bingo here," Gunter said stoically.

No shit. "Where's Tom?" Matt asked.

"Are you ready? Got your cards lined up? Ready to play a little B-I-N-G-Oooh?" the announcer sang.

"Hasn't shown up yet. But there goes Rebecca," Gunter said, and nodded at a figure darting through the crowd toward the dais.

That was Rebecca, all right, but it was little wonder Matt hadn't noticed her before now—her hair was coming out of its braid, a towel or something was hanging like a handkerchief from her pocket, and she was carrying what looked like a giant eraser. She raced up the three steps to the dais platform and a big white erase board there, which she frantically rubbed as the announcer pulled a ball from the popping bingo machine.

"The first number in game four is B-11. That's *Beeee*-eleven. Which reminds me—and I don't think I can say this often enough—Joe Hampton has warned that we all stay away from the *beeeeeans*. Says they're delicious but lethal." The crowd laughed as Rebecca wrote, in perfectly straight and giant letters, *B-11* on the white erase board.

"You're kidding me," Matt said flatly.

"I'm not kidding," Gunter said as he crossed his arms over his concave chest.

"What happened to a meeting?"

"Hey, I'm just here for the pics, dude."

Well, he was here for a meeting, and Matt was instantly striding for the dais. When he reached it, he stood off to one side, by the stairs, just below Rebecca. "*Rebecca!*" he hissed as the old guy called *I-20.*

She hardly even spared him a glance as she erased the board and wrote *I-20.* "*Where's Tom?*" she hissed back at him. "He promised he'd be on time!"

"I-20, where I almost met my maker once, pulling a fifth-wheel trailer." Appreciative moans went up from the audience as everyone carefully marked their I-20s.

"Perhaps Tom was confused," Matt loudly whispered back. "Perhaps he expected a *real* meeting and not a bingo game!"

"Bash."

"Excuse me?"

"It's a bingo *bash*," she corrected him. "And it is a real meeting."

"Ready, gang? The next number is O-66. Get your kicks on oh-six-six…"

Rebecca dutifully erased the board and printed a neat *O-66.*

"I thought you said you got Tom a gig in front of the political committee of the Silver Panthers, not their bingo club!"

"I did get him in front of them, if he'd only show up!"

"In *here?*"

The announcer looked over his shoulder at Matt and Rebecca; Rebecca quickly walked to the edge of the dais and squatted down. A hint of her perfume wafted over Matt, and damn it if it didn't instantly stir up all the stuff he'd worked so hard to push down. And she looked, he noticed, very rattled, which instantly made him feel weirdly protective of her all over again. "Matt," she said, with what sounded like a tinge of hysteria in her voice, "I'll be done in a moment. Jo Lynn was going to do this, but she wanted to play a few games first—"

"Jo Lynn?"

"Listen—do you *see* those Q-tips out there?" she whispered frantically. "They can't *hear* and they can't *see*, and

I have to write the numbers on the board. Just give me a minute. One minute. That's all I am asking."

When she asked so imploringly, he could imagine giving her as many minutes, hours, days, or nights as she wanted, and backed off. That, and the entire sea of sno-cones were staring at him. "Okay, all right," he said, and backed away.

"Well, lookie here, we got us a G-56. Gee-five-six, folks."

"Go sit with Grayson," she ordered him, and stood up, walked back to the white board, and violently erased it.

Matt stepped away, shoved his hands into his pockets, and strode down the row of tables, spotting her kid for the first time since he had come in. He was sitting at the very end of the table, next to woman with bottles of colored liquid and several stuffed bears.

As Matt neared the boy, he noticed that every number on his sheet had been marked. The kid saw Matt looking at his card, and instantly threw his arms and head over it so Matt couldn't see it.

He grinned at the kid and continued to the back where Gunter and his photographer were taking pictures of the group. And there he remained until the announcer said the next session would start in twenty-five minutes. "In the meantime, help yourself to a delicious brisket dinner. Remember, it's free! Just don't forget to stay away from the beans, folks— be considerate of your neighbor," the old man reminded them as they made an instant and mad stampede for the smaller room, practically flattening Matt against the wall.

When the biggest group had passed, Matt spotted Rebecca at the table with her son and started toward her. When he reached her, Rebecca looked up, smiling a little deliriously. "Hey!"

"When you said you had this thing lined up, I thought you meant you had it greased," he said. "I don't believe the words *crash a bingo hall* ever passed your lips."

"A cheery hello to you, too," she said. "We are not crashing a bingo hall. I set up the bingo," she continued matter-of-factly, pausing to flash a smile at a trio of leering old men in Sansabelt slacks floating by in the river of people headed for the free buffet. "These people like bingo."

"I noticed. Like it so much that we hardly have their undivided attention, do we? And Christ, I don't even want to imagine how much money—"

"Yo. Dude. He's here."

They both looked past Gunter, who had appeared from thin air, and to the door, where Tom, Pat, and Angie had managed to squeeze past the thundering herd. Gunter was already moving, quickly cornering Tom, making him pose for a couple of pictures before he took one more step, which, naturally, Tom was happy to do.

"Parrish! What the hell are you doing here?"

Matt stifled a groan. He knew that voice.

"Someone wants you," Rebecca said, and turned around to her kid and the two old ladies he'd obviously been assigned to this evening.

Suppressing a sigh, Matt turned around to face the top of Judge Gambofini's head. He'd never seen Gambofini without his robes—the judge was wearing a red, horizontally striped polo shirt, only the stripes were much smaller on the top than those stretched across his enormous middle. Even more noticeable was that Gambofini was actually grinning for the first time Matt could remember. "Judge, how are you?"

"Almost had bingo a couple of games back. Saw you up at the dais. You're a little young to be hanging out with the Silver Panthers, aren't you?"

"Actually, I—" What he was about to say was interrupted by a strong slap to his shoulder that almost knocked the wind out of him.

"Parrish! There you are!"

"Senator," Matt said, rubbing his shoulder. "You know Judge Gambofini, don't you?"

"I do," Tom said, and eagerly stuck out his hand, although Matt knew damn well he didn't have a clue who Gambofini was.

"Ah," said Judge Gambofini, eyeing Tom as he shook his hand, then slanted a gaze at Matt, clasped his hands behind his back, and rocked back and forth on his tiny feet. "So I guess the rumors about your political aspirations are true."

"What rumors are those?" Tom asked, planting his hands on his broad hips to better consider both men.

"Nothing but a little courthouse gossip," Gambofini chuckled. "If you boys will excuse me, I'm going to get me some of that brisket before it's all gone," he said, and smirked at Matt as he walked on.

Great. This would be all over the courthouse come Monday.

"Hey, this is fantastic," Tom said, looking around at the decorations. "What a crowd! This is exactly the kind of thing we need to be doing. I want to congratulate this girl," he said as Rebecca turned around. "You've outdone yourself again, Mrs. Reynolds!"

"Lear," she reminded him as he wrapped a big burly arm around her shoulders, squeezing so tightly that Rebecca winced at his strength. "It was really very easy to do." She looked at Matt and said, "People make these things out to be a lot harder than they actually are."

"Ain't that the truth?" Tom laughed, and let her go. "So where's our hostess?"

"She's in the dining area. Let's go find her," she suggested, and the two of them walked off without sparing so much as a glance at Matt.

"Is this for real?" This, from Pat, in the company of Angie, who had walked up to stand next to Matt and gape at the place. "I thought this was a meeting," she said, tugging at the jacket of her plain gray suit.

"You and me both."

"I think it's totally cool," Angie said. Her hair was jet black for the occasion. "I've never played bingo before," she added as she wandered off to have a look around. Pat and Matt looked at each other; Pat shrugged, tugged on the jacket again. "Oh well...I guess when in Rome, right?" She followed Angie.

"When in Rome, my rosy red ass," Matt muttered, and turned around, noticed Rebecca's son again. The kid was arranging new cards and was apparently getting a jump on the competition by marking some numbers before the game began. "Hey," Matt said.

"Hey," the kid responded without looking up.

"Remember me?"

He frowned a little. "Sort of."

"I sort of remember you, too," Matt said, and gave in, pulling up a chair. "Remind me what your name is."

"Grayson. What's yours?"

"Matt."

"Ex-*cuse* me? Hello?" One of the old women was peering down at him through enormous pink-rimmed glasses. "I'm Lil Stanton. And who might you be?"

"Matt Parrish," he said, coming to his feet and extending his hand.

Lil Stanton looked at his hand, then at Grayson. "Do you know my great-grandson?"

"Sort of. Right, buddy?"

Grayson shrugged.

"I work with his mom on Senator Masters's campaign."

"*Oooh,*" Lil Stanton trilled, brightening instantly. "That's so lovely. I so enjoy meeting Rebecca's friends! I'm her grandma. You can call me Lil—and that's her grandpa up there on the stage," she said, her smile fading a little. "Just loves the limelight, that old fool. And this is Rebecca's good friend Jo Lynn."

"Speaking of which," said the other woman, who was wearing, Matt couldn't help but notice, a tie-dyed shirt, "I best get up there. I'm marking the board next session."

Lil Stanton smiled at Matt, then made a show of arranging her next session sheets. Matt and Grayson sat in silence for several minutes, watching her align her stuffed bears, until Lil suddenly said, "Oh my..." She looked at Matt, blinking big blue eyes magnified through thick glasses. "I think Elmer was right about those beans. Would you mind watching Gray for a moment?"

Matt never got the chance to answer—Lil was off like a shot, one hand on her belly.

Grayson watched her disappear into the hall, then turned his attention back to his cards and methodically went down a row of *N* numbers, marking them all.

"So, you having any luck?" Matt asked.

Grayson shrugged. "I don't really like this game."

"I don't like it, either," Matt confided. "Too weird."

Grayson stopped marking his card and looked at Matt from the corner of his eye. "Mom said there might be someone to play with, but there's not."

"Someone to *play* with?" Matt twisted around, saw that Rebecca and Tom were back in the bingo hall talking to a lady on a scooter. He shoved his hand in his pocket, withdrew several peppermints he had picked up at lunch. "Want one?" he asked Grayson as he popped one into his mouth.

The child eyed the candy very closely. "I'm not supposed to eat it."

"Oh, yeah? Why not?"

"'Cuz there's something wrong with my teeth. Candy hurts them."

"Ah," Matt said, and unwrapped one, holding it out. "Live dangerously. This won't hurt you."

Grayson peered up at him, assessing him.

"What, you don't believe me?"

The kid responded by fixating on his tie.

"Trust me, there's nothing wrong with your teeth. Your mom just says stuff like that because she's a mom," he said. "Moms can be a little strange, and I won't lie to you kid— your mom may be a lot strange." He extended his hand a little farther. "Come on, she'll never know."

Grayson took the peppermint, put it in his mouth, and smiled. Matt fished in his pocket again, pulled out a few more, and opened his palm. Grayson took four, unwrapped them, and popped them into his mouth along with the first, which was not exactly what Matt had intended, but the kid's cheeks puffed out like a chipmunk's, and he couldn't help but laugh.

Grayson smiled, flashing a peppermint instead of teeth.

"So what kind of games do you like?" Matt asked, smiling.

"Ooogeeah."

"*Ooogeeah?*"

Grayson laughed, his lips and tongue peppermint red. "Yu-Gi-Oh! And Barbie."

Matt's testicles seized. "Barbie, huh? How come?"

Grayson shrugged. "I just like her," he said through the mouthful of peppermints.

"You go to school, right?" Matt asked uncertainly. "What, second or third grade?"

"Preschool."

"Cool." He glanced over his shoulder again and started a little. As if she'd been summoned by some spooky maternal radar, Rebecca had turned around, was peering closely at them. And then she said something to Tom, started marching in their direction.

"Uh-oh," muttered Grayson through his mouthful of peppermints, looking over his shoulder, too.

Uh-oh was right. "Okay, stay cool, buddy," Matt muttered. "I got your back."

Rebecca reached them as the announcer gave them the five-minute warning. She stood in front of them, her arms folded tightly, looked at Grayson first, then Matt. "So what's going on?"

Grayson looked helplessly at Matt. "Hey!" Matt said, plastering a smile on his face, "We're just a couple of guys hanging out. So, Vanna, don't they need you up on stage?"

"Grayson?" she asked, ignoring Matt. The kid tried to be nonchalant about it, but his cheeks were bulging. Rebecca frowned at Matt, then leaned over her son, so that she was, literally, in his face, and held out her hand. "Spit it out."

"Ah, come on, let him have it," Matt whined as Grayson obediently spit out the five peppermints.

"One would have been okay, Grayson. But five?" She frowned at her son, but gave Matt a look that effectively put him on notice, and for a moment, he saw Tanya Kwitokowsky before him, arms folded, pinafore perfectly pressed. *You're in trouble, Matthew Parrish!*

Rebecca very primly put the peppermints in a napkin.

"So this is family night for the Lears, huh?" Matt asked, feeling a little on the reprimanded side.

Still frowning, Rebecca asked, "You met Grandma?"

"Yes, I did. And she pointed out Grandpa, too."

Rebecca winced. "The announcer didn't show, so Grandpa stepped in."

"So when is Tom up?" Matt asked.

Rebecca didn't answer, just stepped over him and fell into Lil Stanton's empty seat as her grandpa announced that the first game of the next session paid a double bonus for a bingo with an *I-15*, the response to which was a collective and appreciative gasp from the crowd that was beginning to filter back in, paper plates piled high with brisket, beans, and cole slaw. "Where's Grandma?" she asked.

"Something about beans," he said. "So about that campaign speech," he continued, scooting over to Grayson's seat, next to Rebecca, and ignoring the announcer and the gray hairs that were all atwitter over the *I-15* twist. "When is that, by the way? Before or after the ballroom dancing?"

"During this session," she said, and elbowed him in an apparent signal that he was to move over, which he refused to do. "Until then, you could make yourself useful and help me do this," she said, perching on the end of her seat, taking one of the colored markers.

"But—"

Rebecca pierced him with another arresting blue-eyed look. "Matt. If you'll just stop talking, I promise we'll see if we can't do your ballroom thing," she said impatiently. "But Grandma will die if someone doesn't watch her cards."

Matt opened his mouth to speak and tell her it was a joke, that the last thing he would ever suggest was ballroom dancing, for heaven's sake, and that they really just needed to get on with Tom's speech. But then he realized her thigh was pressed against the full length of his, and he recalled that lovely thigh in all its firm, fleshy splendor, and before he realized what was happening, he was searching for the *B-21* Grandpa called to kick things off.

CHAPTER SEVENTEEN

Politicians are interested in people. Not that this is a virtue.
Fleas are interested in dogs.

P. J. O'ROURKE

This wasn't exactly turning out as Rebecca had visualized—somehow, she had ended up sitting dangerously close to Big Pants and playing bingo for Grandma. She'd done everything else, why not? Not that she was playing all that well—she hadn't actually heard Grandpa say much of anything since she had made contact with Matt's body and the deep-sixed memory of last Friday night was flooding all her senses again, just like it had last night when he called.

No more than five numbers had been called, but she'd already lost her place. And while she was desperately trying to catch up, Matt was sitting there, watching her mark her cards, his thigh pressed against hers as if this was no big deal, like he made women howl like hyenas every other day. Just casually letting his thigh burn right through her skirt, right through her skin and bone, right into the marrow.

"Missed one," he said, and leaned across her, his head startlingly close to hers, pointing to a *B-4*.

"I know," she lied, slapping his hand away so she could mark it.

"Can he slow this down a little?" she heard someone behind her grouse. "He's going too fast!"

Everything was going too fast, spinning furiously around Rebecca's brain, muddling her thoughts and all her self-preservation techniques.

"Amateurs," Matt muttered, pointing to another number under the *G* column on Rebecca's card. "You missed that one, too."

Rebecca scooched up to the edge of her seat and quickly marked it. "Perhaps you'd like to get your own bingo sheet," she suggested.

"Nah," he said, and reached for one of two extra markers Grandma had laid out for an emergency, and marked another *G* number on two more of her cards. "I like playing yours. And you obviously need all the help you can get."

That was definitely the understatement of the year.

"Here we go, folks! Here's an N-32! Don't believe we've had a 32 yet...not with an N, anyway," Grandpa said.

Matt reached across her again to mark numbers, his arm inadvertently brushing against her breast. "Beg your pardon," he said with a half-cocked grin.

Rebecca's body responded to that brief contact with a gut-sinking shiver of anticipation. She tried to shift her chair away from Matt, but Grayson had wedged his chair in between hers and Jo Lynn's so he could stand to draw pictures on the back of the bingo card sheets.

"Come on, Mork, you're losing focus," Matt said to Rebecca, and casually slinging his arm across the back of her chair, leaned forward to mark more. His spicy scent filled all of her senses and sent her into a cloudy panic.

"Give me the marker," she demanded, holding out her hand.

"No," he said, studying the cards.

"Look, these are my grandma's cards, and if you screw them up—"

"I got the picture, thank you, which is why I am helping you. I figure if you mess this up, Grandma will shoot first and take names later."

"Who am I shooting?" Grandma asked behind them, pushing and shoving her way down the aisle to get to her cards. "Okay, okay, I've got it," she said, snatching the marker from Rebecca's hand. "Y'all help Grayson or someone. What does that say up there? Jo Lynn needs to write bigger!"

"N-32," Rebecca said.

"Will you lookie here? We got us another B. B-9, that is. As in, good news, Elmer, looks like that growth on your butt is beee-nign! That's a B—"

"*BINGO! BIN-GO, BIN-GO!*" a man shouted.

"God-*dam*-mit!" Grandma cried, and threw down her marker.

"*Mom!*" Grayson gasped. "Grandma said a dirty word!"

"Don't you worry, Boo-boo," Grandma said soothingly. "God is punishing me as we speak." She looked at Matt and smiled. "I still wish he hadn't said it to the entire world, but I'll tell you what—Elmer was right about the beans!"

"Thanks for the heads-up," Matt said cheerfully.

Okay, so if a hole in the ground would please present itself, Rebecca thought. To make matters worse, Grandma dazzled them with one of her big I've-got-an-idea smiles that Rebecca and her sisters feared. She leaned across and gave Matt the once-over. "So, you work with Becky?"

Rebecca immediately stood up. "Grandma, will you watch Grayson? It's time for Tom's speech."

"Sure, sweetie! You and Matt run along," she said, grinning broadly as she turned her attention to the next bingo sheet. Rebecca quickly stepped around Matt, paused only to tell Grayson to stay put with Grandma Lil until she got back.

She paused in the middle of the room and looked around. "Where's Tom now? I left him back by the sign-in table."

"Let's hope he's not testing the beans," Matt said jovially. When Rebecca gave him a dark look, his smile faded a little. "Okay," he said, putting up a hand. "I'll find him."

He went one way, Rebecca went the other, to the dais to tell Grandpa it was time. Only Grandpa wanted to review with her some of his better jokes, which he did until Matt showed up with Tom. Tom had obviously been enjoying the free food, judging by the bit ol' barbecue sauce on his shirt. Angie was with them, too, as were Gunter and the photographer. Pat was right behind them all, looking very disgruntled. "I think the whole thing is rigged. I lacked only one number for three calls and still didn't bingo!"

"Okay, is everyone here?" Tom asked, gleefully rubbing his hands together as Gunter's photographer bounced around them, snapping pictures. "This is our big moment, the reason all these folks came out tonight. So!" He looked at Rebecca. "Do you have my remarks?"

The question stunned her. "Didn't Gilbert prepare some remarks for you?"

"Yep," Tom said congenially. "He said he was faxing them to you."

No one uttered a word; Rebecca could only gape. Pat muttered, "Good God."

"The rainy day fund," Matt said quickly. "Talk about how we need that fund to meet the needs of everyone in case of an emergency, to ensure that we are never in danger of cutting back on services."

"Yeah, that's good," said Tom, jotting it down in his pocket notebook. Rebecca silently agreed, recognizing instantly that she wouldn't have come up with that in a trillion years. Which begged the question of what, exactly, she would have come up with.

"I can talk about how I'm a huge advocate for saving money," Tom said. "Not that I can save my own damn money, but they don't have to know that, right?" he asked, laughing easily. Pat groaned again.

"Okay folks, we have a real treat for you tonight," Grandpa said. "The Silver Panthers' president, Francine McDonough, is coming up here to tell you all about it."

Francine, eager for the microphone, pointed her scooter toward the dais and punched it. Matt likewise nudged Tom toward the dais, made him take two steps up behind Francine when she parked her scooter and inexplicably bounded up the steps.

"And health care initiatives," he said to Tom. "Mention that. Remember, don't take any questions, and for God's sake, be vague!"

Tom laughed. "Don't worry, Parrish! This ain't my first rodeo." He jogged up the steps and began sauntering toward Francine.

Rebecca looked at Matt from the corner of her eye. "Okay... the rainy day fund was close to brilliant. Thanks. I really owe you one for bailing me out."

Matt grinned down at her, his gray eyes sparkling with delight. "I do not believe sweeter words were ever spoken. Great thing, debts—"

"Stop it—"

"First I owed you one—"

She laughed nervously as Gunter's photographer turned and suddenly took several shots of them.

"Now you owe *me* one."

"Excuse me!" Rebecca whispered to the photographer, and pointed at Tom. The photographer shrugged, turned back to Tom. She could hear Matt's deep chuckle, but she refused to look at him, lest she lose what was left of her composure, and refused to think about debts or bets in any direction. But while they waited for Francine (who seemed to like the limelight as much as Grandpa) to finish her long spiel, the feel of Matt standing so close to her, his body radiating delicious energy, she could not keep the seductive thoughts of debts from her mind. By the time Francine turned it over to Tom, Rebecca was so uptight that she feared she might actually twist off and spear herself into the ceiling.

Tom strutted across the stage, thanked Francine, and began to speak about why he had come tonight and how important the Silver Panthers were to the state and to candidates like him. He then launched into a little well- rehearsed speech about what he hoped to accomplish as lieutenant governor—which consisted, when one cut through the rhetoric, of not raising taxes. And then a plug for a new superhighway, from Dallas to Old Mexico, with a gas pipeline running beneath that would bring commerce to Texas.

"Huh," Matt muttered. "That's new."

"You know, he looks like a sausage," Gunter said thoughtfully as Tom spoke extemporaneously. "He's really not very photogenic."

"Okay!" Rebecca said, feeling better as the crowd clapped. "This is going pretty well!" She glanced hopefully at Pat. Pat shrugged.

"Now about that rainy day fund," Tom continued from the dais. "I've heard a lot of talk about that. Everyone's concerned, myself included. And I have a lot of colleagues who would like to take a bite here and there. But I say *no*! I say we jeopardize our future and the future of our children by messing with our savings account. As residents of Texas, we need to make sure that the rainy day fund goes untouched so that *all* needs are met, and if we should hit a rough patch—God forbid—services are not cut!"

That was met with strong applause. Rebecca turned a beaming smile to Matt at the very same moment Tom said, "And oh, by the way, today I pushed a fun little bill through that I think you'll enjoy."

Pat instantly threw her head back and closed her eyes. "No, no, no," she groaned. "Please tell me he is not going to say it."

"My bill designates chips and salsa as the official state snack of Texas!" Tom said, raising his arm into the air in some sort of half-cocked victory pump.

"Wow," Angie said, shaking her head.

"Maybe they will think it's cute," Rebecca said hopefully.

"Political suicide is not cute," Pat snorted.

Pat was right. Rebecca peeked around him; the crowd noise had definitely fallen to a low pitch. Dozens of wizened faces—*voting* faces—were upturned to Tom, waiting for the punch line that was, apparently, not going to come.

"So! Wander on into the dining room and get some chips and salsa!"

"Who's going to tell him there are no chips and salsa on the buffet?" Pat asked of no one in particular.

There was another smattering of applause; Grandpa shuffled on stage and took the microphone from Tom, beaming from ear to ear. "Thank you, Senator! Okay, ready for the last session of bingo?"

Tom came striding off the stage, grinning. "Well done, Senator," Angie said as he jogged down the steps and paused for another photo.

"Ah, Re-be-*caaaa!*" Tom said, stretching his arms wide for a hug, into which Rebecca reluctantly walked. "Thanks again," he said, squeezing tight. "Thanks a million for putting all this together."

Honestly, sometimes she thought Tom would gush if she stood up and belched. "No problem, Tom," she said, wiggling out of his embrace.

"We could all take a page out of your book," Tom continued, and Rebecca couldn't help notice that Pat and Angie, standing to one side, looked as if they might barf all over his shoes. "You and Matt be safe getting home, now. Come on, girls," he said to Pat and Angie. "I'm going to treat you to a beer on the way home." He moved to the exit with Angie, Pat, Gunter, and his photographer trailing behind.

"I have to agree," Matt said, shoving his hands into his pockets as they watched Tom glad-hand his way to the door. "Pretty amazing job you did here."

Rebecca smiled in spite of herself. "Thank you, I think."

"But you know he hasn't even begun to ramp up, don't you?"

"Meaning?"

"Meaning, we aren't going to have the time or luxury of this sort of setup again. You might want to adjust your expectations for the long haul."

"You know what you are?" she asked. "A rationalist."

"A what?"

"A *rationalist*," she repeated, casually picking at a nonexistent piece of lint on her jacket. "You know, the kind of person who likes to be in command, likes lots of rules and boxes to put people into and doesn't like people stepping out of their cages."

"You have no idea what you are talking about. I fight against rules all the time."

"You sure stick to them like glue when it comes to the campaign."

"Where do you get this stuff from? I'm not trying to keep you in a box, I am trying to help."

"It's not a bad thing."

"Well, it doesn't exactly sound like a good thing, either," he said gruffly.

"I was merely making a friendly observation," she said, enjoying seeing him on the defensive. "I only mention it because the more you know about someone's personality type, the easier it is to work with them. Here's another observation…" she said, and clasping her hands behind her back, she went up on her tiptoes to almost look him in the eye, and said, "You can dish it out but you can't take it."

Matt's whole body seemed to light up when he grinned down at her. "Wanna bet?"

A surge of heat raced up her spine; Rebecca eased back down.

"So tell me," he said, still grinning, "What personality type can't play bingo? The perfect type?"

"Compared to you, at least," she said buoyantly. "But if you really want to know, I'm a traditionalist, and there's a huge difference between a traditionalist and a rationalist. We might as well be on different planets—"

"Oh, I think we are," Matt said, nodding emphatically.

"Okay, folks! Fifteen minutes to the next game, so get your snacks!" Grandpa called. "By the way, the kitchen has asked me to inform you that there are no chips and salsa. I'll say that again—no chips and salsa tonight."

"You know what your problem is?" Matt said. "You think too much. Just let yourself go. You know, run with your gut and not your head...with or without panties."

"Oh, how very helpful," she drawled as they began to walk back to the table. "Never short on advice, are you?"

"Why, no. It's my job," Matt replied, walking alongside her as if they belonged together. "You're not the only psychoanalyst in the room, you know. I know about people like you, people who use self-help books like a bible, searching for something."

Rebecca paused next to the sign-in table and looked up at him with a laugh. "Oh, please. I'm not searching—"

"It's a cover for what's really going on inside that perfect body of yours."

"There is nothing going on inside me—" Wait. That wasn't quite right, as she could certainly feel the heat stirring her up. "I mean, nothing like you think."

"What I think is that something is bubbling away in there, creating chaos in your otherwise perfectly ordered little world.

I can see it in your eyes," he said, and leaning into her, added in a whisper, "And I saw it when you let go. So why don't you just let go and let it out, especially since you have someone as handy as me standing by, ready to assist in any way he can?"

She thought they had called some sort of truce, but this didn't feel like a truce, this felt like a long untangling into something she feared she could not extract herself from. "Okay. All kidding aside, I thought we weren't going to go there," she reminded him.

"A guy can hope, can't he?"

A smile spread across her lips. "If I were you, I'd hang on to the hope," she said, leaning into him. "Because it's as close as you're going to get." With that, she gave him a little push and started walking again.

But Matt laughed and caught her hand before she could escape—just a touch—but it felt as if a thousand volts of energy surged through his fingers and into her body. "Hey, aren't you forgetting something? You *owe* me. Come with me now, and I'll make it fast and painless."

"God, Matt, that's crude, even for you."

"But I'm in a hurry," he said with a wink, and pulled her to his side to follow him.

"Wait! I've got Grayson—"

"I know, I know, but trust me, it won't take more than a minute. He and Grandma won't even notice you are gone."

"But I—"

"Rebecca, calm down," he said, the light in his eyes burning bright. "We're not going there. But I want to show you something, so just come with me for a couple of minutes, okay?" He put his hand on the small of her back, gently urging her along with him.

He'd asked nicely. Rebecca glanced furtively around her and let him lead her out of there. But as he pushed open the door leading to the main hallway, she collided with his back as he came to an abrupt halt—Tom and company were still in the hall; Gunter's photographer was getting a few last shots. She and Matt looked at each other. An unspoken agreement passed between them; they shared a conspiratorial smile as he firmly slipped his hand around hers. They turned as one, hurrying quickly to the doors at the opposite end of the hall.

In the parking lot, Matt still had her hand, would not let go, and laughingly told her to hurry up. Her heart was beating a wild, uneven tempo, and as clueless as she was to what she was doing, it was nonetheless exciting in a bad girl, very unperfect way. When they reached his car, he quickly opened the passenger door and all but shoved her in.

"Make yourself at home," he said, and shut the door, walked around to the driver's side, got in, and turned on the radio. A jazz CD.

"Mood music. How classy," Rebecca laughed.

"Only the best in my crib."

"I haven't hung out in a car since I was in high school," she said, shifting so that she could face him.

"Then you don't know what you're missing," he said with a grin.

"I'm missing the bingo bash—"

"Okay, all right, just hold your horses—I have something for you."

"For me?" she asked laughingly. "Your book of campaign rules?"

Matt smiled enigmatically. "Actually, no," he said, and reached behind him, pulled out a leather-bound sketch pad and placed it carefully in her lap.

A sketch pad.

Rebecca stared at it, a little confused, a little alarmed by whatever it was that was swirling in the cavity around her heart.

After a moment, Matt moaned. "Please take it, Rebecca—if you don't, I'm going to feel like a complete idiot."

She lifted her gaze, her eyes searching his, looking for the joke, the catch. "What is it?"

"Has it been so long you don't remember what they look like?" he asked with a sheepish grin. "It's a sketch pad."

"For me?" she asked, feeling warm. God, she couldn't even remember the last time someone had given her a gift for no reason. "Oh, my," she murmured, picking it up and carefully turning it over. "Oh, *my*." She looked up at Matt again in wonder.

His smile had faded; there was a strangely tender look in his gray eyes. He suddenly reached behind him again and handed her a red velvet box. "I, ah…I didn't know if you still had pencils or not," he said, thrusting them toward her. "The guy said these were the best."

Rebecca took the box and folded her arms tightly over her gifts, holding them against her chest as a smile lit from a place deep inside her and spread throughout her entire body. She was touched, genuinely and deeply touched. And for someone who walked around so cocksure all the time, Big Pants suddenly seemed so vulnerable, fidgeting around, looking for something to do with his hands.

"Excuse me," she said softly, "but could you tell me what happened to Matt Parrish? You know, the popinjay?"

"Well," Matt said, shoving a hand through his hair, "unfortunately, he's taken complete leave of his senses. He's gone off to have his testosterone checked, because the fact of the matter is," he said, sighing a little, "that if you owe him anything, he wants you to draw again." He dipped his gaze to the box. "At least try, will you? You might be surprised at how good it feels," he said, lifting his gaze to her again. "I want you to get it back, Rebecca. You deserve to have it back."

She wanted it back. She wanted it in this moment like she'd never wanted anything in her life. "Matt...thank you," she said. "This is so nice."

"Yeah, well, please don't say that too loud—wouldn't want that going around town, you know."

She smiled.

Matt paused as if he was searching for something to say. His eyes reflected the same desire she could feel churning inside her, a desire so strong that it frightened her. She could feel that internal dam cracking, and she impulsively leaned across the console, surprising him with the touch of her lips to his cheek.

Startled, he caught her face with his hand. Rebecca slid her lips to the corner of his mouth, landing there for the breadth of a moment, enough to make her heart flutter like a thousand winged birds.

Matt turned a little more, sliding his lips to hers, soft at first, then more demanding, deeply, until he was coming over the console to her. As he deepened the kiss, his hand pressed against the side of her breast, kneading it softly. The sketchbook and pencils slipped, in her clumsy groping about for them, she brushed against his trousers. And her hand lingered there, lightly stroking his erection, marveling at the feel of him, hot and hard beneath his clothing.

Matt groaned into her mouth; he cupped her breast, filled his hand with it as he drew her bottom lip between his teeth. His kiss was electrifying; Rebecca felt wildly out of control again, felt things happening inside her and between her legs that she didn't want to happen. She knew she was about to slide off into the deep end of that rough, unbridled passion, and the thought of her son and grandparents suddenly flashed into her mind. She pushed Matt up at the same time she slid deeper into the seat, gasping for air. "I have to go," she said hoarsely.

"You can't. My testosterone is back and begging for a do-over," he murmured against her lips, nipping at them. "Forget drawing and art..."

"Oh, I've forgotten them, trust me," she said with a coy laugh, and pushed him again. "But my son is in there."

"Yeah," he said, and with a heavy sigh, he reluctantly sat up. His tie was crooked, pulled around to his shoulder, and she wondered for a crazy moment if she had done that as she gathered up the sketch pad and pencils.

"Be careful of those blue hairs," he said, pushing both hands through his hair. "They're pretty vicious when it comes to bingo."

"And free brisket," she added dreamily as she opened the door. She paused, smiled at him once more. "Thanks, Matt."

"My pleasure," he said.

She got out, a little shakily, and closed the door. She watched him back out of the parking space. But before he could drive away, a burning question suddenly popped into

Rebecca's mind, and Rebecca waved at him to stop, running to his car as Matt rolled down the window. "What's your sign?" she blurted breathlessly.

"My what?"

"Your sign. Are you Aries? Taurus?"

He laughed. "Cancer. What's yours?"

"Umm…Pisces," she muttered.

"Glad we got that out in the open," he said, and with a final wave, turned the wheel and drove off.

"Ohmigod," Rebecca whispered as his car turned onto the highway. "Ohmigod."

CHAPTER EIGHTEEN

If confusion is the first step to knowledge, I must be a genius...

LARRY LEISSNER

Rebecca didn't sleep at all that night, no thanks to Matt Parrish and his gift of a sketchbook that had gone straight to her heart, or that hot we-aren't-going-there kiss that had gone straight to her groin.

It was a good thing that at the crack of dawn they were all headed for Dad's show palace, the family ranch in Comfort, because Rebecca couldn't think straight. She really needed a diversion.

Fortunately, Robin and Jake, and Jake's nephew, Cole, would be there, too, because frankly, there was no better way to see Dad than in the company of many. Her only regret was that Rachel couldn't come, as she was off in England studying some manuscript or something like that—honestly, the last time Rachel had called, Rebecca had been a little distracted and couldn't remember what she said. Except, of course, that bit about the Cancer.

Grandma, Grandpa, Rebecca, and Grayson, plus the dogs, piled into Grandpa's massive RV, and they were off, crawling down the highway as Frank and Tater moved from side to side, pressing their noses against the windows in a desperate attempt to smell the scenery slowly passing them by while Bean slept, sprawled across the floor like it was a porch.

Grandpa seemed to have a hard time fitting the Queen Mary into a lane—even worse, he seemed oblivious to the stark terror on the faces of other drivers as they squeezed past, because he was too busy reliving the glory of having been a bingo announcer at a charity event. At the same time, Grandma was grousing about the unusually low pots and the inability of a certain announcer to call any number on her sheet.

"It was a charity event, Grandma. You couldn't have kept the money," Rebecca reminded her from the enormous living area of the RV.

"I know that, honey, but it still would have been fun to win. But *nooo* we've got to have Mr. Saturday Night over here. I bet he called that blasted B-9 in every game!"

"Now, Lil, no one likes a sore loser," Grandpa said.

"I certainly am *not* a sore loser, Elmer!" she huffed. "Anyway, I am sick and tired of talking about that stupid bingo bash. It's just a silly game." She didn't say anything else for a moment (and wisely, neither did anyone else). Then suddenly, she pivoted in her big bucket seat and peered at Rebecca. "Now tell me again about that nice young man with you last evening."

Oh great, here they went. "Ah...you mean Senator Masters?"

Grandma was, unfortunately, way too smart for that. "*Nooo*, I mean the nice man who helped you keep my cards when I had that attack of diverticulitis."

"Oh. Matt Parrish."

"Who?"

"MATT!" Grayson shouted helpfully, having discovered that his great-grandparents were hard of hearing. "She means Matt," Grayson said to Rebecca, as if she didn't know.

"That Matt was such a nice and handsome young man," Grandma said, her smile getting a little too pushy with all its brightness.

"He's just a guy working on Tom's campaign, Grandma," Rebecca said. "No one to get excited about."

Too late. Grandma was a veteran at prying, and almost wrenched her back trying to see Grayson in the captain's seat directly behind her. "Do you like him, Boo-boo?"

Grayson nodded.

"He's a very nice man, isn't he?"

"You have to admire a man who will try and make friends with a five-year-old boy. Probably means he has a great affinity for children. A man who has an affinity for children is a good candidate for being a solid family man."

"Where's my peanuts?" Grandpa asked.

Where's my gun? Rebecca thought, and lay down on the couch, watching the little balls on the ends of the curtains swinging above her as she tried to think of three positive affirmations for the day that might possibly help her endure this excruciatingly slow drive to Comfort:

1. Grandma and Grandpa, notwithstanding how annoying they can be, and what is with this RV anyway?
2. The Masters Bingo Bash that really did happen, and raised $3,600 for charity, thank you very much.
3. Sketch pads and sketch pencils. In a purely artistic sense, of course.

At Blue Cross Ranch, Aaron Lear heard the motor home the minute it turned into the gate almost a mile away. From the sound of it, he figured that Elmer was running in too low a gear, which didn't surprise him in the least. He wasn't too keen on having the Stantons for the weekend, but as Bonnie's very own daughters weren't helping him reconcile with their mother, it seemed prudent to stay on the good side of her folks, as much as that pained him—Elmer drove him nuts.

On the porch, Aaron groaned aloud at the sight of the RV doing a smooth five miles per hour as it wended its way down the caliche road lined with live oak and pecan trees until it lumbered up into the circular drive. The man could be the poster child of the impractical, for who else but Elmer Stanton would drive a huge RV to a ranch house with more bedrooms than the White House? But Aaron plastered a smile on his face nonetheless, walked down the limestone steps and onto the flagstones to greet them. His grandson was the first out of the thing, flying forward with shouts of *Grandpa!* that warmed Aaron all the way down to his toes. He bent down, let the boy run into his arms, grimacing with the pain of it, but lifted him up all the same, holding him tight, clinging to him. "Hey, Ranger," he said. "I've missed you."

But the pain was quickly unbearable, and he put the boy down, just as Rebecca elegantly disembarked from the RV, an honor guard of three dogs on her heels. Two of them raced immediately into the front lawn, sniffing trees and bushes. Behind them, a big ugly yellow one wandered out and walked right into a tree in his quest to find the perfect spot to relieve himself.

Rebecca seemed to think nothing of it, just kept walking toward Aaron, smiling that deep smile of hers that reminded him so much of Bonnie. "Hey, baby," he said, reaching for her.

"Hi, Dad." She hugged him, then held him at arm's length. "You look good!"

He didn't look good and he felt like shit. "Thanks. So do you. Except you're too skinny—"

"Dad." She released him with a sigh that sounded just like Bonnie did when she was irritated with him. Aaron ignored it, turned toward Lil.

She threw her arms around him in a painful bear hug. "Oh, Aaron, it does my heart good to see you looking well," she said, grasping his shoulders and squeezing tightly.

"Thanks, Lil," he said, dragging his hand across the sheen of perspiration on his brow.

"Well, he sure don't look any worse for the wear," Elmer said behind Lil, squinting up at Aaron. "I always knew you'd beat it," he said with a broad grin as he extended his hand in greeting. "You're too damn mean to die."

Aaron could only smile—he hadn't found the guts to tell his family that it was back, had crept into him when he wasn't looking and sunk its tentacles to root in him again. "I had Lucha make some iced tea," he said, and gestured toward the big porch where several groupings of furniture were placed beneath ceiling fans turning at a lazy spring pace. Aaron followed the others, biting down so no one would see how it pained him.

They sat awhile, Elmer and Lil boring him to tears with the intimate details of the bingo something-or-other Rebecca had thrown the night before. He wanted desperately to ask about Bonnie, wanted to know what she was doing, if she was happy, if there was anything he could do or say to make her listen to him one last time. But he couldn't find his opening in Lil's endless chatter, and idly watched Grayson on the lawn, playing with the dogs. The boy looked so much like him (he'd always thought that—Bonnie said he looked like Bud, but the kid looked like his grandpa), and now Aaron wondered if Grayson would remember him at all. Would any of them really remember him? Or would their memories of him fade away over time, like the wallpaper in his mother's kitchen, fade so badly that no one would remember his original color?

After a dinner of prime rib—Dad always insisted on the best—they all went their separate ways while waiting for Robin and Jake to arrive from Houston. Grayson was upstairs with Grandpa, hunkered down over a video game. Grandma had gone in to take a "soaking" bath, and Dad had disappeared into his office with the excuse that he needed to make a few calls.

Finally free of what was feeling a little like an ever-present family, Rebecca escaped outside, to the east side of the huge, six-thousand-square-foot ranch house, sat on a porch swing with Frank, Bean, and Tater forming a living, but exhausted, dog shield around her feet.

It was the first clear moment she'd had all day to think, and to try to make sense of all the thoughts about Matt that were jumbling around and crowding her mind. Unfortunately, she didn't get very far—she heard the screen door open behind her and glanced over her shoulder; it was Dad walking slowly toward her, a newspaper beneath his arm. He motioned for her to scoot over, then stepped over the dogs to sit next to her. Bean instantly adjusted so that he could prop his head against Dad's leg.

"What the hell is wrong with that dog?" Dad asked, pushing him off his leg. Unfazed, Bean patiently resumed his position.

"Who knows?" Rebecca said. "Old and warped, I think."

Dad smiled a little. "That ol' dog doesn't know old and warped." He dropped the paper onto his lap, lifted his baseball cap, and ran his palm over the top of his head. His hair had come back coarse and gray and thin after the chemo. He'd been in remission for six months now, so she was surprised it hadn't grown in more than it had.

Dad put his cap back on, smiled at her. "So how's that campaign going for you? What's he running for, again?"

"Lieutenant governor."

"Ah," Dad said, nodding thoughtfully. "A big gun. Too bad he's a Democrat. I might actually be interested otherwise. So how's it going?"

"Pretty well," she said cautiously. "I'm learning a lot and meeting new people."

"Learning anything useful? Or is this all about meeting new people?"

The tone in his voice quashed her hope for a pleasant conversation—she knew damn well questions like that never had a correct response. "I'm doing this for a lot of reasons. Mostly to experience new things and learn where my talents lie."

"Your talents lie in raising my grandson," Dad said, and in the dark, Rebecca rolled her eyes. "Don't forget he's been through a lot."

Like she hadn't? "I *know* he has been through a lot," she said wearily, feeling like she'd had this conversation a million times before. "But so have I, Dad."

"I know you have, and I'm not criticizing. But you're my daughter and I have been trying to get through to all you girls that you need to learn what's important—"

"Yes, Dad, I know—that's what I am trying to do."

"Come on," he scoffed. "You're trying to find a feel-good fix. But these are precious years for Grayson, Rebecca. Don't do what I did and squander them, because trust me, you can't get them back."

"I am not squandering them," she said, with equal exasperation. "Just because I don't do it your way—"

"You think you aren't, but I know that of all my girls, you are the one afraid of…of life. So afraid that you won't stand out there on your own. You think you have to have a man do it for you—"

"What in God's name are you talking about?" Rebecca exploded. "I am standing out there on my own. I am living alone with my son—"

"You got another nanny."

"She's not a nanny! She helps me out a few hours each week so I have a little free time to explore who *I* am. You may not care, but I sort of lost *me* in all that mess!"

"So you're just doing all this to *find* Rebecca?" he asked, taunting her, then opened the paper, turned several pages. "So you're not looking for some man to take care of you, is that right?" Rebecca jerked her gaze to him. Dad pointed at the paper. "Because you sure look like you're involved with this clown."

Confused, she leaned over to see what Dad was seeing in the paper, and he was more than happy to show her—he held it up, pointed to the three pictures. They were all of Tom at the bingo bash, with the whole crew in the background. But there was one of Tom, holding up a bingo sheet, and directly behind him were her and Matt, looking at each other. No—*gazing* at each other. Rebecca grabbed the paper from his hand and stared at it. Impossible. *Impossible!* That picture looked like there was something between them, something—

"I don't care what it looks like," she said angrily.

"I don't care, either," Dad said, and uncharacteristically patted her knee. "I don't care if you get yourself a boyfriend, Rebecca. You're only human, and a woman like you? I imagine you can't beat 'em off with a stick. All I am trying to say is, don't make the same mistakes again."

She lowered the paper and glared at him. "You think I want to make mistakes? You think I haven't learned a thing or two?"

"I don't want you to latch on to some guy you think is going to save you. Or keep you. I never really understood what it was with Bud, frankly."

"Give me a little credit, Dad. I don't latch on to men who are going to save me or keep me. I was with Bud because in the beginning I loved him."

"I give you more credit than you could possibly know." he said, infuriatingly calm. "But I know you, honey, and I know you married Bud out of some perverse fear. It was obvious to the entire state of Texas what *he* was after, but you just couldn't or wouldn't see it. 'Oh no, we're in love,' you said." Dad shook his head. "The sad truth is men are dogs. And there are a whole lot of them out there who see a woman like you and they want only one thing, whatever the cost. But only you can decide what the price is."

This was nothing new, really. What was new was that she was sick to death of his criticism and visualized stuffing a sock down his throat. "Is that all you think anyone sees? Just the outside of me?"

"I think that's all you *let* them see."

The remark stunned her; she should have been incensed, should have marched off the ranch like Robin did the time Dad had told her to quit seeing Jake, but honestly, she heard a hard clang of truth in his statement that left her feeling numb. She abruptly stood up, stepped over the dogs, and walked to the porch railing.

"I'm just trying to help," Dad added.

"You have a strange way of helping," she said sorrowfully. "You could be a lot more helpful if you would ask about what I was doing on the campaign and tell me how I might use it to find a job," she said. "It would be helpful if you would think about what *I* want, what *I* feel, what *I* think instead of what *you* think I should do. And it would be a whole lot healthier if you saw me as an adult, not a twelve-year-old girl, maybe took some interest in what I've been doing. You could not have been less interested in the bingo bash, but that was a fund-raiser that I put together. *I* did it."

"Tell you what," Dad said through clenched teeth. "The next time you have something you want to show me, you just give me a call. Did you ever think to do that? Pick up the phone and call your old man? Show him what you're so proud of?"

"Oh, I will, Dad, you can count—"

"What's that?" he abruptly asked, interrupting her. "Was that a car? I think Robbie's here," he said, coming to his feet and tripping over Bean. "Goddamn dog!" he snapped as he began walking for the front of the house, leaving Rebecca to stare at his back. He hadn't heard a word she'd said.

She and Dad never really talked again that weekend; after all, his advice was dispensed, and he seemed more interested in what Robin and Jake were doing, what Grayson and Cole were doing. Where Mom was, what Rachel was doing in the UK again.

It was, strangely enough, as if that weekend was meant to point up a few fundamental facts to Rebecca, like what was wrong and had been wrong about her relationship with her father since she could remember. He had never cared what was going on inside of her. For all of his philosophical bullshit, the bottom line was about appearances. Her looks, her marriage, her son…

This business about not wanting her to make mistakes was a lie—the truth was that he didn't want her to embarrass him. She was so sick of appearances.

When Dad and Jake took Grayson and Cole fishing, and Grandma and Grandpa were out on the porch having lemonade one afternoon, Rebecca asked Robin, "Have you ever noticed that Dad is more concerned with appearances than he is the real us?"

"Have I noticed?" Robin laughed. "Did you forget? He hired me for appearances. Don't tell me you're just now figuring that out—didn't you ever wonder why he was so hot for you to do the Miss Texas thing?"

"Yeah," Rebecca said solemnly, "guess I'm just now figuring it out."

With a playful punch to the arm, Robin asked, "What's with you, anyway? You're so *mopey*."

"I don't know. Remember when Dad was really sick, and he handed down that ultimatum?"

"Ah, but there were so many," Robin said with a roll of her eyes. "Which one?"

The one about how we had to learn to stand on our own two feet, figure out the important things, or he'd cut us off.

"Right. Well, I am trying to stand on my own two feet, but he's worried that I am going to be a kept woman or some ridiculous thing like that. He doesn't really care who I am or how I feel, just how I look to the rest of the world. He wants me to set up as some retiring social butterfly and do nothing but look after Grayson, because in his mind, that's what I am supposed to be doing."

"So? What else is new? Dad has always known what's best for us without bothering to know us at all," Robin said, almost cheerfully, having come to her conclusions about the old man and having moved on with her life.

It wasn't so easy for Rebecca. "But I want him to care, Robin. I want him to see me for who I am."

Robin shook her head. "My advice? Don't care. Dad is never going to see you like you want him to see you. He's never going to see anyone or anything other than exactly what he wants to see. But it doesn't matter what he thinks.

It's your life, and you aren't living it for him. Be who you are, Rebecca. And be happy. Life is too short to do anything else. If you give what he thinks a second thought, you will only make yourself crazy. Trust me on this one."

Rebecca nodded, but she couldn't do what Robin suggested, because she was already crazy.

"So what about that guy?" Robin asked, munching on some of Grandpa's peanuts.

Rebecca glanced at her from the corner of her eye. "*What* guy?"

"The gorgeous one," Robin said, nudging her with her shoulder.

"Nothing," Rebecca said, and picked up her sketchbook and pencils and walked outside.

"Chicken!" Robin shouted after her, but Rebecca kept walking, out onto the porch, down the steps and across the lawn, where Frank, Bean, and Tater picked up her scent and came trotting out from their nap under the porch. They walked down to the river, where Rebecca propped herself up against the smooth bark of a weeping willow. From this vantage point, she had a vista of spring wildflowers, grazing cattle, and tall cottonwoods rustling over the river's edge. The sight of it so soothing, bringing back myriad youthful memories of when she and Robin and Rachel would come down here, talk about boys, paint their nails, and dream of happy ever after.

She opened the velvet box, took out a pencil, and picked up her sketchbook.

She stared at the thick paper, trying to dredge up the memory of how it felt to take a pencil in hand and let whatever it was inside her flow out onto the page. There was a time that it had taken no conscious thought at all, just pencil and paper. Now, it felt impossible. She didn't have the slightest idea where to begin.

Tears clouded her vision, and she was struck with the desperate notion that she had given up all that she was to be Bud's wife, including this part of her. She had believed his promises, had believed in their future. Now she had nothing left that she didn't have to rebuild.

Rebecca looked at the tops of the cottonwood trees, bending and swaying in the afternoon breeze. *Get it back*, Matt had said. *Just be.*

Easy for him to say because he could just be who he was—arrogant and kind all at once, caring in a weird, fascist sort of way, she thought with a little smile. Smart. Competent. Sexy. Of course he could believe in himself. She wished she could believe in herself like that instead of stuffing her spirit down, leaving it to lurk in her thoughts and heart.

A flicker of light caught her eye, and Rebecca looked up to the tops of the cottonwood trees again. Miraculously, her hand began to move. She blinked, looked down at the pad she was holding, and saw the first marks of a tree. She dropped the pencil, wiped her eyes, picked up her pencil again, and looked at the leaves impressed against a bright spring sky.

The rest of the weekend passed uneventfully—save a very heated argument between Robin and Dad about the Houston Astros, which drove Rebecca outside again. By the time Rebecca returned to her lake house, she was emotionally exhausted from her family and all the blasted introspection she had done.

She said good-bye to Grandma and Grandpa, then made hot dogs, Grayson's favorite, for supper. Later, when Grayson settled down in front of taped episodes of *SpongeBob SquarePants* with the dogs, Rebecca went to her office with a pint of Ben & Jerry's to check her phone messages.

The first was left bright and early Friday morning by Tom. "Hey, did you see the piece in the paper about us? Great job, Rebecca! Listen, could you come in next week? I'd like to talk to you about a bigger deal. I'm thinking of a big summer fund-raising bash that will leave the competition gasping. You know, one with some great live entertainment like Lyle Lovett." He rattled on about that; Rebecca jotted down a note to call him.

There was another early call from Bud, who, among other things, made a remark about the picture in the Austin paper. "I hope you are finally moving on with your life, Bec," he said, which made her cringe, and then, "And I hope you got a chance to mention Tom to your dad." Typical.

The last message, left just after ten on Friday, was from Matt. She smiled when he said, "Mork, you home?" Just the sound of his voice made her feel warm. "Ah…well. This is Big Pants in case you hadn't figured that out. So…" He paused there, drew a breath. "Look, I know we're not going there, but I've got a couple of tickets to the lyric opera and I thought you might enjoy it. The thing is, I'm not the most lyric guy in the world—you probably already knew that—and I could use someone to translate for me…" His voice trailed off again. She heard a faint tapping in the background. "Okay, so if you're interested, it's Sunday at six. Give me a call if you want to go. Okay. Talk to you soon. Bye," he said, and hung up.

Rebecca glanced at the clock. It was almost eight. She debated calling him, but decided not to, to stick with her instincts, and her instincts said this could never really go anywhere. Her curiosity about him was really nothing more than the usual curiosity that comes after divorce. She'd read enough self-help books to know that a rebound affair was really not healthy, and this couldn't possibly be more than that. So no matter how much her heart was leaning in one direction, her mind was yanking her in another. *Just don't go there...*

When Bonnie Lear returned to her Los Angeles Brentwood home from the gym Monday afternoon, there was a note on the door. *Bealman Florists,* it said. She turned the card over; a delivery man had left a message for her to call. Bonnie dug out her cell phone and dialed the number. The guy said he needed to come by and deliver.

"Flowers?" she asked.

The guy laughed. "You could say that."

Bonnie looked at her watch. "I've got to run a few errands. Why don't you just leave it on the porch?"

"It's too big to leave on the porch, ma'am," he said.

"Too big?"

"This isn't one order. It's like, dozens."

Bonnie paused in trying to fit her key in the door. "Dozens? Dozens of what?"

"Roses. Listen, I'm not too far. If you can just stay put for a half hour, I'll be there."

"Okay," she sighed, and clicked off the phone. She walked into the kitchen, stared out at the backyard pool.

A quarter of an hour later, she heard a vehicle in the drive and walked out onto her front porch. It was not a small van, but a big delivery truck. The man hopped down out of the day cab, walked around to the back. Bonnie joined him there, peering over his shoulder as he reviewed several pages of a bill of lading. Then he unlatched the back and pushed the roll-away door up.

The sickly sweet scent was overpowering, knocking them both back a step. The truck was full of roses. Yellow, white, red, pink...dozens and dozens of roses.

"Someone must really be in the doghouse, huh?" the delivery guy remarked with a grin.

Damn him. *Damn him!* "Is there a card?" Bonnie asked, and the man handed her a stack of them. She opened the first one.

Please forgive me. I love you. Aaron.

She crumpled it in her hand and damn near threw it at the delivery man.

CHAPTER NINETEEN

If we don't change our direction we're likely to end up where we're headed...

CHINESE PROVERB

On the Friday after the Tom Masters Charity Bingo Bash, at the same moment Rebecca was suffering through the RV trip from hell, Matt was in his office, staring at the phone instead of getting stuff together for a hearing on the Kiker case.

He had already picked up the phone twice and put it down. This was a really stupid idea. Nothing was different with Rebecca—it was a thank-you kiss that he tried to take a little further than she'd intended. Nothing to get all excited about and certainly nothing to make a fool of himself over. He told himself he should really forget the whole thing and move on. Maybe call Debbie Seaforth. Which was why, then, when he picked up the phone a third time, he dialed Rebecca's number really fast before he talked himself out of it.

One ring. Two rings. Three rings. Matt was just about to hang up when the answering machine picked up and her silky calm voice was asking him to leave a message. He hadn't thought about that, and the piercing beep signaling it was time to leave his message rattled him badly. "Ah hey, Mork, you home?" he blurted, wincing, and continued to wince until he had stopped blathering into her machine and had hung up.

Then he pounded his desk with his fist. This was bullshit—he was acting like a kid! Since when was he so unnerved by a woman? Never, which was why he really had to stop letting his balls do all his important thinking.

He got up, started going through the files, but was interrupted by the buzz of his interoffice speaker. "It's your mother, Mr. Parrish," Harold said over the intercom.

Oh no. Matt loved his mom, but the lady could talk. "Tell her I'll call her later," he said, clicked off, and walked across the room to a file cabinet.

The buzzer rang again.

With a sigh, Matt walked back, punched the button. "Yes?"

"I'm sorry to bother you, sir, but your mother is very insistent."

Harold would never know what an understatement that was. "Okay, put her through," he said, and picked up the handset. "Mom? What's the matter?"

"Nothing is the matter, Matthew. But I was not in the mood to wait to find out who this lovely young woman is!"

"What woman, Mom?" Matt asked absently as he thumbed through some files.

"The one standing beside you," she said, all chipper. "In the paper."

It worked; she definitely got Matt's attention. "The paper?"

"The *Statesman*, silly," Mom giggled. "This morning I open it up and there you are, big as life smack-dab in the middle of the Life section, standing behind that friend of yours who is running for office. But you're not looking at him. You're looking at her. And what an interesting look it is!"

Oh man. Matt's first instinct was to play dumb. "Mom, she's just someone working on Tom's campaign. You know how it is. You've seen me in the paper with different women."

"Yes I know, my darling son, but you're usually more interested in the camera than your date," she purred with all motherly privilege. "And besides, *I* am not the one who is excited."

The little wave of panic was now spiraling into full mast. "Okay, well, this is a delightful conversation, but I've got to go. I've got a hearing in an hour and I can't find the damn file—"

"Oh, you run right along, honey. I'm going to cut out the pictures so that you can look at them later. Three in all, if you're interested. Bye now!"

Matt frowned at his mom's little chuckle as she hung up. He sprang out of his chair, strode across his office to the door, and yanked it open. "Harold!" he barked. "Bring me today's paper!" He pivoted sharply and marched back to his desk.

Harold appeared almost instantly with the folded paper in his hand, which he laid in front of Matt, the Life section conveniently on top. "You and Miss Lear look really marvelous together," he said admiringly. "Page six."

"He and who?" Ben asked from the door, wandering in as Matt yanked the paper open to page six.

"Miss Lear."

"The beauty queen?"

"Do you guys mind?" Matt asked testily. "I've got to get ready for a hearing in less than an hour—"

"Hey, I wanna see," Ben said, waltzing across the room to have a look.

"They're fabulous pictures," Harold said. "I take it the Bingo Bash was a success."

"The *what?*" Ben exclaimed loudly.

"Long story," Matt muttered, turning to page six to see what the rest of the world had apparently already seen this morning. *Judas H. Priest,* there they were, gazing into each other's eyes. When the hell had that happened?

The second photo was of Tom and company, but once again, just off to the right, Rebecca was smiling suspiciously at Matt, and he was smiling as if...he couldn't even think straight. He couldn't breathe, especially with Ben hanging over one shoulder and Harold drooling from across the desk. He looked at the last picture, the one that really made him feel sick. Tom in the hallway, standing next to that old woman on that deadly scooter (she'd almost taken him out twice with that thing). And over the top of her steel wool head, you could see Matt and Rebecca, slipping out the back door. She looked a little nervous, but he had a shit-eating grin plastered on his face.

"I thought you didn't like her," Ben remarked, peering closely at the last picture.

"I don't," Matt responded, perhaps a little too sharply. "At least not like that."

"Don't like her?" Harold gasped, horrified. "But what about the art festival?"

"Jesus, it must be love!" Ben cried, banging Matt on the shoulder. "Bingo *and* an art festival?" He laughed, strolled toward the door in a definite swagger as Harold followed behind in a definite swish, "So what's the hearing this afternoon?" Ben asked before walking out.

"Uh-oh," Harold murmured, and went out.

"Discovery for Kelly Kiker," Matt muttered.

Ben sighed to the ceiling, shook his head. "I thought you were going to give her a referral. In fact, I think you promised. So when is it that we start lining up cases that actually make us a little money?"

Matt shoved the paper into the drawer and stood, returning to the file cabinet to look for the papers he needed. "I'm doing this pro bono—"

"Like I said—we need cases that make money. Look, it's great you want to help this chick out, but it takes you away from cases that might actually make us a little something."

"Okay, Townsend. You've made your point a million times over, but I really don't have time for the refrain right now. I need to get to court."

"Whatever," Ben muttered, and walked out the door. "But it would be nice if you could remember how we pay the salaries around here and try and chip in with a few profitable cases."

"Yeah, yeah," Matt muttered under his breath as he searched for the wayward file, and thought Ben would probably bust a gut if he knew Matt had given Kelly five hundred dollars out of his own pocket to buy some suitable clothes.

He found the file a moment later, grabbed up his briefcase, stuck the file under his arm, and headed for the courthouse. It was a quick two-block walk, and as he came up to the last crosswalk, he saw Debbie Seaforth coming from the opposite direction.

He smiled.

Debbie looked away.

Whoa. The light changed; Matt began striding across the street. Debbie tried to pretend she hadn't seen him, but Matt stepped directly in front of her in the middle of the crosswalk. Debbie gave off a sigh of irritation; her eyes narrowed as she looked at Matt.

"Deb, what the hell?" he asked, stretching his arms wide.

"You're blocking traffic," she said, and stepped around him, ducking under his arm.

Matt pivoted, caught up and walked with her, bending his head to get a look at her face. "Okay, what's the matter, Deb? Did I forget an important date? Did I say something I shouldn't have? What did I do that you won't at least pretend to be glad to see me?"

"Oh, please!" She reached the curb and stepped up on the sidewalk. "Why would I be glad to see you?" She punched the pedestrian button to cross the next intersection. Four times. In furiously rapid succession.

Granted, Matt was not wholly unaccustomed to The Wrath of a Woman, having been the recipient of it on many occasions. But he'd be the first guy in line to confess that he rarely had a clue as to what brought The Wrath on. Seriously. No, *seriously.* And in this instance, he risked what he instinctively knew to be a monumental blunder and tried to get at the root of it, instead of turning around and walking straight to court like his gut told him to do. "Maybe I think you'd be glad to see me because the two of us had such a good time together."

Debbie slowly turned her head, demon-style, and gave him one of those prosecutorial, I'll-bite-out-your-jugular-and-eat-it looks that made his balls cinch up and reminded him how thankful he was that he did not practice criminal law. "That's just the problem, Matt," she said, breathing fire. "We've been together. Just like you and every other chick in town, apparently. Seen the paper lately?"

Yow. Matt never got to answer. The light turned green and Debbie was striding across the intersection, leaving him to bob like a rubber duck in her furious wake.

He looked at the paper again that night as he waited for her call. And when she didn't call, he looked at the paper several times over what turned out to be a very long weekend, where, in a new twist of the saga that was his life, Matt never left his penthouse loft. Honestly, he couldn't remember the last time that he had stayed in for two solid days...maybe back in '08, when he'd had a horrendous case of the flu. But even then, what's-her-name had come and stayed with him (what *was* her name?).

It didn't matter anyway, because this time was nothing like that time. He felt fine. He just felt sort of...*blah*. Unsettled. Weird. Nothing sounded appealing. Not chasing women, or hanging out with his pals who liked to chase women. Bars, restaurants, and houseboats did not sound appealing. Not golf, not basketball. Nada. Zilch.

What was bothering him, Matt finally admitted to himself (with the help of a couple of vodka martinis), was the goddamn pictures. The goddamn pictures and the uncomfortable and disquieting fact that he really had been gazing at her, looking deep into those blue eyes, lured in by that glimmer of light behind them. He looked almost devoted, and really, he'd never considered himself the devotee type.

This was a problem.

It was a problem because Matt was a serious high flyer, someone who had always told himself that he had neither the time nor the inclination for a long-term, serious thing. He did better with many women at a time. There was no space in his life yet for a wife and lots of kids—he had always thought those things would come in the future. When he was a little older. And had made a name for himself.

But he was thirty-five years old. And he'd made a name for himself. He had, in fact, met all of his self-imposed criteria. So what was it, exactly, the thing that he was so afraid of?

Oh yeah, right, like he didn't know what it was. He knew exactly what it was. Didn't understand it, not why, or how, or even what any of it meant. But still, he knew what he was afraid of, and it was a fear that gripped him right down to the bottom of his heart.

It was that warm glimmer of light deep in those blue eyes.

By the time Monday rolled around, Matt was ready to get out of his house before he drove himself crazy. Fortunately, he was snowed under getting ready for the Kiker trial, so he really had little time to dwell on the fact that she had not returned his call. In fact, he couldn't even focus on the campaign at all until midweek, when Doug and Jeff called from Dallas to discuss Tom's platform, and more importantly, Matt's work to get the Hispanic vote. "This is going to be key to the DA office, you know," Doug reminded him. "Maybe even as key as it is to the lieutenant governor's office." At the end of the conference call, Jeff said, "Great work with the Silver Panthers. You're even getting a little press up here."

That was mildly surprising; one event at the Silver Panther conference didn't seem worth reporting, particularly as it had nothing to do with the agenda they had just discussed over the phone. "Oh, yeah? What are they saying?"

"That it was a good tactical move by Masters, preempting the incumbent and the independent. Which reminds me—we've got a tight schedule of statewide fund-raisers coming up, with a really big one between a couple of candidate forums. We'll send the stuff to you and Tom this week!"

"Okay," Matt said, and had hardly hung up when Harold ushered in two new potential clients. Matt greeted the Dennards, who were both beaming, helped them to a seat, then asked what he could do to help them.

"I've got an invention," Mr. Dennard said. "It's going to make millions when I get it marketed and produced. It's a shoe insert that actually helps you walk and won't let your arches down."

"He's real smart with his hands," Mrs. Dennard said proudly.

"I see," Matt said carefully. "And why do you think you need a lawyer, Mr. Dennard?"

"Why, for a patent, of course! And I have to get one right away, because the minute some of them big company fellas see this, they're going to try and steal my idea. That happened to a golfing buddy of mine."

"I don't do patent law, Mr. Dennard. Did someone tell you I did?"

"Well, no...we just asked for a lawyer," Mrs. Dennard said.

"Mind if I ask who referred me?" Matt asked.

"Rebecca Lear!" they both chimed at the same moment.

"Ah," Matt said, nodding, silently wondering how many more ways the woman could possibly complicate his life. "I'll have to thank her," he said, and began to explain to the Dennards what they probably would have to do to get a patent, and the name of another lawyer who might be able to help them. It took a full, unbillable hour before Matt was confident that the Dennards understood what they needed to do.

The next afternoon, Matt finally found the time to get by the campaign offices, and when he did, Angie was out front, manning phones. She had tipped her hair in green this week, which Matt thought a much better color for her than the pink of last week. "Yo, Ang," he said, strolling through.

"Matt!" she all but shouted, jumping up from her chair before he could manage to squeeze through the tiny entry. "Hey, listen—can you do me a favor? Can you watch him? I've got to get to the post office before it closes, and they've been behind closed doors a lot longer than I thought," she said, motioning toward the back.

Matt stopped, confused. "Watch who?"

Angie pointed beneath her desk. Matt bent over, saw Grayson sitting in the little cubbyhole of the desk. "Hi, Matt," he said solemnly.

"Hi, Grayson. What are you doing under there?"

"Reading," he said, and held up a book, *My Best Dog Friend.*

"You like dogs?"

"I have three. Frank and Bean and Tater."

Matt and Angie looked at each other. Angie shrugged. "So? Will you watch him? He's really no trouble, but if I don't leave right now—"

"So what's the big meeting about?"

Angie was scraping stuff off the desk into a green canvas backpack. "I don't know. Some fund-raiser or something like that." She dipped down on her haunches, peered under the desk. "Grayson, will you let Matt watch you? Please, please, pretty please with a cherry on top?"

"Okay."

"Okay," Matt echoed, "but how long?" he asked, following Angie as she threw the backpack over her shoulder and stuffed a box of campaign letters under her arm (all hand-addressed in perfect calligraphy, naturally. God forbid someone should feel like they weren't *personally* involved in Tom's campaign).

"I don't know. I'll be back as soon as I can. Pat's coming later—if you have to take off, hand him over to her." She pushed the glass door open. "Bye!" she yelled, and was outside before Matt could say anything else.

Grayson crawled out from beneath the desk. He was wearing khaki cargo pants that pooled around his ankles. On his feet were some sneakers that looked disproportionately enormous. His polo shirt hung to his knees, and the kid's hair...*man*. That was some bad hair, no two ways about it, poor kid.

"Wanna play something?" Grayson asked.

Matt sighed, started toward the back. "Like what?" he asked over his shoulder with Grayson following solemnly behind.

"I don't know."

They walked into the larger office next to Tom's, the one with a blackboard on which the daily tasks were written by some enterprising campaign staff member. Anyone who had extra time tried to tackle any of the tasks listed there. Today's list included getting quotes for air time from various media outlets in the major metro areas. Some helpful soul had left some phone books, an empty McDonald's bag, five million catsup packages, and a list of TV stations with lines drawn through them, quotes per minute of air time listed on the side, and a list of radio stations beneath those that hadn't been touched.

"Looks like we've got radio," Matt said, and tossed his stuff aside. "This is like searching for a needle in a haystack, you know," he said to Grayson, shaking his head.

Grayson shook his head, too.

"I mean, here the party has hired that big-ass public relations firm out of LA. Why don't they get Gunter and his people to do this stuff?"

"Maybe he's sick," Grayson suggested.

"Maybe," Matt said with a shrug. "Still seems to me there would be someone out there to do this grunt work instead of wasting our time with it, right?"

"*Right*," Grayson emphatically agreed.

"Right on, bro," Matt said with a wink. "But you have to play the hand you were dealt. So why don't you sit over there and read your book while I make a couple of calls?" he suggested as he sat down and opened a phone book.

"But I don't like this book anymore," Grayson said.

Matt glanced up. "Okay, so...do you have another one?" The kid shook his head.

"Toys?"

"Hot Wheels."

Cool. Matt hadn't seen a Hot Wheels in about twenty-five years.

"And Rescue Heroes."

Dude, even cooler. "Okay. Why don't you get them out?"

"They're with my mom's stuff," Grayson said anxiously. "Can I go get them?"

"Sure," Matt said, and Grayson instantly dropped his book and rushed out the door.

Matt had just dialed a local radio station when Grayson returned, backing into the room, dragging a huge bag. Matt ignored him, turning his back as he asked to speak to the sales department. From there he had an uninformative and thankfully brief conversation with the sales rep, wrote down some figures, and hung up. Only then did he look up and see what Grayson had brought. There were the Hot Wheels, lined up, bumper to bumper, by color. And the Rescue Heroes, which he had also lined up, like a little army on the edge of the desk.

And then there was the vacuum cleaner.

Matt closed his eyes, rubbed one, opened them again, and yessir, that was a toy vacuum cleaner. "What the hell?" he asked, pointing at the vacuum cleaner.

"My fackum cleaner," Grayson said, looked at him with great expectation.

"No. No, no, *noooo,* kid," Matt said, shaking his head as Grayson looked curiously at the vacuum cleaner beside him. "You can't play with a *vacuum cleaner.* That's a girl's toy. Don't you play boy games?"

"Like what?" he asked.

"Like…hunting for frogs, or digging holes. Don't you do stuff like that with your friends?"

"You mean with Jo Lynn?"

"No, I mean with your pals."

"I don't have any friends where I live," he said apologetically.

This wasn't right, not right at all. She was going to warp a perfectly cool little kid and turn him into a girly man. Matt put his hands on his waist, stared down at Grayson. "What about your rescue guys?" he asked, gesturing at the four of them lined up there. Grayson followed his gaze and looked at them. "They hate vacuum cleaners, you know."

"They do?"

"Oh, yeah," Matt said, shrugging out of his coat and loosening his tie. "This is what they think of them," he said, and walked around to the front of the desk, picked up the fireman, and dive-bombed him into the vacuum cleaner. Only he must have used a little too much force, because the piece of plastic snapped off.

But it made Grayson laugh, and he got the gist of the game, kicking the sweeper.

"That's what I'm talking about!" Matt said, and handed Grayson the paramedic Rescue Hero and blithely watched the kid go after it. In fact, he was having such a good time watching him that he didn't hear Tom's office door open, didn't hear them at all until Rebecca exclaimed, "What are you doing?"

He and Grayson both jerked up, staring with horror at each other before turning toward the door where Rebecca was standing, gaping at what was left of that stupid cheap vacuum cleaner. Tom stood behind her, shaking his head. "That's not cool, man."

Rebecca looked at Matt with the same blue eyes that were haunting him on a fairly routine basis, looking for an explanation. "Okay," he said, holding his hands out. "The vacuum cleaner doesn't hold up to some army tactics. So, ah, what have you guys been doing?" Matt asked in a blatant attempt to change the subject.

Tom slapped his hands together and rubbed them vigorously. "That bingo thing was so *great!*" he declared. "I've asked Rebecca to set up a big star-studded fund-raiser for me this summer. Statewide invites."

Matt bent down to pick up the pieces of the vacuum cleaner. "A fund-raiser?"

"Yeah. I'm thinking one with all the big stars of Texas, like Renée Zellwegger," he said, and looked at Rebecca. "Do you think you can get Renée Zellwegger?"

"I've never met her—"

"Yeah, but maybe Bud or someone knows her. Maybe your dad?"

"I don't think so," Rebecca answered, looking puzzled.

Tom shrugged. "Okay, just ask around. Tell your dad you're trying to get her, and maybe he can help."

"But my dad—"

"Wait, wait," Matt interrupted, still trying to absorb it. "Jeff said they've already set out a schedule of fund-raisers."

"Yeah, but this is going to be even bigger and just for me. I've got my own backers, and I told Rebecca if she could find a big outdoor venue, we could do like a barbecue and dance, something like that. You know, make it a thou to fifteen hundred a plate, more for the inner circle."

"But, Tom," Matt tried again, "the party has carefully planned the fund-raisers. As in when and where and who... you can't just insert a big bruiser in the middle of all that."

Tom laughed. "Hey, pal," he said cheerfully, "who's running for office, you or me?"

"Matt, can we go hunt for frogs?" Grayson asked, oblivious to the conversation around him.

Why? There was a huge toad and his pretty little lily pad standing right in front of them.

CHAPTER TWENTY

*And it is precisely these variations in behavior and attitude
that trigger in each of us a common response: Seeing others
around us differing from us, we conclude that these differ-
ences...are but temporary manifestations of madness, bad-
ness, stupidity or sickness...*

PLEASE UNDERSTAND ME

So here she'd spent several days romanticizing his gift
and thinking about little else but him, and he shows up
to bust Grayson's vacuum cleaner and get all bent out of
shape because they had planned a big gala fund-raiser? The
man seriously needed to get over himself...or maybe she
did. Definitely one of them did.

Rebecca picked up a piece of Grayson's little Hoover,
which, incidentally, he loved until this afternoon, and his
Rescue Heroes, and shoved them into the portable toy box
that accompanied them everywhere. Big Pants squatted
down to help her, and they both reached for the paramedic
at the same time. Rebecca slapped his hand away.

"*Ouch,*" he whined.

"Where's the SWAT guy?" she asked Grayson. He shrugged
his shoulders.

"I think he's over here," Matt said, and fell over himself—
literally—getting it off the desk to hand her.

"Matt, let's talk about the Hispanic Democrats. Jeff says you've got some ideas?" Tom said over her head.

"Ah…yeah. Just give me a minute—"

Rebecca stood up, gripping Grayson's portable toy box with the pieces in it.

"Come on back to the office," Tom said. "Rebecca, you keep up the good work! And don't forget to call your dad and tell him all about me!" With a jaunty wave, Tom started back to his office.

Matt shoved a hand through his hair, winced at Rebecca's cool expression. "Will you wait one second before you take off?" he asked, following Tom.

Rebecca waited exactly one second as she watched him stride down the hall, feeling very baffled by Big Pants, but what else was new, and a little baffled by Tom's sudden interest in her father. During their hour-long meeting, he had asked her twice if Dad knew about the campaign, what he thought of it, and if he was going to come to any of the events. She tried to explain to Tom that her dad really wasn't political (and didn't even attempt to explain his aversion to Democrats in general, or her reservations about him showing up anywhere she was trying to work), but Tom was insistent. "Tell him about me," he had said without an ounce of self-consciousness.

In spite of her very best efforts to keep the old girl down, Doormat Rebecca reared her ugly head and said, "Sure!" God, she was too polite sometimes! And gullible. And entirely too easily pushed around. She looked at Grayson. "What happened here? You broke your toy."

He shrugged. "Matt said it was a girl's toy."

"Did he," she breathed. She was going to stand up for herself and stomp on Big Pant's humongous he-shouldn't-be-playing-with-vacuums ego. She envisioned doing it, in slow motion and really hard, like they did in the *Matrix* movie.

She found the Rescue Hero policeman and the fireman, asked Grayson if there was anything else. He pointed to his book, tossed aside. She put that in the sack, too, then returned to the small office where they normally stashed their stuff, gathered up her purse and briefcase and her son, and walked out to her Range Rover. She loaded the stuff into the back, then went around to the passenger side where Grayson was sitting, kicking the dash. "Hop onto your booster."

"Rebecca!"

Great. She glanced over her shoulder as Grayson climbed over the console and into his booster seat. Matt was jogging toward her, his tie flapping behind him. When he reached the Rover, he stopped, flashed that heart-melting grin, and said, "Hey, I'm really sorry." When Rebecca didn't respond, his grin just got deeper and whiter. "I had no right to do a number on the vacuum cleaner. I'm an idiot."

"I'm with you so far," she muttered.

"Grayson and I promise to never do it again, don't we, buddy?"

"I promise, Mom!"

Dammit, but she could feel a small, hairline crack in her anger.

"Let me make it up to you—"

"It was just a toy. There is nothing to make up——"

"Want some ice cream, kiddo?" Matt asked Grayson, blowing right past her.

"YES! ICE CREAM!" Grayson shrieked.

Rebecca gave Matt a withering look. "That's cheating."

"I know." He casually propped his arm against the car door and grinned down at her. "But it was the only way I was going to win. And I have to win this time because I was really an idiot, and if you don't let me make it up to you now, I may never have another opportunity. So how about it, little girl? Want some ice cream?"

She debated, but his easy smile was making it difficult to think. "I might be talked into a soda." She lifted her chin a smidge higher. "And you have to ride in the back with the Rescue Heroes." She stepped back, out of his strong magnetic field, the one that could suck her in and seize her before she knew what was happening.

"Thanks," Matt said cheerfully, and climbed in beside Grayson.

He directed her to Amy's Ice Cream, which was located, rather conveniently, just across the street from his penthouse apartment. Grayson got double fudge chocolate with Reese's Peanut Butter Cup pieces, Matt got butter pecan with extra pecans thrown in, and talked Rebecca into a small cup of chocolate ice cream, which she took with some reservation. She had a small problem with ice cream, much like a drug addict had a problem with cocaine. It was completely out of her control, and she really preferred Matt not hear any of the terrible oinking sounds she could make when she ate it.

They ended up taking their ice cream to Matt's apartment after he asked Grayson if he wanted to see his room. The man was wily, she'd definitely give him that. They sat around his big glass dining table; Matt devoured his ice cream in about three bites, tossed the container into a nearby trash bin, then leaned back, stretching his arm across the next chair. "So how was your weekend?" he drawled as he watched Rebecca pick at her ice cream.

Small talk. She hated small talk, had never been any good at it, and was really no good at it when her skin was on fire just because of the proximity of a man. "Fine."

"Fine? That's it? Did you hit any bingo halls? Vacuum anything? Maybe hand-address a few thousand envelopes?"

Obsess about him, maybe?

"We went to Grandpa's house," Grayson answered for her. "He has horses and cows and some sheep. But no pigs, because Grandpa says they stink."

"Excellent!" Matt exclaimed, and shifted his gaze to Rebecca. "So I guess I can assume you have nothing against the lyric opera, but were out of town?"

Rebecca smiled into her cup. "You may assume that."

"Well paint me relieved," he said, smiling. "I thought I'd done something wrong. So with all those animals around, did you find time for drawing?"

"Mom drew *lots* of pictures," Grayson chimed in again. "And then she made Bean take about ten baths!"

Matt's chest puffed a little. "You took your sketchbook, huh?"

Rebecca stabbed her chocolate ice cream, wondered why answering that question made her feel like she was pulling her skirt up and exposing herself. "Yes," she said at last. "I took it. And I drew a little."

"She drew some trees and some cows," Grayson clarified.

"*Ah*," Matt said, drumming his fingers against the table top. "Trees *and* cows...so? How did it go?"

With a soft laugh, Rebecca shrugged. "I'm no Renoir, that's for sure. I'm very rusty…but it started to come back to me," she said, and glanced sheepishly at him. "Thanks again."

That made Matt positively beam. "This is great news for me, you know. It means maybe I'm not a complete idiot."

Rebecca shook her head; her gaze fell to his mouth, her heart filling with the memory of his kiss, how it felt to be held by him, how it felt—

"Mom, did you tell him about Tater?" Grayson asked, jerking her back to reality.

"Who's Tater?" Matt asked, still beaming.

"He's *my* dog."

"So dude, what is up with all those dogs?" Matt asked, playfully punching him in the shoulder. "You have Frank, right? And Bean—"

"And Tater!" Grayson cried. "But we can't help it 'cuz they come to live with us."

"They're dumps," Rebecca clarified at Matt's quizzical expression. "People dump their dogs in the country when they don't want them anymore. We've had as many as five dogs at once."

"That sucks," Matt said, his smile fading. "That really sucks. You wonder why people get a dog in the first place."

Rebecca nodded her complete agreement.

"Bean came first," Grayson said. "He bumps into things."

Rebecca laughed, told Matt about Bean's arrival, how disoriented he was, walking into walls and lying on his food bowl, and before she knew it, she had launched into a tale of all the dogs that had sought refuge with her. Matt didn't interrupt—he seemed genuinely interested, appalled by the behavior of man, amused by canine antics, and shaking his head as she described how she'd wash them, feed them, and then pull the ticks from their coats. And how she and Grayson would take them to the local grocery in Ruby Falls and try and give them away, but how the worst of the lot—like Frank and Bean—were hard to place. They talked about how many animal shelters were full of dogs just like Frank and Bean, and probably Tater, too, how no one wanted throw-away dogs.

"It's worse when they're kids," Matt said, and told her that he served on the board of a nonprofit organization, Children's Aid Services. The organization tried to find services and clothing for children placed in foster homes. He told her a little about how hard it was to find services in general for the unwanted, and how he'd participated in clothing and toy drives for the organization.

That both surprised Rebecca and warmed her. It felt almost as if they shared a feeling of despair about the unwanted, and moreover, from the sound of it, Matt had spent his professional life trying to lift up people who had hit rock bottom. He confessed sheepishly (and rather charmingly, Rebecca thought) to being in quite a bit of trouble with his partner for taking on too many pro bono cases. "I just can't turn my back on them," he said, running a hand through his hair. "They need...someone. You know what I mean?"

She knew. Possibly better than he could ever understand.

When Grayson grew bored of their adult chatter, Matt set him up in the guest room with a remote and a TV. When Rebecca checked on him a few minutes later, he was fast asleep with Nickelodeon blaring in the background. She returned to the living room—Matt was sitting on *the* leather couch and patted the cushion next to him. "I won't bite you, I promise."

"It's not you I'm worried about," she said, and Matt laughed as she walked forward and gingerly took a seat on the couch.

He playfully grabbed her hand. "By the way," he said, "speaking of the unwanted—I can't thank you enough for the Dennard referral. I always wanted to get involved in shoe insert patents."

Rebecca laughed roundly. "Serves you right for busting vacuum cleaners and being so mean all the time."

"Me? *Mean?*" Matt playfully protested.

Rebecca laughed again, looked down at her hand in his. It felt nice. Human. "I don't get you, Matt Parrish, I really don't," she said. "You can be so charming."

"This afternoon is getting better and better. Now you think I'm charming?" he asked, shifting a little closer to her, his hand sliding around her wrist.

"But you're so…" She shook her head.

"So what?" he asked absently as he leaned forward to take in her scent.

"So full of yourself. I'm afraid you'll float off at any moment."

Matt laughed, turned her hand over, and traced a line down her palm and up her wrist, his fingers moving lightly on her pulse. He lifted a brow. "Your pulse is racing, Mork."

Yeah, and her heart was about to come out of her chest, too.

"If I've been mean to you, I'm sorry," he said, sounding sincere, and the little smile that turned up the corner of his mouth began to fade. "And if I've been charming, I hope you can tell me when that was so I can keep doing it." He moved his hand to the crook of her elbow, a long, nonchalant stroke of her arm that caused another tremor to shoot straight to her heart. "But I'd be lying if I didn't admit there is something about you that makes me feel…"

"Bossy?" she murmured.

"A little confused. And a lot good." He lifted his gaze to her then; the smile was gone. Matt was not kidding around, he was speaking from his heart; she could see it. "Actually, you make me feel so good that I want to do the protect-and-defend thing; you know, be a man," he said sheepishly and shifted closer, dropping his hand to her bare knee, caressing it. "The God's honest truth is that I can't remember a time I ever felt like this."

The headiness she was suddenly feeling was not relieved with a sharply drawn breath. She was uncertain what to say or do. "I thought…I thought we weren't going there?"

"Yeah." He flashed a lopsided smile. "Remind me why, again?" he asked, and brushed his fingers across her temple.

Funny, but she couldn't think of her many good reasons at the moment. "Because you're bossy and I am stubborn. I think that's the way it went." She smiled and reached for the bottom of his tie, flipped it around with her fingers.

"And you're uncommonly horny. Don't forget that," he said low.

That she could hardly deny, and blushed, tugged on his tie a little. "See what I mean? Charming, then full of yourself."

"I'll try and be less full," he said, and brushed her hair back over her shoulder. "But I should get extra credit for the fact that I can't take my eyes off you when you're around. Or when I go to bed, your image follows me into sleep."

He made her feel sixteen all over again, alive and vibrant and worthy of a man's dreams. But she wasn't sixteen, she was in her thirties. "Sure you're not just saying that...you know, because of the horny thing?"

Matt dipped his head a little to look directly into her eyes. "Did you see the pictures in the paper?"

She nodded; her blush sank deeper into her cheeks.

"Then you say how I was looking at you. If you didn't, you're the only one in Austin."

She risked a look at him. She had seen the way she'd looked at him, too.

"This is the point I'd usually make a joke, Rebecca. But it's true—I can't stop looking at you or thinking of you."

Oh. *Ooh...* What was that she heard, the distant sound of a freight train headed right for her? His gray eyes seemed to darken; the way he was looking at her made her believe he could see inside her, could see the desire raging, could see how much she *wanted* him to look at her.

"I look at you and think of the Rebecca that's beneath that gorgeous exterior, the one who accuses people of stealing quesadillas and takes in stray dogs and buys a vacuum cleaner for her son and befriends crazy senior citizens."

Her blush was fire now, racing through her veins, licking at her heart.

"And I say to myself, dude, this isn't you. You don't fall all over yourself for a woman. But I have, Rebecca, and I want to know you, I want to be with you, and I am hoping like crazy that you want to know me, too."

His admission startled her—she couldn't think, couldn't answer, and unthinkingly touched her face, felt the cool skin of her hand against the heat of her cheek. "I don't know what to say," she started, but Matt silenced her by touching his lips to hers.

It was enough to paralyze her. Desire raced through her as Matt kissed her, right there on the leather couch, with deep, thirsty passion, as if he was actually trying to reach the Rebecca beneath. He cradled her face; his finger stroked her brow, her temple, and fluttered to her neck. Shaky, Rebecca grabbed his wrist, was holding on so tightly that she could feel his pulse, pounding in rapid rhythm with her own dangerously explosive heartbeat.

And then she was sliding, drifting down and down, Matt with her. His hand was on her knee, then her thigh, slowly sliding up, his tongue dipping between her lips as his fingers brushed against her panties.

A warm, liquid lust surged through her. Her hands were suddenly around his neck, her lips moving across his, urgently feeling and tasting them, then her tongue inside his mouth, feeling his teeth, the smooth skin of his mouth. When his finger slipped inside the silk of her panties, dipping into the damp cleft, she gasped into his mouth, and her hands fell to his shoulders, clinging to them, then his muscular arms, and his waist...and his erection.

Rebecca was heedless of anything but his body, his strong, hard body. Matt's hand tangled in her hair at the nape of her neck; his other thrust inside her panties, stroking the wet heat between her legs. Purely sexual instincts took hold—she couldn't think, couldn't feel anything but the longing for him to be deep inside her. And she was just moments away from feeling that very thing, because in the fog that shrouded her mind and all common sense, she felt Matt drawing her panties down her leg as he pressed his erection against her—

"Mommy!"

Rebecca jerked away, gasping for air. "Ah...just a minute, honey!" she called as she frantically clawed her way up and from underneath Matt. He fell away from her, melting into the couch, straightening his clothing and dragging the back of a hand across his mouth as Rebecca quickly pulled up her panties.

"I've got to go," she whispered, fixing her blouse as she hurried back to the guest room.

But she felt as if she was moving in a blind fog; her mind was awash with risky thoughts and confusion. She did not trust herself when it came to matters of the heart; she felt that in some respects she was still too raw, and perhaps too weak—and when she saw Grayson sitting on the edge of the guest bed, she felt a huge wave of guilt. The kid was still having such a difficult time coming to terms with his parents' divorce—how could she ignore that? But then again, it had been so long since someone had cared for her that Rebecca was afraid to let go of it. She wanted to cling to Matt, to feel his need and his want for as long as she could.

Her maternal instincts took hold, and she kept moving, gathering Grayson's things. When they returned to the living room, Matt had collected himself, and he picked the boy up when Grayson complained. Grayson put his arms around

Matt's neck, his head on his shoulder. *Safe and sound—Grayson felt it, too.*

They made their way down to her car, where Matt put Grayson into his booster seat, then got in the front passenger seat. As Rebecca started the Rover, he reached across the console, put his hand on her knee. "Maybe we should quit trying not to go there and at least check it out, huh? Maybe you and Grayson could come to dinner sometime next week."

"Maybe," Rebecca said, smiling softly, thinking that would be really nice, thinking that maybe she could even feel something again after being so numb for so long.

"So I'll give you a call, okay?" he asked as she pulled away from the curb and headed for the campaign offices.

"Okay," she said.

They came to a light; Rebecca slowed to a halt, debated telling Matt that she really wanted to try, but before she could, he said, "Before you drop me off—that fund-raiser thing you are doing for Tom? Not a good idea. Just let it drop."

Her warm, light feeling evaporated. "Let it drop?"

"It's not a good idea. The party has all the big-ticket events lined up." He said it amicably, as if he were in charge. Rebecca looked at him, tried to fathom how he could go from such a passionate speech and dangerous kiss to telling her what to do again.

"Light's green," he said.

It was green all right, and she punched the gas pedal, bucked Matt and Grayson into their seats. "Tom *wants* this fund-raiser," she reminded him.

"Right," Matt said as he reached for the overhead hand grip. "But I've been talking to the party leadership, and they aren't going to be able to squeeze it in. I mean, every moment of this election is wired."

"I've already lined up the Three Nines Ranch—"

"I, ah…there's the turn," Matt said, motioning toward the offices.

Rebecca made a hard right.

"Look, you did a great job with the bingo thing," he said, as if that was some anointment from the gods of social events. "And I'm sure you would with this deal, too, but that's not what we want to do. If you want, I can hook you up so you can help out with some local events."

Help out. *Help out.* Like she was some little assistant, pouring coffee and *helping out.*

"Hey…are you going to stop?" he asked carefully, and Rebecca realized she had just blown past his car. She hit the brakes.

"*Mo-om!*" Grayson complained from the back.

"Sorry, honey," she muttered, threw the car into reverse, and punched it backward, braking to a stop behind Matt's car.

He looked at her a little wide-eyed and a lot puzzled. "Are you all right?"

"Matt, please listen to me for once, will you? Tom asked me to put together a big gala fund-raiser, which I am happy to do. I think if you don't want to do it, then you should speak directly with him."

Matt nodded. "Fair enough. I'll do just that." He opened the car door, slid out, then shut the door and indicated Rebecca should roll the window down. He popped his head back in and looked at Grayson. "Later, kid."

"Bye, Matt!" Grayson called.

He looked at Rebecca. "So about that dinner—"

"I'll have to see about our schedules," she said automatically.

"Oh," he said, a frown darkening his face. "Your schedule. I see."

No, he didn't see at *all*, and that was the whole roblem.

"Just one question—should I take it from your current demeanor, which seems to change almost as often as the clock by the way, that you are doing the fish thing again?"

"I really don't know what you mean," she said, gripping the steering wheel tightly.

"The fish thing—you know, Pisces. The thing where you bump up against the side of the fishbowl where I am, then swim like hell in the other direction."

"I have no idea what you are talking about."

"Oh, yes you do, Rebecca—you know *exactly* what I'm talking about."

She put the Rover in drive. "We'll see you later," she said as she pressed the gas.

She saw Matt rear back, then in the rearview mirror, saw him staring after her, and thought the fish analogy was about the stupidest thing she'd heard in a long while, and in fact, her alter ego urged her to say so. So Rebecca circled back around.

Matt was standing in the same spot she had left him. "*Yes?*" he drawled when she let the passenger window down.

"I am not doing a *fish* thing."

"All right. Then what are you doing?"

"Excellent question. I don't happen to know at the moment, but if you will kindly step back, I have a forty-five-minute drive to think about it. I'll let you know."

Matt sighed, shook his head. "That's all I can ask for, I guess. But I gotta tell you, Rebecca, this yo-yo thing is not good. Let's agree that the ball is officially in your court. I've made it clear that I'd really like to explore this thing between us, take it deeper. You've made it clear that you don't know what you want—but I won't press you. It's up to you."

"Great. Maybe we can start with you not telling me how to participate in this campaign."

"Are you serious?" he asked, and leaned over, propped his arms on the window to better gape at her. "Come on, Rebecca, that is a whole different issue—"

"No, it's not—"

"Of course it is! That's my *role* in his campaign. It's nothing personal, it's just politics."

"It's bullshit," she said evenly. "You know what, Matt? I think I know what the problem is here. I think you are jealous of my relationship with Tom."

Matt just snorted like that was the most absurd thing in the world. "Get real!"

"Good *night*, Matt," she said, and pressed the gas again and headed for the street. And as she drove away, she saw Matt still standing there, one hand on his waist, staring after her in bewilderment.

He couldn't possibly be as bewildered as she was starting to feel.

CHAPTER TWENTY-ONE

Women! Ya can't live with 'em and ya can't get 'em to wear skimpy little Nazi outfits...

EMO PHILLIPS

From almost the moment she had called him cheap, Rebecca Lear had managed to turn Matt Parish, formerly known as the most unflappable guy in the world, upside down and inside out. He did not know which way was up. He was confused about many things, but he knew one thing beyond certainty—he was not jealous of her relationship with Tom. Preposterous.

Jealousy would imply there was something to be jealous about, which there was not. If Tom chose to spend all his time in the company of a beautiful woman, more power to him. Matt had a job to do, and he could not care less that every other time he came to the offices, Grayson was there with Pat or Angie while his mom was off playing the beauty queen role with Tom.

Okay, maybe he didn't give a shit where *she* was—sort of—but it was beginning to piss him off that the kid had to suffer through her little ego trip. "It's not all the time," Angie had said one day when Matt complained about it. "But would you mind watching him? I've got to get to the post office again." Funny how often Angie had to get to the post office. She was out the door before Matt could say anything, so he shouted after her, "It is so all the time!" as she disappeared into the parking lot.

He and Grayson had stood, side by side, watching Angie take off. "Got any candy?" Grayson had asked once she had pulled into the street.

Oh yeah, he and the kid were spending a lot of quality time together. Enough that Matt knew that Grayson's favorite cartoon was SpongeBob SquarePants, and Grayson knew who Kelly Kiker was. Matt had even visited the children's section of a bookstore to get more suitable reading material than *My Pal the Dog*, or whatever it was (his pick, *The Day My Butt Went Psycho*, was hilarious, thank you), so that Gray would have something to do while Matt tried to work on Tom's campaign. He knew which were Gray's favorite pants (the cargo ones with the hole in the knee), his favorite food (mac and cheese, hello), and what time he had to go to bed (eight). He knew what Grayson wanted to be when he grew up (a fireman. Or a policeman. Or an astronaut. Or a nanny, for Chrissakes), knew that he missed his nanny Lucy like crazy, and even penned her a touching I-heart-Lucy letter with fangs and dogs and a man who looked a little like Matt. Well, okay, looked like him and about five million other guys. But still.

Matt also knew that Grayson loved his mom, but thought she was sort of weird sometimes. The kid was very perceptive that way. "Mom has a *lot* of shoes, like five or six thousand!" he had confided in Matt one day, all wide-eyed.

"Yeah," Matt had sighed. "The sad news is, she'll get five thousand more, and so will your wife, which you'll have one day if you go the astronaut path instead of the nanny path like I'm telling you. This is something you might as well learn early on, pal. Women really like their shoes."

That obviously horrified the boy, and he had asked in a whisper, "But where will we *put* them?"

"You might have to build a barn."

Grayson had considered that for a moment, and then asked, "How come you don't have a barn for your wife?"

"Okay, I've got work to do. Read your book," Matt said.

Matt also knew that the dog-loving Grayson had a new one named Tot. But of all the dogs, Grayson loved Tater the best, because his father had given the dog to him. And while the kid spoke of the man in reverent terms, Matt couldn't help wonder what sort of dad could leave a kid as cool as Gray hanging, but apparently he did. Matt liked to keep an open mind, but based on the evidence thus far, Grayson's dad was sounding like a humongous prick.

When Matt wasn't watching SpongeBob with Grayson, he was working very diligently on getting a meeting with the Hispanics for Good Government, or HGG, which was a grassroots organization that had grown into a voting force to be reckoned with. According to the poll stats Doug and Jeff held, the Hispanic vote was one area where Tom was lacking votes. And while HGG did not like to be lobbied, Doug and Jeff were adamant that Matt finagle a meeting with them for Tom. His opponent had managed it, and they feared that if Tom didn't get in front of organization, they might endorse his opponent. That would be a critical loss, a potential showstopper.

What really chapped Malt's ass was that Tom didn't seem to care. He was forever off at obscure constituent meetings or working on campaign issues that no one else was privy to. He was not what one might call a hands-on candidate. The only thing Tom *did* show interest in—intent interest—was campaign contributions. He subscribed to the theory that the biggest purse won the pot, and toward that end, he hounded anyone who might contribute a little something. And it seemed to Matt, being just one innocent bystander, that he was using Rebecca to get those contributions, carting her around and letting her charm the pants off some of the big spenders.

Rebecca.

What could he say? He was truly crazy about her, like he'd never been crazy before—which was pretty sad seeing as how she treated him like chocolate one day, brussels sprouts the next. Short-term, long-term, any way he sliced it, he did not see how she could do anything but end up deranging his life in one enormous way or another. Like her referrals to his law practice. The shoe inserts had been just the beginning (the seniors had quite a network), and now Ben was absolutely beside himself, and had reiterated, emphatically, by slapping his hand on top of Matt's desk a half-dozen times, that he DID NOT WANT TO BE KNOWN AS THE PATENT KING FOR A BUNCH OF OLD GUYS WITH HALF-BAKED INVENTIONS.

And what about Rebecca's funky contributions to the campaign? The big giant gala aside, she had lots of really cute, no-place-in-a-political-campaign ideas. Like the e-mail newsletter Gilbert had set up, which she thought would be a lot better received if it was more folksy instead of a just a bunch of blah-blah boring campaign news (her words, not his). So she and Pat started attaching recipes to the weekly newsletter, made it sound like they were coming from Tom's wife, Glenda (who, insofar as Matt knew, didn't even boil water). In spite of his arguments that a man running for the lieutenant governor's office really shouldn't be disseminating recipes, they went out, every week.

Then, Rebecca took Tom along to Eeyore's birthday party. Now, anyone from Austin knew that the annual Eeyore's birthday party was the opportunity for a bunch of aging hippies to hang out in strange costumes. Rebecca, who had only recently moved to Austin, mistakenly thought it was a good opportunity for Gunter to shoot Tom with lots of frolicking children. Gunter got Tom with frolicking children, all right, but most of them were in their forties. Worse, the local paper shot him in a staggeringly huge top hat, standing arm in arm with a wolf in sheep's clothing. Of course Matt had tried to educate Rebecca about how that was going to play. "They'll take those pictures of him and make him look like an idiot."

"Who will?" she had asked, genuinely surprised.

"The Republicans. Heard of them?"

"Only in passing," she said with a cheerful smile, and continued stuffing envelopes (hand-addressed, of course) with the latest campaign literature. "Besides, you're so particular about everything; it's hard to know what's real and what's just another of your weird idiosyncrasies."

"My idiosyncrasies?" Matt echoed in disbelief, but Rebecca ignored him. So he put his hand on top of the stack of envelopes, leaned across the table so that she had to look at him—which she did, with those dancing blue eyes that always managed to get him right in the gut. "They're not idiosyncrasies, Rebecca. I'm just practical, and you have to admit I have a little more experience with this sort of thing than you do."

"Oh really?" she asked, happily wrenching the envelopes free of his palm. "And how many campaigns have you worked on?"

"That's a mere technicality—"

"How many did you say?"

"None," he said through gritted teeth.

"That's what I thought," she said, smiling pertly.

"The point is, I've been around campaigns, I routinely work with elected officials, and I know how this thing goes down. *You*, on the other hand, have been too busy running up and down the runway blowing kisses to the crowds to know that Eeyore's birthday is not the sort of venue where we want our candidate!"

"Ah. So you'd have him down at the courthouse with all your cronies?"

"I prefer to think of them as elected officials with statewide contacts."

"I see," she said thoughtfully, and, Matt thought, she was finally getting the picture as she picked up her envelopes and carefully straightened them into a perfect stack. "Did I tell you?" she asked, standing up. "We got a very generous contribution from Judge Gambofini at Eeyore's birthday party. He said to tell you hi." She flashed a proud little smirk and prissed out of the staff office.

Dammit.

It was obvious that Rebecca was enjoying his frustration, and maybe, just maybe, getting a little too big for her britches. She was taking advantage of the fact that he had, in spite of all the heretofore improbable, if not impossible, emotions bubbling to the surface (which could only mean an increasingly likely possibility of a major devotion, for Chrissakes), gone and done something insane and confessed he was nuts about her. Matt had taken his big old dusty heart and laid it out, salted and peppered it, and served it up to her on a platter. And just when he thought there was hope of getting close to the object of his great affection, she'd find a reason to be mad at him again, and they'd go round again. It was almost enough to make a grown man cry.

What was funny, particularly since Matt didn't know it, was that this was precisely what Rebecca was thinking of him He could be so terribly charming and witty, so very sexy. She would believe there was really the possibility of something between them—taken, of course, in baby steps—and then he'd bug her about some little thing she had done. He seemed to think he was the Central Authority on All Things Campaign, giving her a hard time about silly things, such as how she was wasting time hand-addressing the campaign envelopes (but did he volunteer to generate labels? No). She was taking Tom to all the wrong events (Eeyore's birthday party was for hippies...and distinguished judges, apparently). She couldn't possibly pull off a bigger gala than the party was organizing, so why waste her time (but he didn't actually have any of the details of A Big Party Fund-raiser, did he?), and he thought Grayson was in the campaign offices too often. He had actually said to her, and these were his exact words, because there was, apparently, no end to the list of topics about which Big Pants was an expert: "Grayson is really bored. Don't you think he could use a friendlier after-school environment?"

Augh!

She had politely but firmly informed him that Grayson was fine, and politely but firmly ignored the little voice in her head that said Matt was right, because she *hated* when he was right.

The confusing part about Matt was, when he wasn't trying to mow everyone down with his ideas, he was really great to have around. Like the day he helped her, without any smirking or sarcastic remarks, put up drawings of America Grayson's preschool class had made for Tom and they stood there, side by side, admiring the drawings and laughing like old friends. Matt even pointed out that Grayson's drawing had a monster in it, which he said made Grayson's stand out from all the rest.

That was another obvious and huge selling point—Matt seemed genuinely interested in her son, which was very cool, particularly since Bud wasn't.

And not only was Matt's concern for the underdog real, but well known. He had been overly modest when he told her about his involvement with Children's Aid Services. Gilbert told her about Matt's reputation for taking on some difficult and heart-wrenching cases and said he'd once read that Matt donated several thousand dollars of his own money to the Children's Aid Society.

That made her heart skip just a little.

She had to admit that he was unusually chipper about the string of seniors that were still calling after the bingo bash. He was a good sport, too, would always laugh when she messed with him. One day he asked her about the stars she was lining up for the big to-do he was so adamantly against. "So, do you have the Dixie Chicks lined up?" he'd asked.

"No," she had sighed wearily, glancing at him. "I could only get Lyle Lovett." That, of course, was a lie.

Matt had chuckled, his eyes glimmering with amusement. "Only Lyle Lovett? That's a tragedy. How'd you manage?"

"A friend of a friend of a friend," she had said, waving her hand dismissively.

His smile had brightened then—he was on to her—and he walked closer to where she was standing next to the bulletin board where they posted all the news. "What about Renée Zellwegger? A friend of a friend?" he had asked low, his breath skimming her ear.

"She wasn't available."

"Tom will be crushed."

"Oh no, he was okay with Sandra Bullock." That was *not* a lie.

Matt laughed low; Rebecca turned partially around to look at him. His eyes crinkled appealingly in the corners with his appreciative smile, and his gaze fell to her lips. For a moment, Rebecca toyed with stealing a kiss from him, just taking it…but she was too indecisive. Matt was already walking away, chuckling softly. "Can't wait to go to this shindig," he said cheerfully as he walked out the door.

She was attracted to him. Very attracted. Weak-kneed-butterfly-belly attracted. That was a confusing place to be, because true to his word, Matt had left the ball in her court. He didn't press her; he didn't make her even remotely uncomfortable like so many men in her life had done. But sometimes, she would catch him looking at her, his eyes as soft and deep as the river, and he'd smile as he turned away.

Thankfully, Rebecca continued to convince herself (with help from *Protecting the Inner Child While Searching for the Exterior Woman*) that she didn't need to be involved with any guy right now. After all, she had just come out of a long-term, toxic relationship, and lest she forget, that toxic guy had been terribly charming at first, too. Worse, she feared that Dad could be right about her, that she was too afraid to be alone.

So the ludicrously topsy-turvy upshot of all this was, when she saw Matt, her heart did a funny little dance. She had a raging desire to see him, talk to him, and touch him that she felt, for the most part, completely at odds with the universe. But she was not so numb that she didn't recognize that slowly and surely, she was falling like a shooting star, falling fast and headlong into that lovely chasm, at which point she'd slap a big mental red circle and line on him. The practical Rebecca understood why; the real Rebecca often wondered if she wasn't just completely nuts.

After several days of dancing around their mutual attraction, Matt was growing weary. He did everything he knew how to do to get her to cross over to his side. And while she showed signs of wanting to make that leap, she'd quickly back off. Actually, he couldn't help but feel a little sorry for her. He'd never really suffered the pangs of love, but he figured Rebecca must have suffered them to death. Rather than allow himself to feel the pangs of rejection—that sounded like a root canal to him—he focused his attentions on getting a face-to-face with HGG. He was bound and determined to make it happen, and he hounded that group, called in all the chits he could think of. So when he finally got the call, he was ecstatic. He called Tom's capitol office, told him that the meeting was on, at four thirty at the Four Seasons.

"Today?" Tom had asked.

"Today. That's the only time they would give me. This could be a huge boost toward getting the Hispanic vote, you know," he reminded him.

"Yeah. Okay, I'll rearrange a couple of things. Four thirty at the Four Seasons. Great...just swing by the campaign office and pick me up."

Matt was thrilled to have finally snared the big fish they said could not be caught. But he'd been around long enough that he should have known, when his morning took a nosedive at court, that things were not going to go as he had hoped.

Kelly Kiker's discovery hearing went badly. The ruling against him was especially bad because Matt had not seen it coming. He had arrogantly believed that they would win access to some of the employer records that they both thought were critical to her suit, and therefore, had not been fully prepared when they did not. He apologized profusely to Kelly, but the words sounded empty and hollow, a big fat lie.

"Dude, it's okay," she had said, stuffing her papers into her enormous black bag and lighting a cigarette. "We tried our best, and that's what counts, right?"

He thought about that when he got back to the office, and came to the conclusion that no, it didn't count, not when people like Kelly Kiker got hurt. Trying just wasn't good enough and the truth was that he'd been too caught up in Rebecca and this campaign crap to pay proper attention to the case. Matt rarely let a client down, but he had let Kelly down, and to add insult to injury, Ben gave him another speech before he left the office. That, he did not need, and he was, therefore, in a pretty foul mood when he pulled up at campaign headquarters.

He stalked into the offices. There was no Angie. He continued on to the back, saw Pat sitting at a break table with Grayson.

"Hi, Matt," the kid said, his face brightening.

"Thank God," Pat said. "I'm going to be late. I have to pick my daughter up from band practice."

"Where the hell is his mom?" Matt snapped, ignoring Grayson.

"With Tom somewhere."

"You mean I finally get a meeting with HGG and he's late?"

Pat stood up, slung her purse over her shoulder. "Is that where he went?"

"What do you mean, where he went?" Matt demanded.

"Hey!" Pat exclaimed, holding up a hand and scowling mightily at his tone. "Tom left earlier, said he had a meeting at the Four Seasons. He said you could meet him there when you got in. You don't like that, take it up with him, not me."

The information shocked Matt so thoroughly that he could only stand there, immobilized, as Pat walked past.

"You want to read my book with me?" Grayson asked.

"Wait!" Matt said, pivoting sharply toward Pat. "Are you telling me that he left without me? That he went to that meeting alone?"

"He didn't go alone. He took Rebecca with him. Look, I really have to go," she said, and walked out, leaving him standing there, his blood percolating up to a full cauldron boil.

He could not believe it. After all he'd put up with, after all the time he had devoted to Tom's campaign, *gratis,* and this was the thanks he got? Matt felt a rage coming on like he had only felt once or twice as an adult, and both times in a courtroom. Slowly, he turned and looked at the kid. He frowned darkly.

Grayson took a step back, his hazel eyes widening slightly.

"You wanna go for a little ride?" Matt asked.

Grayson thought about it for a moment, then nodded.

CHAPTER TWENTY-TWO

In accordance with our principles of free enterprise and healthy competition, I'm going to ask you two to fight to the death for it...

MONTY PYTHON

Rebecca glanced at her watch a second time, worried that Tom was getting a little carried away. She had only intended to be gone a half hour, no more, and she thought of Grayson with Pat, his least favorite of the campaign staff. "She smells like milk," he had once told her, wrinkling his nose. Rebecca thought she'd have to excuse herself, send someone back for Tom when he suddenly looked up, beaming. "Matt Parrish!" he called loudly, and Rebecca's tummy did a funny little flip. Smiling, she instantly glanced over her shoulder—but her heart seized when she saw the look on Matt's face and Grayson beside him. *Something had happened.*

Tom turned toward the three men he had come in "to say hello to," and as Matt reached them, he said, "I'd like you to meet Matt Parrish. You may have spoken to him on the phone."

"Of course!" Mr. Martinez said. "Many times!"

"Mr. Martinez? Pleasure to finally meet you in person," Matt said, unsmiling as he extended his hand.

Rebecca leaned over Grayson, ran her hand over the top of his unruly hair, and asked if everything was okay, to which Grayson dropped his gaze and shrugged.

"I'm sorry I'm late," Matt said to Tom and the three men. "I ran into a little problem."

"Late?" Tom asked, looking at his watch. "Oh no, you're not late! Rebecca and I are a little early."

They were early? But Tom wasn't even certain these three gentlemen would even be at the Four Seasons.

"But now that everyone is here, I guess we should get a table and talk about this little campaign thing I have going," Tom laughed, gesturing toward a table.

"Be right with you, Senator," Matt said. "I need to give Ms. Lear some of her son's things."

Ms. Lear? That didn't sound very promising.

"Take your time," Mr. Martinez said pleasantly. "We'll order a Mexican martini for you, if you'd like."

"That would be great," Matt said, and forced what almost passed for a smile.

"Gentlemen, what do you think of a superhighway running from Dallas to Brownsville?" Tom asked as he ushered the three gentlemen toward an empty table.

Matt turned his hard smile to Rebecca; it faded to a sneer.

She did not like that look—it made her feel cold and vulnerable. "I'm sorry you had to bring Grayson," she said, attempting to smooth over whatever was annoying him.

Matt released Grayson's hand. "You probably thought I'd just sit around and babysit for you all day, didn't you?"

"I left him with Pat," she said. "I didn't mean—"

"I know exactly what you didn't mean," he said, gesturing for her to walk. "If you don't mind, I'd like to give you his things and get on with my business."

"All *right*, Matt." She took Grayson's hand, started walking. "I'm sorry you thought you had to bring him down here, but I was going—"

"Save me your lame excuses," he muttered angrily.

Rebecca sucked in her breath. She and Matt had had their moments, but she had never seen him like this, and she didn't like it. "I am not making excuses," she said tightly. "I know you don't like the fact that I have to bring Grayson with me, but I've told you, I am volunteering, and sometimes—"

"What you are doing is letting other people use you so you can flit around and be some ex–beauty queen," he rudely interrupted her as they strode across the marble floor, side by side, Grayson working to keep up between them.

The remark went all over Rebecca. No matter what he was upset about, she did not deserve that. "What is the matter with you?" she demanded angrily. "I'm not doing any such thing, but honestly, it's none of your business what I do."

"It is when you start interfering with my business," he said coldly as they reached the elevator.

"How could I possibly be interfering with your business?" she retorted as he punched a button. "How could I possibly interfere in something I know nothing about? I couldn't possibly care less about your business."

"Mom?" Grayson asked nervously.

"It's all right, honey. Matt's just grouchy, that's all," she said irritably, and stepped into the elevator with her son.

"Oh, I'm grouchy, all right," Matt said, coming in behind her. "You and Tom have lost all sight of what's important. I don't care, personally, but there are a lot of other people who are working hard to get him elected, and when you dash in, drop your kid, and take off with Tom, you are screwing up a lot of that hard work. You think everything revolves around you and what you want. How you and Tom look to everyone out there. But this campaign is a little bit bigger than you."

She didn't know if she should be angry or confused. "What are you talking about?" she demanded as the elevator landed on the bottom floor. The doors opened; Matt put his hand on her back, steered her none too gently out the door and into the underground garage. "I'll tell you," he said low as they strode toward his car. "I am talking about that fact that it is time for you to grow up and stop resting on your beauty queen laurels—"

"Stop accusing me—"

"Let me finish!"

"*Mom!*" Grayson cried, clutching at her sheath dress.

"You need to learn how to use your brains rather than your looks, and you damn sure shouldn't let others use your looks!"

That stung. A swell of emotions, old and bitter, rose up in her. "This is ridiculous. I don't know what you think has happened, but there is nothing going on. I was just running errands with Tom and—"

"I am talking about that meeting upstairs!" Matt shouted, pointing at the garage ceiling as they reached his car. "I have worked for *weeks* to get that meeting, and the first thing Tom does is trot you out there! Look at you!" he said, gesturing wildly at her as he tried to fit the key into his Jag. "You look great, Rebecca, but you don't know anything about the issues facing this campaign, or even what Tom stands for. All you know is which recipe goes with what newsletter. You spend all your time running around on stupid little chores and you have no clue what Tom's record is in the senate. If you were really interested in this campaign, you would learn about your candidate and the issues, but no, you want to walk around like a fucking beauty queen. This whole thing is about how *you* look, how *Tom* looks, and not about a political campaign."

Rebecca gasped—he couldn't have hurt her more if he had punched her. She couldn't speak, she could only gape at him. All her fears and insecurities, all her hopes, bubbled up into some toxic mix. She felt queasy and pulled Grayson into her side. Her son buried his face in her dress.

Matt paused for a moment, looked at Grayson, then angrily yanked the car door open. He reached inside, got a book and Gray's backpack, and shoved them at Rebecca. She took them, still unable to speak, the burn in her heart spreading to her throat.

"There's just one more thing," he said, his voice dangerously low. "This is your kid, and you need to be the caretaker."

"Mommy, I want to go home," Grayson said into her leg.

Rebecca was too stunned to move at first. Whatever feeling she might have had for this man was effectively destroyed, stomped right into the ground, along with her pride. "Fuck. *You*," she said calmly.

"*Mommeeeee!*" Grayson sobbed. "*You said a bad word!*"

She dropped his backpack and covered Grayson's ears. "You arrogant, *arrogant* asshole! How *dare* you think you can mow me down! For your information, Tom never said anything about your stupid meeting, just said he was going to run in and see if these guys were around and say hello. Second of all, if you would get down off that high and mighty throne of yours and quit trying to top everyone on staff, you might know a little more of what was going on. Do you think we're all mind readers? How could we possibly know what you've been working on? All you ever do is complain about what *we're* doing! You waltz in, bark your opinions, and then you waltz out. But do you ever ask what anyone else is doing?"

"That's not so—"

"Let *me* finish," she said, seething. "You think you're so special, Matt? All I see is a hack lawyer who thinks more of his title than his work. And you know what the *worst* thing is about you?" she asked as a hot tear burned her cheek. "You made me believe you. You made me believe!"

Matt's face turned dark; his eyes glittered with fury. "You didn't believe," he said, spitting out the word. "You've held me by a string like your personal little puppet, playing with my feelings. You're perfect on the outside but miserably incomplete on the inside!"

His words slapped at her conscience and she felt on the verge of sobbing uncontrollably. "You think I'm empty? Take a look at your own life, Matt. But hey, say or think what you will, because you know what? You win. You can have it all. In fact, you can shove it up your ass," she said, and dropped her hands from Grayson's head. "Come on, honey," she said, peeling his arms from her legs. "Let's go."

She grabbed Grayson's hand. "And one last thing—I never, *ever* want to see you again."

She turned her back on Matt and marched away from him as quickly as she could while Grayson struggled to keep up.

CHAPTER TWENTY-THREE

Habit is habit and not to be flung out the window by any man, but coaxed downstairs a step at a time...

MARK TWAIN

Rebecca and Grayson cried all the way home.

Rebecca cried because she felt like she had been dumped all over again, which of course she hadn't, because you can't be dumped if you're not involved, but nonetheless, it felt pretty darn near the same. And Grayson cried because he had witnessed a horrible fight and rarely saw his mom cry. Rebecca's repeated and blubbering attempts to tell him it was okay were not enough to make him stop. Plus she was so angry, so *very* angry—with Matt, with Tom—but mostly with herself and the universe in general.

As she and Grayson turned onto the two-lane road that would take them to the lake house, Rebecca swiped at the tears beneath her eyes, then dragged the back of her hand beneath her nose, took a deep breath, and stopped crying. After forty-five minutes, her tank was completely empty. Now she could just be angry in peace.

What pissed her off more than anything was that she was so fragile. Oh sure, after suffering the astounding humiliation of being dumped by Bud, she'd pretty much figured out that she didn't have a lot of chutzpah to cling to when the going got rough. Which was why, of course, she'd spent all that money and time—to build chutzpah! Well obviously, transformation seminars, subliminal motivational tapes, videos and stacks of books about eastern philosophies and self-awareness practices had all piled up and up until she was a huge bundle of Pick Up Sticks. And all it took was for someone like Mr. Big Pants to pull the wrong stick out of the pile, and there she went, literally collapsing into one huge mess.

Thank you, Matt Parrish.

Rebecca hated him. Hated him, hated him, *hated* him so much that at that moment, she thought she might really, genuinely, HATE him. How could someone be so charming and so in tune with her while at the same time be a gargantuan dick? And the thing that made it hurt the worst? That deep down, she knew Matt was right. He was so damn right. Campaign issues bored her. She had no idea what Tom's record in the senate was, or what he hoped to achieve. All the times she'd sat in meetings with Angie and Gilbert and Pat (and yes, with HIM), while they talked about platforms, issues, a new superhighway and pipeline, she had been somewhere else in her head—usually doing self-visualization exercises, or wondering what Grayson was doing. She'd been so eager to sign up and prove something that she'd forgotten the basics, like, who is this candidate? The bottom line was, in spite of all the effort she'd put into improving herself, she had gone into this deal doing the one thing she was trying not to do—look fabulous and put on a killer party. And she'd gotten so caught up in trying to prove something to herself that she hadn't even realized she hadn't changed.

It occurred to her that Tom was more like Bud than she had even realized. They both cared more about appearances above all else, and that was exactly why Tom always wanted her to come along. A pretty face to bring in the contributions. Why could she have not seen it before Matt had to point it out to her?

But he was wrong about one thing. She wasn't empty. No, no. She was a million pieces. How could he not see the difference?

Rebecca pulled the Range Rover up into the drive, slammed the thing into park. Grayson, still upset, was out in a flash, running around to the back and to the comfort of his dogs before she could say anything to him. That was just as well, she supposed, because at the moment, she really didn't have the energy to talk about what had happened. Where was Lucy when she needed her? Matt was right about that, too—she was a rotten mother.

Rebecca got out of the truck and went into the house. She tossed her purse onto an antique bench in the entry, then proceeded into the great room, where she paused, hands on hips, and looked around. Everything was so neatly arranged; books on shelves according to height and thickness. Her lap rugs were artfully arranged on the backs of couches and chairs, each one perfectly color-coordinated with the piece of furniture it graced. Her selection of candles, likewise color-coordinated, were arranged with short ones in front of tall ones, fat ones in back, skinny ones in front. Fruit fragrances on one end of the room, flower fragrances on the other.

Yep. Everything perfect.

Disgusted, she walked to the kitchen, where her spices were alphabetically arranged, her dish towels ironed and stacked by color, and her glasses arranged by purpose in sparkling glass cabinets. Juice glasses on the bottom, wine-glasses on top, and tumblers in the middle. Not to be con-fused with iced tea glasses, which had their own separate shelf. Even the apples in her fruit bowl were arranged so that no two reds or two greens were together.

He was right—perfect on the outside, miserably incom-plete on the inside. How had she managed, in the course of her life, to order and sort and arrange everything about her so that it was all pleasing to the eye and masking all the imperfection underneath? All this time, she had been try-ing to break the bonds of being Rebecca while at the very same time she had been working just as hard to maintain her perfect little world. And in that perfect little world, she *had* held Matt at arm's length, treating him like a puppet, toying with his affection.

Rebecca walked into the great room, wearily collapsed onto a couch, not caring that she still had her shoes on.

That night, after putting Grayson to bed (*No, honey, Matt's not mad at you, he's mad at me*), Rebecca scarfed her dinner (Ben & Jerry's Making Whoopie Pie ice cream), and went to bed, too. But she lay there, wide-awake for what seemed like forever, staring into darkness as a storm tossed the world outside her window. Her mind was blank. Empty.

The next morning, she felt as if she'd been on a bender the night before, but she was up at sunrise nonetheless and on the back porch, a steaming cup of coffee in one hand, her journal on her lap, and pen in hand. She had come to several conclusions in the wee hours of the morning that were still holding with the light of day, and Rebecca wrote:

Positive Affirmations of My Life:
1. Gray is so young he can't be too warped yet. If there is still hope for his mother—and God please say there is—then there is still hope for Grayson.
2. The next time I allow my life to be guided by appearances, pigs will fly.
3. I promise myself to rise every morning and recite the only unqualified applicant mandate worth remembering: Rule 1: Believe in yourself. And starting today, I believe in myself!

Now that she'd hit rock bottom, she thought she might as well confess one more truth—when Rachel had asked if she ever wanted to fall in love again, she had been less than honest. The truth was that she dreamed not of the falling, but of *being* in love, of feeling true love once more before she died; the kind of love that felt all warm and prickly on her neck. And she had thought, once or twice in the small hours of the morning when she was alone and there was no risk of just thinking it, that maybe, just *maybe*...maybe Matt could have been the someone to make her feel that warmth again. That Matt could have been worth the emotional capital. That she could have loved him.

Maybe she already did.

Well, there you had it. Now the real Rebecca could kick her own ass, because it was never going to happen now. He thought she was callous and empty. It was perhaps the cruelest thing anyone had ever said to her. It hurt far worse than anything Bud had ever said, because Bud always lied to get his way. Matt, on the other hand, was telling the truth. He had looked inside her and seen for himself, and the hurt was so deep, she feared she could drown in it.

Yes, well. No point in mourning her pipe dream any longer.

Later, while Grayson watched cartoons, Rebecca heard the phone ringing from her post on the porch. She got up, went inside, and grabbed it. "Hello?"

"Rebecca..." His hoarse voice cut through her like a knife. "Rebecca, listen—"

No. She clicked the phone off and laid it on the kitchen counter. The time for talking had come and gone—she was done. She numbly walked into the great room where Grayson was. He turned to look at her. "Come on, sweetie. There is some stuff we need to do," she said, and Grayson followed her to his room.

In his room, she slowly turned in a circle, taking it all in with a grimace. There were no toys out, because Grayson had been trained from an early age to put them all away. She walked to the closet, pulled open the doors, and glared at the contents. His shirts were on the top rack, hung together by primary color and level of dressiness. Beneath them, shorts on one side, pants on the other, all hung by color. His shoes were in a shoe tree, formal on top, casual on bottom.

Grayson stood by the door watching as Rebecca reached into the closet and removed all the shirts and turned, dumping them on the floor. His jaw dropped as she did the same with his pants and shorts.

"Mom!" he cried, looking at the lump of clothing as Bean wandered in, sniffed the clothes, circled three times on top of them, then dropped down. "What are you doing?"

"Let me ask you something, Gray," she said, walking across to his bureau and opening the first drawer where all his little boxer briefs were ironed and put away. "When Lucy used to hang up your clothes, how did she do it?"

"She just hanged 'em up."

"By color?"

"No," he said instantly. "She didn't care about colors."

"Well, guess what. Neither do we. You pick out what you want to hang up, and I'll hang them any way you want."

Grayson didn't say anything for a moment, just watched her closely, assessing her. At last, he walked to the middle of the pile of clothing she had made, squatted down, pulled a red Yu-Gi-Oh! T-shirt and a pair of blue-green Jams from beneath Bean, and held them up to her. "Can I wear this today?"

"You can wear whatever you like." Together, they shooed Bean away, then bent over the pile of clothing and started, working for an hour or more, carefully choosing different shirts to go with pants and shorts.

But in the end, in spite of Rebecca's best intentions, as she stood back and looked at the first effort to dismantle her perfection, she was dismayed to see that they had somehow rearranged the clothes back in the closet by color. Shirts were mixed with pants and shorts—at least that was one small concession—but, the two of them had unwittingly stuck with what was ingrained in their heads.

By now, Grayson had lost interest, had returned to the great room to watch cartoons. Only Bean remained with Rebecca, looking up at the contents of the closet along with her.

"What do I do now, Bean?" she whispered. "Try again?"

Bean wasn't listening; he rambled toward the closet, just barely missing the door, and lifted his huge head and snout to have a good sniff of a shirt.

That was when Rebecca saw it—Bean was sniffing a *purple* shirt. A purple T-shirt, in the middle of the yellow and khaki dress clothes, completely out of color scheme and character.

"Oh, Bean, thank you!" she cried, landing on her knees and scratching Bean behind the ears. She beamed up at that purple shirt—there it was, her first real step toward imperfection. A baby step, okay, but a step all the same.

And as she hugged Bean, the phone began to ring again.

CHAPTER TWENTY-FOUR

IDIOT, n. A member of a large and powerful tribe whose influence in human affairs has always been dominant and controlling. The Idiot's activity is not confined to any special field of thought or action, but "pervades and regulates the whole." He has the last word in everything; his decision is unappealable. He sets the fashions and opinion of taste, dictates the limitations of speech and circumscribes conduct with a dead-line...

THE DEVIL'S DICTIONARY

It was a couple of days before Matt could admit to himself that what he had done at the Four Seasons was remarkably callous and reprehensible—he'd been a jerk to the one person he would never want to treat reprehensibly. Rebecca wasn't empty; she was full of vibrant life. But he'd been very determined and very angry, and really, at the time, his cutting remark had not seemed that cutting.

Fool.

Now she wouldn't even talk to him. He'd tried three times to get her on the phone, and three times, she'd hung up. On the fourth and fifth attempts, the answering machine had picked up. Which left him with the image of Rebecca's face when he called her empty. And oh, lest he forget, her sobbing "*You made me believe*" had haunted his sleep for three nights now, and okay, his days, too, because he had believed, too. Now that belief felt dashed to pieces.

It made his little triumph with HGG look asinine by comparison. But at least he had pulled that off—HGG was now leaning toward an endorsement for Tom. Which pretty much left Matt standing smack-dab in the middle of the huge hole Rebecca had created when she quit the campaign.

He once thought he'd be happy if she was gone from the campaign, but he wasn't even remotely happy. He was pretty miserable, actually. All this time, he'd thought Tom was treating him like a second-class citizen when he was, in actuality, the Anointed One. Tom had even allowed him to be bumped off his anointed pedestal by a former beauty queen.

It wasn't Tom, it was Matt's own jealousy and arrogance that had put him there. Maybe Rebecca was right—he'd mowed everyone over as if he was somehow entitled to do so. Pat had great ideas about education, which he could not recite today if his life depended on it. Angie had done a great job with the phone bank, in spite of his early misgivings about her. Had he even once commended her? Hell, no. Even Gilbert had written a couple of excellent speeches, yet Matt continued to think of Gilbert as a kid who needed his guidance.

And in the process of reviewing his more outstanding character flaws, he'd have to admit that he never really gave Rebecca any credit. She had worked extremely hard, pulled off an improbable bingo fund-raiser, and was always thinking outside the box. But he'd lashed out at her for being the kind of woman Tom wanted to hang with instead of him, and now, thanks to his supersized ego (which he had not heretofore known was *that* big), he was standing in the hole, missing her.

God yes, he missed her. He missed her smile, her carefully hand-addressed envelopes and children's drawings. Missed hearing the latest diet or recipe tip for the e-newsletter and her motivational office decorations. And Matt missed Grayson. That kid slayed him. He missed green slime candy and Hot Wheels and SpongeBob SquarePants.

With Rebecca and Grayson gone, the whole campaign felt empty, and Matt cursed himself for having such a fat mouth. This was a mess he had no clue how to climb out of—before, on those rare occasions he'd gotten himself into trouble with a woman, he'd never really cared enough to get himself out. He damn sure had never said such hateful things to a woman before, even the one or two who probably deserved it. The whole deal was pretty remarkable for a former all-star ladies' man and left him feeling very uncomfortable and uncertain, like he really didn't know what he was doing anymore about anything.

Matt sort of muddled through the days after that bad scene with Rebecca, feeling very weird. He skipped Sunday dinner with the folks, not feeling up to their usual cheerful interest in his life.

It wasn't until the following Friday that he actually got Rebecca on the phone. He had, in a moment of desperation, tried one last time, and much to his great surprise, she picked up. "Rebecca? Rebecca, how are you?" he quickly asked when she answered.

His question was met with cold silence.

"Listen, I really need to talk to you about the other night—"

"Matt?" she quietly interrupted, her voice sounding hollow and far away.

"Yes?"

"Please don't call me again," she said politely, and the phone went dead.

That was when Matt decided to make the drive out to see his folks, because he needed something solidly familiar.

He met his sister, Bella, on the drive, holding her baby girl. "Where's Bill?" he asked, reaching for the baby.

"Golf, where else?" Bella said. "Cameron, will you let your Uncle Mattie hold you?" she cooed, handing her nine-month-old daughter over to Matt, who smiled at him as he gazed down at her chubby cheeks.

"Look at her smile," Bella said. "She really likes you, Matt. Doesn't that make you want one of these for your very own?"

Yes. Oh, yes. "Maybe someday," he said noncommittally, and together with his sister, walked inside.

Sherri Parrish, Matt's mom, was watching her two oldest children on the drive and saw the wistful look on Matt's face as he looked down at his niece, which she thought was a little odd. Of all her children, Matt was the least interested in marriage and children. Kept complaining that he hadn't found The One.

She met her kids at the door. "Oh my, what a beautiful picture that would make!" she cried.

"Listen, kiddo, I'll be straight," Matt said to Cameron. "Your grandma fell off her rocker a long time ago. You want to say hi to your silly grandma?" he asked, and handed the baby to Sherri, who playfully pinched Matt's cheek before hugging the baby tightly to her. When Bella had first mentioned she was pregnant, Sherri had been very alarmed— she was too young to be a grandmother! But then Cameron had come into the world, and she had done a complete about face. Now she wanted all her children to provide her with precious babies, and lots of them. She peeked up at her handsome son, the brightest lawyer in all of Austin, hell, maybe even the state, and saw that strangely wistful look again as he gazed down at Cameron. It made a mother's heart flinch a little.

"I was going to call you and tell you to invite your friend," she blurted (and honestly, she never really knew where these little verbal strikes came from).

Matt looked startled; his gray eyes widened slightly as he dragged his gaze from Cameron to her. "Who, Debbie? I'm not seeing her anymore."

"No, not her," Sherri said. "The pretty one from the paper."

"Ooh, she *was* pretty," Bella chimed in.

Was it Sherri's imagination, or did the blood just drain from her son's face? "I—ah, I don't know what you mean. She's just a campaign worker," he said, and immediately looked away. "Where's the judge?"

"What's her name?" Sherri asked.

"Mom, I'm not seeing her!" he protested as he walked over to the kitchen bar and looked at some mail.

"I didn't say you were. I just asked her name, that's all."

"Rebecca."

"Pretty name," Bella said absently. "If I hadn't picked Cameron, I would have picked Rebecca. I've always liked that name."

"Okay, where's Dad?" Matt demanded.

"In the study," Sherri said, and chuckled as Matt beat a quick retreat in that direction.

With a look of confusion, Bella watched her brother stride toward the study, then looked curiously at her mother. "What was *that* all about?"

Sherri flashed a fat smile before smothering her granddaughter with kisses. "Don't look now," she said, pausing to laugh at the baby, "but I think your brother might have finally stumbled on The One."

Bella gasped, looked at the door to the study. "No way!"

Matt emerged from the weekly dinner relatively unscathed, and went through his Monday in a fog, which he'd really done every day since the blowup with Rebecca. He stood in front of a judge, arguing the merits against a summary judgment while his mind was full of thoughts of her. On Tuesday, he had lunch with Ben and two prospective new (paying) clients and wondered if Grayson was having any trouble with his arch nemesis, Taylor. And on Wednesday, while he reviewed the staff billings, he wondered where Rebecca was, if she was smiling at someone, those damn blue eyes sparkling like they had sparkled at him.

At the end of that tedious day, he drove over to the campaign offices and was met at the door by Gilbert, who looked frantic. Gilbert, a former slacker, was never frantic, even when he needed to be. He was holding a little notebook, his pen pressed against it. "This is totally wacked, dude! Do you have, like, a diet tip or something?"

"Excuse me?"

"The newsletter, man! We're getting thousands of hits a day, and a bunch of people are e-mailing, asking what happened to the lifestyle section. I need a diet tip!"

"Okay...how about, 'push away from the table'?" Matt offered.

Gilbert groaned beseechingly. "These ladies don't want to hear that! Pat!" he cried, as Pat came in behind them. "Pat, you've got a diet tip, right?"

"Do I *look* like I have a diet tip?" Pat asked. "Anyway, that's your problem, not mine. My problem is this stupid luncheon."

"What luncheon?" Matt asked.

Pat rolled her eyes. "Well, Matt, an *important* luncheon. Rebecca was in the middle of setting it up with the Dallas Women's League, and I can't find any of her files or notes!"

"We may have to cancel," Matt said. But Pat and Gilbert looked at him like he'd lost his mind.

"*Cancel* the Dallas Women's League luncheon?" Pat repeated, as if she perhaps hadn't heard him correctly. "Are you insane? You think Hispanics are the only vote we need to worry about? You think the women's vote isn't just as big? You think women voters *like* getting stood up by anyone, much less a *candidate*? What the hell is the matter with you, anyway?"

"Ah—"

"Matt!"

The sharp edge in Tom's voice startled Matt; he leaned backward, looked down the hallway to where Tom was standing with his hands on his hips. "Hey, Tom. What's up?"

"If you will join me in my office, I'll tell you exactly what's up." Tom pivoted, disappearing into the office.

Matt looked at Pat and Gilbert. They returned his look with twin glares. "What's his problem?" he asked.

"What do you think, Einstein?" Pat said. "The same problem we all have."

Matt felt a little like he was twelve again, summoned into his father's office for some misdeed. He stuffed his hands into his pockets and strolled back to Tom's office. As he entered, Tom rolled in his chair, lifted his leg to kick the door shut, and rolled back. "You've really fucked this up, you know it?" he asked, his voice cold as ice as he glared at Matt over tented fingers.

"What?"

"You couldn't keep your hands off her ass until after November, could you? You just had to go and run her off!"

Okay, the picture was getting a little clearer. "Shut up, Tom. What's the problem, anyway?"

"You want to know the problem? I'll tell you the problem. Since she quit, the whole goddamn campaign is going in the toilet!"

"Oh, God—Tom," Matt said, straining for patience, "you've got three people completely committed to you. Are you going to try and tell me that we can't do what needs to be done along with the public relations firm and the party folks? You think Rebecca was your key to the election?"

Tom laughed derisively and shook his head. "You think campaign contributions just fall from the sky? I'm not talking about the campaign anyway. I am talking about the bunker buster fund-raiser we were planning. Do you have even the *slightest* idea how much I stand to lose? How much in dollars? Hell, her father alone could have brought in fifty grand! She was lining up every major player in this state, and you had to go and ruin all that with your dick."

"Watch it, Tom," Matt said hotly.

"You watch it, Parrish. Rebecca is worth bucks to me. *Big* bucks. And now people are calling here, wanting to talk to Rebecca, and she's not here. Know what else? She won't take the calls at her house. I am about to lose the biggest infusion of cash this campaign has seen yet, and if you think for one minute that we don't need it, think again. We're going negative, and *that*, my friend, requires some serious scratch!"

"You're not serious," Matt said angrily. "You're going to put attack ads out? Why can't you let your record speak for itself? Why do you need to drag Harbaugh through the mud? You've got enough of a track record and you've been touting that damn superhighway as the answer to everyone's prayers!"

"Get real. Do you think anyone gives a shit about my track record? The only thing they care about is who I've *fucked*, which is why *I* kept my hands *off* Rebecca!"

The thought of Tom's hands anywhere on Rebecca made Matt sick with revulsion, and Matt felt one step away from putting a fist down Tom's throat.

"Now look, I need this gala deal. I need Rebecca. Once it's over, you can have her, but right now, I need her and her dad!"

Matt's revulsion was growing. "She's not a thing, Tom."

"Until November third, you're all things to me," he retorted, sweeping his arm in the general direction of the offices. "And before you get on your soapbox, just remember—you're gonna be thinking the same damn thing when you run for DA. Think you can do it better? Well try doing it without money! And if you think anyone in the party is going to give you one red cent, then you better think of a way to fix this crap. So are you going to fix it?"

"I don't know if I can," Matt answered truthfully.

"You damn sure better try."

Matt had to get out of there or kill the next lt. governor. He turned around and yanked the door open.

"Where are you going?" Tom barked.

"Where the hell do you think? To talk to Rebecca!" he shouted over his shoulder.

CHAPTER TWENTY-FIVE

If I've done anything I'm sorry for, I'm willing to be forgiven...

EDWARD N. WESTCOTT

Thursday morning, Matt called the office and asked Harold to reschedule his appointments, as something personal and pressing had come up.

"But, Mr. Parrish," Harold said urgently. "You have that motion to compel in front of Gambofini on the Rosenberg case. If you miss that—"

"Harold. Please reschedule," he said calmly, knowing full well that Harold was right—his ass was grass as far as Gambofini was concerned, having been told no less than two dozen times that if he screwed up again, he'd personally work to see Matt disbarred. Of course, Gambofini threatened that each time Matt was before him, so he wasn't really too worried, at least not this time. He was more worried about Ben, actually, because Ben usually made good on his threats to kick his ass.

Nevertheless, Matt had more important matters on hand at the moment. He changed into a pair of Levi's, a white cotton button down, and his black ostrich boots that matched his belt, put his cell and pager on his dresser, and left his penthouse. In the garage, he put the top down on his Jag and shoved some Maui Jims on his face. It was a gorgeous day, and if he was going to go search the Highland Lakes area for one royally pissed off Miss Texas just so she could hand his head to him on a platter, he was at least going to enjoy the drive out.

When the phone rang, Rebecca was wearing a cut-off T-shirt and jean shorts over a two piece bathing suit, and had just fought off a horde of bees she had inadvertently discovered in the old barn she had decided to convert into an art studio…depending on how things looked once she got all the junk out.

"Hello?" she said breathlessly, using the cordless handset to swat at one last attacking bee as she backed out of the barn.

"Bec? What's the matter?"

"Nothing, Dad," she grunted, swatting one last time as pulled the barn door shut. "Just cleaning out the barn. So what's up?"

"Does something have to be up for me to talk to my daughter?"

Honestly, that's what she preferred, and in general, didn't most people have a purpose when they phoned? "Of course not. But you usually don't call just to discuss the weather."

"So have you heard from your mom?" he asked, and Rebecca suppressed a groan. "Not in a couple of weeks. She was talking about going to Chicago to work on a project for the Heart Association fund-raising drive. Maybe she went."

Dad made a sound of disapproval. "She's been really busy," Rebecca added in her mom's defense.

"Oh, yeah? Well, she wasn't too busy to box up the flowers I sent her and return them to me dead."

Rebecca lifted her brows in surprise. "She *did* that?" she asked, incredulous.

Dad muttered something she couldn't quite catch, and then, "Where's Grayson?"

"He's with Jo Lynn."

"Figures. By the way, I heard from your ex today."

That got her attention. Why would Bud call Dad? *She* had heard from her ex three days ago, and that was enough to last a lifetime. "You're weak, Rebecca," he'd offered out of nowhere. "You quit in the middle of Tom's campaign like a kid and left him in a bind. What the hell is the matter with you?"

"Why in the hell did he call you?" she asked, perturbed.

"To tell me that you quit what's-his-name's campaign. Right in the middle of it, he said. Just up and left them in a bind. Is that true?"

"Sort of," she said slowly. "So what did you say?"

"I told him to mind his own goddamn business. What do you think I said? I don't know who the hell he thinks he is, but he's got some balls to call *me* up and say anything about *you*, that's for damn sure!"

With a smile, Rebecca sank onto the broad stump of an oak that had been chopped down years ago. "Thanks, Dad."

"Don't thank me—I've always hated that bastard. Why'd you quit, anyway?"

She sighed. "I wasn't working in the direction that the, ah…the senior member of the team wanted to go. And it became apparent that we didn't see eye to eye, so I thought it was best if I just took what I had learned and moved on."

Dad didn't say anything for a moment. "Did you leave them in a bind?"

"Well…a little one, I guess. I was planning a big fund-raising event—"

"Bud mentioned it. A statewide affair with entertainment and lots of big names, right?"

"Yes," she said, perplexed that Bud was calling Dad with all this information. "What is Bud's problem, anyway?"

"I don't know. Said this guy is a good friend of his. Sounded like the guy was pressuring him and I guess Bud's embarrassed. He ought to be embarrassed he's a Democrat. Nevertheless, Rebecca, did I not teach you anything?" he asked. "Like not giving up when you've given someone your word? Your word is your bond, and if you don't honor it, what have you got?"

God, she was tired of her father. He was so quick to judge, so quick to criticize, without even knowing what had happened. Rebecca looked up at the tops of the blackjack oaks, realized she had finally reached the point where she just didn't want to hear it anymore and was finally willing to say so. "Dad? Could you, just once, call and ask how I am doing without lecturing me? I honor my word. I did what I could for Tom, but in the end, it wasn't what they needed—"

"Well, according to Buddy-boy, your pal needed the fund-raiser. Now listen, if you told him you were going to do this thing, then you need to do this thing. You can't get a job if you're a quitter. And besides, I told you to call me the next time you had something to show. Wasn't I getting an invitation?"

Her pulse was pounding now. She gritted her teeth, thought about all the times Robin had bitched about the old man. She was beginning to see things Robin's way. "I hadn't planned on it," she said evenly.

"What?" he asked, clearly surprised. "Why wouldn't I get an invitation?"

"Because all you have done is criticize my involvement to begin with."

"That's not true!"

"And now that Bud Reynolds has called you up after what, two *years*, to tell you I am not behaving like he wants me to behave, you have turned around and called to lecture me. You have called up without knowing the facts to tell me what I'm doing wrong again. Well, thanks, Dad. Thanks for your expert advice on every little thing in my life. Now that you've delivered it, we can hang up. Good-bye!" she said, and clicked off the phone. And dropped it on the grass like it was on fire.

She was getting pretty ballsy with this hang-up business—now her father? She sat there staring at the phone, waiting for it to ring again, waiting for Dad to build up a head of steam and fry her right to the tree stump.

But the phone didn't ring.

Very carefully, Rebecca leaned over, picked it up with two fingers, then hurried toward the house, almost throwing it on the back porch in her haste to get away from it. She stood there a moment longer, certain it would ring, and could picture Dad, his face red with rage—no way could he live without having the last word!

But the damn thing didn't ring, which was entirely too spooky…and also liberating when she thought about it, and she did a small victory pump for the real Rebecca shining through.

Right. But just in case he did call back…Rebecca swiped up a beach towel from the padded wicker furniture, and stomped off with her new bad self toward the river to join Grayson and Jo Lynn.

Those two had apparently given up the frog hunt, for they were sitting, side by side, on the edge of the dock, their legs swinging freely beneath them above the river. "Mind if I join you?" Rebecca asked as she took a seat next to Grayson.

"How's that barn coming?" Jo Lynn asked.

"Full of bees and lots of junk. It's going to take some work."

"Ah, well. Can't sit around, so you might as well work. We were just going up for ice cream. You want some?" she asked as Grayson put on his sandals.

"No, thanks I'm going in for a swim. Jo Lynn? If the phone rings, don't answer it, okay?"

Jo Lynn looked at her curiously, but when Rebecca gave her a halfhearted shrug, she smiled. "Okay," she said, and took Grayson's hand, led him up the grassy slope to the house.

Matt stopped at Sam's Corner Grocery in Ruby Falls, bought a pack of gum and two huge bouquets of roses, which he pieced together as one. He asked the checker (a big girl who, in her smock, reminded him of a Red Delicious apple), if she knew Rebecca Lear. "Sweetie, *everyone* knows Rebecca Lear," she said.

"Miss Texas, right?" he asked as he handed her a fiver for his purchase.

"Huh?" she asked, squinting up at him beneath a mound of teased hair.

"She was Miss Texas."

The woman, whose name tag read Dinah, gasped, slapped a hand over her mouth as her eyes grew wide. "She was?" she squealed, and immediately whirled around to the only other checker in the store. "Did you hear that, Karen? Rebecca Lear—you know, that real pretty girl that lives down on the old Peckinpaugh ranch? She was Miss Texas!"

"Miss *Texas*?" Karen cried. "You're kidding!"

Both women looked at Matt to see if he was kidding. "I'm not," he quickly assured them.

"How come she never told us?" Karen demanded of him.

"I, ah...I don't know why she didn't. I thought that's what you meant when you said everyone knew her."

"Oh, no, I meant because of the dogs," Dinah said as she handed him his change and receipt.

"Old man Abbot just shoots them strays, you know that?" Karen said while she used her little finger as a toothpick.

"Oh, he does not!" Dinah exclaimed.

"Does too." Karen insisted.

"If you could just point me toward her house?" Matt asked.

Dinah spared him a glance—"Straight down fourteen oh six, big stone fence and wrought iron gate right after the cemetery"—before beginning to argue Karen's source of information on old man Abbot.

Matt ducked out, found the cemetery and old stone fence easy enough, the old wrought iron gate, too, just like

Dinah had said. But Dinah hadn't mentioned the flying pig on top of one of the stone gate pillars. It looked fairly new. And big. And not very Rebecca-ish.

Fortunately, the gate was open, so Matt turned onto the narrow gravel road, drove slowly through a thicket of trees, mesquite, and cactus, until he rounded a bend and saw an old ranch house—limestone, one story, lots of crankcase windows, and a big wraparound porch. Along the front railings were a smattering of azalea bushes, still blooming even thought it was late in the season. In two old cast iron kettles, several antique rosebushes were blooming white and pink. On one end of the porch was an old wooden porch swing, the white paint chipping and peeling, and on the other end, tasteful and expensive wicker furniture.

The house looked very charming. Just like its owner.

Matt pulled up, killed the motor, gathered the roses, and climbed out of the Jag, at which point he noticed that what looked like dirt and mulch between the azaleas were actually lumps of dogs, three in all, who were now rising to their feet to greet him in true dog fashion—by charging forward. A big, mean-looking, one-eyed yellow dog charged the hardest at him, fangs bared and fur standing. Matt thought he was going to have to dive headfirst into his car for safety, but the dog ran smack into the front fender, stumbled backward a bit, then sat. And that, apparently, ended his desire for a manwich.

The other two dogs, however, one black, one red brindle, had better navigational skills than Old Yeller and raced around their stunned compatriot, barking fiercely. Matt put one hand down, fumbled with the roses, and looked at the porch. "Hey, hey! Come on, Frank! Come on, Bean! Tater and Tot, which ones are you?" he asked, his voice friendly and light. It worked. The dogs instantly started wagging their tales, sniffing at his crotch and shoes, and were joined by a little three-legged dog that came racing around the corner of the house. Even the yellow one found his bearings again and came wandering over to have a good sniff.

"Thrilled to make your acquaintance," Matt said to the dogs, and once he was assured no one was going to bite him, he walked up onto the porch, ducking under a wind chime made from old forks and spoons to knock on the door. The dogs all stood behind him, tails wagging, as if they had accompanied him all the way from Austin.

Hearing footsteps and muffled voices, Matt saw a figure behind the opaque glass of the door and steeled himself, adjusting the roses in his arm. But when the door was opened, it was not Rebecca. For a split second, Matt thought he had the wrong house...until he remembered meeting the older woman at the bingo bash. "Ah...hi. I think we met at the Masters fund-raiser—"

"I remember. Matt, right?"

"Right. I'm sorry, I don't—"

"Jo Lynn."

"Jo Lynn, of course," he said. "I was looking for Rebecca."

"MATT!" Grayson shrieked from somewhere in the house, and Matt heard the sound of small feet running across wood floors. "MATT!" he shrieked again as he came skidding into the foyer behind Jo Lynn.

"Hey, pal!" Matt said, grinning down at an anxious little face smeared with chocolate ice cream, surprised by how glad he was to see the boy.

Judging by the way Grayson roughly pushed in front of Jo Lynn, he was pretty glad to see Matt, too, and clasped his hands, stared at him almost pleadingly. "Are you coming back?" he asked breathlessly. "Me and Jo Lynn looked for frogs but we didn't find any. Can we go frog hunting? Are you going to stay here?"

Matt smiled uneasily at Jo Lynn, who was now eyeballing him with a very curious expression, and he quickly squatted down to talk to Gray. "Dude. You can't hunt for frogs in the heat of the day! You have to wait until it cools off. That's when they come out to have a look around."

"Okay. Can we hunt when it cools off?"

"Maybe." Provided his mother didn't send his body floating down the river or hang it from the cottonwood he had seen towering above the house in back. We'll see."

"Want some ice cream?" Gray continued breathlessly, and put his sticky hand on Matt's, tugging him inside.

"Uh...not just now, okay?" he said, standing, but Grayson would not let go of his hand. "I need to speak to your mom first."

"She's down at the river," Jo Lynn said, now standing back to let him enter. "I can send Grayson down."

"Actually, would it be all right if I walked down?" Matt asked. If there was going to be another scene, he preferred Grayson not witness it this time, having recognized, of course, that that was the second most reprehensible thing he'd ever done in his life.

Jo Lynn looked over her shoulder, toward another row of big picture windows on the opposite end of a great room, through which Matt could see a stretch of glimmering river. "I guess that'd be okay," she said after a moment. "Come on in."

Matt stepped inside—or rather, was pulled in by Grayson, who still had a fierce clamp on his hand, and along with the four dogs, moved into the cool interior. He was standing a few steps above a sunken great room, where overstuffed couches and armchairs graced the wooden floor and large woven rug. A massive fireplace was on one wall, and from either side of the room, long corridors shot off in different directions. At the opposite end of where he was standing was a rustic dining table. A bar separated the great room from what he supposed was the kitchen area, given the ice cream container and two bowls there.

It was a lovely room, warm and inviting, right out of the pages of *Southern Living*. But Matt couldn't help noticing, as Grayson pulled him along to follow Jo Lynn (the dogs, too, naturally), that the books on the floor-to-ceiling shelves on either side of the fireplace were arranged by color and height.

That wasn't all. The magazines on the large pine coffee table were fanned out at perfect one-inch intervals, just like a showroom. In the large, spacious kitchen, he could see a cupboard with dish towels stacked neatly by color and folded identically so that they were all of uniform size. Dishes, cups, even salt and pepper shakers were also perfectly placed according to size and color. The stainless steel appliances were gleaming, as if they had never been touched. The wood floor was spotless. It was as if some deranged Williams-Sonoma floor crew had attacked this kitchen.

"She's down there on the dock," Jo Lynn said, pointing through the kitchen window. "Want me to hold those?" she asked, pointing at his enormous bouquet.

"No thanks."

"Can I go?" Grayson asked, still at his side, still clutching his hand.

"Tell you what, Gray. Let me talk to your mom for a few minutes, and then you and I will talk. Okay?"

"But what if you don't come back?" he asked, his little fingers squeezing tighter.

"Are you kidding? Of course I'm coming back. I promise, kid. So let go, okay? I promise I'll come back."

Grayson didn't look as if he appreciated Matt's promise all that much, and Matt couldn't blame him, given what the little guy had seen and heard from him. But Jo Lynn seemed to understand that this was important, and put a hand on the kid's shoulder, reminded him of his ice cream, and he reluctantly let go. "Just right on out there," she said.

Matt stepped through a screen door onto the back porch. He continued on with his canine honor guard, down the steps to the grassy lawn below, past a stone barbecue pit beneath live oaks, past the padded lounge chairs beneath the willow tree, and onward, to the dock, which ended in a big square where boats could be tied around the sides. On the square end of the dock, three big white Adirondack chairs sat facing the river. Strung between the four corners were Chinese lanterns and tiki torches. Giant potted ferns and a small cabinet gave the dock a little class.

It was a perfect place for a beautiful alien to land. Speaking of beautiful aliens, where was she?

Not on the dock, as Jo Lynn had suggested. Matt stopped at the edge of the dock; his helpful companions all lay down in the shade of a cottonwood, their tongues hanging out as if they had run a marathon. Matt looked downriver, saw nothing, not a person or even a boat. He turned, noticed an old barn or shed, thought it was possible she was doing something in there, and started in that direction.

Only the door to the barn was shut tight, the windows were caked with dirt so he couldn't see inside. It looked like it hadn't been used in years, so Matt circled around the other side of it just to be sure she wasn't back there planting watermelons or building a do-it-yourself doghouse.

As he picked his way around the backside of the barn, he caught sight of her...and stopped dead in his tracks.

She had been swimming, that was why he hadn't seen her. She'd climbed up on the dock, where she was shaking the water from her ears. Standing there, one slender leg slung out, her head tilted to the side, a towel hung from her hand and her long black hair streaked in soft, thick waves down her back. She was wearing a two-piece bathing suit, one that covered just enough and at the same time left just enough to his exploding imagination. Matt was so entranced by the vision that he did not realize he was moving, did not realize he was groping his way around the side of the barn toward her until one of the dogs suddenly barked. At which point, the vision of beauty before him looked over her shoulder and shrieked bloody murder.

CHAPTER TWENTY-SIX

Friends will respect your personal boundaries. Lovers will try to make your boundaries their own...

FRIENDS AND LOVERS AND HOW TO TELL THE DIFFERENCE

Naturally, Rebecca's first thought was that a stranger was spying on her. But in the next instant she realized it was Matt and a huge bouquet of roses sneaking around the old barn, and her brief, heart-stopping fear turned to nuclear fury.

In fact, her fury was so nuclear, she could hardly get her clothes on, and was hopping around the dock on one leg like a crazy loon as she tried to stuff the other leg into her shorts without tumbling right back into the river. All the while, Matt was striding toward her, waving his hand and the flowers, saying something she couldn't hear because she was so desperate to clothe herself.

The moment he stepped onto the dock (with her traitor dogs behind him, howdoyoudo), she yelled, "Don't you dare come near me!" And proceeded to get tangled up in the T-shirt she was so frantically trying to pull over her head.

"Rebecca, please just give me a minute!" she heard him say as she managed to get her head through.

With one arm caught in the fabric, she pointed with her free arm. "Stop right there!"

"I'm sorry I frightened you," he said, holding out the roses as some sort of peace offering. "Really. I was looking for you—"

"I don't care," she snapped as she managed to punch her arm free of the T-shirt, pull it down, then dig her hair out of the neck. "You can turn right around and crawl back to the rock you've been living under."

"Okay, I will. Just let me just say a couple of things," he tried again, and stood there, holding the flowers upside down now, looking so goddamn good and completely repentant.

But no, oh *nonono*—he had sorely underestimated the strength of her fury, and her mouth was moving before she could think. "You want to *say* a couple of things?" she seethed. "Like you haven't already said enough? What did you forget? Between I'm a bad mother and I'm trying to stab you in the back, what could there possibly be left to say?" Just speaking those transgressions aloud infuriated her even more, and without really knowing what she was doing, Rebecca gave in to her furious anger as she abruptly picked up the soda can Jo Lynn or Grayson had left behind and threw it at him.

Matt easily ducked it, but looked at her like she was deranged. She threw the core of Grayson's apple at him before he could say a single, solitary word. "Hey!" he shouted as the core bounced off his boot, which caused Frank to rise from lounging in the shade and trot over and have a look.

"Get out!" she shouted, madly looking around for something else to throw. "I told you I never wanted to see you again, and believe me, I've heard everything I ever want to hear from you, you…you—"

"Go ahead and say it, because whatever it is, I deserve it and then some," he offered.

"Dickhead!" she obliged him.

"Ouch," Matt said with a wince. "Good one. I was sort of hoping for your run-of-the-mill asshole, but okay. So now that you've got that off your chest, may I please try and apologize?" he asked, holding up the flowers again.

"Don't you dare make light of it!"

"I'm not, baby, I swear I'm not. I'm just trying—"

"You don't get it, Matt! I don't want to hear your apology," Rebecca said. "I don't want anything to do with you. I don't want your constant judgment, or your bizarre paranoia, or the arrogance you take everywhere you go."

"All right. Okay," he said, dragging a hand through his hair as he helplessly looked around the dock. "You're so right, Rebecca. I've been very arrogant. I feel a hundred times worse, so will you please let me talk?"

"No, no, *no*. You are such an asshole. "

"Wait just a minute," Matt said, putting one hand on his waist. "A dickhead *and* an asshole? I mean, I was wrong and all that, but aren't you sort of stretching it a little?"

Arrogant, impudent backwater asshole—Rebecca heaved a cheap synthetic rubber thong at him, which floated close enough to hit him in the chest before wafting down to the ground. Matt looked down at her thong, then slowly lifted his head with a look that made her heart skip a beat. "That's not helping,"he said low, "so stop it. I am trying to tell you something."

"I told you, I don't want to hear it," she said, and picked up the other thong. Matt instantly pointed a long and menacing bouquet at her. "If you throw that, you better be prepared for the consequences, missy!"

"*Missy?*" She couldn't help herself; she gave a shout of maniacal laughter. "What are you going to do, throw me in the river?"

"Of course I'm not going to throw you in the river."

"Then what? Remind me of how empty I am?" she said, and instantly caught a sob in her throat that surprised the hell out of her— surprised her so much that she lost track of what she was saying and put a hand to her throat, swallowing that lousy sob down as she stumbled back a step. It took a moment before she could look at him again, and when she did, she could see, even across the distance between them, the remorseful sorrow in his gray eyes, and quickly closed her eyes before she let his remorse seep in, desperately reminding herself that she didn't want his stinking apology. She was done with him! She was *done.*

"That," he said hoarsely, "was a horrible, inexcusable thing for me to have said. And even more importantly, it was a lie. I have no excuse, other than to say I was really angry that afternoon, and I...unfortunately, I took it out on you."

"That's not exactly news," she said miserably, looking down at the thong she still clutched in her hand. "Do you always take your anger out on others?"

He shook his head, looked at the flowers for a moment. "No. But I guess I'm like most losers in that regard—I didn't take my anger out on someone I didn't care about, someone like Tom. I took it out on someone who really matters to me. I'm sorry, Rebecca. More than I can say. I was so...*wrong.*"

Even though she could hear the contrition in his voice, she couldn't let it be that easily tucked away. "Give me a break," she said, waving the thong dismissively at him. "You don't care about me. You care about your career and how you come off to the world. And if you and I get along in the meantime, that's great, another notch in your bedpost. You're just like all the rest."

"Hey, what I did was wrong, and you have every right to be angry, but I'd appreciate it if you didn't lump me in with all the rest of the sorry dogs you've known."

"Why shouldn't I? You act just like all of the sorry dogs I've known!"

He pressed his lips together, then blew out a hot breath. "Yeah, well, while we're at it, you can act like a stuck-up beauty queen. One minute you leave me with a promise, and the next moment I'm twisting in the wind."

"That may be your perception, but I never said it was anything more than what it was—a little fun."

"A little fun?" he all but choked. "I felt something more than a little fun when I looked at you and when I kissed you, Rebecca. You did, too."

"I didn't."

His gaze narrowed. He shook his head. "Christ, you know I love you, but you're too chickenshit to admit that maybe you feel something, too. You're too afraid to let your-self just be—"

He struck a nerve in her so raw that she reacted without thinking and hurled the other thong at him.

Matt dodged it, lowered his head. "That does it," he said, and started toward her, gripping the bouquet like a weapon.

Rebecca instantly backed up, bumping into Adirondack chairs. He came striding forward while her worthless mutts rested in the shade, watching complacently instead of protecting her. She tried to dodge him, but he was too quick for her; his fingers closed around her wrist. She tried to wrench free, knocking the bouquet of roses from his hand; they scattered across the dock, some falling to the river below as she struggled to free her arm. But Matt pulled her roughly into his chest, his arms circled around her like a vise, and his mouth crushed down on hers, kissing her with as much fury as she felt, his tongue sweeping deep inside as he curled his fist into her wet hair to hold her head back so that he *could* kiss her like that, kiss her so she couldn't breathe, kiss her until she couldn't feel anything but him, his body hard against hers, his arms locking her to him, his lips brutally soft, and the tendrils of the emotion in his words twining around her heart, holding it captive.

She had never been kissed with such fierce passion, and Rebecca melted, just like in the movies, right into his arms, clinging to him, and if she could have crawled inside him, she would have. Her hands sought his face, his shoulders, his arms, the broad sweep of his chest. She could feel him hard and lean all the way down to her toes, and she remembered, oh God, she remembered that night on his couch, remembered his mouth, his hands, all his painstaking, patient efforts to free her from the four-year curse, and felt the river of desire flowing through her again.

And when she thought she'd simply melt into a puddle on the dock, Matt lifted his head. His gray eyes were swimming with emotion. He traced the pad of his thumb over her bottom lip, kissed her tenderly once more. "You are going to get cleaned up, and I am going to spend some time with Grayson. And then we are all going to get a burger—you, me, Gray, Jo Lynn, the whole damn town of Ruby Falls if you want. Then I am going to teach Grayson how to be a boy and hunt some goddamn frogs. And *then*, Rebecca...you and I are going to talk. Not shout, not throw things, not compete. *Talk*. You and me. You know we have to do it."

Rebecca touched a finger to his lip. "What if I say no?"

"Then you'll just have to shoot me," he said, flashing that fabulous George Clooney grin, "because I won't take no for an answer."

"Okay," she said weakly. "Your gun or mine?"

Matt chuckled, wrapped her tightly in his arms for a long moment, hugging the living daylights out of her.

And Rebecca felt her neck go all prickly and warm.

Matt walked Rebecca back to the house, their arms looped around each other's waists, with a full coterie of dogs to flank them. They said good-bye to Jo Lynn, who had a knowing smile on her face. Probably because Matt was smiling like a madhouse idiot as she jumped on her golf cart and drove away. When she had disappeared into the woods, Matt followed Rebecca and Grayson inside, still smiling that fool's smile as Rebecca washed Grayson's hands and face.

"Why are you laughing, Mom?" Grayson asked, looking at her face, reaching up to touch the wet tail of hair falling over her shoulder. Matt had the incredible urge to touch it, too.

"I don't know, honey," she said, her smile broadening. "Okay, you're all clean and I'm going to grab a shower. Will you be all right with Matt?"

"Yes!" he shouted.

She laughed, tousled his hair, then looked shyly at Matt. "Okay?"

Was she kidding? "More than okay," he said, winking at his young partner in crime. "Come on, pal. Let's go out and see what those ugly dogs are up to."

"Come on!" Grayson cried, already pulling Matt outside. Reluctantly, Matt looked at Rebecca, who was still standing there, smiling like a silly little girl, a wistful expression in her eyes that stirred the man in him. But Grayson yanked hard on his hand, wanting his attention all to himself, and the two of them burst out onto the back porch, where the four dogs came to instant and rapt attention. Only then did Grayson let go of Matt so he could point out his best friends—Tater (his favorite); Tot, the three-legged beagle; Frank, the big brown dog with the John Wayne swagger; and last but not least, Bean. "Mom says he's not very smart," Grayson said. "Plus, he's blind in one eye. And he might not hear, either, but the doctor isn't sure because he's really dumb."

And Bean looked really dumb, poor bastard. "I know how he feels," Matt remarked, which drew a curious look from Grayson.

"Do you have a blind eye?" Grayson asked, letting go of Tater.

"In a manner of speaking," Matt said, to which Grayson screwed his face up with confusion. "The thing is," Matt said, motioning to the tables and chairs that were perfectly arranged, of course, at the end of the porch, "sometimes I get mad and say things I shouldn't. Like that night we were in the garage of the Four Seasons, and I was shouting at your mom," he said, taking a seat.

Grayson followed his lead, scooching up on one of the wicker seats until his feet were a half foot off the ground. He gave Matt his somber attention, was doing that little man thing, and Matt leaned forward, propped his elbows on his knees. "You ever run off at the mouth and wish you hadn't?" he asked earnestly.

"I dunno."

"Man, I have. I don't do it very often, but when I lose it, I definitely let it fly. Like that night—I wasn't very nice, and now I'm trying to make it up to your mom. You know, tell her how sorry I am."

Grayson nodded.

"I want to say I am sorry to you, too, pal. That wasn't cool, all that yelling."

"Mom cried."

The kid may as well have stuck a knife in Matt's gut. "I shouldn't have lost my temper," he said, shaking his head. "There's no excuse for that, ever."

"Okay," Grayson said somberly.

"But you know how it is, you just get some idea in your head and the next thing you know, you're thinking all kinds of crap that isn't right. And the thing is, I really *like* your mom, so it was *really* stupid. You know what I'm saying?"

"Uh-huh."

"I'm really sorry, Grayson."

"It's okay," Grayson said cheerfully.

"So I was thinking," Matt said, "that when she gets out of the shower, we'd all hang out together a little while, then go get a burger. You and me and your mom. After that, if it's okay with your mom, you and I can go hunt some frogs, because dude, you have to hunt frogs at *night*. And when we catch a couple—"

"*Yeah!*"

"—and put them in a box, then maybe you and the dogs can go to bed so I can talk to your mom and tell her how sorry I am, just like I'm telling you I'm sorry. What do you think'?"

"You could get Mom some ice cream," Grayson suggested. "She always smiles when she eats ice cream."

"Ice cream?" Matt asked, surprised. Most women he knew avoided ice cream like the plague, lest it go straight to their thighs. Rebecca said she never touched the stuff, and barely touched the cup he had bought her at Amy's that afternoon.

"Mom *really* likes it. She eats it every day. Sometimes twice. And she has tons of buckets of it. But you have to ask first."

"Wait—back up," Matt said, confused. "Your mom has tons of buckets of *ice cream?*"

"Come on, I'll show you," Grayson said, jumping up from his seat and running for the back door. Curious, Matt got up and followed him into the kitchen, where one of those big, industrial-size refrigerators dominated one wall. Using two hands, Grayson yanked open the freezer side of it.

Matt blinked.

Inside on half of that industrial fridge was container after container of ice cream. Gallons, half gallons, pints, ice cream bars, and ice cream cups. There was chocolate, vanilla, rocky road, butter pecan, banana…lots of flavors with funky names, like Making Whoopie Pie and Blue Lagoonba— every conceivable flavor a man could imagine…*but nothing else.* There was not a single frozen dinner, no meat, no vegetables, no ice even. Just ice cream. "Wait," Matt said, releasing his breath and finding his voice. "Where's the meat?"

"That one," Grayson said, pointing to a small chest freezer next to the dishwasher.

Astounded, Matt turned and looked at the freezer again. "I think you might have a good idea here, sport," he said, scratching his head as he gaped at the freezer, and wondered how in the hell someone as near perfect as Rebecca Lear could hide so much ice cream. In her house *and* in her body.

Which was one of the reasons he was looking at her so intently when she came walking out on the porch, wearing a blue-green slip of a dress that hugged her body. On her feet were matching sandals; her hair was brushed back into a soft, silky tail that fell down her back. She wore just a touch of turquoise jewelry, enough to bring out the pale blue of her eyes. Rebecca looked, as always, absolutely amazing.

Apparently, ice cream was all she was eating, judging by the way she picked at the monster burger he bought her at Sam's Corner Hamburger Hut (which was, as one might have guessed, right across the street from Sam's Corner Grocery and Sam's Corner Video). Matt and Rebecca sat across from each other, listening and laughing at Grayson's amazingly long and convoluted story of a Yu-Gi-Oh! card that he and Taylor had stolen back and forth, which apparently ended with a badly torn card and two kids in the preschool administrator's office.

At the end of Grayson's earnestly told tale, Rebecca looked sheepishly at Matt. "He's having some anger management issues," she confided in him.

"Anger management?" Matt snorted. "He's getting picked on and he's taking care of it, aren't you, Gray?"

"I'm going to pound his face in!" Grayson declared, to which Matt gave him a thumbs-up. "And then I'm going to get on the top of the school and jump on him, and then I'm going to kick him and put dog poop in his face, and—"

"Grayson," Rebecca said calmly. "Remember what we talked about—dog poop does not belong in anyone's face."

Okay, so maybe the kid needed to turn it down a notch, but the bottom line was, he was a boy, and boys figured out their problems with their fists. Grayson would grow out of it; all boys did. But anger management? Sounded like more mumbo-jumbo crap, and if there was one thing Matt wished for Rebecca, it was that she would get that stuff out of her lovely head.

They returned to Rebecca's lake house just as the sun was beginning to set, and Rebecca obliged Matt's request for a pail, a flashlight, and a barbeque fork (although she objected to the fork, but not as loudly as she objected to Matt's attempt to explain its purpose), and away they went, two guys out to do a little frog giggin'.

Rebecca stood on the back porch and watched them walking down the long stretch of lawn, the dogs trailing lazily behind, Grayson struggling with the pail he had insisted on carrying as he looked up at Matt with pure adoration.

She hadn't realized—at least not so clearly as in this moment—that a man like Matt was exactly what her son needed. She had thought he needed his father, but it was more than that—he needed a man he could look up to. That very basic and unfulfilled need was what made Grayson so angry with her when he came home from a visit with Bud.

He wanted a dad and he wanted his dad to be like Matt. And he was too young to understand why he couldn't have both a mom and a dad like he deserved. Rebecca could remember feeling that way, too. She'd been a little older, but the need for both parents had been as real to her as it was to Grayson now.

In Matt, he'd found a male figure to make up for the absence of a rotten father. That Matt didn't seem to mind, and in fact, seemed to *like* Grayson's company, touched her heart so thoroughly that her eyes were suddenly burning with gratitude.

Oh, man. Oh, *man*...she was in too deep, over her head. Grayson's infatuation with Matt could not possibly be a good idea. She wasn't part of Tom's campaign anymore and she feared setting her son up for more disappointment.

But would it be another disappointment? Was she making an assumption that she and Matt could not see each other, could not even be friends, really, after the things they had said to each other that night at the Four Seasons? If she believed they couldn't, then what did she make of that kiss on the dock? What about the electricity that had flowed between them, had *always* flowed between them? And did the man who had a reputation of having been with every woman around town spark that electricity in everyone, or was it hers alone? Was it possible she had fallen under his charming spell once again and was giving in too quick? Was she being played for a fool? Or was it possible that for once, she could trust her instincts? Was it even possible that she could, for perhaps the first time in her life, *act* on her instincts?

This was such difficult territory, such ominous caverns and valleys and peaks in her mind and heart that she had never before explored. Most of her adult life she'd been with the same man. In the last few years, she'd been with that man almost hating him, certainly resenting him, wishing things were different. Her days had been filled with regret, not hope. Was this hope?

She picked up a paperback and sat on the back porch, but her mind was racing; she was too full of doubtful questions and wishful thinking to read. Just a few days ago she had decided to eschew all the self-help stuff—the lifelines she had clung to in the last year. She had decided to go with her gut, whatever may come. And her gut had told her to stay as far away from Matt Parrish as she could get. Now she didn't know what to think; she couldn't seem to find her true north. All she knew was that this man, for whatever reason, lit a fire in her like no man had ever done before, and she really didn't know how to turn away from that. Or even if she should. Or even if she *could*.

Welcome to your life, Rebecca. Nothing is certain anymore.

CHAPTER TWENTY-SEVEN

I know nothing about sex because I was always married...

Zsa Zsa Gabor

When Matt and Grayson returned an hour or so later, Rebecca was still sitting on the back porch, still holding the book from which she had not read a single word, still conflicted by her emotions. It therefore took her a moment to notice that Matt's pants were rolled up to his knees, and that he was carrying his boots. His white shirt was splattered with mud, and Grayson and the dogs were soaking wet.

"Find any frogs?" she asked dryly, while hoping to high heaven they would not actually show her any gigged frogs.

"No," Grayson moaned, clearly disappointed. "They wouldn't come out."

"It didn't help that old Bean here was doing his own version of frog hunting," Matt said as he leaned up against the railing of the porch. "There's something seriously wrong with that dog." Rebecca laughed; Matt smiled. "So what have you been doing while we were watching Bean eat frogs?"

"Reading."

Matt looked at her book. "Must be riveting."

Rebecca glanced down, noticed that her book was upside down, and quickly put it aside. "Well!" she said brightly, gaining her feet and running her damp palms down the sides of her hips. "I know a little boy who needs a bath!"

"I know a bigger boy who could use one, too," Matt suggested. "I have a clean shirt in the car if you would let me borrow a shower."

As ridiculously juvenile as it was, the thought of him naked in her house sent a very warm and unexpected shiver up Rebecca's spine. "Absolutely!" she said. "Yes, sir. A shower. We've got plenty of those, huh, Gray?"

"We only have two, Mom," Grayson said. "The one next to my room and the one in your room."

Rebecca laughed—something like a horse's whinny—and grabbed Grayson's shoulders. "That's right. Just two. Okay, come on, I'll show you where," she said, and pushed her son into the house with Matt following.

They walked down the long hallway to her room, but when they crossed the threshold of her inner sanctum, Grayson squirmed out of her grip and ran to the bath. "Nice," Matt said, looking around at the pale blue walls, the rustic quilt that covered her bed, and the whitewashed furniture. "A person could really hide out here for a few days."

Rebecca shot him a look; he smiled pleasantly. Rebecca walked (or staggered, she wasn't really sure) into the master bath.

"Thanks," he said, looking at the extra-large shower, which Rebecca remembered a moment too late, had been built specifically for *two* people. "I appreciate it."

"Towels are there. Shampoo, soap, that sort of thing in the shower."

"Great."

She tapped Grayson on the shoulder. "Come on, kiddo, we need to get that mud off you." She walked out of the bath, thought she could feel Matt's eyes on her, and as Grayson went darting past her, she casually glanced over her shoulder. He was looking at her, all right, that deep intense gaze boring right through her. "Umm anything you need?" she asked.

A curious smile came over Matt's face. "I think all that I need is right here."

She really had to stop reading something into every little statement he made. But even just standing there her skin was doing that prickly thing. She ushered Grayson out of her room and across the house to his bath.

While she helped him bathe and get the big clump of mud out of his hair, she barely heard his chatter, something to do with the habits of frogs. Her mind was filled with the image of Matt standing in her bathroom, looking at her in a way that made her feel so tingly.

When Grayson finished his bath, she helped him dress in his favorite pajamas, saw him to bed, and was prepared to read to him, but Grayson wasn't interested.

"You don't want a story?" she asked, surprised.

"No, because I went frog hunting and now it's your turn."

"My turn for what?"

"I dunno," he said, settling back against the pillow. "Maybe ice cream, because you really like ice cream."

Rebecca laughed. "I *do* like ice cream," she said, and kissed Grayson good night, left him to dream about frogs while Tater dozed on the floor next to his bed.

As she walked down the hall to the great room, she could hear Matt in the kitchen. He had dressed in a fresh polo shirt, had wiped the mud off his jeans pretty well, and was padding barefoot around the old oak floors of her kitchen. Frank, Bean, and Tot were with him, all lounging, their heads between their paws, their snouts pointed at empty dog bowls.

Matt looked up and smiled as Rebecca walked in. "Your dogs are hungry."

"They're con artists," Rebecca said, sliding onto a bar stool. "They've all been fed." Frank thumped his tail against the floor in acknowledgement of the truth.

"Is that right?" he asked, frowning down at the dogs. "They scammed me out of a couple of biscuits, then." He looked up at Rebecca as he reached into a bag of grapes. "I hope you don't mind, but I sort of invaded your pantry." He paused, held up a bottle of wine for her to see.

"I don't mind," she said, and in fact, thought it was kind of nice, particularly seeing as how he had some French cheeses arranged on a platter, and was now putting grapes around the cheese. "I had no idea you were a gourmet."

"A gourmet I'm not," he said with a laugh. "This is something my mom does. I have no culinary skills, but I copy well. Except," he said, frowning down at the platter, "there's something she always puts with it…"

"Just a wild guess, but maybe crackers?"

"Yes!" he said, snapping his fingers. "So you're the gourmet."

"As it happens, I have dabbled in the culinary arts. Enough to at least know that crackers go with cheese," she said. "I'll get them for you."

"Great. Will you bring them outside?" he asked as he stuffed the wine bottle under his arm and picked up the platter.

Rebecca fetched the crackers and followed him out onto the porch. He'd lit three citronella candles that she kept out back to keep the mosquitoes at bay. There were two wineglasses and a corkscrew, too. Matt put down the platter, took the crackers from her hand, and emptied some onto the platter. He stood back, looked critically at his efforts, and finally shrugged. "I don't know why, but it always looks a lot better when she does it," he confessed, and picked up the corkscrew and wine bottle.

"Do you see her often?" Rebecca asked.

"*Too* often," Matt said with a roll of his eyes. "My folks live in Dripping Springs, and my brothers and sister and I troop out for dinner every Sunday night if our schedules allow. My folks get a little testy if we don't make it. So what about you? See your parents much?"

Well, let's see…Dad's an ass and Mom avoids him like the plague, so no, we don't get together much, she thought, but said, "Not too often. Dad lives in New York most of the time, and Mom lives in California."

"Ah. Opposite ends of the country. I've been handled a couple of divorces like that," he said, as he pulled the cork. "Frankly, I was thinking you and I were going to end up like that," he said as he poured a glass of wine and handed it to her. "Opposite ends of the universe, I mean."

Rebecca sat in one of the padded wicker chairs. "You did?"

"Well, yeah," Matt responded matter-of-factly. "We've been going around and around, wouldn't you say?"

Rebecca's heart did a funny little skip. "Going around and around what?" she asked, forcing herself to take a sip of wine as Matt fell lightly into the seat next to her.

That made him laugh, as if they shared some little intimate joke, and he leaned over, put his hand on her fore-
arm. Involuntarily, her body flinched; how embarrassing
that even the smallest of his gestures could send a shock of
light through her.

"You're stiff as a board, Rebecca," he said softly. "Are
you afraid?"

*Afraid? Ha! Like I have something to be afraid of! Lord, no! I
am just...just what if he says he loves you again?* "Would you like
some cheese?" she asked abruptly, leaning forward so that
her arm escaped his scorching touch, and busied herself by
putting some cheese on a cracker. "Gouda!" she exclaimed,
feeling strangely nervous, and deathly afraid of any silence.
"I love Gouda, don't you? Once, when I was in France,
I found this little cheese shop, and I ordered two pounds
of it. But my French isn't very good—actually, I don't know
French at all, just a few words and phrases, but anyway, the
shopkeeper said he didn't have that much and he'd deliver
the cheese, which, if you think about it, is kind of a funny
thing to say, but anyway, when they brought the cheese
around, it was more like two wagonloads." She thrust the
cracker at him. "It was Gouda."

Matt's steady gaze did not waver as he respectfully put
the cracker down. "Rebecca—"

"It's good you had a clean shirt," she blathered as her
mind raced wildly.

Matt looked down at his clothing. "I always keep an extra
shirt in the car. You never know, right?"

"No. You always know," she said.

Matt glanced up. "What?"

Her heart began to sink, because she realized, as her gaze dropped to his shoulders, that his extra shirt was exactly the problem. "I *always* know," she said, still staring at his shirt. "I always know where I am going to be, without question. And the fact that you don't always know where you are going to be or who you are going to be with is just a little…a little…"

"Disconcerting?"

"Disconcerting."

"But why would that be disconcerting for you?" he asked.

"Because," she said, and put her glass down, "because I always know. At least I think I do, but honestly? When it comes to you, I don't know anything."

"I do," he said calmly.

"Great. I feel like a fifteen-year-old girl again, and wondering how I could have met the one man who really lights a fire in me, and he is the type to carry extra shirts in his car, and I am the type to never need an extra shirt."

"Really?" he asked, looking pleased. "I light your fire?"

Rebecca moaned and sank back against the wicker chair. "I've really, truly, lost my mind."

Matt laughed and playfully squeezed her knee. "It's okay, Rebecca—I don't think an extra shirt in the car is a statement about the way I live. And like you, I've lost my mind, because you really light my fire, too."

"Are you sure?" she asked uncertainly. "This isn't one of those conquest things?"

He smiled a little. "If this was one of those conquest things, as you put it, I wouldn't be doing this much talking."

That went shooting straight to the pit of her groin, and Rebecca smiled. She straightened up in her chair. "How do you know it's not an infatuation?"

Matt sighed wearily. "You're really a lot of work, girl, you know that? This is *real*, Rebecca. Believe me. Look, I know you probably have a hard time trusting because you must get a lot of fawning over you all the time, simply because you're so drop-dead gorgeous—"

"Oh!" She stared helplessly at the fan above her head. "Matt, sometimes I think you are about the smartest man I have ever met, and then you'll come out with some bone-headed comment like that."

"What'd I say?"

"The beautiful thing. Okay, so I won a beauty pageant way back there, but I'm not the same woman I was then, and I am really not so beautiful! I don't get fawning all the time, in fact, I never get fawning. In case you haven't noticed, Grayson and I aren't exactly whirling around with busy social calendars."

"What are you trying to say?"

"That I can't have flings. I have Grayson, and I have... this is going to sound stupid, but I have standards—"

"Like I don't?"

"You're the one with the shirts," she said, nodding at his polo.

He nodded thoughtfully, studying her face. "I also told you I love you," he said. "I really must have lost my mind, because I am sitting here, in the middle of a ridiculous conversation with you, like it means something, but every time I come near you, you freeze up like an ice cube! Why do I waste my breath? Why do I splay my heart open for you?"

Rebecca stood up. She thought of a billion retorts. So many that she couldn't manage to get even one out, and suddenly walked away from the little table and down the steps to the lawn, to where, she had no idea.

Matt was right behind her. "Uh-uh, no way—I'm not going to let you swim away this time," he said. "Stand and declare!"

"Okay, how's this? I'm very upset to learn that I'm the moron in this equation!"

"At least you're the gorgeous one—"

She stopped, whirled around to face him. "Do you think," she asked, stabbing him in the chest with the tip of her finger with each word, "that because I haven't jumped right into your bed then I must be frigid? Is that what you are trying to say?"

"No!" he said, grabbing her hand. "I mean you are scared stiff. Literally."

Rebecca sucked in a breath to tell him that was a lie, but thought the better of it (since it was true), and closed her mouth. They stood there under the moonlight, staring at each other, and all Rebecca could hear was the river running just a few yards away, running slowly, running away, just like she'd been doing from the moment she'd met Matt. "You would be, too," she admitted, and laid her forehead against his chest.

Matt put his arm around her. "Isn't it obvious that I adore you?" he asked. "Four Seasons debacle notwithstanding, of course. Do you know the last time I told a woman I loved her?"

"No."

"I was seven."

Rebecca laughed into his chest.

"And look at it—I came all the way out here to grovel at your feet for having made an ass of myself. And I stood there and let you throw stuff at me, and then I pretty much admitted I've got a thang for ya, baby. I was just sort of hoping you had one for me, too."

Rebecca laughed again, then lifted her gaze to Matt. "I do. I guess it's really hard to explain."

Matt put a hand to her face, cupping her chin. "Try me," he said, and he looked like he meant it. *Try me. Try anything.*

"Okay. For starters, I've never really been with…I mean, I've only been with one—"

"Oh, I get it," Matt said, nodding, and started to sway softly with her under the moonlight. "So you're not quite over him, is that it?"

That was so preposterous that Rebecca snorted loudly through her nose. "Oh my God, I'm going to have to get a blackboard and chart this out for you. *No*, Matt," she said, and with a loud sigh, lifted her gaze to the stars. "I was over him *years* ago and I've never been sorry that it's over. What I've been sorry for is that he left me without any emotion at all. Just up and announced he was leaving one day, like he was going to the store, like ending ten years of marriage was no more than stepping out for a six-pack. And even though I had stopped loving him eons before that, I couldn't understand how two people could have passed so much of their lives together and there be no emotion at all. Just nothing. Unless…" Unless she was nothing, she wasn't worth it.

Matt didn't say anything.

Rebecca's gaze blurred; she blinked. "And now," she said, smiling nervously, "I've met you, and I think you're pretty darn wonderful in spite of all the evidence to the contrary—"

"Careful—"

"—and I guess I'm more afraid than I realized."

"Not of me, I hope."

"Of not being worth the effort." And having voiced her fear aloud, she turned her face into his shoulder, ashamed.

"Ah, baby," Matt said, and wrapped both arms around her, rested his chin atop her head, and together they swayed in the cool night breeze, neither speaking for a long moment.

"That's not something you'd ever have to worry about with me, you know," he said quietly. "If you think about it, it's been pretty emotional between us from the beginning, wouldn't you say?"

Rebecca laughed into his shirt. "Definitely."

"I think this could be all you could ever want, Rebecca. But you might have to let the facade crumble away and just be who you are."

"I am."

Matt instantly shook his head. "Nope. The only time I have seen the real Rebecca was when you were drunk. And all it takes is one look at this house to know the level of hiding going on."

"What hiding?"

"Please, like you don't know what I'm talking about, you self-help guru," he said with a chuckle. "Let me put it this way—I've never known another living soul to alphabetize their canned goods."

"There is that," she sighed. "Did you notice the color coding, too?"

Matt laughed. "I think somewhere in that perfect house and in this perfect body is you, who is not so perfect, just dying to get out and breathe."

Astounded by his insight, Rebecca lifted her head and blinked up at him. "That's so *true!*" she admitted woefully. "But I don't know how. I've tried everything."

"Not everything," he said, and pulled away from her so that he could see into her eyes. "Not. *Everything,*" he muttered again, his eyes all but smoldering in the pale moonlight. "Let me help you, Rebecca," he murmured as he brushed a loose strand of hair from her forehead. "We'll peel some of those layers away and see what lies beneath." He leaned down so that his lips brushed against her ear. "I've seen you come, you know...and I think you can do better."

Just knock her over with a feather now, because she thought she could, too, and if he kept it up, she might do it right there. But Matt's hand was sliding down her bare arm, to her breast. Rebecca slowly drew her breath. "You know you can do better," he whispered. "*Say it.* Say, *I want to come...better.*"

The ground felt like it was shifting beneath her; a damp fog had swept into her head, and she was a slave to his touch. "I...I want to come *harder,*" she whispered. "*Matt.*"

He made a guttural sound deep in his throat, and in that dangerous fog, Matt took her hand, started for the house. Rebecca's heart was pounding. He mounted the porch steps in twos, walked right through the mess of dogs in the kitchen and down the long hallway to her room. Once there, he easily pushed her into the middle of the room, then shut the door and turned around, pressing his back against it and smiling devilishly. The bathroom light was still on; it was just enough light that she could see the hard glint in his eyes as his gaze casually roamed her figure.

"I'm going to help you really let go, if you think you can handle it."

Could she? She felt light-headed, almost dizzy. His way with words was intoxicating, and when she nodded, her head felt loose on her shoulders.

Matt smiled. "Then take off your shoes."

That was not exactly what she had expected. Rebecca looked down at her sandals and kicked them off her feet, across the room.

"Now let your hair down."

She thought about making a quip, but obediently pulled the band from her hair, letting it fall in silky waves to cover her shoulders.

The smile on Matt's lips faded; he just looked at her, taking her in, then said, "I want you to light some candles and place them on the nightstands. Then turn off that light."

"Yes, sir," she said with a playful salute, then padded over to her dresser, lit several candles, and moved them to the nightstands on either side of her bed. When she had turned off the bathroom light and returned to the middle of the room, Matt put a finger to his lips. "Don't talk," he said softly.

Rebecca smiled, mimicked zipping her lips, locking them, and tossing away the key.

Matt slowly pushed away from the door, his arms still folded, and walked toward her. "Are you wearing panties?"

"Of course!"

He quickly pressed a finger to her lips and shook his head. "Take them off."

She lifted a brow; Matt nodded. With a little laugh, Rebecca managed to push her panties down to midthigh without actually lifting her dress, then very delicately reached under her hem and pulled them down. As she moved to toss them aside, Matt caught her hand and took them from her.

"Now your bra."

"Ah—"

"No talking, Rebecca—you said you could handle it, didn't you?"

She nodded.

He smiled approvingly. "Take off your bra."

Her skin felt warm with anticipation; a little shaky, she reached behind her, fumbled over the fabric of her dress with the clasp of her bra for a few seconds while Matt gazed at her breasts, then slipped her arm out of one strap, and the other, and let her bra fall to the floor beneath her dress.

"Good," he said. With his gaze on hers, he lifted his hand and let his fingers dance across her nipple, tweaking it beneath the fabric of her dress. "Go ahead," he said low, watching her closely. "Take off your dress."

"My *dress?*" she asked, awakening from her pleasurable fog.

"Your dress. Are you afraid to expose yourself? To let me see you?" he asked as he lifted his hand, traced a soft line from one ear, across her jaw, to the other ear. "Aren't you just the least bit curious to know what she looks like?"

"Who?"

"The real Rebecca," he said. "Don't you want to know who I see when she will let me? How she appears to me?"

Rebecca pressed down the strange urge to hit him. Damn him. *Damn him!* How could he know so much about her that she didn't even know about herself? Yes, she wanted to know what she looked like to him, if he found her attractive, if he found her sexy, if he felt that goddamn fire racing through *his* veins. She wanted him to see her with his naked body, wanted to feel him, on her, in her, around her. Just thinking about it had made her wet; desire throbbed between her legs.

"Are you going to retreat into your fear?"

No, goddammit! "To hell with you," she said, and grabbing the hem, she lifted the summer dress over her head, tossed it aside, and stood there before him, naked as a jaybird. *Starkly* naked.

To her surprise, Matt did not act the least bit smug. In fact, he dropped her panties along with his jaw. And his breathing, she noticed, was getting heavier, like hers. That was empowering, and she unthinkingly stood a little straighter.

Matt drew a long, ragged breath. "Turn around."

Rebecca turned slowly, until she was facing him again. His expression was hard; he swallowed, muttered, "*Touch them.*" Rebecca hesitated; he lifted his gaze to her eyes. "If you can't even touch yourself, how will you feel good about me touching you?"

Self-conscious, but wanting this strangely erotic experience, Rebecca put her hands on her breasts, and the moment she saw the light in Matt's eye, her self-consciousness slipped away. She gripped herself firmly, squeezing the stiffened nipples between her fingers.

Matt swallowed again. "What are you thinking?"

"That I like the way you are looking at me."

"And I definitely like looking," he growled, and pulled the polo shirt over his head. He stood before her, admiring her naked body, and remarkably, Rebecca didn't feel ashamed. She felt alive. Without thinking, she reached out and touched his chest, felt the heat of his skin beneath her finger, heard him draw a ragged breath that sent a flame of pleasure licking her groin. She liked this.

Matt stepped closer, but didn't touch her in return, just leaned in so that his lips grazed her temple, and whispered, "*Lie down.*"

Rebecca slowly backed away from him, bumped into her bed. This was so different than anything she had ever experienced. Her senses were vibrant, wanting more, wanting it all. She sat on the edge of the bed and slowly leaned back until she was lying on it.

Matt walked over to the bed. He stood a moment, gazing down at her...and shook his head. "Not like *that*," he softly chided her, touching her knee. "Lie back like a woman who wants a man to make love to her."

Yes, yes...She scooted up until her head was on the pillows. She draped one arm above her head, let the other one fall open at her side, bent one knee over the other. "Yes," he breathed. "Now close your eyes."

Oooh, this was going to be good. Rebecca closed her eyes, heard Matt moving, heard the drawers of her bureau being opened. "Ah," he said, and she heard the drawer shut again, then a moment later, felt Matt's weight on the bed, then the silk of something across her eyes as he lifted her head. "A scarf," he said as he tied it behind her head. "Don't take it off, don't move. I don't want you to see anything. Just feel. I'll be right back."

"Wait!" she said anxiously.

"*Rebecca*," he whispered, his hand touching her cheek and floating to her neck. "I adore you, remember? I promise you are safe. Trust me," he murmured soothingly, stroking her arm. "And think about what you want me to do to you while I'm gone," he said as his fingers skimmed down her belly to the apex of her thighs.

And then he was gone.

Rebecca lay there, her eyes closed and wrapped in one of her scarves, listening to the trees rustling outside, thinking, as Matt had instructed, of what she wanted him to do to her. Delicious things she had always wondered about, imagined occasionally, but never dreamed she'd actually experience until now.

Just as quickly as he disappeared, Matt was back; she heard him enter the room, heard the door close softly behind him.

"What are you doing?" she asked, and jumped, gasping softly at the feel of his hand on her face.

"*Ssssh*," he said. "Just lie back and enjoy."

How could she not? She had been stripped clean of all her clothes, was lying, bare-ass, on the top of her bed. There was nothing left to hide, nothing left to do but let him have his way with her. The words sounded terribly decadent in her head, but they felt exhilarating, and she could actually feel her body quivering with anticipation.

She didn't have to wait long; the first flush of cold was on her lips and startled her so badly that she almost choked on it. But it slid off the side of her mouth, to her neck. And then it was again on her lips, and Rebecca opened her mouth, let it slide in, and smiled, spreading her arms wide on the bed. "*Rocky road,*" she said. "My *favorite.*"

Matt chuckled above her; and then his lips were on hers, sucking them clean of the ice cream. She waited for the next sweet assault; felt the cool river of it on her chest, followed by Matt's mouth and tongue, slowly licking up the rivulets that ran off either side of her, beneath her breasts. When his lips closed around her nipple, Rebecca involuntarily arched into him with a jolt; the resulting tremor reached all the way down to her sex.

He was gone again, and in the next moment, she felt another drizzle of ice cream from her breastbone to her belly button, followed by his tongue, lapping it up, following the trail and dipping into her navel as Rebecca lay there, panting, using her hands to search for him in the dark. She found his chest, his shoulders, trailed her hands down his body, gasping a little when she felt his naked hip.

"Don't stop, let yourself go," he said, and Rebecca reached around to the patch of wiry hair and his thick erection. Matt moved so that he was beside her, his mouth still on her belly somehow, nipping her, licking up the ice cream, sending another drizzle of delicious cold to simmer in the heat between her legs. Rebecca squealed with the sensation, squeezing him in her hand. His smooth skin felt like silk over marble; she could feel his erection pulsating in her hand, could feel the pearl of moisture at the very tip. And as Matt's tongue dipped between her legs, sucking up the ice cream and sending her into another surreal orbit, Rebecca lifted off the bed, groped in the darkness for his face.

"*Let me*," she said, gasping for air. "Let me try. Give me the ice cream."

Matt made a sound that was something like a groan and a laugh, but he took her hand, dipped her fingers into the ice cream canister.

Still blindfolded, Rebecca came up on her knees, scooped a little of it out, and reached into the dark, until she found him. Uncertain as to what part of his body she managed to hit, she leaned forward, ran her tongue along the creamed skin, delighting in the decadence of it, feeling the hard nub of his nipple on her tongue. She laughed, found the container, took more, slowly rubbed it on his body, smiling broadly when she heard Matt groan and felt him fall onto his back.

Something snapped in her then; she could feel the sticky sweetness everywhere, and wasn't certain if it was all ice cream or the swell of her own outrageous desire mixing with it, too. She groped about, her hand fluttering until it found the container, and she scooped more of the melting ice cream, rubbing it into her mouth, then more, which she rubbed on Matt, on his torso, his hips, his penis. She reached forward, her tongue seeking him, finding his erection, drawing it into her mouth and sucking the cream from his skin.

Matt was moving beneath her, restraining himself, she thought. She could feel him hardening in her mouth, could feel his testicles burgeoning in her hand, could taste cream and salt and his body.

And then suddenly he grabbed her. She had the sensation of flying. Rebecca gripped the scarf that covered her eyes, yanked it free to see Matt looming above her, a bead of perspiration on his brow, his eyes dark with lust.

"Are you ready to come better?" he asked her through gritted teeth. "Are you ready to know how it feels to be completely free?"

She laughed, licked her lips. "Ready."

Matt kissed her then, a desperate kiss of pure lust, then broke away, grabbed the ice cream container, and dipped more of it out, pushing some into her mouth with his fingers, then maniacally spreading it on her skin while Rebecca laughed. Then he surprised her by smoothly flipping her over onto her belly and spreading it on her hips, lapping it off one cheek, then the other. Giddy with desire, Rebecca reached down to feel the ice cream on her body, to feel the sticky wet sweat on them, and Matt's arm snaked around her waist, lifting her up as one thigh went between her legs.

His entry brought a shock of raw pleasure to her; she didn't breathe, didn't move as he slid, slow and easy into her, letting her body adjust to him. The sensation of it was startling, so cool and hot all at once, and so intoxicatingly provocative that Rebecca's breath came out in one long and heavy sigh. She instinctively lifted her hips; Matt slid in deeper, to her core, and Rebecca felt a surge of sensual gratification so deep she threw her head back against his shoulder, moaning.

Matt's hand slipped from her waist to her sex, and as he began to move inside her—slow and smooth at first— he toyed with her, teasing her toward the climax he had warned her about. Rebecca's breath was coming in spurts now; she was gulping for air, lost in the sexual bliss that surrounded them as he slid deeper and harder into her, pushing her toward release with his body and his fingers.

She reached the point where there was no going back, where she could feel it nearing the surface, and Matt said hoarsely, "*Let it go, Rebecca, let it go…*"

She let it go with an animal cry, her arms flailing, knocking the last of the ice cream onto the bed, her body shuddering from the sheer weight of her orgasm. Rebecca let go, came harder and better than she ever had in her life, falling headlong into pure rapture. And as it rained down all around her, she heard Matt cry out with his release, and thought, almost giddily, that he was louder than her.

Several moments passed before either one of them seemed to breathe; several more before they could untangle themselves from each other. They laughed later; laughed at the ice cream everywhere, laughed at the scarf, which Matt confessed had been a last-minute idea. They lay together on sticky sheets, their arms and legs entwined, Rebecca feeling so wonderfully vibrant and alive that she wanted to explore it all, to know everything there was to know. Matt obliged her, even while joking about the beast he had unleashed, and when they had at last exhausted themselves, they spoke low to each other about little things, and somewhere between talking and giggling at their toes, that blissful night passed into a blissful dream.

A dream that was brought to an abrupt end when the faint strains of "*Who lives in a pineapple under the sea?*" drifted into Rebecca's consciousness.

CHAPTER TWENTY-EIGHT

When you're in love it's the most glorious two and a half days of your life...

RICHARD LEWIS

At the sound of that familiar refrain, Rebecca's eyes flew open; beside her Matt shifted and groaned lightly in his sleep. Carefully, she moved his arm that was slung across her torso, slipped out from the sheets that were now impossibly sticky thanks to their adventure in ice cream, and darted into her bathroom, where she quickly cleaned up, pulled her hair up into a ponytail, and donned a silk robe.

When she stepped into the bedroom again, Matt was still out of it, sprawled across the bed facedown—it looked as if his cheek might actually be stuck to the pillow—the sheet covering him from the waist down. He did indeed possess a beautiful body, a magnificent form that she'd like to paint someday, but at the moment, she really didn't have time to admire him, and tiptoed out of the room.

Grayson was in the great room, sitting cross-legged in front of the television, glued to his favorite cartoon. Surrounding him were the dogs, who all clamored to their feet when they saw Rebecca, and all came charging forward, tails wagging.

"Hi, honey," she said, trying to wade through a pack of snorting and hungry snouts.

"Hi," Grayson mumbled.

"Did you sleep all right?" she asked, pushing Bean away.

"I dunno," he said, and inched closer to the television in a clear sign that Rebecca was interrupting.

She walked out onto the porch and fed the dogs, pouring whatever came out of the container into their bowls without any thought. Fat little Tater looked up at her in wonder, as if she were a doggie food angel sent from heaven. Rebecca laughed, squatted down to scratch him behind the ears. "That's right, Fatso. It's a new day," she said, and left the dogs scarfing their food to go back inside, where she took a seat directly behind Grayson.

*Speaking of new days...*there had to be a proper way to broach the subject of a man in Mommy's bedroom, but it wasn't exactly a situation Rebecca had anticipated dealing with anytime before he was eighteen. Now she wished she'd had the foresight to at least look it up in one of her parenting books. But she had to think of something quick, because Patrick and SpongeBob were grabbing balloons and floating away as the theme song played to an end. "*Hi, kids! We'll be right back!*"

Grayson stood up, started toward the kitchen.

"Ah...Gray, come here, will you?" she asked, reaching out for him.

He looked at her hand very suspiciously. "Why?"

"Because I want to give you a hug."

"Ah, *Mom*," he complained, but stumbled forward nonetheless, dragging his feet, until Rebecca could reach him and wrap him in a strong embrace.

"Mom! You smell like ice cream!" he complained, pushing away from her.

Rebecca grabbed his hand before he bolted. "Grayson, honey, listen...you know Matt and I are friends, right?"

He nodded.

"Well...sometimes, grown men and women like each other. You know...like mommies and daddies like each other."

"Okay," he said agreeably.

No, not okay. He was supposed to sit down, ask questions. Assuming, of course, a five-year-old could really ask those types of questions. "Well, Matt and I...Matt and I sort of...like each other."

"Did he spend the night last night?" he asked solemnly.

Rebecca reared back—honestly, how did he *do* that? "Umm...yes. Yes, he did, Grayson. Sometimes, when adults like each other, they like to spend the night. It's natural. It's what people do. Someday, you'll want to spend the night with someone, too."

"I want to spend the night with Taylor."

"Taylor?" she said, pushed slightly off task by that. "I thought you didn't like Taylor!"

"Maybe I'd like him if he spent the night. You didn't like Matt and he spent the night."

"That's a little different," she said. "How did you know Matt spent the night?"

"His car is outside," Grayson said. "Is he going to be here today?"

So here it was, the defining moment, the instance in which she might screw the kid up forever. Rebecca bit her lower lip as she looked at a stoic Grayson. What answer did he want? Did he want Matt to stay? To go? Was this when she made him understand what spending the night meant?

Grayson tugged on her hand.

"Okay. All right. Listen, Grayson, Matt is…well, he's—"

"Hey, pal, ask your mom while she's trying to figure out what I am if she has any coffee," Matt said from the kitchen, finishing up with a big yawn.

"Matt!" Grayson wrenched his hand free of Rebecca's. "Can you take me on the boat today?" he shouted as he ran to where Matt was standing.

"Tell you what," Matt said, and Rebecca realized that he was wearing only a pair of jeans, "find me some coffee before I slit my wrists, and if your mom says it's okay, I'll take you out on the boat."

"Mom! *Moooom!*" Grayson screeched from five feet away. "Can Matt take me on the boat?"

That was it? That was all it took? No sit-down talk, no review of what grown-ups sometimes did together? Relieved, Rebecca fell back against the couch. "Honey, he can take you all the way to the ocean if you'd like."

"Yeah!" Grayson cried, jumping up and down and clapping.

"Wait—we had a deal," Matt said gruffly. "Before you go getting your swim trunks all blown up, where's my coffee?" He grabbed Grayson and turned him upside down like he weighed nothing and shook him until Grayson broke into a fit of giggles.

It was, Rebecca thought, exactly the way Matt made her feel. Upside down and full of giggles.

So Matt knew he was in pretty deep, like up to his neck, because he did not leave that lake house until Sunday evening, and even then, he had Rebecca and Grayson in tow. This was not like him at all.

He'd come to Rebecca's special little lake house Thursday afternoon just to talk, but Friday morning, when he went back out to his car, the world was a whole other place than he'd known before, all shiny and new. And as he stood there, Rebecca's phone in hand, he knew that the world would never be the same again. He hadn't been the same since he'd looked up and seen her gliding toward him in the capitol park, all demon-eyed.

He also knew, all the way down to the pit of him, that he had, after more than thirty years, found The One. Not that he was entirely certain how he knew—but one night of fabulous sex did not usually make him feel all mellow and protective and part of a unit, and that was exactly how he was feeling at the moment. Definitely a feeling unlike any he'd ever had, and even though the lawyer in him would argue against it on principle, history, and his typical, dog-like practices when it came to women, Matt knew it was true. He really, truly, knew.

Still barefoot, he hopped up the gravel road a ways, for a little privacy, and phoned the office. Naturally, Harold answered crisply on the first ring.

"Harold, how's it going?"

"How's it *going*, Mr. Parrish?" Harold echoed, the surprise evident in his voice. "Well…I suppose it's going exactly as it ought."

"Listen, I'm not going to make it in today. I'm feeling a little under the weather."

There was a long pause. Then a muffled cough. "Excuse me, Mr. Parrish—if I may…are you calling in sick?" Harold asked incredulously.

"What, aren't I allowed the same courtesy we extend to all twelve employees? Am I not human? Do I not bleed?"

"Certainly, Mr. Parrish, it's just that…well, sir, I'll just walk out on a limb and say that as you've never called in sick even once in the eight years I have worked for you, I am very surprised."

"I guess there's a first time for everything," Matt said, smiling. "Get Townsend to cover my docket, will you? He can do it with one hand tied behind his back."

"Ah…I beg your pardon, sir, but Mr. Townsend said if you called, I was to put you through—"

"On Monday, Harold. Have a good weekend," he said, and clicked off before Harold could say more. Ben would be mad as hell come Monday, but at the moment, Matt couldn't care less. He was too busy falling in love, man.

The next order of business was clothes. He did maintain the one-shirt rule, as in always have an extra shirt in the car. But he did not, however, maintain the extra pair of boxers rule, and donning his polo, Matt hopped into his car and drove to Ruby Falls, where he found Sam's General Store. Among various pottery and dolls and frilly little things that he assumed old ladies bought, Matt found a rack of men's golf clothes, picked up some pants, shorts, a couple of shirts, and a pair of sandals. The only thing he couldn't find at the general store was underwear. The high school kid at the checkout told him he could get some undies at Sam's Corner Grocery. Why was he not surprised?

He found them there, all right. On the "other" aisle.

Dinah was at the same register when he came through with a pack of gum, another huge bouquet of roses, and a package of three boxer briefs. She glanced at him from the corner of her eye as she rang them up. "I guess you found Ms. Lear's house all right," she drawled.

With his underwear and flowers, Matt flew down the two-lane to Rebecca's, through the gate with the flying pig, up to the lake house with the flowering pots and charming crankcase windows and rustic planters and big wraparound porch and thought, for the first time in his life, that it would be nice to come home to this. He loved the smell and sound and feel of this house.

Rebecca never asked him when or if he was leaving; he figured if she wanted him to go, she'd say so, but he had the definite sense that she was just as entranced with the little world they had stumbled into as he was.

In truth, she even seemed a slightly different person after their earth-shattering lovemaking. Even as early as this morning, he noticed dog food pellets on the floor, unswept. When she cheerfully offered to make breakfast, she dropped a clean dish towel to the floor and stuffed it back onto a stack of them, without regard to color or texture or shape. And as that magical weekend wore on, the various facets of her perfection began to slip away, like so many pieces of leaves scattered to the wind.

Matt made good on his promise to take Grayson out on the boat, and in the end, all four dogs and Rebecca went along. She packed a lunch, said she knew a little place upriver, which turned out to be a small island where someone had gone to great pains to make a grassy picnic area under the boughs of old pecan trees. It was perfect for a lazy afternoon like this.

While Grayson threw sticks in the water for the dogs to fetch—those that would, anyway, as Bean never saw the stick, Tot was afraid of the water, and Tater was disinclined—Matt and Rebecca lay on a quilt beneath a pecan tree and talked. About everything. Stuff he hadn't thought about or mentioned in years. Like they had been stranded on a deserted island, had come into human contact after a long absence, which, in a metaphorical sense, Matt figured was right on target.

Rebecca told him about Bud, how she had fallen in love with the high school football star and had followed him to college, then given up her dreams of an art degree because he wanted a wife and a beauty queen. And how Bud had grown disenchanted with her when she became pregnant, even found her changing shape off-putting. It was then, Rebecca casually reported, that the affairs began, one after another, and that even some of her so-called friends thought nothing of screwing her scum of a husband in the garage while Rebecca was inside nursing their son. She said it so matter-of-factly, so numbly, that it sent a cold shiver down Matt's spine. He was beginning to understand how a woman like Rebecca could be so stiff, so afraid of life and of love.

She was much more animated when she talked about her sisters. She laughed as she told him about Robin, headstrong and ambitious and finally out from "under her father's thumb." Rachel, the baby, who was still in school studying ancient British literature and battling a weight problem, brought on after years, Rebecca said, of her father's criticism.

Her father, Matt quickly understood, was the central character in their lives, whether they wanted him to be or not. "Sounds like a hard-ass," he reflected, after Rebecca told him of the rift that had developed between him and Robin over her place in the family company.

Rebecca shook her head. "That's really too nice—he's a bastard," she said, without rancor. "When he found out he had cancer, he called my mother, even though they had been separated for years. She dropped everything in LA to come and care for him. For a while, it looked like things were going to work out. I thought maybe he had grown up a little, that maybe his mortality had shaken something lose in him." She gave a long and weary sigh. "But, as soon as the treatment started to take, and the cancer went into remission, he was back to the usual—bossing us all around, running our lives. And even though Mom dropped everything to be with him in his hour of need, he started ignoring her all over again."

"I take it you don't get along with him."

"Oh no, we get along," she said. "I mean, in spite of all I've said, he can be a decent man. He adores Grayson, and I think he truly wants my happiness…it's just that he wants to define it for me. I do love my dad, but I don't like him very much."

Matt changed the subject, asked her about her reigning year as Miss Texas, which made her snort in that funny way she did and roll her eyes. "Another great chapter of my life," she said caustically.

"Then you weren't kidding when you said you never wanted to be Miss Texas?"

"God, no. Never!" she said emphatically. "It was great after it happened, but it was all Bud's thing, not mine," she said, and confessed that she had been a stupid young woman who was more interested in pleasing everyone around her than in doing what was right for Rebecca. Good ol' Bud, Matt gathered, cared more about the way things looked than what they were, and in particular, his wife. He knew the type—men who were so insecure with themselves that they insisted their wives were perfect, their houses, their kids. It all went into feeding their own sick egos.

Rebecca was a gracious, kindhearted, and determined person. Even though she could be confoundingly stubborn, she was appealing in a charming way. The fact that she was gorgeous was just icing on the cake. So if there was a man out there who thought that wasn't enough and wanted more, he had to be an a prick to Matt's way of thinking.

Whatever she thought of her ex, Matt couldn't say—but she seemed to be well past any feelings about Bud, grateful to be out of that dysfunctional relationship and now was anxious to become someone in her own right. All by herself. Just as soon as she figured out who or what.

"Any ideas?" she asked as they lay on their bellies, side by side, while Grayson and the dogs napped.

"Bingo bashes?" he suggested.

"No!" she said, laughing (and oh, her eyes sparkled when she laughed).

Matt sobered a little, asked in all seriousness, "What about Tom's campaign? I have to tell you, he is about to come unglued. Your big fund-raiser? The people calling don't want to talk to anyone but you." He smiled sheepishly. "I almost got lynched at the office. Everyone misses you, Rebecca. Tom wanted me to come out here and repair the damage, but it was too late."

"Too late? Why?"

"Because I missed you ten times more than they did, and I had already gotten out my knee pads to make the crawl to Ruby Falls."

Rebecca laughed, playfully shoved him. "I figured as much, silly. Tom's left half a dozen messages on my machine."

"Will you come back?" Matt asked.

Rebecca smiled thoughtfully, pulled wild rain lilies from the grass and made a pile. "I don't know," she said at last. "I'll have to think about it. You were right about me—"

"No. Rebecca, no—I was so wrong. I can't even begin to say how wrong—"

"Matt," she said, with a hand to his arm to silence him. "You were *right*. I never bothered to learn anything about Tom or the issues. I thought all that was boring. I just saw a chance to do things, maybe find a job, maybe make some friends. But I should never have used his campaign like that. I never should have signed up without asking a few questions and agreeing with what he was doing."

"You aren't the only one," Matt grumbled, and told her how he had joined the race because they said he would make a great district attorney. "That thought had never once crossed my mind until that night, and there I was, lapping it up like ol' Bean."

"Yikes," she said with a sympathetic smile.

It was amazing, Matt thought later that evening, when they had come back to the lake house and Rebecca was in the throes of preparing a gourmet meal, how easily his life story had come tumbling out of him today. He could honestly say he wasn't the kind of guy to tout his accomplishments or talk about himself. But that wasn't the half of it—as he talked, he heard himself say things that he had never really, consciously realized before now. For example, how it chafed him that his partner was in it solely for the money. "There are people out there who get used up, and they aren't smart enough or sophisticated enough or old enough to fend for themselves."

"There's your reason to run for DA," Rebecca observed, and Matt realized instantly that she was right. Not because he had connections, not because he could raise the money, and not because he looked good to voters. Because he'd always looked out for others, as far back as he could remember, beginning with the special-education student he had befriended in the sixth grade, and for whom he received a sound beating from a couple of his classmates when he stood up for the kid.

"You're right," he said, his voice full of awe.

Rebecca laughed, shoved a sautéed julienne carrot into his mouth. "Don't look so astonished."

He also told her about his family, heard the pride in his voice as he described them. His father, a retired judge, who had been his inspiration to go to law school. His mom, who was in her sixties now and at last free to do as she pleased—which was, apparently, to pester all her children about grandkids. His sister, Bella, his brothers, Mark and Danny, and the summers they had spent in and around Austin, swimming in the springs, watching the bats at night, and exploring old limestone caves.

Dinner was fun and relaxed, with an absolutely delicious salmon and asparagus (which Grayson deemed yucky). Afterward, Matt made a point of spending some one-on-one time with Grayson. Rebecca had told him that Grayson's adaptation to his parents' divorce had been rocky; that he was always angry when he came home from seeing Bud, and that he missed his nanny, Lucy, although Rebecca said that he was mentioning her less frequently now. Matt had noticed that when he and Grayson were together, he did not want to share Matt's attention with anyone else, not even with Tater, his favorite dog. It was also obvious that in spite of how much Rebecca loved her son, Grayson craved a man's attention.

But Matt also saw a stocky little kid with a great imagination (cool), a great sense of humor (bonus points), and a good throwing arm (which was really good news, because if Matt was going to be around, he had to have someone to play sports with). The kid was great. The only little thing that alarmed him was his room, and what Matt saw as his alarming, Mom-like leanings. Not one toy was out of place. His clothes were hung by color. In his dresser, his underwear was neatly folded and stacked.

"Gray, we can't have this!" Matt exclaimed, shaking his head in disgust when Grayson obliged him by opening the sock drawer, and they were all lined up in little army formation, and, big surprise, color coordinated.

"What's wrong?" Grayson asked, looking at his socks with genuine concern.

"Boys don't line their socks up. Boys shove 'em in there however they can get them, and when their mom gets mad, they say, 'Sorry Mom!' but just keep doing it."

"Oh," he said, his brow furrowed. in serious concentration.

"Let's do something about these socks right now!" Matt said, and stuck his hand in the drawer, messed them all up.

With a shout of laughter, Grayson did the same, then asked eagerly, "What about my underwear?"

Matt grinned. "I knew you'd see it my way."

After the underwear, they rearranged his little closet ("Mom already did that," Grayson said, which just proved there was something terribly wrong with the kid), and when they were done, Grayson asked him, "Are you going to spend the night again?"

Matt shoved a hand through his hair. "What do you think I should do?"

The kid fingered the hem of his shirt and stared at his feet before muttering, "I wish you'd stay forever."

CHAPTER TWENTY-NINE

But love is blind, and lovers cannot see the pretty follies
that themselves commit...

WILLIAM SHAKESPEARE

Positive Affirmations of My Life:
1. Can now count myself among the sexually liberated. Did I really put up with Bud's clumsiness all those years? Wondering if his lack of finesse might be part of larger issue – like maybe he's a closet homosexual, which would really explain a lot.
2. Grayson is happier than I've seen him in a long time, adores Matt – didn't even care that Bud blew off their weekend again. And he hasn't fought with Taylor in more than two weeks! Yes!
3. Saved the best for last – I am happy, too, happier than I can ever remember being in my life, so happy that I don't think I really need to do this shit anymore. Sayonara, you stupid Affirmation Journal for life! I am free!

It was true—Rebecca felt like a completely new woman. After years of numbness, and just going through the motions, it seemed like she had woken up one day in never-never land, where things actually were falling into place and she was, at last, her own person, warts and all.

She agreed, reluctantly, to finish out the fund-raiser for Tom. She had balked at first—it seemed a little disingenuous to plan a fund-raiser for a candidate she really knew little about, but then again, it seemed much worse to promise to do it and then renege at this late date. And Tom was so frantic on the phone that she almost believed it was a life or death situation for him. She determined it would be worse for any chance at future employment to dump the project, and agreed to do it on three conditions: "I want to do it from my house."

"I don't care where you do it, just as long as you do it," Tom insisted.

"And I need help."

Tom had hemmed and hawed at that one, but in the end, Matt had come through with Harold, who had practically begged Matt to recommend him when Matt had casually mentioned it. He was, Rebecca quickly discovered, a godsend.

The third condition she kept to herself—but she had promised herself to learn about the campaign and the issues before she finished the gala, and toward that end, had penciled in a series of candidate forums over the next month. By the time her killer fund-raiser came around, she was determined to be the most informed person on staff.

From that point forward, Rebecca put all her energies into her new sense of purpose and experiencing, no holds barred, the absolute, heart-stopping, all-consuming positively joyous process of falling in love.

Falling! As in, off a cliff, a nosedive right into the thick of it. Now it seemed so amusing that she could go from despising Matt half the time to adoring him all the time. She loved how he cared for Grayson and paid attention to him. She loved how he loved her dogs. How dedicated he was to his principles and his practice. And she was held in thrall by how the man could turn her into a quivering heap of raw flesh with a single touch.

"What in the hell is the matter with you?" Robin had demanded on the phone one afternoon when Rebecca called to invite her and Jake to her fund-raiser.

"What do you mean?"

"I mean you're all giggly and flighty. That's so unlike you. It's almost…ohmigod. It's that guy, isn't it? That lawyer you couldn't stand?"

Rebecca laughed. "Maybe."

"Maybe? That's all you're going to say? Tell me, or I will drive down there and make you tell me."

Robin had never been very subtle. So Rebecca confessed all.

Except, of course, how Matt had liberated her, had led her across new boundaries and had coaxed her to climb up to new horizons. Each time they were together (which was frequent, because frankly, she wanted it all the time, and that was definitely a new Rebecca), it seemed she was lifted higher and higher, freed at last from insecurity and secret despair.

And oh, what a willing and cheerful partner Matt made in her journey to find herself. The night she pulled out a Kama Sutra book, one of the myriad self-help and philosophical books Rachel had passed along, Matt laughed, put his hands over her eyes, made her flip through the pages, then choose one, sight unseen. Afterward, lying there half on, half off the bed, Matt had whispered the words that had made her heart shine as bright as the sun: "Baby, you're gonna kill me!"

Yeah, well, she was certainly going to die trying.

And there were times, such as when she and Matt would sit on the back porch and watch Grayson and his new pal Taylor play with the dogs, that she wondered if she was kidding herself or if it was really possible to feel this way about another person, to be so totally in tune with another human being. She didn't have the need to analyze it anymore, just the strong desire to feel it. This was, she recognized, the best time of her life.

Matt, too, was having those tender and shiny feelings of love, and just like Rebecca, he found them rather remarkable. He could honestly admit that he was glad he hadn't missed this, being part of another person's life. He never would have guessed it could be so pure and so fulfilling. When he thought about the meaningless flings he had had over the years, he even felt a little sorry for himself. What a dumb bastard he'd been.

But now Matt was so happy with the new twist of his life that he didn't even mind when Ben made fun of him and Harold was beside himself every time Rebecca stopped by his office.

He didn't mind that copies of *Bride* magazine were popping up at his mom's house, and that on more than one occasion, when he walked into the room, his mother and Bella would suddenly stop talking and pretend that they weren't planning a wedding. He supposed the thought had even crossed his bachelor's mind. How could he not think about it? Rebecca was impossible not to love. Her presence was gold—bright and warm and soothing, particularly on those days he bombed in court. She knew instinctively what to do, how to bring peace to him again. He could see why her sisters relied so heavily on her.

He was surprised at how artistically talented she was. One day, she had dragged him out to the old barn to ask his opinion of whether or not it could be converted into a studio/office. That was when he had seen some of her paintings that she had stored there and he'd been stunned by them.

"Oh, those," she said with a shrug. "I did those a long time ago, before Grayson."

"You should *definitely* paint, Rebecca," he had declared emphatically.

Rebecca had laughed that gentle-rain laugh, kissed him on the cheek, and walked out of the barn. And he knew—because that was the way it was between them now, that sixth sense of knowing another person well—that she would paint again, in her own good time.

Yep, ol' Matt Parrish, former player and ladies' man about town, was having a wonderfully new and exciting time in the company of Rebecca. He was discovering new things about himself, as well. Too bad this little epiphany he was having about love and life was not extending to work or Tom's campaign.

Or perhaps he was experiencing the same sort of epiphany there, too, but without the positive light shining on it. For the first time since Matt and Ben had partnered up, he was seeing their firm differently. It was a slow dawning, happening over time, beginning with a talk he had with Rebecca, when he had said out loud for the first time what he'd known deep inside for a long while—that he and Ben were at opposite ends of the spectrum when it came to their business. Ben was Matt's best friend, and this dawning reality was a hard one to own up to. Together, they had been through a lot of good and bad times, both personally and professionally. And all of a sudden, it was as if the heavens had opened up and shone a light right on the crux of the uneasiness buried in him—Matt knew he could not spend the rest of his life in a firm that was all about chasing the buck.

Where exactly that left him, he wasn't entirely sure. He supposed he could begin a practice on his own, which wasn't so appealing at this stage of his career. Or pursue the DA thing. But even that was beginning to look a little shaky, thanks to his exposure to Tom's campaign.

Tom had calmed down quite a bit once Rebecca agreed to continue the fund-raiser, and now that the legislative session was over, they were heading into the critical late summer months of the race, and Tom was coming on like gangbusters. In fact, he had called Matt at the office one day and asked him to dig up some dirt on the Independent guy, Russ Erwin.

"Why?" Matt had asked. "He's no threat to you."

"We're going negative, I told you," Tom had snapped. "There's got to be something in that fruitcake's background to exploit."

Biting back a more stinging retort, Matt had managed to calmly ask, "Did I hear you correctly? Did you just ask me to find something to exploit?"

"Yeah, why?"

"Why? Because you know how I feel about that, Tom. I spend my days representing people who have been exploited. I just don't understand why this campaign can't be about the issues, not what you can exploit. That leaves a bad taste in the mouth."

"For God's sake, Parrish, when are you going to climb down off that ivory soapbox and back off and let me run my own campaign?" Tom had shot back. That had worked, had definitely struck a nerve Matt had not known existed before Rebecca accused him of doing the same thing. Mowing everyone down, she had said.

"I'm not asking you to invent something," Tom continued testily. "I'm just asking you to take a look."

And Matt wondered why he was still supporting Tom Masters, and if he hadn't perhaps exploited himself with the words *district attorney* dangling in front of him.

The moment he hung up the phone, Harold was at his door, smiling like a Cheshire cat. "What is it?" Matt had asked absently.

"Miss Lear to see you, Mr. Parrish," he had intoned in his best professional voice.

Matt smiled broadly when he saw Rebecca standing in the waiting room, talking to Ben. By the look of things, he was going to have to roll Ben's tongue up and stick it back in his mouth. But he could certainly understand his partner's reaction—Rebecca was wearing a form-fitting pale yellow silk skirt that showed her fabulous legs to their fullest advantage, which, he couldn't help noticing, were accentuated with the help of a pair of three-inch heels that made her almost as tall as Ben. Her black hair was pulled back in a sleek ponytail, and she had black, Jackie Onassis–type sunglasses on top of her head.

When Matt cleared his throat, she turned toward him, flashed a gorgeous, all-white smile that made both Ben and

Harold swoon. "Matt!" she exclaimed prettily, oblivious to her admirers. "I'm sorry to bother you, but Harold and I were just wrapping up a little meeting, and it's the lunch hour, so I was hoping you might have a moment."

"For you, I have all the time in the world," he said. "Why don't you come into my office before they drool all over you?" he suggested, motioning for her to come inside. Rebecca laughed, tapped Harold lightly on the arm with what looked like a rolled-up brochure as she walked by.

"Just like you, Parrish, taking all the fun out of everything," Ben complained as Matt gave him a jaunty wave and shut the door.

Behind the closed door, Rebecca slipped into his arms and kissed him passionately.

"Hey," he said, grinning like a lovesick pup, "what a great surprise. I didn't know you and Harold were meeting."

"Yep. I went to a candidate forum this morning and had some ideas, so I dropped by. I hope I'm not intruding on any lunch plans."

"If you were, I'd dump them," he said truthfully, thinking how much fun it would be to go the usual watering hole with her on his arm.

"Well," she said, slipping from his arms and walking to the window that overlooked the capitol, "I am *famished*. I hope you don't mind," she said, closing the blinds, "if I have a little lunch on you?"

"Absolutely not. Where would you like to go?"

"Right here," she said, pointing to his desk. Matt looked at his desk, then at her. She arched a dark brow, pointed to the desk again with the rolled-up brochure, and dropped her handbag on a chair. "Do you remember when you said we could explore all my fantasies?"

Little Matt sprang to instant and rapt attention. Big Matt could only nod as he quietly turned the lock behind his back.

"Well..." She paused and shyly dropped her gaze. "If you wouldn't mind having a seat at your desk, I have this fantasy where I come in, and...*you* know."

"You're kidding," he said flatly, but he was already moving to his chair.

Rebecca came around to his side of the desk, very gracefully went down on her knees, and slipped in between his legs, and slowly unzipped his pants. "Be very quiet," she said. "Or Harold will know what's going on." With a sly wink, she stunned Matt into silence; he gripped the arms of his chair as she closed her lips around the head of his penis, thought wildly that this could not be happening, that he was a professional, that he did not do this in his office. But then she moved her lips down the shaft, Matt turned to jelly and thought *what the hell.* His head fell back against the chair, and he was sinking into a vat of pure, unadulterated bliss, sinking and sinking as she began to move on him, licking and sucking and nibbling her way to his climax.

Which came very quickly. Illicit sex in the office had that effect on him. "*Wait,*" he said hoarsely, not quite able to move yet, as she very carefully cleaned him up. "What about you?"

Rebecca smiled as she came to her feet, leaned over him and kissed him on the lips. I'll see you later," she said, and walked around to the other side of his desk, picked up her bag, pausing only to straighten her skirt and sweater before prissing right out of his office like she owned the joint. Damn, if she wanted it, he'd give her the keys, the deed, and the brand-new coffeepot.

There was no denying it—this was *definitely* love. Still grinning like an idiot, Matt zipped his pants, turned, and planted his elbows on his desk and dragged his hands through his hair in an effort to regain his composure. That was when he noticed the rolled-up flyer Rebecca had been carrying and left on his desk.

Matt picked it up. *Russ Erwin, the Man with a Conscience*, it said. The tree-huggers anthem—*We're the only ones who care.* Socialist assholes.

He tossed it in the trash can without another thought.

CHAPTER THIRTY

*I have come to the conclusion that politics are too serious a
matter to be left to the politicians...*

CHARLES DE GAULLE

Rebecca worked hard to rid herself of the trappings of
the old Rebecca. She rearranged her furniture, let Jo
Lynn change things around in the kitchen (even though she
had to go out on the porch, unable to watch), and boxed up
all her self-help books and mailed them to Rachel. She even
went to Ruby Falls one afternoon with no makeup, wearing
shorts and a T-shirt.

And one morning when Bud proclaimed loudly on the
radio, *"No one can beat a deal at Reynolds Chevrolet, so come on
down to the motor mile,"* she went. Not to Bud's dealership, of
course, but to a rival Ford dealership. She had decided that
her Range Rover was perfectly pretentious, and what she
really needed was a pickup truck for hauling dogs (which
now numbered five with the addition of Cookie, although
Jo Lynn had dibs on Cookie, just as soon as Cookie grew out
of eating shoes).

The truck salesman had nothing but smiles for Rebecca's
breasts, and talked her into a red king cab pickup, the one
with the heated leather seats and a surround-sound Bose

speaker stereo. When Rebecca finally said okay, he ushered her into his cubicle to do the deal. Only he hadn't counted on Rebecca having once been married to a car dealer, or having done her homework. He certainly hadn't counted on the fact that she was no longer a doormat and was, at that very moment, visualizing herself kick-boxing him around the cubicle as she politely, but firmly, maintained her ground.

A few hours later, mentally high-fiving herself, Rebecca pulled off the lot with a brand-new, cherry-red pickup, knowing damn well that Bud couldn't beat the deal she had just gotten. With her new radio blaring, she drove north to a neighboring county seat, where a candidate's forum was being held.

Rebecca groaned when she saw the arrangement—in someone's deranged opinion, it wasn't too hot to have an outdoor forum. Nothing could be further from the truth, but nonetheless, in honor of Pioneer Days, a raised stage and podium had been built at one end of the town square. The candidates sat on the stage beneath a canopy, fanning themselves, while the people who had come out to hear them stood in the sweltering sun beneath umbrellas and big panama hats. Rebecca managed to squeeze in with some others to share the thin shade of a little tree, and from there, she could see Gilbert standing off to one side, making last-minute notes on a piece of paper.

Candidates for the legislature went first, all of them promising great things for the future of the state and their districts. No new taxes was a common theme, and several seemed to think bigger pots on the state lottery were the answer to revenue problems. Each one, to a candidate, promised program cuts. But not programs to do with children. Or the elderly. Or teachers. Or criminal justice. Or special needs populations. Who exactly that left, Rebecca wasn't sure.

When it was at last time for the candidates for lieutenant governor to speak, Tom was up first. "I urge you to look at my record in the senate," he said, and stabbed his forefinger against the podium to make his point. "My opponent has made a mess of the state budget with all his special interests, and now he wants to take the dollars out of *your* pocket to pay for *his* special interests!" he bellowed as his opponent shook his head vehemently. "I promise you, as the next lieutenant governor of this state. I will provide the leadership necessary to make sure that does not happen!"

That earned him a huge round of applause. "I will make commerce a *top* priority! More commerce means more revenue for our state coffers!" he said, getting another thunderous round of applause.

His Republican opponent, Phil Harbaugh, was next up. Harbaugh thanked the crowd for coming out, said he'd rather have worked for special interests than not to have worked at all like his opponent, and would continue to work to improve funding for education and competitive insurance rates. He took his seat to a smattering of applause.

Up last was the Independent candidate, Russ Erwin. He unwound his lanky self from his seat, stood up, and strolled to the podium. He wasn't wearing a suit like the others, but had on boots, Wranglers, a rodeo belt, and a cowboy shirt. He respectfully removed the cowboy hat from his head, and bent over the microphone.

"My name is Russ Erwin," he said to the crowd. "I'm a rancher. Got me about a three-section spread out by Lampasas. I mostly run livestock, but I grow a little sorghum, too." He paused, shifted the hat to his other hand, and bent over again. "Now, I never set out to be a politician, that's for darn sure. I wouldn't have given you a plugged nickel for 'em. Then I got a little notice on my gate one day, delivered by the State of Texas, telling me they was gonna run a superhighway and gas pipeline from Fort Worth all the way to Old Mexico, and that it would bring jobs to the area, and all of us in Lampasas County would prosper because of this highway." He paused again, ran his palm over his temple. "Now, had I known all it took was a highway to prosper, I'd have said yes a long time ago."

The crowd laughed; several of them nodded. Of course, Rebecca had heard Tom mention this on more than one occasion, always as the next best thing since sliced bread.

"Anyway, I got that piece of paper, and I guess I had a slightly different take on it. I could see what they had planned was going to displace a lot of ranchers whose families had been working that land since before Texas was even a state. And I could tell that superhighway was gonna flat out ruin our landscape. 'Course, there wasn't a word about any of *that* on the paper," he said, chuckling. "So I called up my representatives, said I had a problem. I went through the whole darn list and not one of 'em could help me. I'd call up one, and he'd say, 'Well, now, Mr. Erwin, I'm not on that committee, you need to call so-n-so.' This went on until every last one had pointed to the next guy. That was enough to get my dander up, so I started looking into these committees and such, and the more I looked, the more I saw stuff happening that I didn't much care for.

"Now, Mr. Masters here," he said, indicating Tom with his hat, "he says, just look at my record. Well, I did. And about the only thing I could find was a resolution he got passed naming chips and salsa the official state snack. I like a good bowl of chips with some salsa like anyone, but I don't see what that has to do with protecting our land, or making sure we get teachers paid enough to educate our young, or even making sure that the fine people assembled here today in this heat don't have to spend every last dime they got."

Tom laughed with the few hearty members in the crowd, but shifted anxiously in his seat.

"There's plenty of stuff like that for Mr. Harbaugh, too, but I won't take your time now, because it's too damn hot to listen to a bunch of political talk. I'm not trying to cast aspersions on these two gentlemen. I figure they done the best they knew how to do. But like my ol' daddy used to say, if you want something done right, you just 'bout have to do it yourself. So folks, I am running for lieutenant governor of this fine state because I figure if I want it done right, I'm gonna have to do it myself. Thank you kindly for you time." The crowd went wild with applause; Mr. Erwin stepped back, put on his hat, and sauntered to his seat, where he sat with his legs crossed and his hands folded neatly on his lap.

Both Tom and Phil Harbaugh looked like they wanted to bolt.

This was the fourth candidate forum Rebecca had been to, the fourth time she'd seen the plainspoken, straightforward Mr. Erwin, and she liked his style. When the event was over, Rebecca pushed through the crowd to the stage, slipping behind a couple of men so Tom wouldn't see her as he tried to get off the stage and into air-conditioning. But there were several people standing around Mr. Erwin; he was taking the time to speak to them all. When at last he turned to her, she stuck out her hand. "Mr. Erwin. I heard what you said and I'd like to help in some way if I can."

"Well, now," Mr. Erwin said with a grin, shaking her hand. "We always got room for one more."

That weekend, Matt asked Rebecca and Grayson to come to town for a change. Rebecca arrived at his building and parked in the second of his two parking spaces, but her truck was so big that it left just a slip of a space for his Jag.

She and Grayson were already in his loft when he came in, looking chagrined. "I'm sorry," he said, after greeting Grayson with a high five and crossing the room to kiss her. "I'll call the management right now and get someone to move that monster thing. That's never happened before—it must be a new tenant," he said, reaching for the phone.

"Don't you like it?" she asked, shoving her hands in the faded work jeans she'd worn all day.

"Like what?"

"My new red truck!"

Matt's jaw dropped; he paused in the reaching for the phone.

"Mom got a pickup," Grayson said, "so we can take our dogs with us."

A look of panic came over Matt, and he quickly looked around the room. Rebecca laughed. "We didn't bring them here, silly. Jo Lynn is looking after them."

"Wait—you bought a king cab truck?" Matt said as his gaze swept her from head to foot. Rebecca nodded. Matt grinned. "I think you must be the best-looking Farmer Fred I've ever seen in my life," he said, folding her into a big hug.

That night, Matt took them out for his version of a gourmet meal, to Guero's Taco Bar. As they helped themselves to the fajita fixings—and Grayson built a volcano made of cheese and guacamole—Rebecca mentioned the candidate's forum.

"You went?" Matt asked, only mildly surprised, having grown accustomed to her attendance at all the candidate events. "I thought about going up, but I had a hearing I couldn't get out of."

"It was interesting," she said as she carefully selected a strip of chicken from the cast iron skillet. "Tom's really pushing revived commerce."

Matt glanced up. "The party's platform is education."

Rebecca shrugged. "The best speaker of them all was Russ Erwin, the Independent."

"Oh yeah?" Matt snorted before taking a swig of his beer. "Now there's a tree-hugger looking for an audience." But as he drank his beer, he saw that Rebecca's fork had frozen in midair, and slowly lowered his bottle. "What?"

"He's not just a tree-hugger looking for an audience. He's a rancher who is fighting big government's encroachment on his life."

Matt was groaning before she could even finish. "Rebecca, honey, you're kidding, right?"

"I am *so* not kidding, Matt. I am very serious. Russ Erwin makes the most sense of any of them, and I like him. I think he has what it takes to be lieutenant governor."

"Mom, are you gonna eat that?" Grayson asked, pointing at the chicken on her plate.

Matt planted his elbows on the table, and leaned forward. "Rebecca. I admire the fact that you are learning about the issues. But organic fruit is not the way to go."

For a moment, Rebecca could only glare at him.

"What?" he asked, seeming clueless as to how patronizing and arrogant he was. "Do you understand what I mean?"

"Oh, I understand," she said, barely able to speak. "I understand that when you told me I should get involved, you really meant, Rebecca, you're just a former beauty queen, so let me give you my expert guidance and maybe you can begin to understand—"

"Rebecca!" he said quickly, laughing a little as he reached over to put his hand on her wrist. But Rebecca moved her hand just as quickly so he couldn't do it. Matt's eyes narrowed; he slid a look at Grayson, who was busy sticking meat in his volcano, oblivious. "I am not telling you what to think. All I am trying to say is, that if you listen to him for more than a moment, you will probably hear him advocate something that comes really close to socialism."

Rebecca really couldn't remember from tenth-grade government class what socialism was, precisely (but she'd definitely be looking it up as soon as she got home), yet as far as she knew, this was a free country. She sniffed, straightened in her chair, looked away from him.

"So what, you're not talking to me now?"

"Of course I am talking to you, Matt," she said in the same patient voice she often used with Grayson. "I just believe, being an American and all, that I can listen to whomever I want, and you can go straight to hell. Or listen to Tom if you choose, providing, of course, you're ready for a superhighway-slash-pipeline in your backyard. And in the meantime, we can go on our merry little way, being a little democratic unit, each of us free to think and vote as we please." She glared at Matt, daring him to argue.

He sat for a long moment as if he was actually debating whether or not to argue, tapping his fork against the side of his plate as he considered her. But then he suddenly grinned, stabbed more chicken, and put it on his plate. "You're right—I can't argue with an impassioned plea for the right to vote our conscience. So I am going to change the subject. Tom says that we have almost three hundred affirmative replies to this shindig you're throwing."

"Three hundred and twenty-five," she said pertly. "And about fifty calls from people wanting to get their friends in, I can't believe it, but I think this is going to be one very cool and hip event."

"What about your dad?" Matt asked, rolling a tortilla.

Dad. "Don't remind me," she moaned, and moved to dismantle Grayson's second volcano.

Rebecca hadn't spoken to Dad since the afternoon she'd hung up on him. She should call him and make amends, she knew that, but she had no desire to do so, and ended up putting the call off in favor of another fabulous weekend, where the subject of Russ Erwin did not come up again. Nor did the campaign. On Saturday, Matt and Rebecca took Grayson to the new Texas history museum, then on to Barton Springs, where Grayson and Matt swam in the cool spring waters while Rebecca lazily read a romance novel (which, she smugly noted, had nothing on the nights she and Matt spent together). Saturday evening, Matt's sister happily took Grayson until the family meal on Sunday so that Matt and Rebecca could have an evening alone.

Matt was excited about the date he'd planned at an old-fashioned supper club. They dined on sea bass, listened to some great jazz, and crawled home in the early-morning hours. As exhausted as they were, both of them were still anxious to put their hands on each other's bodies, and made slow, languid love until they drifted off to sleep in each other's arms. And in that unearthly place between wake and sleep, as Matt's breathing began to deepen, Rebecca smiled, whispered, "This is love…I love you, too." He didn't speak, just rolled over and wrapped his arm around her.

On Sunday afternoon, while Matt was dozing through a baseball game on TV, Rebecca padded into his office and dialed her father in New York.

"Yeah," he answered gruffly.

"Dad?"

"Rebecca," he said quietly. "So you finally decided to pick up the phone and speak to your old man again?"

She closed her eyes, preparing herself. "Yes."

"Great minds think alike, I guess. I got tired of waiting for you to make the first move and I've tried to get you all weekend, but you won't answer the phone."

"That's because Grayson and I have been in Austin. With a friend."

There was the dead silence on the other end while it sunk in. And at last Dad said, "Aha."

Rebecca sighed, stared at a picture of Matt at some event somewhere. "Dad, you remember the gala? Well, I thought about what you said, and I put it together after all. I am calling to invite you. I was hoping you would come and see what I've been doing, and…and meet Matt."

Dad didn't say anything at first. "That's his name, huh?"

"Matt Parrish. He's a lawyer in town."

"*God,*" he groaned, then sighed wearily. "Are you happy, Bec?"

The question surprised her. "I…yes, Dad. I am. But why don't you come see for yourself?"

"What, come to Austin?" he asked in a voice that sounded, remarkably, almost hopeful.

"Yes, to Austin. I think this gala is going to be really fantastic. I've pretty much done it on my own, but I'd really like…" She stopped, hearing the words in her head and not wanting to say them.

"You'd like…?"

"I'd really like to know what you think," she said at last.

"That," he said, "is encouraging. Yes, I want to see it, Bec. I want to know what is important to you, in spite of what you believe."

Amazing what a little hanging up could do, Rebecca thought, and smiled. "Thanks, Dad," she said. They talked a little longer about Grayson before ending the call. Rebecca was still sitting in Matt's office, staring at the picture of him with her feet propped up on the edge of the desk when Matt came in, looking for her. "Hey," he said.

"Guess what? Dad is coming."

"Great," Matt said, but Rebecca thought he looked a little pale.

CHAPTER THIRTY-ONE

Men and women, women and men. It will never work...

ERICA JONG

Sometimes Matt felt as if he were on a seesaw. Things would be going along so great, and then someone would accuse him of being pushy, or opinionated, or somehow superior, and lately he had been getting it all from sides. Enough that he was seriously reassessing—reassessing everything.

First, there was Ben, who, when he found out Matt had taken on Charlie, a transient who had been hit by a public bus, went ballistic. "What in the hell is the matter with you? Are you *trying* to ruin us?" he had railed in Matt's office one afternoon as Matt had calmly perched himself on the windowsill and let him have at it.

"Yes, that's what I am doing." At Ben's wide-eyed gape, Matt snorted. "Of course I am not trying to ruin us, but buddy, I have to tell you that your song of ruination is getting a little old. We've done pretty well for ourselves. I brought in the Rosenberg case and the Wheeler White case, and they were both big money settlements. Now you just sound greedy."

"And you sound like you think you have some superior cause and the rest of us attorneys just can't understand your higher calling," Ben had snapped so sharply that Harold had quickly jumped up and pulled the door shut. "I am sick to death of this save-the-world crap you have going, Matt. You may think you are bringing in the money, but take a look at the books. I am the only one consistently bringing in paying clients while you are taking on homeless drunks."

Matt really wanted to throttle Ben, but he managed to remain calm. "Charlie has a right to seek legal counsel. He got hit by a *bus*, Ben. He wasn't doing anything but standing there when a big fat-ass bus with a big orange longhorn painted on the side came barreling around the corner on a red light. I know you don't give a shit what happens to him, but look at it from a humanitarian standpoint. If there was a chance in hell this guy would have ever gotten off the streets, it's gone now—he can hardly walk, much less work. Cap Metro knows they hit him, they know that their driver was at fault, yet they have practically told Charlie to go to hell."

"That's because," Ben said, barely able to control his seething, "your charity case had a blood alcohol content of point one four, almost twice the legal limit. Cap Metro will have no problem convincing a jury that the bum was so drunk, he stepped off the curb in front of their bus. You know that, and still you go looking for this kind of thing."

"I didn't go looking for him," Matt said, quickly reaching his limit of patience. "Kate Leslie in the drug diversion court called me. I had a hard time pretending that because the guy is homeless and an alcoholic, he was not entitled to the same laws and protections that we enjoy. So what if we lose the case? Doesn't he deserve legal representation?"

Ben threw his hands in the air. "There's not a thing I can say to you, is there? We're at opposite ends of the universe."

There it was, the truth said out loud and now lying there, like a corpse, between two old friends. Neither of them said anything for a long moment, just stared at each other as the truth sunk in. "Yeah," Matt said at last. "I guess we are."

Ben had turned and walked out of his office.

That's the way they left it that afternoon and for days afterward, a philosophical argument hanging over them like a death knell, affecting everyone in the place. Even Harold, unflappable Harold, was making little mistakes, the type for which he normally would have offered his resignation. And that alone, Matt thought, was reason enough for him to do something. The only problem was, he couldn't figure out what, exactly, he was supposed to do.

So he just kept working, hoping the problem would go away, or that a solution would magically present itself.

Fortunately, there was Rebecca to keep him afloat. He was enjoying her metamorphosis, watching her chip away at her perfect little cocoon and seeing her true self shine through. In sharp contrast to the perfectly put together house he had first entered, now there were books strewn all over her house, haphazardly dropped in one place or another, without regard to color or height. There were days at the lake house she never donned even a smudge of makeup—which made no difference to him, frankly, because there was something naturally seductive about her, whatever she wore or did. But the biggest sign of change had to be the evening Grayson spilled ice cream on a very expensive rug. She didn't freak out, she didn't scream with horror, she didn't cry. She laughed and made some remark about how much the boy was like his mother when it came to ice cream—a real pig.

The more Matt knew Rebecca, the lovelier she became, and he knew, of course, that he was head over heels for her. Completely and totally captivated, obviously and permanently bewitched. Obvious to him, anyway, because when she began to exhibit her newfound enthusiasm for politics, he really couldn't think of anything to say, especially since he had, in a heated moment, encouraged it. And then having subsequently learned, on those rare occasions he actually *did* say something, like, *Why are you doing this*, the new Rebecca could bust his balls like nobody's business in the course of reminding him why she was doing it.

Matt chalked up her absurd infatuation with Russ Erwin to that gentle quirkiness about her he found so endearing, and listed it as one of the frighteningly few things in the *con* column, along with *hogs the covers*, which she audaciously denied.

But there was, admittedly, another part of him that was mildly alarmed she could be so easily taken in by a bunch of grass-eating, tree-clinging, salamander lovers. Rebecca was exactly the type those environmental goofballs preyed on— big-hearted, overly concerned about things like stray dogs and spindly tomato plants and trash on the roadside. He could just hear them now: *Please, Rebecca, please help us save the universe! Corporate America is stealing our air! Your son and your dogs and your tomato plants will not have air to breathe and we will ALL choke to death!*

Matt had been around this race long enough to know that if it wasn't one gimmick, it was another, and this Russ Erwin, whoever he was, had landed on a pretty good one. Normally, he would have ignored it, but normally, he wasn't working on the opponent's campaign. And normally, neither was she. There was just a little too much conflict of interest there for the lawyer in him to ignore. And furthermore, he had a personal stake in the outcome of this race—a stake that, given his rift with Ben, was beginning to emerge as very important. If running for district attorney was really an option for him, he was going to have to see this bullshit through.

So when Rebecca called him up one day, asked if she could tag along that evening to one of the last candidate forums, he said yes, thinking it would be a good opportunity to point out a few things about Tom and Phil Harbaugh that might perhaps move her off the Russ Erwin dime.

She was at his loft at precisely six o'clock in the evening, armed with a small notebook and a sheaf of study papers. They took her new king cab pickup to fetch Pat and Angie. Both women looked at Rebecca as if she'd lost her mind.

"What did you buy this for?" Pat demanded, struggling to climb up to the backseat in the tight, but securely fastened, dull gray skirt she always wore.

"To haul dogs and other stuff. Do you like it?"

"It's not really you," Pat said flatly. "It's more like...I don't even know who it's like."

"I think it's totally *awesome*," said Angie, whose hair was neon blue today, almost an exact match to the new tattoo of a bluebird on her neck.

"Thanks!" Rebecca chirped. "Where's Gilbert?"

"He went with Tom. They needed to go over his opening remarks one last time," Angie said.

"Meaning, Gilbert is writing them as Tom decides them on the way over," Pat translated, then made a sound of disgust. "Sometimes, I wonder who's really running the show."

"Why do you support him?" Rebecca asked, looking in her rearview mirror at the more-dour-than-usual Pat.

She shrugged, looked out the window. "Oh, he's not that bad. And he's definitely the lesser of two evils."

"You mean three," Rebecca corrected her

"No, I didn't mean three. I meant two. The Independent guy hasn't got a snowball's chance in hell."

Fortunately, Matt thought, Rebecca didn't argue.

They reached the auditorium where the forum would be held and trooped in together but the place was packed to the gills and they had to separate to find seats. Matt and Rebecca managed to snag two end seats on the aisle, one directly behind the other.

After a series of deadly boring speeches by local and state politicians (what was it about politicians that made them promise to keep remarks brief, then proceed to talk until they were blue in the face?), the candidates were finally introduced. The lieutenant governor candidates would go first, followed by the gubernatorial candidates.

The first one up was the incumbent, Phil Harbaugh, who made a couple of very lame jokes that Matt didn't even get before he launched into a little speech about the lack of revenues to keep state government running—without noting, Matt thought wryly, if all the state government apparatus *needed* to keep running—and talked about his plans to increase revenue that would NOT RESULT IN A TAX INCREASE TO THE AVERAGE, HARDWORKING TEXAN! His solution? Increase the gas and/or grocery tax, which, to Matt's way of thinking, amounted to a tax increase to the average, hardworking Texan, no matter how you sliced it.

Tom was next. Matt winced when he began his speech with an off-color joke about how these debates were a little like his wife—no matter how logical you were, you could never really win—and then proceeded to explain to the audience that he wasn't going to talk about taxes and program cuts, but how to strengthen the economy. Matt braced himself. Surprisingly, Tom had a couple of realistic things to say and had gotten much more articulate on his plan for economic growth: the superhighway, with a major gas pipeline running underneath, from Dallas–Ft. Worth to Mexico, all five hundred some-odd miles. This, Tom argued, would provide jobs and a new high-speed route for commerce around an already congested traffic corridor.

Of course Matt knew Tom was a proponent, but what surprised him was that his speech was suspiciously articulate, full of facts, and so unlike Tom that Matt had to wonder how he'd done it. He looked at Gilbert standing off to the side, noticed the look of shock on his face, too, which bolstered his feeling that something wasn't quite right. And as he sat in stunned amazement as Tom actually argued—with *percentages*—for economic growth, Rebecca tapped him on the arm.

Matt turned slightly. She was holding up a thin magazine to him; he could see her manicured finger jabbing at something he was to look at. He took the magazine, glanced at the front—*Southwest Region Engineering and Construction*—and then the article Rebecca was so rabid for him to see. It was entitled "The Superhighway Gas Pipeline—Boon or Bust?" Granted, it was dark, and he couldn't read all of the fine print, but he understood what had excited her: Tom's speech advocating the superhighway was almost identical to that article.

At least it explained Tom's sudden articulation.

As Matt was trying to scan the fine print, Tom finished his remarks by telling the audience he was the best man for the job and to vote for him in November. He got a fair amount of applause as he took his seat, and the next candidate, Russ Erwin was introduced. Matt looked up, saw a lanky cowboy in jeans, blue blazer, and boots saunter to the podium, and had an image of him sitting on a split rail fence, spitting tobacco as he watched the ranch hands work the cattle. The man casually put one hand on the podium, one in his pocket, and said, "Hello, folks. My name is Russ Erwin and I am running for lieutenant governor."

It was easy to see, Matt thought as the man talked, why Rebecca was taken with him. He had a down-home folksy manner about him that was appealing. He talked a little about government, how he didn't need any more of it in his life, a point with which no one could disagree. He talked about how he had gotten into this race because he couldn't find a government agency in all that huge bureaucracy that could help him, and he didn't think that was right, either. And how he was all for economic development, but that a superhighway and gas pipeline would displace ranchers—and he reminded the audience that Texas was built on ranching. He said the plan for the highway and pipeline was short-sighted in its economic thinking. The jobs would be around temporarily, and then what?

By the time Russ Erwin finished his speech, Matt was impressed. And wondering, like Tom had earlier, if there was something in Erwin's background that could derail his plain look and plain talk. Because it was a dangerously successful look and talk.

That night, after they had dropped Pat and Angie (having listened to Pat gripe about the seating, the lighting, and the fact that she couldn't hear anything) and were driving back to his place, Rebecca playfully poked him in the ribs. "Well?"

"Well, what?"

"Did you look at the magazine?"

"Yes."

"*Well?*"

Matt laughed. "What is it you want me to say?"

"I want you to say that it's odd Tom was making a speech that was almost identical to that article."

"Okay, Tom's speech was almost identical to that article."

"And?" she asked, sparing another look at him.

"And what?"

"Matt! Don't you think it's a little strange Tom is spouting almost word for word what some huge construction and engineering firm says are the benefits of this superhighway and pipeline?"

"I don't think it's uncommon to take information from a variety of sources."

"Okay. Then don't you think it's a little strange that Tom is suddenly taking information from *anyone?* I mean, you are the one who was so adamant he shore up his platform, and he wouldn't do it."

Matt had to agree—that was a little strange. "He's probably one of those candidates who glad-hands for money first, and then decides what he's going to say," he said, voicing his thoughts aloud. "He's a procrastinator."

"A procrastinator?" Rebecca laughed. "Is he that, or someone who stands to make a lot of money on the highway deal?"

That observation startled Matt so completely that he jerked his gaze to her. "What are you implying?"

"Just what you think I am implying. That Tom stands to gain a lot from engineers and construction firms if he's elected and sees that highway project through."

She spoke so matter-of-factly. "Do you know what you are saying?"

She rolled her eyes. "Yes," she said forcefully. "Do you think I speak without understanding my own words?"

"Rebecca, I've known Tom a long time. He's a lot of things, but he is not a crook," Matt said, but wondered why he was defending Tom. It wasn't as if he held such huge regard for him. And hadn't he sat in the same auditorium as Rebecca wondering what the scam was?

"I hope you're right about Tom, I really do," she said. "But it seems odd to me that a candidate who has not been able to put two words together before tonight suddenly comes up with a great speech. You don't have to buy into my theory," she said as she turned the truck into the garage of his building.

"Thanks," he said. "And now, maybe you'll tell me where a former beauty queen picked up such an obscure trade magazine?"

Rebecca pulled into a slot, put her cark in park. "Believe it or not, this former beauty queen can read. You can find that magazine at any library or bookstore. You'll be surprised what you might find in a bookstore, Matt—lots of information to help you make an informed opinion. Know what that is? Or do you think that law degree makes all your thoughts golden?"

"Good night," he said, and climbed out of her pickup and thought for once, he was glad he was going to bed alone.

CHAPTER THIRTY-TWO

It is dangerous for a candidate to say things that people might remember...

EUGENE MCCARTHY

Rebecca had just said good night to Jo Lynn and watched her drive away in her golf cart when the phone rang. "You're right," Matt said when she answered. "There was something a little strange about Tom's speech."

"Okay," she said, nodding thoughtfully. "Is that all?"

"Are you going to make me grovel?"

"Yes, I am. I love it when you grovel," she said, grinning.

She heard him sigh. "Okay, you're right; I should visit a bookstore sometime."

Rebecca waited for the rest. "That's it?" she said after a moment passed.

"What more do you want?"

"Oh, I don't know...something like, 'I am one notch below dog shit for ever suggesting that you couldn't think of those ideas on your own,' or, 'When I say ugly things like that, please know that I am really just insecure about the size of my—'"

"Okay, okay!" he said, laughing. "So what about you?"

"What about *me?*"

"Don't you want to make at least a little apology?"

"For what?" she demanded as she studied a cuticle. "Because I found a candidate to believe in, but am still working on his opponent's campaign? Or how about for being afraid to back out now because I've invested so much of me and my future plans in this stupid gala?"

"Well, I was just hoping for a little 'I'm sorry,' but I'll take all that."

"I don't know what to think anymore," Rebecca said, running her hand through her hair. "I mean, I really have put a lot into this gala, and it's less than a month away. Tom was pissed the last time I quit—can you imagine how upset he'd be if I quit now? And that's not even the thing that bothers me, to be honest. You know what I really fear?"

"What?"

"That it would be disastrous if I up and walked away from the biggest fund-raising gala this state has ever seen. I'd be labeled a quitter. No one would hire me."

"It seems to me that you can finish what you committed to doing, but you don't have to vote for the guy," Matt said. "In the end, it's your vote that counts, not the money raised."

"That's a stretch, isn't it?"

"A huge one," he admitted with a laugh. "But I think you're right. Austin is still a small town in some respects, and it could affect you down the road if you quit now."

"It's funny in a way—just a few months ago I was explaining to everyone on the invitation list that Tom was the best man for the job. Now I'm pretty sure he's not."

"I know," Matt said wearily. "I've known this guy for a long time, and I'm starting to have more questions than answers."

Neither of them spoke for a moment, until Rebecca at last asked, "What do we do?"

"I don't know," Matt said. "I'm going to look into a couple of things this week, see if I can ferret out what's really going on. But I do know one thing, Miss Priss...the next time you drive that badass truck into town, we're going to have a little tête-à-tête"

Rebecca laughed. "I love you, too," she said and sighed dreamily.

All the doubts in her head were shoved aside in the next few weeks in favor of the gala. There was so much to be done. The event was to be held at the Three Nines Ranch, an old spread, but more of a scenic conglomerate than working ranch anymore, with a few hundred head of cattle, a dude ranch, and lots of old pecan and oak trees. Caterers had to be consulted—barbecue for five hundred people took ten masters. Lighting had to be arranged, plus seating. A stage and dance floor had to be constructed, which the Three Nines was happy to contribute, as they had planned to create an amphitheater for the local performing arts scene, anyway. But the construction company hired to do it was slow as molasses, and Rebecca was fearful that the construction would never be finished in time. The entertainers had to have contracts, which Tom's publicity firm was slow putting out.

And then there was the matter of major contributions needed to pay for the event, which was Rebecca's primary concern; and contributions needed to fill Tom's war chest, which was his primary concern. Tom called Rebecca daily for a head count and openly speculated who would give more than the price per seat. Not a day went by that he didn't ask about Rebecca's father, to the point that it was grating on her nerves, and at last, Rebecca asked, "Why the great interest in my dad, Tom?"

"Are you kidding?" He snorted incredulously (Tom had, in these last weeks sliding toward the election, gone from good ol' boy to hot-tempered candidate). "What do you think? Your old man could make a sizable contribution to my campaign, Rebecca. You've talked to him about that, right?"

"No, Tom, I asked him to come, that's all," she said through gritted teeth. "He's not a fan of politics and even less so when it comes to Democrats. If you want more, you'll have to ask him yourself," she said. It galled her, because she knew her father would contribute if Tom asked, if only for her sake. That is exactly what she would have hoped for a few months ago—but now she couldn't think how to explain to Dad that she'd done all this for a man she wouldn't vote for.

"Don't think I won't ask," Tom said with all confidence. "You just get your old man there. I'll do the rest."

Oh, that's right, you'll do it all, won't you, you silver-tongued devil? And which magazine will you be reading from? Whatever. She charitably chalked up Tom's testiness to a general state of being keyed up, and besides, her mind was already racing ahead to the phone call she needed to make about ushers. So she hung up, shook it off, went on with the dozens of calls she needed to make before she and Gray and Harold could take their routine trip out to see the site.

As those weeks flew by, Rebecca and Matt saw each other as often as they could, but they were both terribly busy. She missed him. She knew he was up to his neck—he had hinted at some trouble at the firm—but when she asked, he shrugged it off, saying he wanted to talk about sunnier subjects. And she knew that Tom was demanding as much of Matt's time as he was of hers in advance of this gala. Most recently, Matt said over dinner one night, Tom had asked him to investigate Russ Erwin's background, and even though Matt had found nothing untoward, Tom was relentless. "I don't know, Rebecca, there is nothing to suggest that Russ Erwin isn't as exactly what he appears to be: a stand-up guy with a real concern about what is going on in Texas."

"Did you tell that to Tom?"

"I did," Matt said. "But have you seen the ads the Republicans are putting out on Tom, the one from Eeyore's birthday party where he looks like a clown?"

"Yes," she said with a wince—just one more thing Matt was right about. The list was beginning to pile up so high she'd have to ride a crane to the top.

"The whole race is going negative. Tom and Gunter are putting out an ad in the next few days that shows Phil Harbaugh laughing at some joke, only he looks half drunk. The caption is going to be something like, 'This is what Harbaugh thinks about Medicare.' And that's only the beginning," he warned her. "Russ Erwin has managed to stay off the radar screen until now. But there is a new poll next week, and if he's gained any ground—which I suspect he has—then he will become the target of the nasty ads, too."

"I am beginning to detest politics," Rebecca said, putting down her fork, her appetite gone.

"You and me both," Matt grimly agreed.

"Once this gala is over, I'm through," she said resolutely.

"And *that*, sweet cheeks, is just a week away. Is everything ready?" Matt asked, picking at her plate from across the table.

"I think so," she said, crossing her fingers. "The entertainment is lined up, at last. The caterers are all set. We got the temporary liquor license through, but Tom had to make some calls for that to happen. And the site is finally completed. The only thing I have left to worry about is what to wear," she said.

Matt laughed. "That's funny. You're going to knock them dead, Miss Texas, even if you wear your work jeans."

"I wish I could believe it. There will be some people who would like to see me fall flat on my face."

"Like who?" Matt demanded, pausing in his scavenging of her dinner. "Give me their names and I'll kick their ass."

She flashed him an appreciative smile and said, "Like Bud. And some of our so-called friends from Dallas with lots of money. And then there are some who just make me really nervous, like Dad."

"Don't worry about him. He'll be so proud, he'll bust," Matt said confidently.

"Not my dad. And I thank my lucky stars your parents will be out of town."

"My parents love you, girl," Matt said with an impatient frown. "You couldn't do a thing wrong if you tried."

"I just don't want to mess this up. I feel like my whole life has come down to this one event and everything I ever was or thought I could be is going to be proven by its success or failure."

Now Matt put down his fork. "That's just crazy. It's a party, Rebecca. Are you really that fragile?"

She looked at her wineglass, then at Matt, and said hopelessly, "Yeah, I think I am. Self-help books and transformation seminars notwithstanding, I am neither confident in my abilities nor prepared to pick myself up and dust myself off."

Matt reached across the table, gripped her hand in his. "I'm confident in your abilities. Whatever you think is going to happen, it won't, because I know you, and I know this will be a grand success. But if something happens, whatever the fallout, I want you to know you can fall on me and I will be there to pick you up and brush you off."

Rebecca felt a rush of warmth as his sincere sentiment swirled around her heart. "Why, Matthew Parrish," she said, squeezing his hand, "that's the nicest thing anyone has ever said to me."

"I *mean* it." Matt lifted her hand to his mouth and kissed it, then asked, "Are you going to eat that?"

CHAPTER THIRTY-THREE

Happiness is having a large, loving, caring, close-knit family in another city…

GEORGE BURNS

When Robin, Jake, and Cole arrived at the newly named Flying Pig Lakehouse (it said so above the gate) the night before the gala, Robin noticed immediately there was something different about Rebecca. *Very* different. What, exactly, she couldn't quite put her finger on. She was pretty sure it wasn't the dogs, although there were four or five (Robin couldn't be sure), all of them looking a little knocked around by life. And Rebecca's lack of makeup was highly unusual for her, being a former beauty queen and all, but Robin didn't think that was it, either.

She watched Rebecca closely as Jake's son, Cole (a few months shy of his seventeenth birthday and along to babysit Grayson, for *big* money, as he put it), handed Grayson a paper bag.

"What is it?" Grayson asked.

"Well, open it up, goof, and check it out," Cole responded.

Very carefully, Grayson opened it, peeked inside, then gasped loudly as he turned to Rebecca. "It's *green slime!*" he said in a reverent tone, and looked up at Cole with open adoration.

"Ever seen a dog eat green slime?" Cole asked, ushering Grayson out back, where the dogs were frantically awaiting any attention.

Something was different, all right—Rebecca was not the sort to beam so broadly at green slime. Quite the opposite, really. And the house. Sure, it was clean, picked up, as would be expected. But it was not...perfect. That was it! It wasn't perfect! *Rebecca* wasn't perfect. Robin had figured it out, and gleefully went about the rest of the afternoon looking to see how many imperfections she could find, sort of like looking for Waldo.

There were plenty—mismatched towels in the cupboard, one of Rebecca's old oil paintings hanging slightly askew, a TV remote tossed carelessly onto the floor. Some life-changing thing had happened to her sister, and Robin figured she knew what it was. After all, the same thing had happened to her not all that long ago.

Naturally, Robin wanted all the gory details, but she had some news of her own she was dying to share. So when Rebecca was preparing a sumptuous supper of pork tenderloin, and asked Robin to open a bottle of wine and taste it, Robin sighed.

"You might as well tell her," Jake said, pausing in the repair of a door hinge to frown at Robin, also anxious to have the news out in the open. "It's not like you can hide it, you know."

"I'm not trying to hide it, thank you, Mr. Fixit," she said irritably.

"Hide what?" Rebecca asked. "You're on the wagon?"

"Very funny." Robin grinned. "But not exactly."

"Then what?"

"She's pregnant," Jake announced matter-of-factly, and shrugged when Robin shrieked.

"I was going to tell her!"

"Not until you had tortured her."

"Robin! *When?*" Rebecca cried.

"Due in the spring," she said, with a whimper, however, as Rebecca had flung her arms around her.

"Who knows?" Rebecca asked breathlessly as the dogs barked excitedly. "Does Mom know? Rachel?"

"I told Mom before she headed for Seattle. She was out of her mind excited. And I told Rachel on the way down yesterday, who said she knew, of course, because my horoscope said something about big changes." She laughed.

"And Dad?"

Robin's grin faded a little. "Umm...not yet. I thought I'd tell him this weekend."

"Rob-*bie*!" Rebecca cried. "This weekend?"

"I thought it would be better to do it in person, because you know what he is going to say. When—"

"—are you getting married," Rebecca chimed in with Robin. "So? Are you?"

"Yeah," Robin said, smiling softly at Jake's back.

"*Maybe*," Jake corrected her, deadpan. "I'll see how you conduct yourself this weekend and then decide."

"He'd die without me," Robin said, shrugging. "So what about you?" she asked, hiding a smirk when Rebecca almost dropped the knife she had just picked up.

"What about me?" Rebecca asked, but Robin noticed she was avoiding eye contact.

"Come on, Bec. It's obvious."

The blood drained from her sister's face, and she immediately began stirring a sauce for the pork with a vengeance. "I am not pregnant, if that's—"

"That's not what I mean," Robin laughed. "But come on—are you getting married?"

Rebecca did not look up from her stirring of the sauce, refused to look at perhaps the one person on the face of the earth who would know if she was lying or not. How lucky for Robin, then, that the doorbell rang at that very moment. "I knew it. You're in love!" she exclaimed as she whirled and started for the door. "Rachel was right!"

"Robin, don't you dare answer that door!" Rebecca cried, and Robin heard a clattering of utensils as she reached the door before Rebecca, flung it open, and stood, hand on hip, sizing up the new guy from the top of his head to the tips of his polished loafers, almost pitching right into him when Rebecca collided with her back.

The new, very handsome guy clasped his hands behind his back and patiently waited for Robin to complete her inspection, at which point, he asked, "So what do you think? Do I pass?"

"Oh my God," Rebecca muttered helplessly behind her.

"Oh, you pass, all right," Robin said, smiling brightly. "I mean, *dude*—"

"She means," Rebecca said, elbowing her sister sharply, "that she's pleased to meet you."

Robin could only nod violently in agreement that she was very pleased to meet who she was now firmly convinced was her future brother-in-law.

"Hey," Jake said, stepping around and in front of Robin to extend his hand. "I'm Jake, this one's keeper. Come on in and I'll get you a beer, and if she gets out of hand, just give me the sign, and I'll handle it."

"Thanks," Matt said, "might have to take you up on that." To Robin, he grinned as he shook her hand. "I've been anxious to meet you," he said, and paused briefly to kiss Rebecca, at which point Robin saw The Look, the very same look she often saw in Jake's eyes, the look of love, but hello, it was nothing compared to the look in Rebecca's eyes. Robin could not recall ever seeing Rebecca so... *happy.* "So," she said to Matt, batting her eyes. "You've heard about me?"

"Yes. And I've been retained to represent Rebecca Lear in a very old dispute. Does a certain pair of red, high-heeled shoes mean anything to you?"

Robin laughed. "Does a black eye mean anything to you?" she shot back, just as Jake dragged her inside with an arm around her waist, rolling his eyes as he handed Matt a beer and Robin complained that certainly after twenty years, Rebecca should let bygones be bygones, and besides, the last she saw, the red shoes were still hanging from the high wire above River Oaks.

It was one of the best dinners Rebecca had ever had—Matt fit in so easily, and the four of them laughed and carried on until well after midnight, long after Grayson and Cole had turned in.

Matt was finally coaxed into telling a nosey Robin how he'd met Rebecca, and watched Rebecca's face flame with shame as Robin and Jake doubled over with laughter.

"Come on, Robbie," Rebecca pleaded. "Haven't you ever made a boneheaded mistake before?"

"Nothing like that! You thought he stole your quesadilla?" Robin doubled over again.

"Ah...beg your pardon, Robbie?" Jake asked. "You *haven't?*" And proceeded to tell, above Robin's objections, how their first face-to-face meeting occurred. In jail.

"Long story," Rebecca said to Matt's curious look.

"You have no idea how long," Jake said, laughing.

When Matt finally said he had to leave, Rebecca followed him outside. "Great night," he said, opening his car door. "I really like Robin a lot. She's...well, she's..."

"I know," Rebecca assured him. "Don't try and explain it. You'll never think of the right word, trust me."

Matt leaned over, kissed her good night. "Get some sleep. I know you are in knots about this deal, but everything's going to be fine."

She watched him drive away, walked back into the house where Robin was waiting for her. "He's the one," her sister said flatly. "And before you give me some song and dance, you better say yes, because he's perfect for you! I adore him! And he's smart, and funny, and he's so laid back—"

"All right," Rebecca said, laughing. "I will admit that he's definitely the top contender for the rest of my life. There's just one little thing."

"What?" Robin demanded.

"Dad," Rebecca said, pushing her sister toward the kitchen. "He hasn't met Dad yet."

"*Oooh,*" Robin said, and sadly shook her head. "Jesus, I hope he doesn't dump you. Where is Dad, anyway?"

"In town," Rebecca said with a roll of her eyes. "He said he was getting in too late to come all the way out here, and said he wouldn't come out tomorrow, either, because he doesn't want to be stuck and have to stay all night." She sighed loudly. "I think he's really looking forward to this!" she said in a sarcastically singsong voice.

"Consider yourself lucky," Robin said. "You won't have him in your hair all day."

It turned out that Robin was right; the next day was too wild to have tried to fit Dad in—there were so many last minute details to attend, so many sudden cancellations and sudden requests for tickets.

Rebecca made a run out to the ranch, went over everything one last time with Harold, who had proven to be the best stage manager in the western hemisphere. "Efficiency is my middle name," he'd once told her in all seriousness. He was also terribly excited to be part of the event, and when they began to set up tables, he told Rebecca to go home. "I've got it under control, Ms. Lear," he said firmly, turning her about and, hands on her shoulders, marching her toward the parking lot. "You just come back as your divine self, and your stage will be ready."

Rebecca couldn't argue—she barely had time as it was to get home and change. It seemed like one moment she was feeding the dogs in the early morning, and the next, she was getting dressed for the night and a stellar event for a man she couldn't vote for.

Rebecca dressed carefully; she chose a pale turquoise silk chiffon dress, with a deep, draping neckline and beaded shoulder straps. It hugged her figure, then flared at the hips into a full skirt that swung above her knees over an underskirt of magenta. She wore Stuart Weitzman pumps that were the exact match of turquoise and aquamarine and diamond drop earrings and matching pendant necklace that rested at her throat.

Robin helped her put up her hair in a chignon, which she held in place with two diamond-studded pins. "Oh my... you look gorgeous, Rebecca," Robin said as she stepped back to admire her, a look of awe on her face. "God, you still piss me off after all these years!"

"How so?"

"Because," Robin said, smiling as she checked her reflection in the mirror, "you were always so much prettier than me and Rachel, and all the boys drooled over you—"

"Honestly, Robbie. You were the one who went through them by the dozens."

"Yeah, because I found out all of them really wanted to be with my little sister."

Rebecca laughed. Robin had a vivid imagination.

They finished primping and went to meet the guys, who were waiting for them in the great room, both dressed in Texas formal per the invitation. Jake looked very dapper in his tuxedo coat and cummerbund over Wranglers and black boots. But Matt looked even better in his tails and formal waistcoat over a pair of Levi's and boots.

As Robin and Rebecca walked into the room, Jake let out a low whistle for Robin, but Matt seemed to have trouble rising to his feet. He couldn't take his eyes off Rebecca and stood there speechless for so long that she felt herself begin to color.

"Matt, say *something*," Robin urged him, voicing Rebecca's thoughts out loud.

"I can't," he said. "I'm at loss to say how beautiful she looks. God, Rebecca...you look like you walked right out of a movie." Rebecca smiled self-consciously, did a little curtsey of thanks. "I mean, it's stunning," he said again. "*You're* stunning. You're…"

Robin tapped him on the shoulder. "Roll your tongue up and put it in back in your head. We don't have all day." And then she yelled for Cole and Grayson while Matt shoved a hand through his hair, still unable to take his eyes off Rebecca.

The four of them arrived early, as Rebecca wanted to make sure that everything was in order and that the groundsmen, supplied by the Three Nines Ranch, had put everything up like she and Harold had instructed. Of course she knew what the place was supposed to look like, but she could not have prepared herself for the sight of the party grounds where the event would be held under an evening summer sky…it had been completely transformed, just like Harold promised. They walked through stone gates to the party area, and all of them came to an abrupt halt and stared at their surroundings as Harold came forward to greet them in a stunningly royal-blue tuxedo.

Rebecca had wanted the place to look like Texas, with lush greens to represent the coastal plains and eastern pine forests, reds and browns to represent the canyons in the west, and dark blues and grays to represent the mountains around El Paso. Dozens of round tables had been set up, all draped in those colors. The centerpieces at each table, made by local art students (and for sale after the event) were three-dimensional representations of Texas; barbed wire and horseshoes for ranching, oil rigs and oil pumps, skylines of the major metropolitan areas, cattle…and in the pecans and live oaks that formed a canopy over the dining area, hundreds of small star lights had been strung to create the illusion of a big Texas night sky.

The stage was a long, rectangular raised platform, behind which a canvas was draped and painted with the Austin skyline—Rebecca had asked a woman she had once taken an art class with to do it, and she had been happy to oblige. The result was outstanding; one felt as if he or she were standing on a hilltop, overlooking Austin. The dance floor, made of oak planks from the original Three Nines Ranch house porch, was off to one side, and was covered in peanut shells and sawdust for the boot-scooting tunes the live entertainment would provide— Rebecca had lined up four separate and well-known country western bands.

At either end of the dance floor, and behind the dining area, were three bars fashioned out of wooden barrel horses, used by ranchers and rodeo enthusiasts to learn how to rope. And at the far end of the grounds, but within a short walking distance of the dining area, were the barbecue pits.

"It's fabulous, Bec," Robin said. "You've done such a fantastic job."

"Thanks," Rebecca said proudly. "I had no idea it would turn out so well."

"You know, you ought to do this for a living," Jake said. "You're really good. There's a huge market for it in Houston. I bet there is here, too," he said. "I'm going to check out the barbecue—a man can't ignore a scent like that," he said, and offered his arm to Robin, leaving Rebecca with that stunning idea.

As the two of them trotted off in the direction of food, Rebecca turned slowly around, taking in the creation that had begun as an idea in her head one afternoon in Tom's office, had been sketched and sketched on paper so many times that she could almost recite the exact number of chairs. As she came full circle, she noticed Matt was gazing at her.

"So what do you think?"

"I think," he said softly, "that I am incredibly proud of you. It's wonderful, Rebecca. Masterfully done. Bravo," he said, applauding softly. "The party could never have created such an intimate feel to this venue, particularly on the budget you had."

Rebecca grinned up at him as Matt encircled her in his arms. "Thanks, Big Pants—that actually means a whole lot coming from you."

"Yeah, well, Miss Priss..." He paused to kiss her. "Jake's right—you ought to give his idea some thought, because you can do as well as the big guns. Better, even. And if Tom Masters doesn't give you the praise and glory you deserve, I will personally put this fine ostrich leather boot up his ass."

"I'm sorry, I'm certain I didn't hear you correctly. Would you please repeat that, only a little louder?"

Matt grinned broadly. "That's what I like about you—all modesty." He kissed her until they heard Harold's desperate call. She was needed in the ranch house, he said, as he flew by to direct those arriving early.

The next couple of hours went by in a whirl; waiters and bartenders began to show up, along with dozens of guests. Harold manned the front gate with the ushers while Rebecca spent a half hour sorting out confusion over the playbill with the bands. When that fire had been stamped out, she went back out to the party area to find Matt, and ran into Pat, who was looking rather spiffy in a pink mother-of-the-bride gown. But even more intriguing, Pat had a surprisingly younger man in tow. "This is fantastic!" she exclaimed when she saw Rebecca. "I never thought you—I mean, I never thought..."

Rebecca laughed and squeezed the old girl's hand. "I know what you thought, Pat, and you weren't alone. I wasn't sure I could pull it off, either. Have you seen Tom?"

"He and Glenda are on their way. He wants to make an entrance you know," she said. "He said to call him when the first band starts to play."

"Hey, Pat," Matt said behind her, "You look great."

Pat beamed. "Thanks!"

"I'm going to have to take her now," he said, touching Rebecca's arm. "There are some people she needs to meet." He introduced her to Doug and Jeff, two men who, he said, were part of the Democratic Party apparatus in Dallas. And several senators and representatives were in attendance, all ooohing and aahing and generally jealous that they hadn't been part of this fund-raiser.

And last, but certainly not least...Dad. Robin found Rebecca and Matt in conversation with Mr. Holt Peterson, the man who had used his collection of vintage Cadillac convertibles to shuttle people between the airport and the ranch. "He's here," she whispered, "and Bec—he doesn't look so good."

"What do you mean?" Rebecca asked, instantly fearing that he had misunderstood the dress code on the invitation.

"I mean he looks *sick.* Come on—they've seated us and he's asking for you."

Rebecca looked at Matt as he turned from two men he'd been speaking to. "My dad is here."

"About time," he said with a confident smile, and with his hand on the small of her back, they followed Robin through a growing crowd, struggling to pass through the rich and famous of Texas, men dressed in formal tails and jeans and boots and cowboy hats; women in brightly colored slips of gowns, the richness of the fabric rivaled only by the size and sparkle of their jewels.

When they at last came round to the table where Jake and Dad were sitting, Rebecca saw what Robin meant—Dad looked awful. He had lost quite a bit of weight since she had seen him a couple months ago; he was gaunt, his face leathery and his eyes sunken. She walked quickly to the table as he used his hands to push himself up and out of his chair. "Dad?" she said, trying to keep the alarm from her voice.

His eyes lit up and he smiled broadly, standing back to admire her dress. "Becky, you look beautiful. Times like this, you remind me so much of your mother. She was the beauty of the plains, you know."

"Thank you," she said, surprised and touched by the compliment. "Are all right?"

"I'm fine. Just lost a few extra pounds, that's all," he scoffed, waving a hand at her, but no amount of scoffing would change the fact that he looked sick, like he had when they had done all the chemotherapy—

Rebecca suddenly looked at Robin, saw the same fearful thought reflected in her sister's eyes.

But Dad was eyeing Matt, moving around Rebecca to have a better look. "Well, Becky, are you gonna let the ol' boy just stand there, or are you going to introduce us?"

Rebecca looked at Matt, who was, as usual, looking completely at ease. "Dad, this is Matt Parrish. He's a lawyer—"

"I know, I know," Dad said, extending his hand. "Aaron Lear, of Lear Transport Industries. Heard of us?" he asked, squinting as he peered up at Matt.

"It's a pleasure, Mr. Lear. And yes, of course I've heard of you. What Texan hasn't?"

"Uh-huh," Dad said, studying him "Never hurts to kiss a little ass, does it, Parrish?"

Matt laughed. "Can't say that it does."

"So you're a lawyer, huh?"

"That's right."

"Never had much use for lawyers," Dad remarked, clasping his hands, gauging Matt's reaction.

But Matt just laughed again, said cheerfully, "Most folks don't."

A slow smile cracked her father's face "Ever been married?"

"Dad!" Robin cried. "Leave him alone!"

"Nope, sure haven't," Matt answered amicably.

"Then get me a drink and I'll tell you why you never should, son," Dad said, and pulling out a chair, sat heavily, waiting on his drink.

"Honestly, Dad!" Rebecca moaned. "Matt, I'll get it—"

"No, Rebecca. Let Matt do it," Jake said, grinning at Dad. "This is how Aaron likes it—put 'em to the test, see who's still standing when he's done toying with them."

That remark prompted a rough bark of laughter from Dad, who slapped the table with glee. "Now see? Here's a man who's learned his lesson. Have a seat, Jake. You paid enough for it," he said, patting the seat next to him, then looked up at Matt again. "You weren't planning to take all night to get that whiskey, were you, Parrish?"

"No, sir," he said.

At least, Rebecca thought, as Matt casually strolled away after asking if anyone else wanted anything, the worst was over. Dad and Matt had met.

But then she saw Bud and Candace standing near the stage with Tom chatting it up.

CHAPTER THIRTY-FOUR

Man, unlike any other thing organic or inorganic in the universe, grows beyond his work, walks up the stairs of his concepts, emerges ahead of his accomplishments...

JOHN STEINBECK

Matt was also thinking the worst was over, and really didn't think Aaron Lear was going to pose any problem for him. The man honestly looked too sick to be anything but a pain in the ass, which was obviously what he had set out to be.

He got the whiskey, ran into Gilbert wearing a T-shirt with a tuxedo drawn on it, black jeans, and high tops. He was with Angie, who had chosen a vintage thrift-store dress to accent her boots and black lipstick. She had jet-black hair, too, with tints of blue and red. But Matt could honestly say she looked a whole lot better than the guy she had come with—he looked as if he had just stepped out of a coffin.

"This deal is so tight!" Angie exclaimed. "We're going to get a drink," she added, and said to her date, "*Free* bar."

"Awesome," he said, and the two of them sauntered off.

Matt looked at Gilbert. "Speech ready?"

"Yeah, and dude, he's got the whole thing on three-by-fives in his coat pocket!"

Now that was unbelievable. "Have a drink, then, Gilbert," Matt said. "You've earned it." Gilbert chucked Matt on the shoulder and followed Angie and her beau.

By the time Matt got back to the table with the drinks, Rebecca was missing. He wasn't surprised—she had an awful lot going on this evening. With a smile, he handed the whiskey to Aaron Lear, a beer to Jake, and a glass of soda to Robin, who caught his eye, rolled hers, and took a long, fortifying sip.

Mr. Lear leaned back, wet his lips with the whiskey. "Not bad. Thought it would be standard bar crap." He put the glass down, looked at Matt. "So, Parrish, what are your intentions?"

"Oh, for God's sake, Dad!" Robin exclaimed. "Why do you *do* that?"

"I don't know what you mean, Robbie," he said, feigning innocence. "When a man comes sniffing around my daughters' skirts, I like to know what he's after, that's all. And Matt here, he doesn't mind answering a few questions, do you Matt?"

"Not at all. I have nothing to hide," Matt said, looking him square in the eye.

"Is that right?" Mr. Lear said with a definite smirk.

"That's right. I don't mind telling you up front that I'm after her money. Every last red cent."

Robin choked so hard on her soda that Jake had to slap her on the back—but not before flashing Matt a look of pity, as if he expected to see him eaten alive. Mr. Lear just laughed, flashed a crooked little smile, sipped his whiskey, and said, "You know what, Parrish? I think I'm gonna like you. I *know* I'm gonna like you a hell of a lot better than that asshole," he said motioning with his head toward the stage.

Matt, Robin, and Jake all turned to see who he was talking about.

"Oh, God," Robin muttered.

"Who is it?" Matt asked.

"Bud Reynolds. Rebecca's ex," Mr. Lear said. "You've heard him on the radio, haven't you? *Come on down to Reynolds Chevrolet,* yada yada yada."

Yeah, he'd heard him, all right, and had thought, long before he knew Rebecca, that the man's voice grated. While the blonde on his arm was predictably pretty, Reynolds sure didn't look like the big, strapping, handsome man Matt had expected, the sort of man worthy of Rebecca's attentions. No, Bud Reynolds was the opposite of that. His barrel chest slid to belly flab. And he had a thick face with a ruddy complexion that suggested either he drank too much or the exertion of walking to the stage had almost done him in.

"How she stayed married to that ass for so long is a mystery," Robin said.

"*Why* she ever married him is a mystery," Mr. Lear said. "I'll tell you the truth, Matt." He paused to down the last of his whiskey and shove the glass back across the table to him, "That's what worries me about Becky. She's pretty, but she's not the sharpest tack on the board when it comes to men."

"Come on, Aaron, that's not fair," Jake said instantly. "She was fifteen when she met Bud, nineteen or maybe even younger when she married him—"

But Mr. Lear cut him off with a biting, "*So?*"

"So, she's a lot older and wiser, just like all the rest of us. She knows what she is doing. And Matt here is a good guy."

"Thanks, Jake. I'll remember you said that," Matt said with a wink, and took Mr. Lear's glass. "Would you like another one, Mr. Lear?"

"If you don't mind."

Matt swiped up the glass, stopped short of crushing it on Lear's head for having so little faith in his daughter, and began striding to where Rebecca was standing with Tom and her jerk ex-husband.

She must have felt him coming, because she glanced over her shoulder as he approached, and he saw a look of relief on her face as Tom began to wave at him.

"Matt!" Tom cried, extending his hand. "I was just telling Rebecca that she's done an outstanding job. I've heard from several of my supporters that this is a great party."

"The best I've seen," Matt said.

Reynolds was eyeing him closely, too. "Don't believe we've met," he said through the cigar in his mouth. "But I've seen you in the paper," he said with a sly wink. "Bud Reynolds, Reynolds Chevrolet and Cadillac."

What was the deal with announcing your business? Some sort of lame plug? "Matt Parrish," he responded without offering his hand, and instead, put it possessively on the small of Rebecca's back.

Reynolds didn't miss that obvious signal, and chuckled as Matt greeted Tom's wife, Glenda, then turned to the blonde with Reynolds. And as Reynolds didn't seem inclined to introduce him, Matt introduced himself. "I'm Matt Parrish," he said, offering her his hand.

She looked at his hand as if she wasn't certain what to do with any of them and reluctantly took it. "Candace."

"I was just going over the program with Tom," Rebecca said, looking up at Matt, the anxiety evident in her blue eyes. "He has some, *new* friends he'd like to have sit up front. They are planning to do standing ovations and maybe ask some look-good questions."

"You mean, friends other than the contributors who have paid two thousand dollars to have front row seats?" Matt asked, frowning at Tom.

"Yes," Rebecca said, her voice full of frustration. "I'm not sure how we can do that."

"Well, we can't do it," Matt said to Tom. "Those folks paid for the entertainment and the privilege of looking right up your nose."

"Can't you just find a couple of tables and squeeze them in?" Reynolds asked, smiling darkly at Matt. But whatever message he thought he was sending, Matt was not the least bit intimidated—he saw that oily smile in the courtroom all the time.

"We could. But that sort of defeats the purpose of charging different plate prices, don't you think?" he asked, returning that dark smile with a thin one of his own.

"Yeah, it does, doesn't it?" Tom asked, now looking confused.

But Reynolds was obviously a man used to getting his own way. "Come on, buddy," he said, clapping Tom on the back. "We're just talking a couple of tables. You think those folks are going to know the difference? Hell, just tell them we got the *three*-thousand-dollar plates!" He laughed as if it was funny.

"There's no room," Rebecca tried to explain. "We could barely squeeze the ones already there."

"I wouldn't do it, Tom," Matt advised. "It's dishonest and unfair, and trust me, it won't go unnoticed."

Reynolds snorted a laugh at that. "Did you make this poor guy pay, Tom? 'Cuz he's sure acting like he had to cough up a couple of grand."

"Oh, God," Rebecca muttered beneath her breath; Matt could feel his pulse racing, probably from the strain of keeping his fist out of that man's nose.

"You're right, Bud," Tom said, not sounding very certain at all. "No one will notice." But he looked expectantly at Rebecca. "You can get a couple of tables, right, Rebecca?"

"Sure she can," Reynolds said.

Rebecca's blue eyes turned to ice. "I'll see what I can do," she muttered. "If you'll excuse me—"

"Ah, before you go round up those tables for us, Becky," Reynolds said. "Is Aaron here? Thought I might talk to him a minute."

Rebecca stiffened, but spared the ass a glance. "He's here somewhere," she said, and turned, walking away before Reynolds could say anything else.

Reynolds laughed, snaked his arm around the blonde. "Women," he said, shaking his head. "Especially that one... she'll turn to ice so fast, you'll think an arctic wind has blown up your shorts."

At least Glenda had the decency to gasp, and even Tom looked a little appalled. As much as Matt would have liked to turn Reynolds's fleshy face into dough, he forced himself to say nothing, to turn and follow Rebecca, who was striding away at a clip.

He found her with Harold, who, true to form, delighted in the challenge of squeezing extra tables up front. "I'll get right on it!" he assured her with a snap of his fingers, and was off.

"What's going on?" It was Pat, who had seen them talking with Tom. Matt told her, and Pat's irritation was evident. "Is it those high rollers from Houston?"

"Who?" Matt asked, unaware of anyone from Houston in Tom's back pocket.

"I don't know…a couple of guys from some firm down there. They call him pretty regular. Franklin and Vandermere, something like that."

The name, Matt thought, sounded vaguely familiar. But at the moment, he couldn't think; he was too busy trying to rearrange expensive seating for whomever it was Tom wanted to impress. In the meantime, the music had started up; people were dancing in between trips to the barbecue pits, and drinking plenty. The event was going exceedingly well, Matt thought, and figured, doing a rough head count estimate, that it had probably raised tens of thousands, not to mention the amount Tom was gathering by walking around and glad-handing everyone in the crowd. Including Rebecca's father, Matt noticed, in the company of the man's ex-son-in-law. From where Matt stood, Mr. Lear looked even unhappier than before, and in fact, when he made his way to the table with the forgotten whiskey, Mr. Lear was sneering something fierce.

"Bastard is still after my money," he groused, taking the whiskey from Matt. "Wants another ten grand, like the first wasn't enough. Let me tell you something right now, Matt. If you ever decide to run for office, leave me out of it. I don't like politicians and I don't like bloodsuckers."

Seemed like a good time to dance, Matt thought, and when Rebecca returned, a frown on her gorgeous face, he intercepted her. "Dance with me," he murmured in her ear. "I want to dance with the most beautiful woman here."

Rebecca's eyes widened. "Really?" she asked. "You want to dance?"

"I want to make love. But as that doesn't seem doable at the moment, I actually know how to waltz."

Rebecca was happy to dance, and they fell in with a crowd doing a slow country waltz while Matt whispered in her ear that she was the most beautiful woman on the planet. And Rebecca, giggling, whispered back, "How do you know? Have you met all the women on the planet?"

"Educated guess," he said, pressing his thigh between her legs to twirl her around. And for a moment on that summer evening, the world faded into background noise, and it was just the two of them, a lucky guy with the most beautiful woman in the world, turning round and round in their own little happy fog, smiling at each other. They were, in that moment, perfect.

But then the music ended, and the band announced a break, and they reluctantly made their way back to the table, and the perfect moment ended.

Rebecca was dreading the conversation with Dad because of what he might say, dreading looking at him again because of what it might mean. She was desperately worried about him; he looked like hell and was drinking like a fish. But when she tried to ask, he said there wasn't a damn thing wrong with him and to quit asking. Conditioned from years of having Aaron Lear as her father, Rebecca did what came naturally and just stopped talking.

Which left Dad the opening he needed to grill her—*What are you going to do after the election? Are you going to stay home with Grayson? Too many women rush out in the world and leave their kids spinning.* That remark had, of course, infuriated Robin, who interjected with her own, *How would you know? You weren't around so much. And how come it has to be the mother who stays home?*

That in turn prompted a rather heated discussion between Robin and Jake and, of course, Dad, who finally demanded to know why they were arguing about it.

"This isn't how I wanted to do it, but what else is new. Dad, there is something I want to tell you," Robin said.

"Ladies and gentlemen, if we might have your attention please!" Gilbert suddenly called from the stage.

Ah, for the love of God! "Robin, not now!" Rebecca cried.

"Tell me what?" Dad demanded as Harold walked up, whispered to Rebecca they were next.

"Will you calm down?" Robin said to her father.

"Ladies and gentlemen!" Gilbert called again, and the crowd began to simmer down and turn their collective attention to the stage.

"Great. Your timing is impeccable, Robin. We've got to go," Rebecca hissed as Matt reached for her arm, urging her up and toward the stage.

"Please welcome Mr. Doug Balinger of the Texas Democratic Party, for a few remarks," Gilbert said. Polite applause went up as Doug took the stage.

"Good evening, folks. I am much honored to be here tonight representing Texas Democrats," he began, and while he expounded on what the party thought of the future of Texas, Tom's little team gathered around him while he reviewed his notes.

"So how do I look?" he asked, sounding nervous, which surprised Rebecca greatly. Of all the times she had been with him and seen him do his thing, he hadn't exactly been articulate, but he had never been short of completely full of himself.

"You look great," Rebecca responded with a reassuring smile, reaching to straighten his bolo tie.

"Remember, nothing about Medicare!" Pat reminded him.

"And everything about donations," Matt added.

"Right, right," Tom said, and looked at his note cards again as Doug wrapped it up by announcing, "It is a great honor for me to introduce to you the next lieutenant governor of the great state of Texas...Senator Tom Masters!"

Amid the applause and whistles, Tom took the steps two at a time, pausing to bow like a prizefighter, then waved to the crowd as he strode to the microphone like a superstar. "Thank you, thank you!" he shouted as the applause and whistling began to die down. "This has to be the best-looking crowd in the Lone Star State."

That sparked another round of thunderous applause, through which Matt, Rebecca, Pat, and Gilbert made their way up front to a small table reserved for staff.

"Before I get started, I'd like to thank a few people who have made this night possible," he said, shuffling through his note cards. "The fine people of the Three Nines Ranch," he started.

Matt leaned toward Rebecca and muttered, "Stand up and wave to the crowd when he calls your name."

"And Matthew Parrish, a personal friend and confidant," he said, which, Rebecca thought, seemed to startle Matt. He came only halfway out of his chair, waved quickly to a smattering of applause as he sat again. "I'll tell you what, if I don't know the answer, my pal Matt does," Tom continued as Matt sank in his chair and looked at Rebecca and Pat, shrugging with bewilderment. "And Pat Griswold. Where are you, Pat? Oh! Stand up, Pat," Tom urged from the podium. "Now, Pat here, she's dynamite. She's helped shape my position on several key issues you'll hear about tonight."

Pat stood and sat quickly, blinking in shock.

"Nor can I forget our emcee this evening, Gilbert Ortiz," Tom said, gesturing for Gilbert to stand. But Gilbert was already on his feet, clasping his hands and shaking them like a victory dance above his head, much to the delight of the crowd. Through the microphone, Tom laughed and said jokingly, "Gilbert, you're taking my spotlight." The crowd laughed again as Gilbert sat down.

Tom glanced at his notes. "Many of you have spoken to Angie Rush on the phone. Angie's helping herself to barbecue—there she is!" he said, and they turned, saw Angie near the pits, jumping up and down and waving. "Angie is my right hand," Tom said. He paused, then glanced at the staff table as if he couldn't remember anyone else.

Rebecca felt her pulse racing. Tom looked directly at her, then said, "And Rebecca Reynolds—I mean Lear. I'm going to get that straight one of these days." He chuckled. "Rebecca's been a help to my campaign...speaking of which, I want to talk to you about the vision I have for Texas," he said, and shuffling his cards around, began to talk about Texas under his leadership.

Not that Rebecca heard any of his tripe—she couldn't hear anything with the blood pounding in her ears. *Rebecca has been a help to my campaign?* That was it? What happened to thanking the people who made this night possible? What happened to all the things she had done for his stupid campaign, even when she had lost faith in him? That was all the recognition she was going to get, and he couldn't even remember her damn name? And across the front row, she saw Bud, and she felt something implode within her.

She didn't even realize that she was gripping the edge of the table until Matt put his hand on hers. Only then did she notice how the rest of them were looking at her—Pat, with horror; Gilbert, with confusion; and Matt...damn him, but Matt was looking at her with, what, *pity?*

That did it. Every self-help seminar she had attended, every self-help book she had read, all of them were suddenly bubbling up, frothing inside her, shouting—no, screaming—at her not to accept this horrible, unconscionable slight lying down. The real Rebecca, who slowly and surely had been climbing out of her hole, was suddenly clawing and scratching her way out, fighting for air.

As Tom droned on, Rebecca pulled her hand free of Matt's and, glaring at him, she leaned across and whispered hotly, "Do not pity me!"

"Honey, I don't pity—"

But she had already jerked back into place, her back ramrod stiff, feeling as if her head might literally explode off her shoulders. She debated getting up and walking out in front of everyone, but decided that was too easy for Tom. So she waited. For what, she had no idea. Just sat there, gripping the table, her heart beating harder and harder as her fury raced.

And then Tom handed it to her on a silver platter. He mentioned "his" idea for a superhighway and pipeline across Texas, one that would bring jobs to struggling areas and new lanes for commerce from north to south. "Now, my opponents are going to argue against it," he said, shaking his head with a sad little laugh. "But you know my opponents, Phil Harbaugh would sell this state to Mexico if he could, and frankly, Russ Erwin has his head so far up a tree, he's sucking sap. It's hard to listen to someone who'd rather do good for all the lizards in this state than the people," Tom added, and nodded his appreciation of the loud applause to that statement.

That was the moment Rebecca realized she was standing, her arm raised high in the air. "*Rebecca!*" Pat hissed at the same moment Tom noticed her standing there with her arm raised high above her head. But Rebecca ignored Pat and glared at Tom, who seemed startled, and looked around for someone to tell him what was going on.

"Senator Masters!" she called in a voice that was, remarkably, as clear as the summer night.

Tom could not ignore her now, and said unevenly, "I think Rebecca has an important announcement. Is that right?"

"No," she said, lowering her arm. "I have an important question."

A murmur went through the crowd, and Tom cleared his throat, glanced helplessly at Bud, and thereby signed his own death warrant. "Okay—"

"About this superhighway pipeline you have planned… what do you say to all the ranchers out there who will be displaced in the name of progress? You know who I'm talk-ing about, right? Ranchers whose families settled Texas and have known nothing but a ranching way of life for genera-tions? And then, as a follow-up question, could you please tell us what you will say to all those economically depressed areas when the thing is built and the jobs go away?"

A hush fell over the crowd as everyone waited for his response. Tom glared at Matt as if he had asked the question.

"I'm sorry, Senator, but I didn't hear your response," Rebecca continued, wildly out of control and loving every minute of it. "Oh, and another thing—have you told the Three Nines Ranch, our host for the evening, that the superhighway will cross the southern corner of their acre-age where they still graze cattle?"

Tom laughed nervously as he glared at Matt. "All good questions, Rebecca," he said. "I think we've got some answers for you, right, Matt?"

Matt looked up at Rebecca. She couldn't read his expres-sion as he slowly came to his feet. It didn't matter, she tried to tell herself. She had done what she had to do. He could be mad, but she had to do it for her, not anyone else. Matt could do that smooth speak and get Tom out of trouble like he was good at doing, Rebeca didn't care. She'd had enough.

But she wished, that just once, someone would stand beside her. Just *once.*

"Well, Tom, I'd like to say that we have some good answers," Matt said, looking at Rebecca, and then, so sub-tle that she almost missed it, he winked at her. *Winked* at her! "But I don't have any, and frankly, I'd like to hear your answer to Ms. Lear's questions. Personally, I think a pipeline that long is a pretty dangerous idea. And I don't understand why this highway is such a good idea. I mean, we've already got a major interstate running from Dallas to Brownsville. You think there is enough over-the-road commerce to support two superhighways?"

A buzz had started in the crowd; people around them were talking excitedly, and Tom looked as if he had suddenly awakened to find himself in a foreign land. He madly looked about for someone to help him out of his mess, but everyone around him was confused about what was happening.

Not Rebecca. She had never loved anyone as much in her life as she did that moment, and she tapped Matt on the arm, smiling gratefully. "You wanna blow this pop stand?" she asked.

Matt laughed. "You think we have a choice?" he said, and with another wink, put her hand on his arm and escorted her through a sea of tables, a sea of people who had paid a small fortune to be here. She smiled at them all as if she were a reigning beauty queen on her last walk as someone took the stage behind them and announced the music would begin again shortly.

Matt attempted to lead her out of the little park, but Rebecca tugged on his arm, pointed to her father, who was, she couldn't help noticing, the only one standing. She walked over, smiled at her family. "I'm sorry. But then again, I'm not," she said cheerfully.

"Don't ever be sorry, baby!" her father said. "I'm so proud of you, girl! You finally stood up for yourself, and that's what I've been trying to get across to you these last two years—stand on your own two feet," he said, and grabbed her in a fierce bear hug, holding her tightly. And when he released her, she thought she saw a glimmer of a tear in his eye, but he quickly turned to Robin. "You could take a page out of her book, you know." To which Robin groaned as she came to her feet and hugged Rebecca.

"Way to stir up a party!" she said proudly.

"Are you coming with us?" Rebecca asked.

Robin looked at Jake, then both of them looked at Dad, who was beaming at Rebecca. Robin shook her head. "Are you kidding? We can't wait to see what happens next!"

"We better go," Matt said low, nodding to where Tom, Doug, and Jeff were making their way through the tables to reach them.

"Yeah, get the hell out of here and enjoy yourselves," Dad said, and put his hand on Rebecca's cheek, smiling at her again before pushing her to leave.

Hand in hand, she and Matt walked quickly out of the gates, headed for her truck.

But once they were out of the gate. Matt abruptly stopped her.

"Come on," she urged him.

"No. I have to say this. I mean, what you did back there…" He paused, shook his head, his gray eyes dancing with laughter. "When you take the silk gloves off, you're one tough cookie. You know, I love how weird you are, how beautiful you are, how righteous you can get. I love everything about you. And I realized tonight when you had the guts to stand up and ask what we've all been wondering, that I don't think I can live without you."

She laughed, flung her arms around his neck, and kissed him. "And I never loved anyone as much as I loved you when you stood up for me. Thanks for standing by me, Matt."

"Are you kidding? I should have stood up a long time ago. I knew there'd be trouble the moment I met you, but now I am prepared to follow you all the way to the ends of Planet Rebecca if I must."

With a grin, she grabbed his hand and tugged. "The way things are going, it might at least be Mexico," she said, and laughing, they ran for the monster truck.

CHAPTER THIRTY-FIVE

When you get to the end of your rope, tie a knot and hang on...

FRANKLIN D. ROOSEVELT

Robin and Jake brought an enthusiastic Dad back to the lake house with them a couple of hours later, and Rebecca broke out the champagne and ice cream.

Dad looked a hell of a lot better having heard the news of Robin's pregnancy. After the usual interrogation about marriage and college funds (which earned a groan from everyone), Dad turned his attention to what Rebecca had done, giggling like a schoolboy.

Robin said that Senator Masters spent the rest of the evening going from table to table, frantically assuring his sponsors that he did indeed care about ranchers. And she added that Pat Griswold had asked her to tell Rebecca that she wished she had said it. Dad said again he was so proud of her for standing up, and proclaimed the bastard Tom Masters had it coming, and the five of them laughed and made a game of thinking up new campaign slogans for Masters the Bastard.

But the next afternoon, when her family had left and it was just the three of them again, Matt and Rebecca pored over news from around the state, slowly realizing that they had effectively ruined any political aspirations for Matt. He said he was glad, that he didn't think he had the stomach for it and thought he could do more good elsewhere.

"Like where?" Rebecca asked.

"I'm not sure," he said honestly. "But I'd like to give people who don't have money a chance at decent representation," he said. "That's what I want to do." It helped when Matt's father called later and asked him about all the flack. He told Matt he was relieved and heartened that his son wouldn't be going into politics. "I spent my career there, and son, you're above politics," he assured him. "You deserve a better life."

As for Rebecca, she felt exhilarated, scandalized, enlightened, and most importantly, finally and completely free to be herself. She felt shiny and new on the inside. She felt like her own person, one who was less than perfect, the evidence of which was played up in the local papers for several days following the event while she and Matt hid out at the lake house.

It was surprising to her that Matt seemed like a new person, too.

Matt didn't see how he could ever be the same again having witnessed firsthand what it meant to stand up for one's principles. Once the furor had died down and he returned to his offices, he quickly began looking into some questions he'd had for a few weeks, particularly after hearing the names Franklin and Vandermere. In the middle of one night, he had awaked with the answer—Franklin and Vandermere was a big road construction firm, and several years ago, they had been party to a lawsuit in which he had been peripherally involved. His memory was that they had paid themselves for contracted work on a toll road near Houston that was never completed. The details were foggy, but he recalled that they were a shady outfit. After the events of that night—the closeness between Rebecca's ex-husband and Tom, along with Franklin and Vandermere reps, he knew there was something rotten going on, and he was determined to unearth what it was.

While Matt was quietly looking into Tom's ties to Franklin and Vandermere, Rebecca had begun to pull things out of the old barn in her quest to return to her artistic roots. She told Matt that maybe she would create and sell pottery, or paint for a living until she figured out what she might do, and who knew? At the moment, she was just ecstatically happy being free of the old Rebecca and planning on her life as the new Rebecca.

But a couple of weeks after her astounding fall from grace, Rebecca's phone rang, and a male voice asked for her. "Ah, Ms. Lear, my name is Russ Erwin, and you and I met at a little candidate deal up there in Georgetown," his deep voice rang out.

"Yes, of course! I remember it well."

"Well, now, I'd be less than honest if I said I hadn't followed with some glee what happened out there at Tom Masters's big fund-raiser, and I thought I'd just touch base, see if you were interested in coming over to our side. You sound like the type of lady we want."

Rebecca sank onto a bar stool. "You want me to help you with your campaign? But the election is less than a month away."

"It's creeping up, isn't it? Still, I'd like your help—not without some study on your part, though. What I'd like to do is send you some material, and after you look it over, see what I'm about, maybe you can call with any questions you have and we can decide if there's a fit, and what sort of place we might have for you in our organization, before and after the election."

She grinned broadly at Grayson, who was sitting at the bar eating a peanut butter and jelly sandwich. "I'd like that, Mr. Erwin."

"Please, call me Russ. We're just a few folk who came together and are trying to do the right thing. Where should I send the material?" he asked.

Rebecca gave him her address, and they talked a little longer about what had happened at the Three Nines Ranch. When she at last hung up, she was thrilled, as was Matt when she called to tell him. "It sounds like a great opportunity," he agreed.

"But I thought we'd sworn off politics," she laughingly reminded him.

"No, we've sworn off politicians we don't believe in," he said. "There's a big difference."

"You're sure you wouldn't mind if I got involved in another campaign?"

"All I want is for you to be happy, Rebecca," Matt said. "Whatever it takes."

She loved that man.

Rebecca did indeed join the Independents and was so immersed in it leading up to the election that she didn't really notice how much time Matt was putting in at the office.

Matt was pretty immersed himself in two issues: the first, and most important, was to come up with a buy-out plan that

Ben could live with. Ben wasn't exactly anxious to split up, but he agreed with Matt that the time had come to go their philosophical ways. The trauma was too much for Harold, and, having branched out a little with Rebecca during the campaign, he decided he had what it took to run a biker coffee shop. Which is precisely what he and Gary moved to Santa Fe, New Mexico, to tackle.

To each his own, Matt thought.

The second issue Matt had on his mind was Tom's campaign, and he quietly, methodically, followed up on his suspicions. In the course of his follow-up, he had a chance to study Tom's voting record on hundreds of boring bills, and mentally kicked himself for never having done it before, because there were, indeed, some interesting voting patterns.

In the week before the election, Matt packed up his personal belongings, said good-bye to Ben, and stopped by the attorney general's office on his way out to the lake, where he intended to spend several days, thinking.

That night, he and Rebecca watched TV for a while with Grayson. Tom seemed to be rebounding from the disaster at the fund-raiser as the election entered the eleventh hour, and had bombarded the airwaves with negative ads. Later, when Matt and Rebecca went to bed, he told her about his visit to the attorney general's office. Rebecca listened quietly, nodding thoughtfully as he explained what he suspected. "That actually explains a lot of things," she said, but what, exactly, she did not elaborate. "It's water under the bridge now."

Over the next few days, the TV stayed off, while Rebecca and Matt took Grayson fishing, or sat out on the dock at dusk, or made deep love in the early-morning hours, after which they would whisper about their future. Matt would have a little one-man office, handle cases for the poor. Rebecca would ease into event planning, but also focus on her art. They would live at the lake, where they could believe they were on top of the world, safe and sound and happy. And then they would talk about a brother for Grayson, or maybe a sister. Or two. Or three. And then they would dissolve into laughter and love again.

On the eve of the election, Matt went to Sam's Corner Grocery, had a chat with Karen and Dinah, and when he came back to the Flying Pig Lakehouse, Rebecca met him at the door barefoot, wearing shorts, a dirty T-shirt, and her hair in a ponytail. She handed him a beer as he walked in. "We've got a new addition," she told him after he kissed her hungrily.

"A new addition?"

She grabbed his hand and pulled him out back, where Grayson was busily trying to wrestle a small weiner dog and the hose that Bean was unwittingly lying on. "Meet Radish," she said, smiling.

"Radish? What kind of name is that for a dog?" he exclaimed, and went to help Grayson tackle the feisty little dog while the regular slackers just lay there, panting indifferently.

Inside, on the TV Rebecca had left on when she spotted the little dog, an image of Tom Masters surrounded by lawyers, walking into some courthouse, flashed across the screen.

"*In a startling development on the eve of the statewide election,*" the announcer intoned over the images, "*Senator Tom*

Masters was brought in this morning for questioning about an alleged series of kickbacks from the Franklin and Vandermere construction firm in exchange for state contracts. Sources tell us that in addition to Franklin and Vandermere, other notable firms, such as Reynolds Chevrolet and Cadillac, may also have been involved. An unnamed source at the attorney general's office claims that there is enough evidence to show that the senator solicited contributions from other major Texas corporations with the promise of billions of dollars worth of contracts and prearranged kickbacks, should he be elected lieutenant governor. Early voting has concluded and the polls open at seven a.m...."

CHAPTER THIRTY-SIX

*The world is round and the place which may seem like the
end may also be only the beginning...*

IVY BAKER PRIEST

Bonnie was home from Seattle, had finished putting her
things away and going through her mail. She had just
picked up the phone to call Robin and let her know she was
home when she heard the doorbell ring.

Bonnie put down the phone and walked to the door,
opened up the peephole, and peered out. Then shut it. And
stared helplessly at the door, pressing one arm against it to
hold herself up. After a long moment, she straightened and
opened the door. "Hello, Aaron," she said. But even as angry
as she was, she couldn't help noticing how gray he looked.

"Just give me five minutes," he said, holding up an aged
arm to keep her from shutting the door in his face. "That's
all I'm asking, Bonnie. Please."

"I asked you not to come here," she said angrily as the
tears burned in the backs of her eyes.

"I know," he said, lowering his arm. He looked old, she
thought. "But I couldn't stay away, Bonnie. I couldn't just...
fade away without talking to you, if even for the last time.

Please listen. And after you've heard what I have to say, if you want me to go. You have my word, I'll go, and I won't bother you again. Ever. I swear it."

Bonnie stared at him, wondered how many times in her life would they do this. Ten? Twenty? But looking at him now—*How ill he looks*—she still couldn't bring herself to shut the door in his face and move on with her life. More than thirty years had gone by, thirty up-and-down years, and she couldn't let go of them, no matter how badly she wanted to.

Slowly, reluctantly, she stepped back so that he could come in. "Five minutes, Aaron. That's all," she said, knowing the moment that the words were out of her mouth that it would never be all, not until they both had gone into that long, long night.

ABOUT THE AUTHOR

Julia London is the *New York Times, USA Today,* and *Publishers Weekly* bestselling author of more than twenty romantic fiction novels. She is the author of the popular Desperate Debutantes, Scandalous, and The Secrets of Hadley Green historical romance series. She is also the author of several contemporary women's fiction novels with strong romantic elements, including the upcoming Homecoming Ranch trilogy, *Summer of Two Wishes, One Season of Sunshine,* and *Light at Winter's End.*

Julia is the recipient of the RT Bookclub Award for Best Historical Romance and a four-time finalist for the prestigious RITA Award for excellence in romantic fiction. She lives in Austin, Texas.